35

WE
ARE
THE END

Gonzalo C. Garcia

GALLEY BEGGAR PRESS

First published in 2017
by Galley Beggar Press Limited
37 Dover Street
Norwich
NR2 3LG

Text design and typesetting by Tetragon, London
Printed in the UK by Clays, St Ives

A CIP record for this book is available from the British Library

ISBN paperback: 978-1-910296-79-0
Limited edition ISBN: 978-1-910296-80-6

Pa' mis viejos

1

Dead Leaves

It's 4:17am and Tomás is still smoking out the window and drinking coffee. He drinks it straight from the French press because she took all the tea mugs and coffee cups. She took a lot of other things, too: the chopping board, the landline phone, a wok and the German shower curtain with embroidered chalets and pine trees. He really did like that curtain. But that stuff doesn't matter. He moved into the new flat last week and he bought straws for the cafetière this morning and he was glad, so glad about moving out, although he should probably have built the bed frame as soon as he arrived. It's too late now and he doesn't want to wake his new neighbours up.

He places the needle back at the edge of the record. Those are the only things she left him that were hers: a record player and a *Greatest Hits* Serge Gainsbourg vinyl (presumably because the album's miserable, but most likely also because the needle has no weight and the record's scratched so it gets stuck on the fourth song). The endless looping of three rising chords, Serge going on about dying leaves, dying leaves, dying leaves, oh dying – leaves, makes all the sadness seem pretty fucking ridiculous, a scam, like a dead guy sitting up at his own wake and pointing at a hidden camera, or when you cry in front of a mirror. But

7

despite Serge, today is an OK day. He lifts the needle again and the strings open in dissonance.

Earlier today, instead of working, he went to a museum and looked at stuffed birds and paintings of dead people. Before moving to Santiago, his parents had once told him that cities are places for the young and that he should be happy, like all young people are meant to be but so rarely are. Judging by their smiles, the painted army generals and the dead birds at the museum begged to differ too. Just like always, the streets had been filled with the elderly from very early on. They don't have much time left and they can't afford to share what time they do have with the crowds they live to avoid, and the man who pretends to be blind (Tomás is certain he pretends because he only thanks women who give him change) in a corner of Plaza Italia had been singing about not having any time left either but he'd seemed pretty happy about it, like he'd even moved his hips a little, and the whole thing was depressing as hell. Tomás had been about to give him change because he couldn't give him time, but as he'd stood in front of him, the man thanked him before he'd even dropped the coins in his metallic cup. Tomás pretended he was deaf and walked away.

And before that even, he had sat in the rain on a bench near his office and written his name on it. He's been writing it on trees, benches, bus seats and cubicle doors since he was a child because his sister, Angela, would eat his snacks and steal his pens if they weren't tagged. Although he knows it's a stupid ritual (then again, he can't think of a ritual that isn't stupid), this bench is different because there's someone out there who insists on erasing his name and leaving different ones behind. Today it had been Susi. Yesterday it said Santiago, but it's always the same hand-writing and Tomás wonders if he'll ever meet him or her so that they can agree to own opposite sides of the bench.

This city wears him out like that. He doesn't really know why, but kindness can be unbearable in a city that returns none of it. What does that even... leaves, leaves, leaves, death, fuck... He has to find a way to make Serge finish the damn song or he'll lose it. He lights another cigarette and some of the ashes fall on the record in smooth white spirals that will never reach the centre. At least he has all the time in the world.

He leans out of his window and looks down to the empty visitor's parking spots. Cars in the dark can look like bodies too, and the stack of bins in the corner look like animals, but no one will paint them, no one he has ever known will crowd the walls next to the golden pheasants, captain-general O'Higgins or the Atlantic puffins. No one will paint him either but that's OK because he wouldn't know what to do with his hands. He's also glad he's on the second floor because he can just flick dead cigarettes out and watch them spiral down with the wind until they disappear. The Santiago skyline is brighter than the stars above it, a golden mess with constant strobes of red and green dots on the highest roofs, blinking at imaginary private helicopters no one here owns. He shuts the window and it becomes a blur of amber and he must remember to clean it even if he knows he won't.

So why can't he sleep? He doesn't even try anymore. Getting up, taking a shower, dressing, drying and waxing his hair, cleaning his glasses and shaving... Shaving. Is there anything worse than shaving? He finds it hard to want to do any of it, as if he could predict how tiring every one of those things could be and... God knows he needs to keep himself awake and get to work or he will never finish anything again and...

'But you must eat,' his dad had told him after he broke up with his first girlfriend. It had been a bad breakup because they were both eighteen and she had given him so many symbolic gifts – a fluorescent green piece of string tied up to match her ring size (though it loosened up to the size of her big toe), a school napkin paper boat (which had half-sunk when they tried it on a puddle), and a lot of photographs of full trash cans because she wanted to be a photographer. She had told him to stick the symbolic shoebox up his ass. So he'd kept it. 'Leave that stuff and go somewhere nice and eat,' his dad had said. 'When I was shooting Argentinians at the border, all I thought about was coming home and having a nice *casuela* by myself. A-lone. Away from their fucking accents... *Oh puro Chile es tu cielo azulado*... Tomás, don't be embarrassed about eating alone.'

But that wasn't it. Despite Tomás's first girlfriend being Argentinian, his father had shot no one – outside of his imagination – because his mother had taught him how to break into patriotic songs to manage his anger. Plus, eating at Domino's every day, where they don't even have tables and the cashiers now refer to Tomás by his first name, has made him impervious to embarrassment. It's not like he cooks at all either (and he's closer to Domino's than he's ever been before). No, it's shaving, shaving for yourself, that's far worse. He really does understand why beards have become fashionable amongst lonely men.

He gets his computer bag out of his suitcase and gets the printed paper that says 'HI – I HOPE YOU'RE WELL ☺'. He'd stuck this on the window facing the street in his last place because there was a commuter bus filled with shopping mall workers that passed by that way every morning, and they could see that he could work from home and never even shower, and one of them even middle-fingered him when he waved. It still has the blue tack on each corner and he sticks it on the new window and finishes the coffee. But it isn't for the commuters now. It's complicated (and rather pathetic). Thing is, he really does hope she is well. But not *as* well.

He goes to the kitchen and starts the kettle. It was his birthday on Saturday and he is still pretty upset about it. More dead leaves, dying leaves, needle on track four and play. He had received a letter from her that morning. It was a birthday card and the front was green and yellow spots and she had written 'H.B. Hope you're keeping well ☺. Eva. x.' Her wishes had come in abbreviations and he's sure it's because she couldn't get herself to write the word 'happy' since she must be feeling worse than him. What really bothered him, though, was the part about 'keeping well'.

He had only just turned twenty-seven. Even worse is how his parents' card also said the same thing. 'Keep well, son'. Had he crossed some age gap he wasn't aware of? Would people call him 'Sir' from now on when they first met him? Would they ask him 'what do you do?' so they could use him to confirm how well they were doing in comparison? Would no one notice that, despite it all, he shaves for himself? It doesn't help that there's no special look for mid-twenty-year-olds. You either look like a teenager or your dad and so it's all about 'taking' from other ages, not 'keeping'. Must he now also wear those terrible khakis with a polo shirt (with a random mini-animal embroidered on the chest) tucked underneath? That doesn't even... He doesn't work at a place where that...

He presses down hard on the coffee and puts in a new straw. At 4am it's hard to know if he should give up on the previous day or get ready to start the new one, but he has so much work to finish; so much to start, rather. And so he goes to his desk, lights the half-melted vanilla candle and opens his IDEAS book.

Jaime told him yesterday that their videogame has to be finished by the end of the term. They'd decided (Jaime did) to split the work, so that Jaime would be in charge of programming and Tomás the story design. He's been trying to come up with a story for months now and he lied to Jaime about his progress. He told him 'it was coming', IT, because after all, that's what it takes. One idea, one moment, and it will come, it must, because can you really live your whole life without one great idea? But nothing he comes up with resembles the Big Narratives, as Tomás calls them, of games like *Final Fantasy VII*, or *Chrono Trigger* or *Zelda*... It isn't all his fault though. They only make cheap games for mobile platforms, bad copies of known games filled with product placement, pop-up ads for deodorants, horoscope readings and package holidays to Acapulco. And Jaime can't program anything without a bug either, and the last flash game they finished had to be taken down from the App Store due to its poor quali... It was shit. It was about an elephant called Bimbo, and he defied the laws of gravity, because when he jumped to collect coins he never dropped back down, and all you were left with was an empty screen with moving platforms. Disney bought it in the end, and rehashed it as a cheap mobile game about Dumbo, the flying elephant, and they were both allowed to keep their jobs at the university. The reception for their previous games had always been divided. People either loved the storylines and hated the gameplay or loved the gameplay but hated their storylines. This means that every game Tomás has had a part in currently appears as MEDIOCRE on App Store reviews – 2.5/5 stars, and that's taking into account two of Jaime's 5 star reviews – and he can't stand the fact that game reviews focus only on what the games lack instead of what they have. But what he really means is he hates knowing he's MEDIOCRE, just like everyone else, part of another filled-up bus, heading to another kind of MEDIOCRE shopping mall.

So now his job is to try and find a reason, a story, for any fault that might come up in Jaime's coding. But is that even possible? Can he really write a narrative about all those gaps, all those mistakes that aren't his? And isn't it also unfair that Jaime can set out the conditions, all the mechanics of a world that he must then justify with a simple story? And does it really matter? After all, as game reviewers always point out, if the gameplay's crap, everything else falls with it.

He opens the IDEAS book on the last page. He had been writing a scene about a man who could make rain go upwards because Jaime had messed up the physics engine again. Why on Earth would anyone want rain to go back to the clouds and even worse, how can rain exist if it doesn't fall in the first place? But he will think about reversing rain tomorrow. For now, he must accept that people as simple as Jaime do exist. He walks back into the kitchen and takes the Domino's pizza box out of the fridge. He cuts two slices out and puts them on a cardboard plate that he takes from a stack of cardboard plates. He microwaves the slices for two minutes.

They come out flaccid like wet bread. He turns the radio on even though Serge is still stuck on dead leaves. It's playing 'Sigue sus Ojos' by Caravana. Why are all good songs sad songs? Why must everyone sing about the things they don't have? He doesn't know the answer, but what he does know is that if he had continued playing in the band with Yiyo, he too would be happy playing music for a living and all their songs would be about being young, memories of being even younger, and Santiago, at night, shining for them.

He cleans the grease from his fingers with the kitchen towel and bins the plate on top of dozens of similar plates. He takes out a new packet of post-it notes from the cutlery drawer. He notices that she also took the dessert spoons but that's OK because he never has dessert. He writes 'e-mail Yiyo' on a post-it and sticks it on the cream-coloured cupboard above the kettle (why must all new flats always be cream-coloured?).

He turns the tap on and leans over to drink and then turns off the radio just before the singer repeats *and this time I would like to see you appear*. He knows the lyrics by heart. Or at least he thinks he does. OK, so he's never actually finished listening to the song because it was Eva who had told him to do so. She was always showing him new music and even Yiyo had once said that she had better taste than him. At the time, anything she was better at felt good. It was as if by standing next to her he was making everyone aware of his luck, which is superior to just being lucky. And hell, he knew she was much better at a lot of things. Her parents were obsessed with France and so she was too, and she'd watch (and make him watch) all these French cooking shows like *J'ai Encore Faim* and *Chef Hannibal* where groups of bearded chefs feathered geese and chickens onscreen and always with a smile despite all the blood, and used pans that looked like spaceships from *Battle Star Galactica*, and she took notes and said a lot of French things like *quoi* real quiet so that he had to ask and she had to explain, and they then ate the TV recipes on Sundays and... She always asked how it was and he always said it was good but on the last week that they were together he told her, while she was boiling six pans with different things at the same time, that she should be careful with the gas bill. She didn't say *quoi* or ask him how the food was but she did ask him, 'Tomás, I've been thinking, if I take the Trans-Siberian train, will you come with me?' and he answered, '*Cherie*, let's get the gas bills first,' and there was no dessert. She left a whole feathered chicken on the chopping board and he put it in cling film and stuck it in the freezer. She said he should just bin it and he said he would, but he's been carrying the feathered chicken from freezer to freezer ever since.

He looks out the kitchen window and tries to see the mountains but it's all smog and passing empty buses. When the day starts in Santiago, the city at a distance disappears into a new night, all of it grey-veiled and dark, and the Andes, the great peaks no one ever talks about (can only he see them?), loom above the concrete like secret mirages, pointing not North or South, just Out.

He puts the coffee in the French press and pours in the water. He adjusts the lid but doesn't press it because Eva had once told him he had to let it brew for five minutes – but he's not sure why. If all the grains are instantly suspended in the boiling water and in the end they all gather up at the bottom, right where they started, then pressing or not pressing doesn't change a thing. Plus, all coffee tastes the same and he should really just buy instant… But he'd need a mug for that, which doesn't matter, but neither does waiting five minutes. And so he waits and then presses and turns to go back to his desk and notices (not that he'd ever need any more) that his kitchen only has two electric hobs.

Was it true? Was he just boring? Surely he could have asked for more hobs. The last time he saw Eva it was to hand her the gas bill. He thought it'd make her laugh but it didn't. She didn't even look at it. She had lost weight and told him she had stopped smoking and started going to ballet lessons, and he told her he had stopped smoking too but she just let out a quiet laugh. He asked her why she had left him. The way she had done it too: she called him up (she had left him eight missed calls, eight!) but he'd been sleeping; she left messages with the secretary and she had phoned him up at his office but he'd slept through those too (in all fairness, Jaime likes keeping the office phone disconnected as he says admin gets in the way of what he calls his 'creative trances'). And then Eva knocked on his office door and he got up, though he may as well have been sleeping because when she waved her phone at him, he waved back with his. He showed her the floating elephant onscreen and she said, 'Tomás, I'm leaving you,' and then she just left. And so, when he later asked her why, he expected a story, a big low after a moment of great but flawed happiness, a story arc like the ones he teaches in Games Design 1:

HAPPY AS FUCK

SEX STOPS

TWO ELECTRIC HOBS

But she only said: 'I didn't know I could do better. And now I know.' It was cruelty, Tomás thought. Nothing more. To not give him the full story. And she had lost weight, was wearing a thick eyeliner he'd never seen her wear, and she told him about her new flat in Bellavista, which is most likely not cream-coloured and must have at least eight hobs, all of them gas, all of them cruel.

He sits at his desk and sticks two post-it notes on either side of the table.

REASONS WHY I MIGHT BE BORING:	REASONS WHY I'M OK AS A PERSON:
I don't like working.	I have a job.
2 hobs (electric).	Frozen chicken, head and all, in the freezer.
Dislike travelling.	I enjoy travelling once I'm there.
I make games for a living.	I make games for a living.
I can't sleep.	I never sleep.
Subject to change Subject to change Subject to change Subject	I don't own anything. The possibilities are endless (subject to change).

He gets up and takes a straw from the packet on his desk and puts it in the French press. But did it really matter? Could you really separate a life into favourable and unfavourable categories? He had once Googled 'why do people break up?' and Minxydoucheover9000 said that sometimes it's the things that make one fall in love with someone else that were also responsible for the breakup. But if that were true, then surely good and bad things are interchangeable and they could get back together again. And Jaime did say most lasting couples go through 'rough patches', sometimes more than once, and this one hadn't even been rough (she left him a goddam record player). And sure, Jaime's been single for years, but if someone who didn't know a thing about relationships could tell him that, then surely it means he, who knows much better, should have the evidence to support it. The record does an 80s rap song scratching noise to a beat that never starts.

He tears up the post-its and bins them. He'll have to get in touch with Eva tomorrow. He will thank her for the birthday card and tell her that he hopes she's well and then she'll ask him how he is and he'll say something French, *oulala*, miss all the hobs, *oulala* the taste of non-coffee, *oulafuck* did I just get us two tickets to Paris? He'll also tell her that he's still working on a game about her, even though he's never started it… Which is fine because beginning things is not as important as wanting to begin things and, like shaving for himself, it will show her that he has not forgotten about his priorities.

A note appears under his door and he can hear steps outside in the corridor. It's 5am so it can't be the postman but he hopes it's another gas bill under Eva's name, if only to see her name on a piece of paper that wasn't his, and written by someone other than himself. He walks up to it and takes it. It's the same note that showed up under his door at the same time last night. It's a folded A4 that says:

> You are cordially invited to come to Abdul's vintage madness on Sunday at the Plaza Italia market. We sell anything from kitchenware to voodoo dolls. Please come. The sales are mad on Sunday, mad!
> Cordially, your neighbour,
> Lucas.
>
> (P.S. Please come. X)

Tomás opens the door and checks the corridor but Lucas is gone. He steps out of his flat and hears heavy metal coming from the apartment facing his and then some loud laughter. It's Goat Eater all over again. He had shared a flat as a student with the drummer and vocalist of death metal act Goat Eater. They were both vegans and they slept most of the day and practised all night so as to not bother the parrots that gathered in the trees lining the apartment block. He notices strobes of light on the edges of the door and on the bottom, half of Lucas's note still sticking out. Someone suddenly takes the note and Tomás turns and hears a peephole lid opening so he goes back inside, slowly closing his own door. He hopes that he's not sharing a corridor with Goat Eater fans. Then again, if that were the case, he'd have something to add to his favourable list and it's not like he'd be sleeping.

He goes to the kitchen to turn the heating on. He hates having showers in the cold and he should really be getting ready to take the metro to work. Tomás only teaches at university on Thursdays. That's tomorrow. And after he can try and sleep at any time, usually under his desk, once Jaime goes home. He should really build the bed frame when he gets back though, but only if he gets back early enough not to bother anyone.

He finishes his coffee and sees the beginning of sunrise and the backyards and gardens shine with dew. When grass shines in Santiago it means winter is about to end. Eva used to say that. It makes no sense but it is indeed the end of August and winter has to end, shine or not. He looks at the picture of Eva on his desk. She's holding a miniature Eiffel Tower key ring he got her for her birthday. He turns it so that it faces the door for when he comes back from work.

He gets into the shower once the flat is warm enough. He must remember to buy soap because he only has lavender shampoo. Although he thinks they're actually the same thing in different bottles and there's no such thing as too much lavender. So no, that can also...

He'll thank Eva tomorrow, or today rather, and write a game about her, always to remember, to replay the days she left, the days she came back, the dead leaves dead leaves that are gone as soon as he imagines them and fuck Serge, fuck him to silence, he really does hope she's keeping well ☺.

2

Underwater Physics

IDEAS BOOK P. 18:

It can't just be about rescuing a damsel in distress because it's an indie game and indie hipsters will give us hell and for good... Anyway, the hero has to have shitty powers... Something limited, the ability to only fight in water, but he can't be as restricted as Aquaman because he still has a speck of self-respect. It's a PLATFORMER and he's collecting family heirlooms: a pearl, goldfish statues, purple coral shards and meteorite crystals shaped like people. At the end of the first stage, after killing an eel with a posh accent, you learn that the King of Tides (a crab with an eye patch) needs all these trophies too, in order to use their magical powers to send off waves across the world and let water take over forever so he can teach people a lesson about the power of nature (remember to make the game box fully recyclable to really hit it off with *that* demographic). But you, the hero, you steal it all anyway with the help of a telepathic guide, Mona, who reveals to you that she's been trapped for thousands of years in an underwater volcano (which you will find at the end of a level). But then, suddenly, when you finish collecting everything, the world just dries up, and now freed from the crushing ocean, Mona can save herself. Once she sees the state of the world above, she turns against you because it's your fault, it's your fault and you did this. Why did you not say anything? Did you not see the signs? She would have preferred another thousand... But then you realise that you could only understand her telepathically, and you've no fucking clue what she's actually saying now that she's free. The King of Tides just shrugs when she speaks, a crabby shrug, and it doesn't help you that she only speaks French, and she then beats the shit out of you to bring back oceanic life as we know it.

Though sometimes the plot isn't the problem. The issue here will be getting Jaime to correctly calibrate all the underwater physics and their complicated particle effects.

·   ·   ·

At the metro he takes the line 1 from Manuel Montt to Baquedano. It's only two stops away but he didn't sleep and so he's too tired to walk. He's always found it surprising how tired he is and how little weight he puts on even when he sleeps well. And he never even exercises and eats all that trash. It might be genetic and all, but it's probably his body working overtime to save him the embarrassment of asking for metro space on his way to work. Can positive things also be psychosomatic? Anyway, he likes rush hours in the metro. He's standing by the metal pole in front of the door which he can't even see because of all the people.

He's touching shoulders with this real fat guy who's sweating and reading the *La Cuarta* newspaper, some article about an American model called Jerry-Springs and why her liberal parents called her that, all in a tiny black bikini and smileys on the nipples and CAPITAL LETTERS EVERYWHERE and hashtags EVERYWHERE on the page because it's so #important and the guy keeps sweeping the gelled-up black remains of what his hair used to be to one side with the other hand as if it made a #fuckingdifference. To Tomás's left is a woman with big headphones on and she's carrying a cardboard tube in her backpack. She must be an architecture student because she smells of glue, doesn't look like a tramp (has shoes) and has small cuts on her fingers that end in yellow and red polka dot nails. She bites them and the colours have all cracked. He wonders what would happen if he tapped some random woman's shoulder like hers and asked her a deep question about herself, like, 'don't you think you've dealt with enough?' or something more specific to her, 'do you love symmetry?' or some vague bullshit that only hippies with BAs would answer. He likes to think about this sort of thing because he feels capable of anything, of making people take their headphones off out of awe because he'd have broken the unspoken rule about never speaking to someone you don't know in the metro and… Although really, he just likes it because he knows he would never do it and he'd like someone else to do it to him. But what would they ask him?

He could have studied something useful too, and by that he means essential, unlike videogames design, unlike narrative, unlike coffee, unlike pizza, unlike hobs and bed frames and ceramic plates and cups of any kind. He often asks himself what he could have done instead, but he always just ends up making characters, other people in a Tomás disguise that they don't even want, didn't even choose. Sometimes it's a doctor in a warzone curing people of terrible diseases in a cliché of poverty, stray dogs and limbless kids everywhere, a country called Republic of Developing. But then he comes from that Third World too, which makes the whole thing confusing. Other times he's a banker who's depressed because his working-class friends deleted him from Facebook when he bought pet passports and a yacht he ironically called The Winner. Whoever it is, it's never just Tomás. Eva used to say people were always hoping their lives would change, which she thought was pretty fucking stupid because change, she said, is just a nicer word for loss.

Today, like most days, he's just Tomás, and he's taking the same metro he's taken since he was eighteen and he doesn't recognise any faces, no one, not even his own on the glass doors that shake and pound to echoes in tunnels where no one's been and so he can't lose a thing. He reads the edge of the student's cardboard tube as she leaves and he's sure it says 'Flat: cream-coloured'.

More people get on. The doors close and everyone stops talking and it's just a long buzz, the metal scratching, sometimes even giving out sparks that briefly light the wiring on the walls of the tunnel. A guy in a suit presses against him and Tomás sees him from the reflection in the window. The guy takes out small scissors from his jacket's inside pocket and starts trimming his moustache on the sides and above the lips. Some of the hairs land on the back of an old lady's neck and on Tomás's shoes and they just stay there. He's surprised that inside a tunnel with all this noise and the trembling of the metro there can be no wind at all. No one talks but everyone's touching someone, staring at someone, and Tomás swears this is as close as anyone gets to anybody else in Santiago and why would anyone prefer to walk? The metro lines are all so small and the wait between stations is never more than a minute or two. Eva once said that in Paris the metro was like a spider web and that rush hours over there are hell on Earth, but he finds that hard to believe because she also said instant coffee and hot dogs were hell on Earth. Still, he could have just agreed with her.

Baquedano station. It's a short walk to Bellavista from here but even if he knew where she lived (she said it was better for him not to know), he wouldn't know what to tell her. He could pretend to be one of those American Jehovah's witnesses that plague Santiago and knock on every door until he finds her, but he doubts she'd be impressed by what she'd witness. She'd probably let out a small laugh and say that she knew it, that she knew that what he had was in some way a crisis of faith, but that yet again, he went about it the wrong way, and she would then add that there are deities much more powerful than Jesus… And what do people say to their exes? He has a full page of it. His IDEAS book, written upside down from the last page (page 100), says:

I learnt lots with you. So glad it happened.
If we take it slow this time. I feel it might definitely work.
We were too young.
I feel so delicate now.
Please, let me drink you.
I'm into marching bands now.
It was just too real, you know?
Let's stay friends on Facebook.

God, he hates that word: EX. It makes people sound like an exam mistake or an illegal trespassing signpost. Whoever invented it must have lived in Santiago too.

He gets out of the crowd in the metro station and walks to the *Fuente de Soda* nearest to him to get a takeaway coffee and a fried *sopaipilla*. It comes wrapped in a blue paper napkin that's definitely toilet paper and it's covered in grease stains and mini eruptions of oil now brown from all the use. He sits on the bench facing Yiyo's shop and writes his name on it where it now says 'Lolita Diaz'. He smiles and stretches his legs until well after the yawn has passed. He takes one bite off the *sopaipilla* and he feels full, and all the pigeons in the world start to crowd at his feet because they know it. Eva used to say pigeons were dirtier than rats and should be killed. He told her: if they exist, they must be important. But when you see them crowding around you with all their fucked up feet and necks breaking this way and that with that throaty blipblipblupping and skipping to get your crumbs that they confuse with cigarette buds, convinced of their invisibility and entitled to everything you own at restaurant terraces… You have to wonder if anyone would miss them if they ever returned to their own planets. He should have just agreed with her, the useless pigeons, their useless flights from roof to wire to roof, the useless noise and useless conversations. 'Pigeons are the wisdom teeth of the Earth, useful only to a world without people.' It didn't make any sense but that's what she had said once when they passed out drunk next to the canary cages in Yiyo's garden, where he'd also taken in orphan pigeons. He throws the rest of the *sopaipilla* at the birds that pick on it before disappearing to the street corner where they sell paintings of poets no one recognises.

Yiyo's music shop hasn't opened yet. It's called AudioPop. The shutters are only halfway up. Tomás takes out his IDEAS book and writes,

> Dear Eva,
>   Thank you for your letter. I loved the colourful spots.
> We are getting older. Isn't that funny? And since we aren't
> being spared the time, I think we should meet up and talk
> it all over. Again, thank you for the card. The colour choice
> was fantastic.
>   Love,
>   Tomás x
>
> PS. I have *foie gras* at home. I now get what you meant about subtlety.

He tears out the page and puts it in a used gas bill envelope because he has to make sure she reads it. He takes out a roll of sellotape from his bag and seals it.

He looks up at the shop and waits for Yiyo to open. He wishes he were selling drum kits and guitars too. Yiyo used to offer him work here when they were younger but Tomás just laughed it off. He always said he was working on the new *thing* and that this time it'd be huge. And the truth is that before the breakup, before his last game came out, he really did believe it'd be huge, he'd be HUGE. He used to take notes of the smallest details so he could then include them in his games: when the smog gets bad, everyone in Santiago has dust halos in the sun; the neighbour's dog barks in perfect jazz straight eighths; Eva's fake painting-poster on their wall is called *Sky* but the downward strokes, the blue waves and their unfinished circles that cross over buildings and people, suggests it just didn't know it was an ocean. By the time they split up, Eva didn't want to hear a word about his stories. She even declared herself ANTI-NARRATIVE one night, as if by his doing she'd lost all hope of ever loving any story, any story at all. 'It's the sky,' she said, 'that's what it is and that's what it's called, even if now that you said otherwise we can never see it again. And the yellow silhouettes nose-diving into the edge of the frame, those are all birds.'

He sees Yiyo inside the shop coming to open and waves at him. He doesn't see Tomás at first but when he gets to the door he waves back. Tomás stands but Yiyo signals him to wait for him to roll up the shutter. He comes out wearing a Sonic Youth T-shirt under a red and black flannel shirt and black jeans, like a cheap barista.

'Hey dude, how's it going?' Tomás says.

'It's too early to say. Same as always I guess, man, you?'

'Same really.'

'Actually dude, I'm pretty excited,' Yiyo says rubbing his face with one hand. 'We're recording the guitars for Fármacos tonight. I'm really nervous.' He waves to some guy opening a hat shop behind Tomás.

Fármacos is the band Tomás would be in if he hadn't been so persistent in getting a real job, which is just C++LIFE code for <Function Name='LACKING IMAGINATION'/>. He'd always had better grades than Yiyo through school, even without studying, and Yiyo just took a gap year to play music and travel without any money or anything all the way from Brazil, across the Colombian jungle and into Panama, walking and hitching rides in boats filled with monkeys, underage prostitutes and cocaine, like a hobo just to 'live a little, man. I won't be a suit-and-tie slave yet, you know? I know my dad is rich but I want to be independent, man,' and he even snorted cocaine from a monkey's forehead. Then, this happened on Facebook:

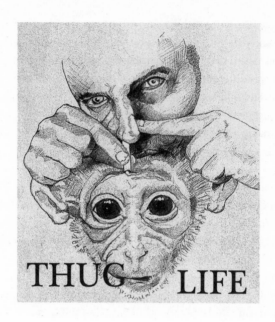

THUG LIFE

And it was that same day that the monkey head-dust photo appeared, following five hundred likes and a fucking meme made for it on 4chan. com, that Tomás decided to send off his university Games Design application. He sometimes wishes he'd taken a gap year too, although he knows that even under different circumstances, even with a meme of his own face doing drugs off of an alpaca's groin, he'd somehow find a way to live through the same decisions all over again, and he'd be sitting right where he is now, five years older, twice the pigeons, half the money, zero memes. <Module Name='Envy' ExceptionImplementation='true'/>. He does really hope for Yiyo's band to succeed.

'Hey man, listen, I have a favour to ask you,' Tomás says.

'Sure man, shoot,' Yiyo says, making a gun with both hands.

'It's about Eva.'

'Come on, it's been long enough.'

'It's just this one last thing.'

'You said that last time when you wanted me to give her that bag full of candles. She didn't even remember having them.'

'That was different.'

'It's always different.'

'She just loved vanilla so much, I thought—'

'So what is it this time?'

'You know where she lives now, right?'

'No.'

'You said you did.'

'I do, but not for you. You looked pretty fucked up after you gave her the candles.'

'It's a bill, man, a gas bill.' Tomás hands him the letter and Yiyo turns it to look at the writing on the front of the envelope.

'A bill?'

'Yeah. Could you give it to her? It's important. She's expecting it.'

'Alright, sure dude, but tonight I got band shit to do.'

Tomás sighs and looks at the shop windows. There's an old blue CJ drum kit with a bent splash cymbal and black electrical tape holding the bass drum skin in place. Christmas lights are tangled around the cymbal stands.

'So you still haven't sold the drum kit, huh?'

'Nope. It is a piece of shit after all.'

'A real shame.'

'I thought the lights would work, but I guess it's August,' Yiyo says, walking back to the door. 'Sorry man, I've got to finish opening up. You want to come in or are you staying out?'

'Nah, thanks. I've got to get to work. I just came to give you the bill.'

'So how's that going?' Yiyo asks.

'How's what going?'

'Work.'

'Well, the next one will be big.'

'Good. Christmas lights might work for you,' Yiyo says, stretching with a smile. 'Good, good,' he says while shaking hands with his first customer who just waits there nodding at nothing.

'Yeah.'

'Bye dude.' Yiyo turns a cardboard sign by the door that now says OPEN and Tomás waves back even though the door's now closed.

He lights a cigarette, stands and turns to cross towards the park that runs along the Mapocho River. In Santiago, anything with more than two trees is called a park, but this one's really great because there's a giant water fountain that sprays red and yellow and pink water and even music, although they mute it in the summer because people use it for pool parties and forget to wear clothes. He sees a young couple flying a kite together, and a stray dog that follows him (stray dogs always follow him) until it finds pieces of bread by a bin. He's always found it funny that the whole of Santiago revolves around the Mapocho, the river of shit that crosses the city and divides it into those who have to live with it, and those who hope to some day sail on it. Plaza Italia cuts Santiago in two, into whites and browns, into rich and poor, into German and misspelt Spanish surnames, and if water could be sliced in half and made to flow in opposite directions, the river would do just that and its whirlpool would be right here, right where he now steps on his dead cigarette.

Then again, the Mapocho isn't too bad because anything can look beautiful next to it, like having an ugly friend with you on a night out in town (which he knows is a shitty thing to think). There's a plastic windmill salesman pulling a cart full of spinning reds and oranges. People sell everything on foot in this city. You'd think it'd be easier to just wait in some corner, let people come to you. That's what he'd do, build a customer base, maybe even promote it online and make business cards with at least two telephone numbers and pay to appear in the Yellow Pages and... There it is again, the pigeons, the *Sky*, the not-doing-coke-on-a-monkey's-head, the river splitting, and him just sitting in the middle, where no one knows if trash is sinking or getting pushed aside by the current, by the spinning colours and the broken Sandro tunes from the tiny speakers that could now spell out forgotten memes about him: *all-your-base-are-belong-to-us, I Regret Nothing*... But they really don't.

The truth is that if it were your job to sell counterfeit Snicker bars and ChocoPanda ice-lollies, you'd also probably develop an instinct to escape, to run, to walk away. In Santiago you never really enter anything but you leave a lot. Tomás stands and the salesman asks him if he wants a windmill and Tomás promises that he'll buy one later on the way home. The salesman tells him that he'll be there all day and then asks another guy the same thing, but the other guy just says no.

He crosses the avenue again and turns on a small side street where his office is. Well, at least it used to be his. When the university announced that they would be cutting down their spending budget and many people lost their jobs, it seemed like the wrong thing to do to complain about having to share an office with Jaime. But there's only one desk, so Tomás has to work on a small flat surface by the windowsill until Jaime leaves. Jaime is always there when Tomás arrives but at least he leaves early too, because creative minds, he says, are attuned to the power of sunrise (though you can't really see the sun at all because of all the skyscrapers blocking it). Jaime once said it was OK that Tomás had to write by the windowsill because good writers can write anywhere. But when Tomás asked if he could work from home, Jaime said that no one really works at home. Either way, Tomás can't complain. After all, Jaime let Tomás stay at his flat for nearly three months after the breakup without paying for as much as a beer. Sometimes though, he wishes the rent had been expensive as hell.

There's a crowd gathering by the main door of the office building. They're all wearing hiking boots, green jungle hats with nets on the back of the neck, and oversized military jackets filled with pins and badges and creases and holes. Some have banners that say 'Blue Peace' and 'Unite against #GlobalWarming or suffer THIS' with a photograph of a volcano erupting into an atomic mushroom cloud of reds and orange sparks in the background. The university shares the office building with Blue Peace, so every week Tomás and Jaime have to watch crowds start their marches towards the La Moneda Square along the river. Last week, the protesters were pissed off by the lack of media attention after their #WeAreJustAnimals naked protest campaign against animal-made clothing failed to get into the evening news. Fighting warmth in winter gets no support whatsoever.

He pushes through the crowd and a woman with a megaphone gives him a volcano banner. He takes it by the mushroom cloud and thanks her because they like being thanked, and she smiles at him as he walks inside. The elevator is still under maintenance, which is really just a Chilean way of saying BROKEN FOREVER since he's never seen anyone come to maintain it. He takes the stairs instead and by the time he's on the ninth floor he can hardly breathe. He should really stop smoking and go jogging and eat organic vegetables. He should ask the Blue Peace people for advice. His father, now sixty, told him once that he already has friends who've died of lung cancer. But, like his father, Tomás will stop smoking when he has his first kid (and then, also like his dad, never actually do it). At least that was the deal he'd had with Eva.

He opens the 934-A door to the offices lobby. He walks past the secretaries because he still hasn't graded the students' Game Ludonarrative Dissonance assignments from the beginning of the semester. He's also not up to date with the attendance sheets for his seminars. They wouldn't take long to do, but that's also the reason why he never does them. He looks at the secretaries as he passes by and Anna sees him and stands to talk to him. He keeps on walking. Ever since she got pregnant, Tomás has found it easier to outwalk her.

'Tomás, the tests, please!' she shouts to him, holding her belly.

'Sorry, I'm joining the protest today. This one's with clothes.' He shows her the volcano banner and he walks past office doors where there are people he's still never even met. At the end of the long corridor is their boss, Pedro Milcock. Tomás hopes that Pedro doesn't know about the assignments, and he probably doesn't because even when *Bimbo: The Elephant* failed to sell, he told Jaime they were doing work that showed promise. Still, he's only ever complimented Jaime for anything they both do, and Tomás is sure that Pedro knows that he doesn't deserve to work there, that he's just another pigeon living on someone else's scraps. Jaime says this is all in Tomás's head, but just to be safe Tomás always avoids Pedro. For example, once, on his way to his office, Tomás saw him starting to come out of a door at the other end of the corridor. Tomás went into the toilets that were next to him and locked himself in the handicapped cubicle. When he was about to come out, someone came in. Tomás looked under the door to see if he could recognise the shoes. He didn't (who could ever do that?) and so he sat and heard that someone piss. FOR. AGES. When he came out, Pedro was looking at himself in the mirror, still pissing, and then frowned at him. Tomás walked straight out but he should have washed his hands first.

He opens his office door, door 405, right next to Pedro's. Jaime turns on his chair and smiles at him.

'Great, so now you're a climate change activist. Cool, man,' he says with a fist in the air. 'You know those hippies are all wrong right? I only wish it were warmer. But hey, some of those girls must look good naked, despite all the hair,' he laughs and Tomás nods and puts the volcano by the bin.

'How are you?' Tomás asks Jaime, but Jaime turns to look at his computer screen again.

'You have to see this. Been trying out a new engine, Unreal 4. Check this out.'

Tomás sighs. 'We don't use Unreal 4.'

'Not yet. Look, check it.'

Onscreen: a dark back alley with an old bar that has a light flickering and no people inside. When the lights turn on in the bar, Tomás can see the rain bouncing on the floor like pebbles, freezing in light before disappearing, as if lightning had struck.

'Pretty cool, huh? Finally got the rain to come down.'

'Looks great.'

'It looks real. Look how big those drops are. Look at how they splash and make puddles. Sure, I don't know how to stop the puddles from gathering water yet, but hey, I'm not sure what I can do with it yet anyway. I was thinking maybe a detective game would go down well with the whole rainy dark alley bar thing. Any ideas?'

'Well, there's already a game like that.'

'Every damn time... Took me all weekend. Shit, so what's this one called?' Jaime sighs.

'*Heavy Rain.*'

'Fuck me...' He closes down the dark alley. 'I guess we still have Bimbo.' He opens up a screen with the elephant, the sad fucking elephant condemned to fly without reason other than coins which can't even buy anything in the game because they didn't have time to come up with any items.

'Hey man,' Jaime starts, 'do you think it would maybe look better if I applied underwater presets on the physics engine instead of flying ones? I mean, without a liquid backdrop, of course.'

'Why would you do that? The game sucks no matter where it's set.'

'I know, but maybe it'll change underwater. Part of the problem is that Bimbo sticks to the jumping animation, but underwater there'd be no jumping, it'd just be swimming.'

'There's still a floor in the ocean,' he says. But what if the puddle gathered so much water, so many pebbles that it covered the whole of

Santiago? What if out of a puddle, a mistake in physics, they could make a whole ocean where lightning is just dust particles that freeze nothing, and Bimbo can finally be the mistake he was destined to be and just float on forever? Playable mistakes are the hardest thing to program though, and Jaime could never pull them off on demand.

'I guess. It's too early for a Bimbo sequel anyway,' he says, turning the elephant model that even underwater flies confused, contorted in choppy animation and low-res greys and blacks that stick out of its head and body in sharp polygons. The more you look at it, the more it kind of starts to look like a pigeon or...

'Well, that's enough for me today,' Jaime says. He opens up the web browser on a dating site called GeeksWithoutKids.com. He scrolls down the PC Master-Race section (which just means old people) to a page full of photographs of women wearing thick black-framed glasses, pokéball earrings and *Zelda* Triforce tattoos over their Xbox Gamerscore points and PC Steam Achievement lists.

Tomás goes to the window and opens his IDEAS book on the small white surface next to it. He starts to open the window but Jaime turns and...

'Could you wait a bit until I'm gone? I can't stand those damn hippies. I feel that if you open the window we might get their BO from here. I'm about to leave anyway.'

'Really? Where are you going?'

'Date.' He points at the screen.

'It's not even lunchtime.'

'Well, they're meant to be geeks after all.'

Tomás nods because he likes to stay alone in the office and use the real desk.

'How do I look?' Jaime asks him, standing up and putting his coat on. He's balding on the sides and you can tell by the dark cracks on his cheeks that he had real bad acne, and why is it that people ask you how they look before doing something important? Can they change it? Would washing your face, rubbing a tissue on it, changing shoes or wearing a nice watch change anything at all if you're an ugly fucker? Repairing Jaime's cheeks would be like building a smooth parking lot inside the ridges of the Grand Canyon. It just can't be done with today's technology. He's also wearing this fucking ridiculous red bowtie because he's the kind of guy who thinks self-hatred is confidence, and those damn braces he isn't ashamed of make him seem honest about it.

'You look great.' Tomás answers. 'I mean, if you put a gun to my head,' he says using his hand as a gun aimed at his left ear, 'I'd lose the—'

There's a bang on the window and they both jump and turn to it. A bird is dying on the other side of the sill after crashing against the glass.

'Dude,' Jaime says.

'Fuck.'

'Should have opened the window after all,' Jaime laughs as he picks up his umbrella.

'I'll clean it up, don't worry.'

'Well, you kind of have to, I have to go, like, now.'

Jaime leaves and Tomás bends down in front of the window to see the bird. It's shaking, black eyes still open, its wings wrapping the body to stillness. It's the second time a bird has died on their window and he really should, once he's done with the new game, print out bird silhouettes and stick them everywhere. He knows it works because he's seen them stuck in other buildings around the city and he wonders why birds are so afraid of their own shadows that they refuse to touch them.

He opens the window and pokes the bird with his pencil. It doesn't move so he takes out an A4 from the printer tray and uses it to grab and wrap it and then leaves it in front of himself on the keyboard. Would it still have crashed under Jaime's ocean preset? Nothing can look painful underwater, even drowning. He takes out a cigarette and rubs the tip to let specs of tobacco fall on the bird. He looks for a pen inside the pen mug, finds a Bic, and takes its insides out to keep the plastic tube. He looks at himself on the black computer screen with the tube up his nose and then looks at the bird with the tobacco.

The climate change hippies are still downstairs shouting motivational slogans amongst themselves. Free our futures, free our futures, free... The bird opens its beak and shuts its eyes, and the pen falls off Tomás's nose, and he stands and leaves the bird by the window and lights a cigarette. At least it's not a pigeon.

He looks at his IDEAS book and writes FREE OUR FUTURES and draws a bird under it, but he knows he could never turn something so abstract into a game. He finishes his cigarette and looks at the time. He still has twenty minutes to kill before class and he wonders if Yiyo's delivered the letter. Would Yiyo free his future? Would Eva write back or just appear at his office? Would they 'talk it over'? He hates that douchebaggery, talk it over, which is really just C++LIFE code for <Function Name='TALKING A LOT'/>, too much and to the point of exhaustion and about nothing in particular, minor annoyances, the way her tone implied this or that, the way he's sorry but he misunderstood that tone (which is like saying he isn't sorry at all), the way she just didn't have as much fun as they once did when tiring others with the same fucking jokes routine they shared for two whole years about this hipster in the metro they pretended to have conversations with and hey, man, yo, man, what's up bro, check my beanie out, man, but there was no one there even wearing a hat... And then there's the way they've both changed just because they're older, which they'll try to make sound like something positive with big words like EXPERIENCED and MATURE, but you're OLD, you douchebag, you're getting older, you're just OLD, #oldandying. And that's what happens when you talk it over. You agree to a wall of noise, and then you agree to silence.

He locks the office door from inside and turns the lights off. He kneels on the floor and crawls under Jaime's desk and lies on his back looking up at the table. It's in moments like these that he recognises himself as a teenager and it really gets to him, because if people can only see themselves as they want in secret, then the whole city is just filled with half-people, ghosts traversing through walls and convinced they can still dream when they're just remembering, and then they disappear and it freaks everyone out, and like in the movies, they just don't know yet that part of them is already dead.

Under the desk it's an astrological display of chewing gum. Someone else has done before what Tomás is doing now. Someone has lain under the desk, just like him, and stuck about sixteen pieces of chewing gum underneath. He or she even took the time to connect some of them and Tomás is glad he's sharing a stranger's secret. They remind him of the times he and Eva would walk up the San Cristóbal Hill on summer weekend mornings and stay there until the stars came out and they would see the whole of Santiago light up for them, just for them, and somehow, in the sudden emptiness of city nights, he would know, he knew, that he could spend all of his life watching the streets and the sky flickering like a dying candle in the dark.

The pieces of gum move overnight. He's sure of it. No one apart from Jaime and himself can get into the office and so who could be coming in (or why) to move them is beyond him but it happens. Could it be Lolita, the remover of bench names? Or was it Jaime's troll droll on the shelf that comes to life at night to do it? It's always turned to face the desk.

'What are you looking at?' he asks the doll but even if it did answer, Tomás likes that their agreement is a silent one.

What yesterday was a perfect circle of seven pieces of gum is now a square. He turns to the troll doll on the shelf that looks both old and young at the same time, which is pretty much what an internet troll is too, and he notices its big toothless smile and bulging eyes. He checks his watch and it's time for him to go to class but he could fall asleep under the desk right now. The rug is comfortable enough and he already used his bag as a pillow once. He must remember to build the bed frame when he gets home but only if…

He puts his jacket back on, gets his IDEAS book from the window and takes four random books from the shelf (Chaos Theory 1, Ludonarrative Dissonance, Physics Engines, and Unreal 4) to make his students believe that he's well-prepped for class. He walks up to the dead bird wrapped in paper, shakes the tobacco dust off of it, and grabs it to put it in a bin outside.

Towards the main door he sees Anna the secretary putting her phone down and standing up and grabbing her belly. Tomás keeps walking and shows her the dead bird.

'Tomás, please, those grades, when will—'

'I can't right now, something died in my office.'

3

Chewing Gum Constellations

There are still forty minutes left of class and Tomás has nothing else to tell them. Maybe if the classroom didn't look like something dreamt up at Google he would make an effort. The walls are red, the desks are bright yellow, the carpet is red and the blipping LED in the projector is red too. The whole thing would be like being stuck in *Doom*'s KILL SCREEN if it weren't for the green-shaded window that opens into the bins. The bins are red too, and so are the bin bags.

He checks his phone without taking it out of his pocket (as if they wouldn't notice, but the important thing is to look like you believe it), and he favourites a NASA post to an article he will never read. It's about a super Earth that just got discovered, exoplanet HD7924d. Planets get discovered and he has nothing to say about it. It sounds like the classroom codes in Tomás's timetable. He's on PH203r but it's no exoplanet because the slight tilting on the floor, the bend on the window that shrinks and splits the bins with its tiny cracks, and the way time just doesn't pass... It means that if anything, it'd be a black hole.

The students stare at him and he stares back at them. It's dark. He had forgotten to turn the lights on when he came in and he can't just walk over to the light switches now without saying anything. All the noise and all the reds are being sucked out by the remains of the dead class star, now just shadows in front of other shadows, tearing through the classroom, their words and thoughts travelling through whole universes but always seeming still, going nowhere, and that is what it is to be young like them, to not notice that what you've said has been said and will be said a million times over, to think yourself safe from PH203r, to appear to go nowhere. He looks back at his phone and in the Twitter responses to the NASA article @RealNicolasCage says to not get our hopes up about the super Earth because it's fifty-four light-years away. It's still closer than the end of class.

He can't come up with anything. He should carry small-talk studio cards, like on those old panel shows where people won washing machines and orthopaedic mattresses. Even then they'd probably give him short official answers: Yes, No, Why of course, I understand. He'd have to lead into new questions, personal questions, even hurtful ones, just to get a reaction like journalists do on news channels. Still, no one would watch it because eighteen-year-olds are not meant to know what they're doing, and the proof is that they're all here. They could just Google their whole fucking degrees, just like he Googles his teaching material. Should he tell them that, how no one great every cared about school, how the best game studios don't give a shit if you have a degree? But teaching is just a job. He doesn't always have to be teacher. He needs it. It's OK. Even light-years end and at least he's getting paid to get older. He knows they're texting each other about the silence, about their lunch plans, about how red everything can be and how his shoes remind them of their parents. Thirty-eight minutes. He presses Follow on @RealNicolasCage.

'What do you think?' he asks, looking at his shoes for a brief moment so that he can put his phone away. Still, no one says a thing. He would be quiet too if he were them because he knows, and they know, that the most important parts of a game are the gameplay mechanics and not the story. They've been talking about *Final Fantasy VII* and the way it manages to critique late capitalism and debate over the existence of God and destiny using a simple love story plot. But all they want to talk about is why Aeries, the girl the hero loves, dies at the end. He can't blame them though. It's fucking ridiculous. There should be a man in every classroom, an old man in a renaissance costume or something that looks official, sitting at a far corner, and his job would be to shout BULLSHIT in a posh accent every time these kinds of subjects come up. And what do they think? Well, they don't and they can't. They are eighteen-year-olds who've never had a lasting relationship and they smoke e-cigarettes because they're safer and one student, a short guy with a T-shirt of Che Guevara wearing an identical Che Guevara T-shirt, even said that if the game was a critique of late capitalism, then there'd be no place for a love story. 'Politics have nothing to do with love,' he said, and his friends agreed and Tomás just nodded. He knows that the convictions of the young can only ever be changed by their own inevitable disappointments and not by some old douchebag who tells them he knows better. Still, he's meant to teach BULLSHIT and there's no man in the corner, just more nodding all in red and at the rhythm of a trash disposal truck dropping small tins and bits of glass that its claw fails to keep and…

'So, any thoughts?' They look at each other and pretend to write. He can see one of them drawing a cock smiley with glasses and a moustache that covers the entire page. Another student's phone vibrates. The boy silences it but then starts texting anyway. There's only one girl who likes to work, but she never says anything, although she keeps sighing and rolling her eyes whenever the others speak. She's a Videogames Design post-grad, but she enrolled to sit in Tomás's undergrad class to write the script for her upcoming game. He checked for her in the registry and her name's Franziska, Fran. She's twenty-four and a German exchange student, which means she must already know it's all BULLSHIT. Tomás looks at her and she smiles back and unzips her hoody. Tomás looks back at the clock. He really could use a smoke.

'OK, that's enough for everyone I think,' he says, but they don't even move. 'So, for next class,' he starts, 'think about *Zelda* and *Super Mario* and the use of the "Damsel In Distress" tropes in gaming.'

'Will we ever look at indie games in the course?' Che Guevara asks, looking around him while they all nod in silence.

'Like which?'

'I don't know, like *The Loop*, or at least *Kink Turbo*. I mean, I just don't see the point in learning about these huge games with corporate budgets. We don't really care about the things we'll probably never do. Not that I want to work for those corporate assholes, but I'd much rather be realistic about it. We'll all be making indie games, small budget titles, and it'd be great to get some tips. We should be looking at *The Loop*. Now there's an awesome story.'

Tomás has no idea what Che is talking about. Other students nod and start whispering and laughing about it, so he shuffles the books he brought in his bag, picks up his IDEAS book, opens it and waits until they all go silent again.

. . .

IDEAS BOOK P. 22:

~~The protagonist is a larva. There are only microbes in the world~~. Earth is microscopic and everyone in it is a microbe. There's only one human, the protagonist, you, and you live alone in another planet filled with purple rings and a pink ozone layer. It's light years away and it rains black paint splatters all the time. In your world, everyone else left to find sunnier planets, but you stayed because you had just built up a shed that you now use as a studio for your paintings. All of your paintings come to life as monsters. ~~They keep~~ You can give them any ability, but you can't give them life for more than a day because, as you learnt from very young,

41

all paint spoils in this black-rain planet, even inside the shed (there's a lot of wind) and you haven't invented glass or proper windows because you like the sound and the smell of rain when you sleep.

One day you paint a man with long arms, wings and five feet but no head. When you finish the monster and it comes out of the canvas, you give it your only working light bulb and your flying shoes so that it can achieve the speed of light. Then, you make it fly into the micro-planet nearby in search of friends.

When the monster lands on Earth, it finds nothing but microbes moving about with no other purpose than to decompose dead things on shallow water. The monster picks up one of the microbes with its long arms, chosen at random, and it starts to stretch it in all directions.

The point of the game will be to make a microbe evolve into a person under a day, so that it can be taken to the rainy planet before the monster disappears. And you'll have to go through all the stages of evolution before you can stretch them further. The microbe becomes a bigger microbe, then a deep-water larva, then a fish, then some kind of crocodile, and then a bird a monkey (the game can't be that long). Up to that stage there is no time, there is no way of dying, there are no items and the monster helps the evolving creature by eating any predators that come near it.

But then the creature becomes a person and the timer starts. He now needs items like fire, a hammer and a wooden pillow. The monster keeps trying to stretch him because he's still not large enough but it just won't happen, because he now only responds to one name in the entire universe, Dan, and the monster doesn't even have a mouth so he has to learn sign language too. Even when Dan just stands there in front of the monster he can't stretch, not without believing it can happen, and so he needs to get the power-up of Belief and Optimism. He builds an altar, and the entrance to it is so small the monster can't come in to stretch him, and its legs are starting to fade with time, and its feet are no longer even there. He keeps growing and that evening Dan finds he's too large for this planet, and his head even lights up from space like a volcano every time he breathes. He begs the monster to take him somewhere new, somewhere large, where he can choose to be by the sea, on earth, or in the sky, but not have to deal with them all at once. Now that he can draw, he draws the monster a face, and asks to fly him out in exchange of a voice. But with its new face, the monster can now see the world and it doesn't want to go back.

That's when Dan fights him, the BOSS BATTLE. And when he wins, the monster takes him to your home, to your shed, and you're waiting there, and you cry, and the monster cries too and his tears rub him out entirely. The guy is confused. He has never seen black rain. He tries to talk to you, but you can only speak French. And now he misses the old monster because you've just painted another one to take him back to the microbes, now all evolved into crocodiles, and he loses all of his power-ups, like sleeping and cooking on more than two electric hobs. The only thing he can do now is paint faces he has never seen on cave walls, but they all just look like microbes. And the timer never ends.

.   .   .

'I didn't like *The Loop*,' Tomás says, starting to tidy his things. 'No particular reason, I just couldn't get into it.'

No one says anything but they start closing down their computers. Fran puts her pens back in her pencil-case. Tomás isn't sure when he's last seen a pencil-case, but it must have been years ago.

They leave the classroom but Fran stays. Tomás closes down his PowerPoint presentation and turns off the projector. The hum disappears and Fran's still sitting. Although he has his back to her, he knows that she's looking at him.

'Anything I can do for you?' he asks her whilst tidying his laptop wires into a ball in the small pocket of his bag.

'Me have one question. Sorry, um, Spanish not so good.'

He turns to her and closes his bag.

'Sure.'

'You know *The Loop*, right, *The Loop* no exist, you know, um, you know it don't exist?' she smiles, standing up and taking out a small black makeup mirror from her purse.

'What do you mean?'

'They make up, they invent up to... um, to mess you.'

'Oh. I thought I saw something called Loop, Lupa, Lupus, something like that...' he says but she just smiles. 'I don't mind it so much. The classes are for you, not me.'

'They think you very weird, you know, like.'

'Like what?'

'Don't know. Like, very creepy maybe? You know? Yeah, it might be dead bird, maybe, yes?'

'Oh.' He looks at the bird all wrapped up in paper on the reading stand, right under the lamplight. It looks red too. He just couldn't get himself to put it in the bin, not with the way they treat the bottles. He will take it out and bury it somewhere. He will give it to the museum with the paintings of dead people and the taxidermists there will love it because they haven't seen a bird so recently alive in years.

'I've got to get going. Nice to meet you.'

'Fran.'

'Fran. See you next week.'

'Wait, give five minutes.' She steps up to him and she looks inside her purse. She takes out a notepad and writes down a telephone number, tears off the page and gives it to him.

'I'm very alone too,' she says. 'Class people, they so very young, make me feel like mother. I hate children, you know? I hate mother too. I mean, have you seen they clothes? Chile bad, bad clothes.'

He doesn't know what to say but her eyes are grey and blue and her lips so red and she comes closer and he can feel her breath on his right cheek and she kisses it, and then the left, and his face is warm and all he can look at is the bird under the lamp.

'See you soon, yes? No complicated, yes?' she asks.

'Why?' he answers but she just leaves and so he says, real loud, 'Make sure you think about damsels in distress!' but she doesn't say anything and he swears he hears her laughing.

It must be some kind of dare and he shouldn't have let her kiss him. Jaime told him that Claudio, a C++ programming teacher, once nearly got fired because a group of girls had kissed him, and at the same time taken a selfie that then went on Twitter and became a viral meme.

Then, when he gave them bad grades at the end of the year the two girls accused him of sleeping with his students. He didn't get fired only, but only because no one else understands C++ like Claudio does. Plus, the meme was so popular people were asking him for autographs and signing into his courses just to see him. 'No matter what we do, we're all programmed to fuck, that's our only certain feature,'

Claudio had said at a late staff meeting, where he had got wasted and explained he had actually been sleeping with one of the students for a whole year and no one gave a shit. He wrote this on the blackboard:
`<Module Name='Humans\Sex\KissingStudents.dll'/>`

Tomás must not let any of that happen. If Eva ever found out! He must be stronger than Claudio, stronger than C++, than the will to be memed, than his certain features. He checks his phone but Yiyo still hasn't messaged him to confirm that he's delivered the letter. Did Tomás tell him to confirm? He will have to tell him to confirm. Yiyo's phone contact picture is still the dusty monkey. Tomás has to tell him. He makes a paper ball with Fran's number and puts it in his jacket pocket; he will bin it outside. He takes the bird and walks out of the classroom, avoiding the purple circles in the red carpet.

Inside the elevator he looks at himself in the wide mirror. He looks tired. His eyes are swollen and although the elevator lights are bright white, he's sure he looks paler today. Why, months after the breakup, does he still look like this? And why would Fran want to kiss that? He should make sure he sleeps before meeting up with Eva. Minxydoucheover9000 from Yahoo! Answers also said that after a period of non-contact, you have to look like the best version of yourself. He lifts the dead bird up near his face and sees it in the mirror.

When he turns to face the elevator doors, he sees the red lip marks on both his cheeks. Two students come in and press 1 and they look at Tomás and his dead bird and he smiles at them.

'*Angry Birds* lecture,' he tells them, but they look away and then at each other. He just hopes they didn't see his cheeks.

The doors open and he heads straight out of the building and onto the street. He rubs his cheeks as he walks across the global warming activists and their volcano pamphlets now soaked in rain as they shout slogans about the world coming to an end and blow piercing whistles. A woman wearing a neon green road-worker windbreaker gives Tomás another volcano banner. The guy selling plastic windmills is in front of the office-building door, and he gives Tomás an orange windmill so Tomás has to give him five hundred pesos for it before going in. The old man doesn't even say thank you.

Back in his office, he drops the banner next to the other banner and the bird back on the windowsill. He lies down under his desk and sees the chewing gum constellations. The square is a circle again, so he looks at the troll doll smiling at him.

His phone rings and he takes it out from his pocket as fast as he can because it should be Yiyo telling him what will happen to his future, his entire life, but it isn't. It's his mother and he sighs before picking it up. Her contact photo is a beige couch.

'Hi Mum.'

'Hi *monito*! My little monkey, how are you?'

'Ugh.'

'Aiii, don't be *jugoso*, son.'

'You don't even know what that means.'

'I know it's a hip thing to say. Don't hate the player, hate the game. Don't hate… Everyone says that at the gym. But hating a game without players, now that's *jugoso*. I'm not that old you know?' He hears his dad mumbling something behind her. 'Did you get our card? Your dad wants to know if you got our card. How are you? The card, yes, yes, I asked him, I think he got it. You got it right? Are you still at work? Your dad wants to know if you're still at work.'

'Retired!' his dad shouts in the background even though no one asked him anything and his mum laughs.

'So you finally did it,' Tomás says, touching the chewing gum stars above him.

His dad picks up the phone. 'Yup, after thirty-eight years. It's a long time. Isn't it a long time?'

'Oh, so looong,' his mum sighs behind him.

'It's a long time.' And it is a long time. His dad had worked at the Clover factory in Graneros for most of his life. When he started, his job was to put toys in cereal boxes. He gradually moved up to designing them, after revolutionising the field. He came up with a string that glued the toy to the bottom of the cereal box so that kids had to eat the whole thing before getting it. It was impossible to unstick so it made people eat faster. It had made Tomás popular in primary school because he could get his classmates any toys they wanted, but as he became older it made him unpopular because his house was always packed with cheap plastic superhero figures that no one cared about anymore. Once, he brought a girl home and she asked him why there were so many toys. He said he had a retarded brother in a care home who only visited on weekends. He called him Nacho because it's what he felt like eating at the time, and he kept up the story throughout most of high school.

'We just called you to tell you some good news. Right *vieja*? We have some good news.'

'Some great news! Oh, look at the flood. Oh my God, a flood on TV, always so many floods in here. Jesus Christ save those poor people, oh my God so many commercials. This country, I tell you, and tomorrow it's hot again!' his mum says in the background.

'What is it?' Tomás asks, leaving nail marks in the chewing gum dots.

'I start flying tomorrow!'

And that is worse for Tomás than a Biblical flood. Every man in the Perez family after Tomás's grandfather, all his dad's cousins, even the distant ones (although they're really all distant), have been, or are, recreational pilots. And Tomás's dad loves saying it, over and over again, that during the dictatorship, he had flown to the border with Argentina, ready to start a war, and that he's been frustrated ever since that he hadn't got to kill any Argentinians. He once told Tomás that even when they screamed their accents were annoying, and that he still dreamt of screaming Argentinians. Tomás still hasn't applied for his license because he's afraid of heights, but his dad keeps bringing it up from time to time. Even Nacho would be flying by now.

'Maybe you can come with me and I'll teach you.'

'He'll teach you!' his mum says.

'I'm real busy with the game, sorry.'

'Ah… And how's Eva doing?'

'She's busy too. Sometimes I don't see her for a whole day. She says hi.'

'Great. Say hi back to her. Tell her I want grandkids.'

'We want grandkids!'

'No.'

'Well, someone's got to buy your games,' his dad says with a sigh. 'Remember, it's the simplest things that are the best. Just keep it simple. Remember the sticky string I invented? It was that simple.'

'Say hi for me,' his mum says.

'Alright, I will.'

'But seriously, you should come and fly with me.'

'Dad, I have to go. Eva will be home soon and it's my turn to cook dinner tonight.'

'Again?' his dad says.

'Well done her!' his mum says in the background.

'OK, well, take care. If you change your mind, just give me a call. I have a cell phone now.'

'I will.'

He hangs up and sits against the wall under the desk. He just can't bring himself to tell his parents about the breakup. They really liked Eva and they'd be so hurt. And his mum would say that it's because he has no patience with other people. And his dad would say it's because he doesn't have a real job like his sister does, who is definitely not like Nacho because she writes the cultural section for *El Mercurio* paper and keeps meeting celebrities. Her work on the contemporary magical realism scene in Chile was called 'revolutionary' by the new magical realist

Adolfo Genuino, although Tomás doesn't know why because he never reads the paper, just as she never asks him about his own work. And his dad would then go on to tell him that to get over Eva he needs to learn to fly and think about shooting Argentinians and sticking strings, sticking them everywhere, at the very end of boxes just like him, just that simple, to make him learn about patience and deserving things you really want and... Plus, if he and Eva end up together again, it would make the whole conversation useless. He's just not prepared to have useless arguments with that beige couch. His dad just retired and he needs to rest and fly and well, retire, and to force him to think about Tomás's own problems would be too selfish.

He hears the key turning on the other side of the office door so he gets up and sits by the windowsill and opens his IDEAS book. Jaime comes in and looks at the bird in front of him.

'Amazing, you've been working here the whole time. Don't worry, I'll get rid of it then.' He takes the bird, puts it in an empty crisp packet that was on the desk, steps on the plastic bin pedal and drops it inside. The speed of the whole thing makes Tomás swallow hard. 'You haven't left then? I thought you had lessons.'

'Yeah, but they ended early. Most of them hadn't even played *Final Fantasy VII*, can you imagine? Sometimes I wonder why we even call them students if they never want to study. They keep telling me what I should be teaching them instead. Something about a loop. They had little to say about the story.'

'*The Loop*? They were on about that in my class too. It's a shame about FF7 though. It's a great game, amazing gameplay mechanics,' Jaime says, putting his scarf on the desk.

'How was your date?'

'It was fine,' he says, going through the post-its on his computer screen.

'Just fine?'

'Yeah,' he sighs, 'she was way too nerdy.'

'Isn't that the point of GeeksWithoutKids.com?'

'Yeah but this was too much. Her name was Agatha. Fucking Agatha. Who the hell is called Agatha nowadays? And her favourite game's *Pokémon* and you know how much I hate *Pokémon*.'

'Yeah, you hate *Pokémon*. That sounds terrible.'

'So, they finally left,' Jaime says, looking out the window.

'Who?'

'The hippies. They're gone. They all fucking love nature but they're allergic to rain. Hey, what's that?' Jaime says, coming closer to Tomás.

'What's what?'

'*Huevón*, that!' He touches Tomás's right cheek with a big smile.

Tomás looks at himself in the window reflection and Jaime leans back in his chair.

'Classes finished early, huh?' he laughs.

'Come on, man.'

'Student?' Jaime asks and Tomás doesn't say anything. 'Just what we needed, *huevón*, you're fucking a student. I've got to tell Claudio. Maybe they'll make a meme out of you now.'

'Could you talk any louder? And no, I don't want a meme.'

'Are you retarded? This is good, the best things that's happened to you for a while. You're finally getting over Eva.'

'She's a postgrad, she's German, and don't mention it to anyone because it was just a greeting and she can't even finish sentences and she's older than the rest and—'

'OK, alright, calm down, I won't, I won't.' He stands and takes his phone out. 'But you should invite her out tonight. There's a Programming postgrad party at ten. It's at my house.'

'I won't invite her. We could lose our funding.'

'Well, you should. It's always just men at these things. I was actually just picking some stuff up before going home to get everything ready.'

'I'm not coming.'

'Every night you don't go out, you pass up an opportunity, my friend.'

'I don't want an opportunity.'

'Come on.'

Jaime leaves and Tomás checks his phone and lies under the desk to look at the chewing gum stars again, No word from Yiyo about Eva so he texts him.

'Dude, what happened?'

Yiyo calls back immediately.

'I have something to tell you and you won't like it. Didn't know how to tell you, but I guess you have to know.'

'What happened?' Tomás looks at the troll doll smiling back at him.

'She's gone, man, Eva's gone for good,' he says and Tomás swears that the circle of chewing gum has turned into a square again, and that its corners are sharper than they ever were before.

4

The Party

'Cut its head.'

'I think it's looking at me.'

'Tomás, dead things can't look at you. It won't mind, I promise. Here, just take the knife.'

Eva puts down the onion, wipes her face with the *Arc de Triomphe* tea towel (though he's the one tearing up), and stands behind Tomás. She kisses the back of his neck, takes his hand, takes the knife.

'Now, just like a guillotine,' she says, pronouncing it in French: *Guilluhteeneh.*

He had done the same with her once. They had played pool at a bar in Bellavista and he'd walked behind her to guide her shots. She'd laughed. But she'd let him do it. Though not for long. Her parents owned a pool table and she was much better, so much better than he was. She had beat him. They never played again, or even spoke about it. But now, with the whole feathered chicken on the chopping board, he wishes he could cut it in one slice, one motion to show her a history of motions because, as she had once said, there's nothing more impressive than seeing the results of years of practice in the space of a second. She'd been talking about the Monet show she had gone to see in Paris when she said that. He'd said he didn't get painting at all. She'd said it was about the immediacy of everything, though he hadn't understood what she meant by that. And she now tightens her grip on the knife.

'On three.'

'OK.'

'*Un, deux…*'

They make a slight dent on the chicken's neck.

'You do it,' he says, smiling and giving her the knife.

'Man do you give up easily.'

'You just do it better, so what's the point?'

Tomás moves over to let her cut everything, and a drop from the leaking ceiling falls on his head. She chops the chicken's head off in a single slash. The immediacy of everything.

And then Tomás wakes up without her, dreamless, as always, unsure of anything but the words *after, after, after* and Serge on repeat, dying and dying again.

.   .   .

To Antarctica. She's gone to the Antarctic. Who the hell goes to the Antarctic? Only people who hate everything must go there because there's nothing, no one to see in a six-month night and… But should it surprise him? Whenever he notices something has surprised him, it stops being surprising. It's the end of a twist-driven movie, their biggest mysteries cheapened because they were always certainties to those who knew but… Did he know? OK, so maybe it's not the place itself that surprises him, maybe it's that he never thought she'd make it to Antarctica. He had once wished that she'd pull it off but not NOW. Is NOW a pure coincidence? She's getting back at him, she's saying 'I am alone and better for it and here's your proof.' Leaving without telling him, sending a birthday card over with an acronym… She wanted him to find out, to hear through other people that her dreams were easier to achieve without him. But surely it hadn't been his fault that it had taken her so long, surely it… If anything, the fact that she's done it can only be proof that he helped her get there. Yes, it's his fault she's achieving so… She had always accused him of being distant, but this is by far a greater gap between them than any argument over gas bills and cooking habits could ever create.

'She did it,' Tomás says in front of the bathroom mirror, while he shaves and shaves only for himself. As a maritime biologist, she had always been drawn to the extreme poles, their topography and their wild life. Once, they drove to Viña del Mar and when they were on the hills, where the ocean suddenly appears white with sun at the distance, she hugged him and told him that she'd been born to be on water. One of the last things he heard of her from Yiyo was that she had joined a group of scientists who are all passionate about this one ice hole that tunnels down into the deep ocean from the frozen surface just outside of the Chilean Antarctic coast. He knew she had been hoping to join the group of scientists on an expedition to study Antarctic ice sheets but had never asked about it because, what's the point of asking about something no one knows anything about? The team would go and study whatever it was they found at the bottom of the world; they still don't know how deep the tunnel goes, or where it leads to, or if there's any life in it at all. Yiyo told him she'd joined the team months ago but Tomás thought she would stay in Santiago. He can only imagine her in this city.

Tomás washes the shaving foam off his cheeks and then goes to his room. He gets undressed and lies on the floor in the bedroom without a bed and looks up at the ceiling. He notices two wet patches over him and one of them lets out a small drop that lands right in the middle of his forehead. What are the chances? He rolls over to one side and in front of him is a pile of clothes and on top of it, a suit bag.

He opens it and takes the suit out. He's only ever worn it once, for a friend of Eva's wedding, and they fought over it because Eva thinks black suits are only good for funerals. He leaves the suit on top of the pile, goes to his living room coat hanger and reaches into the inside pockets of his jacket. He finds the ball of paper with Fran's number and spreads it on the sofa's arm and dials.

'Hey.'

'Hi.'

'Listen, there's—'

'Yes, yes. What time you will be get party?'

'Oh… Ten, I think.'

'OK, see you at party.'

'Bye.'

'Bye,' he says again, but she's hung up.

Tomás goes back to his room and tries to find a white shirt in the pile of clothes. He finds one between the black 2013 Deftones Tour hoody (which Eva hated) and the red and black flannel shirt (which she hated less) and spreads it in front of him. The collar has brown dirt marks on the inside and the sleeves are full of creases. He must remember not to take off his blazer at the party and to wear an obnoxious tie to hide it all, which won't be hard since really all ties are obnoxious.

He takes off his jeans and T-shirt and carries the suit and white shirt to the bathroom. He leaves the suit on the toilet seat, still with the hanger, and looks at himself in the mirror. He spots a white hair and pulls it out and then puts on the suit and the fucking purple tie with the fucking yellow lines and 90s cartoon *Super Mario* faces all over it. Eva's probably right, he *does* look like he's going to a funeral, and if he had to choose whose funeral it was, he'd say it's his career's because he hasn't been able to come up with a single fucking story for the game and he hasn't marked any of the fucking papers and he still hasn't fucking slept and now he's going to have to talk to his colleagues ('colleagues'! What kind of cunt would say that?) and the German who talks like a mistranslated game from the past and then the rest of the postgrad students about… But he already arranged to meet Fran and he can't think of an excuse not to meet her. He will have to keep seeing her in class anyway.

He looks at himself one last time and goes back into his room. He puts on his coat and in his right pocket he can feel the plastic windmill he never binned. He takes it out and blows on it but it doesn't turn. He carries it with him anyway and walks to the front door and sees a folded note on the WELCOME carpet. It says:

> Please come to Abdul's vintage shop at the Plaza Italia market. We sell everything and we really need your help to stay open. Please come.
>   Cordially,
>   Your neighbour, Lucas.
>
> PS. Please man, come on…

Tomás makes a paper ball with it and throws it on the sofa. He opens his door and the corridor is empty and the lights have gone off and he can hear a torrent of heavy guitar riffs and the tiny earthquakes of a double-pedal bass drum from inside one of his neighbour's flats. He sighs and walks along the corridor using his phone to light it up.

Downstairs, he waits for a taxi to drive by and looks up at his bedroom window. HI – I HOPE YOU'RE WELL ☺ he reads. But tonight he's lying to Eva, to the street facing it and every person walking and looking up to it, and to the whole city and its flashing lights and the silhouettes moving about in other flats, and the unfinished skyscraper with the hanging plastic sheets flapping in the wind like the sails of an old ship about to set off, and the mall workers still filling buses now on their way home, the buskers with them too, pouring the same fucking guitar lines back and forth, back and forth, back and always with the deep voice,

57

always with the long strum at the end of a chord meant for the oceans and the mountains and the countryside and change, the always silent begging for change in the smallest possible coins. Tonight, in the noise of Santiago in the dark, which is never dark enough because its nights too are lies, he laughs at the crooked sign and hopes no one he knows has ever seen it.

He lifts his hand to stop a taxi, gives the address, and they drive up the Kennedy Avenue and into Las Condes. He looks up at the balconies of the apartment complexes as they drive by and sees people smoking and partying and kissing and playing guitar and then this one guy, on his own and wearing a bathrobe, looking down into the road. Everyone's moving out of synch, like TV screens stacked together and tuned to different channels. The driver's quiet and the radio's playing a *cumbia* about love lifting people higher and higher. When they drive into a tunnel, the song crackles into static.

'Fuck this piece of shit!' the driver says hitting the radio.

'It's the tunnel I thin—'

'—What are you, a fucking professor now? Fuck this piece of shit.' He hits it once more just before getting out of the tunnel and into the Kennedy Avenue, where the *cumbia* starts again. 'You see?' he laughs. 'Piece of shit knows who's the boss. I'm the fucking boss, right man?' he asks, looking up at the mirror. 'Right man? I'm the boss.'

'Sure.'

'That's right, I'm the boss, you piece of shit,' he tells his radio. '*Love takes me hiiigher, so high.*'

Tomás nods and takes out his phone to text Fran.

'I'll be there in a few minutes. Hope you're keeping well. x.'

They turn into Las Tranqueras and the taxi stops in front of the police station. The driver presses a button on the price counter and the price goes up by a thousand pesos. Tomás doesn't understand why it does that but he pays the driver anyway and tells him to keep the change. The driver doesn't thank Tomás so Tomás thanks him again and then gets off the car. His phone vibrates and it says:

'You quick up here. Death of so boredom. :-) --- :-p xoxoxoxo F.'

Tomás sighs because he doesn't like smileys at all, although he knows it's not her fault that she was born to a generation that replaces words with yellow faces because they can't deal with the silence at the end of a sentence and… Or was it Eva who hated… Still, that could also mean that she'll do most of the talking and he'll just have to smile.

He rings the bell outside Jaime's apartment building and the caretaker in the downstairs lobby looks at him and the electric door opens.

'Hi, and who are you?'

Tomás looks at the caretaker who for some reason doesn't recognise him (is it the suit?) even though he had lived with Jaime for three months. They even had lunch together once, when Tomás got locked out and felt too guilty to eat his food in front of him. But Tomás can't remember his name so he chooses not to mention any of this.

'Hello? Who are you looking for?'

'I'm looking for Jaime Rivera, 1104.'

'Hold on,' he says, sitting back with the phone between his cheek and shoulder while he opens a can of Coke. 'What's your name?'

'Tomás Perez.'

'We have a Tomás Perez downstairs. Tomás Perez. Pe-Rez. Pe – Yes, that's right. Should I tell him to come in? You sure? OK.' He hangs up. 'Come in.'

Tomás goes into the elevator and presses 11. Inside, there's a mirror on every wall and he tidies his hair behind his ears and checks his profile. He finds that he prefers his right side. He remembers reading online about a test that proved that most people usually find the opposite side of whatever they may consider better more attractive. He must remember to stand to Fran's right. Although she did kiss him on both sides, so maybe it's all bullshit and everyone just wishes that they had a better…

The elevator makes a TING TANG and opens on 10. Tomás puts his hands in his pockets and looks at the old guy in white shorts who steps in.

'Going down?' he asks Tomás.

'Up, to eleven.'

'OK,' the old guy says with a sigh, scratching the back of his neck.

The doors open again and Tomás walks out looking for 1104. He can hear electro music and he can feel the bass under his feet. He rings the doorbell but no one comes out and the music and laughter inside just keep going, so he waits for enough seconds to make it seem like it's not desperate to knock. And then he knocks.

Jaime comes out with a champagne bottle and a red and black cardboard crown on his head.

'*Huevón*! You came!' Tomás nods and he looks inside and there are mostly women (he can count four other guys) and some people are dancing and Fran, Fran's on the balcony smoking and talking to an old bald hippie woman who's wearing a shaolin monk toga and smoking a pipe.

'I thought you said it was mostly dudes.'

'I know, right? I figured if I said it was a sausage party then most guys would call their girlfriends to come. But I guess you're alone, right?'

'Yeah.'

'Fran's here, you know? She's been asking about you.'

'Man…'

'Ah,' he sighs spilling some of his drink on his fingers, which he then slurps up. 'Have fun for once. Come in, here have this *huevón*, come in,' he says, opening the wide door behind him and putting his own paper crown on Tomás.

Tomás goes in and looks around and he's way overdressed and most girls look so young in their jeans and tank tops and their fucking Hannah Montana faces and they dance like pros with self-aware asses and sweat and joke and every joke is so funny because everyone laughs so fucking hard and… Tomás hangs his coat by the door and takes out the plastic windmill from his pocket. He then walks up to the dining table and takes a cup of pisco sour. The young girls sitting at the head of the table next to the drinks look at him, at his blazer and at his shoes and the windmill. They laugh and Tomás smiles at them and he wonders if right now, right this moment, he should be having an epiphany about what it means to be old, what it means to pretend to understand younger people and their laughter, and all of it just to be spared of the shame of ageing. He suddenly has the urge to tell his parents that despite his never flying, despite never inventing anything that could come close to the simplicity of sticky tape in cereal boxes, he truly loves them because it's not their fault they're so...

He takes a sip of pisco sour and his lips burn a little. He crosses girls dancing in the living room. Pink confetti lands on him as he walks up to the large window that gives out to the balcony. He can see himself on it, the suit and the tie and the pisco sour and his hair full of pink dots, the crown tilted to one side and the plastic windmill. He knocks on the window and Fran turns to face him and smiles, so he smiles back and waves hello with the windmill that doesn't turn.

She slides the window and kisses him the same way as before. One. Two. The old woman with the orange toga bows towards them and goes back inside. Tomás steps out onto the balcony and lights up a cigarette. Fran slides the window closed and walks up to the edge of the balcony, right by the wooden wind chimes, both elbows resting on top of the safety fence that wouldn't save anyone who actually wanted to jump. He leans forward on it too, and for a moment, they can only hear each other breathe out smoke to the perfect major scales of the hollow bamboo sticks hitting against one another.

'Hi,' she says.

'Hello.'

'You, um, like dress for funeral, king of funeral,' she laughs, touching the crown.

'Yeah,' he says, smiling.

'Well... I guess it's a kind, a kind of party too. Like, not so good. But hope it don't get to that bad!'

'Let's hope it doesn't.'

She raises her pisco sour and downs it so he does the same.

'For you,' he says, giving her the windmill, his back straight, slow hands, wind on his face, the kind of douchiness he knows will be a struggle to live with later.

'Thank you,' she says, putting her cigarette out on the floor and taking the windmill with both hands. She blows on it and it doesn't turn so she looks at him.

'Sorry about that,' he says, unsure of what he's apologising for.

'Jaime right, you promising material,' she laughs and Tomás laughs too.

They both turn towards the city lights and Tomás notices she's shivering, which makes him shiver too.

'Look. I have question. I really do. One question, OK? Can ask you? Very um, weird. But I have to. I'm sorry.'

'What?'

'Um... You know what? Forget. It's very weird, you forget,' she says.

'Go ahead and ask,' he says with a smile.

She comes nearer to him and their shoulders touch and they face each other and Tomás is glad he's standing to her right so she can see his better side even though all her sides are fucking perfect, her nose and cheeks marked with freckles from another kind of sun that will never exist here, the kind that rests and forgives wrinkling, unties the skin, her large blue eyes and their lashes sticking out like miniature sea flowers and himself in them, the walking profile with only one best side, trying to sit still.

'No, no! It so weird question,' she takes his hand. Hers is warmer than his. 'I do not want you freak, freak out. But I think about ever I first meet you, you know?'

'It's fine. What is it?' He waits for her to lean towards him and he throws the cigarette down the balcony, watching the spot of light at the end of it become part of the city before it disappears and then, then he closes his eyes to hear her breathe between the wind chimes. Those lashes, those lashes, the sea flowers, the better side, perfect skin, another kind of sun, forgiving, the king of funerals...

'OK. Here is... um, can me pray for you?'

He opens his eyes and looks at her and she doesn't smile, she doesn't laugh and fuck his life, she really means it. He doesn't say anything and lights another cigarette and then turns to her again, trying to hide his now dying boner.

'Can pray for you? Can I pray for success of your videogame? Can pray for your stories? You look you need God, you know, my king? Is ok, everybody need. And, and I do not means you look bad, you know? You just very look, I do not know how to say, like you not there sometime, like absent maybe?'

He looks back at the people dancing inside. The girls at the table are looking at them and laughing and Tomás wonders if this is a joke, a dare.

'Can I then?' she asks.

'Yeah,' he says turning back to her, 'I guess so.'

'So great. I was scare it weird to you. But is OK if I pray to Jesus? Or you have other preference?'

'Jesus will do.'

'Dear Jesus,' she starts and puts one hand on his shoulder and closes her eyes. 'Please Lord, Oh Lord Jesus, me pray for you for Tomás Perez. I pray so hard right now, the way you like, that you...' He looks at her lips, thick with red lipstick pressing together and opening and closing, opening and closing, opening and they shine with all the lights in Santiago. 'I pray you make that his videogame success and it go well with his stories. I hope you that have good plan set for him because he really need it, Lord Jesus Christ. Thank you so much Jesus. Amen.' She opens her eyes and smiles at him. 'Thank you,' she says to him and he nods and smiles back. 'How you feel?' she asks, taking his hand.

'I don't think I have the words.'

'I know, I know, me can tell,' she says. 'But you still can dance, yes?' She presses his hand with hers and then opens the window and the noise comes out to them: the music, the laughter, the glasses, the dancing, all of it coming for them hiding in the balcony, in the whispers of a prayer and in the sounds of the hollow wind chime that keeps moving although they can no longer hear it.

'Let dance,' she says.

'OK.'

They go in and she takes his hand and pulls him to the middle of the dancing crowd. She takes off her coat and she's wearing a long black dress with a great cleavage. She throws the coat and the plastic windmill onto a sofa, gets two pisco sours and gives him one.

'You're also dressed for a funeral,' he tells her and smiles. She laughs.

'I glad you like it, you know?' she says, looking at her dress and pulling one of her fallen shoulder straps back up. '*Salud,*' she says in a perfect accent, and then downs her drink so he does the same.

They dance and they look at each other and he can't even remember if he ever danced with Eva. He's pretty sure he never asked her to, but he thinks that if they had danced, she would have probably moved just like Fran: up and down, her arms on the sides and her shoulders doing circles at odds with the beat, her neck bent towards him and her face almost touching his. Right now, as he looks at his hands waving to the rhythm, he feels ridiculous and he wishes he were younger, that he didn't have to remember Eva, that he wasn't wearing a suit or the party hat and that he could just sit at the ends of a table and laugh with the rest of them at the older people who are always dressed for funerals. He shuts his eyes and Fran grabs one of his hands and puts it on one of her shoulders, the sharp bones that are always so new when they belong to someone else.

And then the song dies out so they both stop moving and she smiles at him while people clap. She takes his hand away from her.

'I'll be two seconds,' he says, and she nods and starts talking to the guy dancing next to her. He's trying to put one leg between hers but they won't open, so he ends up doing something like the monkey on his own, without anyone to watch him make it ironic. That guy is as old as Tomás and he's also wearing a crown.

He goes into the bathroom and washes his face with cold water. Behind him, the bathtub is still full and Tomás remembers this one party where Eva and himself and one of Eva's friends sat inside it, clothes and all, and poured champagne on each other. They were wearing bright bird masks (his was an owl), and Eva's hair was all wet and pushed back behind the ears and she had smiled at him, she had looked at him and neither of them had said a thing.

Tomás touches the water, now cold. He turns off the light and sinks his right leg into the bathtub. He knows he'd look mental if someone were to suddenly walk in but he's so tired, so tiring, and a bit drunk. He then sinks his left leg and slowly sits inside against the bathroom wall and he shuts his eyes and the music and laughter get quieter until all he can hear are the tiny waves of water spreading around him.

And then he wakes up to a hard knock on the door. He stays sitting in the bath hoping no one will knock again. But someone does knock again, and he gets up and his suit sticks with the water and drips. He steps out of the tub and his shoes sound like wet sponges. He opens the door and it's Fran and she smiles at him, comes in and locks the door. She kisses him and he kisses her and she grabs his ass and he takes her waist. She tastes of pisco and cigarettes.

'Wait. I bring your coat. We can get hell out of here.'

Tomás nods. She leaves and he locks the door again. He looks at himself in the mirror. He looks so small, so thin with the suit stuck to him but that doesn't matter because he knows that when you don't sleep you see the world as it is, the world without yourself in it, just a plain pile of small single objects: the soap holders, the shaving cream, the cotton buds, the electric toothbrush, the wet suit… Everything else is a backdrop: the party, the jokes and the dares, himself and Fran. She knocks and he puts on his coat.

'I call taxi already. We wait downstairs,' she says.

'Aren't you going to ask me about this?' he asks, looking at his shoes.

'No.'

'Why?'

'I afraid I don't like you after. No talk before OK? We fuck first, then talk a lot, but keep the crown, OK?' she says. She leaves and he follows her out.

In the living room a group of girls are finishing a game of musical chairs. One of them sees Tomás's trousers dripping when he walks by, and she stops moving so her friends look at him too. He waits for Fran to get her stuff. The music stops and one of the girls sits on the last chair and shouts 'I win!' but no one gives a shit, so she stands instead. Jaime walks up to Tomás, laughing and leaning on him.

'Have a blast, man. You know, I always knew you were lucky. I told you, didn't I tell you *huevón*?'

'Yeah. Hey, I'm leaving. Thanks for everything.'

'But we're just… Just…' He looks at Tomás's shoes and laughs real hard and then walks back to the dancing people and falls on a sofa.

'Let is go,' Fran says to him and he nods. She takes his hand as they walk to the elevator.

Inside, she doesn't look at him but she looks at herself in the mirror and draws a smiley on the glass with her lipstick. She doesn't say a thing so he doesn't either.

They walk past the caretaker who looks at Tomás's shoes and sighs as he picks up a mop behind them to clean the puddles. They keep walking in silence and the taxi driver waves at them and Fran waves back.

'Where to?' the taxi driver asks.

'Where you live?' Fran asks Tomás, and he notices the sun starting to rise just over the hills, and her thick lips shine red under the streetlight as they split into a smile, the ocean flowers taking in everything, the silhouette of a skyscraper frozen against the waves of a black river, the single man walking back alone forcing laughs at lit-up windows, the stills of birds that appear in the flash of rooftops, the fading print of a plane in the sky, and then the fucking tunnel.

5

The Night The Sky Fell

IDEAS BOOK P. 28:

The game starts off with a rocket launching into space. As Vince (an astronaut) is carried into space with nothing more than a robot companion (that can only talk if it's answering a question), we get the backstory in captions and translucent stills.

The stars and the moon and the sun have all disappeared. It was all very sudden, all without cause. ~~People took days to notice. In fact,~~ No one noticed until the tides, with no moon to calm them, came out in waves to drown out the coasts. Everyone's afraid now. Riots break out for supplies, people kill each other for canned food. They kill each other over bomb shelters to wait out the darkness. Activists appear on news channels happy and smiling because now everyone listens to them. A Blue Peace hippie frees caged animals from the zoo, others make peace with those they spent a lifetime hating. And others pray for the Rapture, head into the streets to preach the end of everything. The chosen ones, the chosen ones will make it, it's too late now and the unchosen people (pretty much the whole world according to the chosen) should get ready for something far worse than darkness.

Then there's a still of the NASA headquarters. Scientists have lost control of their satellites. The International Space Station doesn't answer calls or gives signs of life. Other astronauts in short secret supply missions have their families notified of their disappearances. No one wants to go out into space to check what's happened. That's when they call Vince, the only guy who was still sending CVs over to NASA (had been refused so many times before) even after the blackout, because he understood this disaster as an opening, an opportunity to have less competition over a job he really wanted. He said he'd do anything to see space, and then he got the job, which to his annoyance had no title because there was no clear mission. But even if it meant seeing nothing, moving through plain black, it was worth it just to get out of Earth for a while, and probably forever.

When he breaks out of the stratosphere ~~it's like being submerged under water~~ the engine lulls into silence, and the white LEDs of the ship turn on. There's nothing out in space and Earth looks like a shadow. Suddenly the ship malfunctions. One of the Rapture preachers worked at NASA too, and he had loosened engine parts to make his predictions come true. That's when Vince puts on his astronaut suit, ties himself to the ship and comes out into space. ~~It's warmer than he thought it would be~~ He looks at the metal plates, the engines and the different latches of all sizes... And who is he kidding? He has no idea what he's doing. He should have never got the job. That's when he takes his helmet off, and realises that nothing happens, that everyone just lied about space being dangerous. Now he's better than an astronaut, and he doesn't give a fuck about tidal waves on Earth.

That's when the gameplay starts. After a day of floating about in space, you notice a strange faraway light. The stars are all dead, and you have to give life back to them by solving puzzles and becoming friends with them. Each star values different things: some of them are very private and want to be left alone, some of them want to know that if they die, others will die with them. And so you have to choose the right dialogue options until there are enough stars to make up constellations, and each one you form lights up the Earth just a little more.

The last star is the sun, but it only speaks French and Vince can't understand a thing, which means they can't be friends. It gets so pissed off with your lack of understanding that it decides to live just to burn you out of space. On Earth, no one remembers Vince anymore, but they're glad the sun is back, sad that the Rapture didn't happen, and they're scared for the future of stars.

.　　.　　.

'Was it good?'

'Why you ask this?'

'I don't know.'

'Ah.'

'What?'

'Guys always think the dicks so different. My must be better dick. I be so large, so special,' she laughs. 'Most dick same, you know? They sometime flop, sometime hard, sometime not work, bend right, bend left... But still same dick, even taste same.'

'Really?'

'Yes, really. Men worry very much about stupid dick, get sad if no speech about the dick. Like it only dick in the world. Build dick monument, you know? All should very worry about is hands, the face, the arms, the body, you know? The body, yourself, your body. Dick is smallest part, too small. Even ear more important.'

Fran takes his crown off and puts it on. They had sex four times yesterday. When she had asked him if he was enjoying his day off he agreed and told her she should stay for another night. This means the bed frame still hasn't been made, and so they've had to fuck all around the flat: against the kitchen counter, by the WELCOME rug under the door, in the shower without the German curtains, against his desk. She said his flat was just what she expected it to be. Though she didn't find it funny when a drop from the leak in the ceiling landed on her back. She told him this was a 70s building and that it was designed by European architects; it would remain intact forever.

'I miss Germany,' she says, putting her bra back on, her back against him.

'Must be great.'

'No. But better than here um, to be honestly. People more open, you know?'

'That's not too hard. Why come here anyway?'

'You have brother or sister?' she asks, stretching a pair of tights.

He quiet, he don't know, he wish. Truth is, he and his sister Angela used to be friends. She was addicted to online games and she always asked him how he was doing at university, play-testing his games and reviewing his early builds (she tested the Bimbo alpha and beta and told him it was the worst thing she ever played, which only made him like her more). Then one day, after seeing a therapist, she decided she needed to change. She went off to India to find herself and became someone else – which is pretty much what finding yourself means. The friends she went with, a bunch of new-age asswipes who changed their names depending on the season (Winter, whose real name was Oswald, was his sister's boyfriend at the time), convinced her that if you're dumb and go to India, you come back smart. They all came back the same though, except they now wear weird loose shapeless Nepalese pants that stink of incense. They hate technology, have permanently erased their Facebook profiles (after lengthy Facebook declarations of intent filled with the word 'society' and 'human nature' and so many fucking 'journeys') and now collect typewriters and take pictures of sunsets and their feet. One of these asswipes was the son of a major news editor in town, and Angela got a job interviewing famous asswipes who always hate being famous and having money and everything they buy with it. Her feature articles all have a signature statement at the end: 'and this was today's morsel of society'. This got her a column called Morsels of Society, which has a picture of her sitting on a pillow and wearing an orange scarf. Every fucking artist she interviews talks about journeys and talent and money and capitalism and start-ups and business and racism and violence and stop the war and holidays and childhood and Guantanamo and depression and sex and magic and follow me I'm a fucking @socialmedia guru because I rant about shitty current TV shows and I want people to know that they can connect with me and still know I have an attitude problem, but man, keep writing, man, because #EveryoneCanMakeItIfTheyReallyWantIt and if you don't you're an asshole since I made it and I had nothing but my ass in my mouth and now I own everything so I can't sympathise with the former unless it's about to become the latter, man, you know, man, the journey, the ass in the mouth and... Does Tomás have a sister? When Bimbo failed, Angela told Tomás he needed a change too, and bought him and Eva tickets to India. He never told Eva about it. He was trying to come up with a new game. This time, a huge one. He couldn't just take off to buy colourful Nepalese trousers. And his sister hasn't spoken to him ever since she found out he didn't take the plane. He does however follow her on Twitter @MorselsOfSociety.

'No,' he says. 'I don't. You?'

'Yes. But they terrible people. Too religion. They think videogame is drug addiction, like meth. I needed to get out so I can make game in peace. Got exchange offer from aunt who work in university in the South. Had to take. But aunt now teach religion, is very fucking crazy family. I just would want to work in my game.'

'I know what you mean. What are you working on at the moment?'

'I want make game that is important you know? A game people remember. I want to make game about deep thing. But I like adventure game. Very hard to make deep in adventure game. Always too happy, too hope, jumping around, finding thing. I want adventure game that feel like depression, you know? A game that depress so much people with true adventure. I have good gameplay now in pre-alpha build. I need good story, so I take your class. But all adventure too happy. Sadly, you too happy too.'

'All adventure too happy,' he repeats.

The mall workers are passing by in their white-lit bus. One of them points at the sky from the window and makes eye contact with Tomás. The sky appears to be falling, streaming down, the cracked grey city ceiling letting only the faintest light to cut through, dropping in two pillars so low Tomás could touch them if he opened the window. The icy drizzle swallows the edges of the streets, the walls dividing houses, the watercoloured cars driving nowhere – a pre-alpha build of Santiago. The clouds are getting swallowed up at the edges of the now peakless mountains made of fog, and birds are flying lower than ever because he can now hear them whistle and sing that the world's turning all wrong. They're tired, they sing, tired of migrating. Eva used to say that birds must love the city because they're safe, that even the tallest buildings or the fastest cars can't get them. She was sure some of them overstayed their seasons. Even we need to settle, they sing.

'Hey, you know, I could fuck again. You want fuck again? I want come again. I don't feel like getting dress, you know? But not under ceiling waterfall, cool? Too cold for water.'

'It's really not that big a deal. Just a few drops here and there.'

'No water because cold.'

'Sure, whatever.'

'Much thank you!' she says.

She puts the crown on him again. She takes off his underwear and rubs his dick with one hand while she snaps her bra off with the other. She tilts her head to one side.

'You see, same dick as all in universe,' she says with a smile. 'Don't worry, is OK, is OK.'

His back hurts against the carpet. He should really build that bed frame. She puts his dick in her mouth.

'Wh– Who is– Pictu– Picture at entrance?' she asks after a minute or so, taking a break.

'What?' he asks, folding the crown over his ears.

'Girl. Photograph at entry of flat. She very pretty.'

'No one.'

'Oh. Is OK, is OK,' she says.

He takes off her underwear and she sits on him. Her hips are large, the bones sticking out in triangles at the ends. She moves her ass back and forth, her eyes closed, her hands on his chest.

'Ya, ya, ya,' she starts with a smile, like the German pornos he knows too well. Then again, all sex sounds the same.

'Ya, ya, ya,' he says too.

'Jesus, ya. Jesus, ya, sure is OK if I pray to Jesus?'

'Yes.'

'Much thank you!'

Eva used to fuck him in French whenever she'd cooked a French dinner. Once, after a killer ratatouille she asked him if he liked it, and he said he did so she started saying more stuff than just *Oui*. The accent was great and all but he can't remember the last months of sex because he could never work out what she was going on about. He even downloaded a voice recording app and left it on the coffee table so he could Google-translate it at work, but all he got from the twenty-something minute recording was *oh putain* which at times even sounded angry. He kept the recordings, but he still can't translate them. It isn't the strange words or noises or tenses that make it impossible, it's not knowing where any of them begin or end.

Fran turns and uses his black suit as a blanket.

'Sleep time, yes?'

'OK.'

'Much thanks.'

'No problem.'

'Girl at entrance very pretty. I hope you OK.'

'Yeah.'

'Maybe after all, maybe after all you teach good adventure game. Is OK,' she says with a yawn, patting him on the back. 'Is OK, good night.'

Tomás waits on the floor until he can hear her sleep-breathe. He gets up, goes to the kitchen and turns on the kettle. He looks out the window and the sky's still dropping. It's still snowing and he looks down to see if it has gathered but it hasn't. It's the first time he's seen snow fall but the excitement wears off fast because all he can think about is the Antarctic and how much more impressive snowfall must be there, and how expensive his heating bill will be because of it and...

He waits five minutes and presses the coffee down and puts in a straw. He turns on the radio and sits at his desk and opens his IDEAS book.

Do you love your home?

Do you love turning boring (BOOORIIIING) rooms into palaces?

Then come to El Huaso's

Ta-ta-ta-ta, ta-ta-tum

Two-for-one on any hammer you need:

Ball-pein hammers, claw hammers,

Shingling hatchets, drywall hatchets, rubber mallets,

Carpenter hammers and brick hammers.

All with the ease of double injection (Double Injectioooon!) grip technology.

Come to El Huaso's and tear that nail apart-art-art-art

SubjectToLimitedStockTermsAndConditionsApply.

He finishes writing the ad, lights up a cigarette and lies under his desk where there are no changing chewing gum constellations. Would it be fucked up to go and find her there? What would she say? It would make him the least boring person in the world. Two electric hobs or even the Trans-Siberian train would be no match for him. He'd go down South to Punta Arenas and look for a boat by asking the locals, backpack on, beard on its way, and he'd find a merchant navy boat, nothing fancy, even rough, and he'd make friends on-board, whom he'd introduce her to later by their first names and she'd be there when he arrives, standing on ice, telling him she can't believe it, that she thought he didn't have it in him, that she's glad he knows what she really wants, what she's always wanted. But that's the problem. That's his problem. In his IDEAS book she's always waiting for him.

> Is your dog suffering from post-traumatic stress disorder?
> Meow!
> Is your best friend now your WORST NIGHTMARE?
> Your mother sucks woofs! in hell-ell-ell!
> Speak to Papa Dino, dog psychologist, animal wizard, philanthropist.
> Hi, I'm Papa Dino and I love your dogs.
> But most of all, I love Jesus Christ-ist-ist
> If you like God, call me 927138210

He turns the page. He needs something that Jaime can't fuck up, something without variables, something simple, and he needs it fast. But who can ever guess any of Jaime's mistakes before they happen? So he closes the book and decides to wait and see what Jaime's working on. He stays looking up at his desk and he can hear the hum of the boiler and the water pipes above his ceiling and Fran's breathing and he closes his eyes and sees absolutely nothing and then it's just snow, so much snow, and the remains of the shrinking sky that he can now touch if he stretches on his toes, and points his hands like TV ballet dancers do, and he could even pretend to fly while the birds just settle with all the white powder below him, now turning to ice.

. . .

Tomás and Eva are lighting fireworks from the wine bottles they just drank. In the movies fireworks always make domes of colour, light half-faces in sparks, a build up of strings climaxing as the whole sky just blows up. But here it's only smoke, the invisible screeching travel of a rocket gone missing, the shadow of a trail that gets lost within seconds, the disappointed laughter when no one manages to create rainbows with explosions. The San Cristóbal Hill that overlooks Santiago is made of ice. There are people slipping on it because of all the noise making the Earth shake in reds and greens.

'Do you think lights can freeze in the sky? Do you think colour could take over nights forever?' Eva asks him.

He nods because it already happened. In our frozen cities nothing can be dark again.

'Let's look for it. Right now, let's look for it,' she says.

'For what?' he asks, failing to light the firework in the frozen bottle.

'The hole in the ice, the tunnel. I bet it runs through Santiago and I have to know where it ends.'

They walk slowly down the hill so as not to slip. She looks at the ground after every step and even touches some of the icy cracks. Despite Tomás knowing that this is useless, that you can't find anything by keeping surfaces intact, he follows her down, for what seems like hours.

When they reach the foot of the hill, Eva turns to him and they face the sky and the now frozen explosions and then the people watching them. Everyone's still: kids unable to finish a jump, the tense faces before laughter, the moment in a clap that looks like prayer, stuffed birds in life-like poses, and the river, the Mapocho adrift in chunks of ice which will never carry anything for anyone again.

They cross the useless bridge and the windmill salesman selling to multiple customers at a time. When he sees Tomás he calls to him.

'The wind, man! The Antarctic wind! Just look how they turn!'

He gives Tomás a windmill that won't stop turning. Maybe he needs the wind to make a good videogame too. Maybe he'll write about this, the fireworks, the lacking laws of physics. It would be Jaime's masterpiece too.

When he turns he sees Eva looking for cracks again and when he asks her if she wants the windmill, she takes it to look for the wind's direction.

'If you can read the wind, then you know the currents of the ocean, the shapes of the world beneath us,' she says.

He nods. 'We should really pay for that windmill,' he says, 'if we intend to keep it,' and the reds and greens of the sky slide down Eva's face and people clap and laugh and the jumping children touch floor and dogs bark again and pigeons resurrect, but only until the next rocket freezes everything up again.

'Come on, *nous devons partir*,' Eva says, 'we won't find anything by just standing around!'

She walks too fast. It's not like they even know where they're going. She says the tides lead the way. 'Just be patient and read the water, pay attention to the waves, the currents, you'll see,' she says, and with a smirk, '*tu va voire*, we'll find it.'

They're looking for the boat she bought. She put their apartment up for rent after watching a show about alternative lifestyles, which really just means dirty and uncomfortable lifestyles, or just plain stupid. There was a young guy with a beard on it who liked climbing trees. He had no shirt on but still had braces over both shoulders, aviator sunglasses, trousers high enough for everyone to see that he had no socks on as he jumped this way and that and down from avocado tree branches, like a chimp with a suit. Anyway, he said that if you were really into adventure and all that stuff, then living on the ground just wasn't for you. He had a canal boat that he shared with his wife (who read wooden fortune runes to tourists). Eva went online and looked up the forms as soon as the show ended. 'We'll live on a boat. Can you even imagine?' she asked. He said that he couldn't and she said that this was exactly why it was necessary.

The fireworks they'd set alight at the San Cristóbal Hill are still going. Even all the way South they can see them explode over the Andes, everything still freezing with the blasts: instant photographs that last a second, the stillness of forest fires, the death of frozen birds lasting just a moment longer. And then the pinks and greens that shine on their faces melt from the sky, and the peaks appear black, and their faces are black, and the forest fires burn acres to soot, and the volcano in front of them is a shadow, its smoke invisible.

They arrived in Puerto Varas yesterday because Eva says that the boat she's looking for is in Lake Llanquihue. That's how they'll find it, she said, the hole in the ice, in the ocean. They will live on a boat and search for it every day. She has to know… 'We have to know, and we have to be there first,' she said, because whatever they find inside will never be untouched again.

They walk past empty pebble beaches, empty German chalets filled with alpaca sweaters, wooden wind chimes, and plastic windmills turning in between the explosions in the sky. And then she finds it, the boat, anchored by the empty hotel on the cliff.

'Don't you like it?'

'I don't know how to sail.'

'We'll learn. The guy on TV said it wasn't hard.'

'But it's a lake. How will we get to the ocean from here?'

They get on the boat. It's light and wooden, like a movie prop, and he wonders if it isn't just part of the harbour. Whatever it is, it's still larger than any flat they could ever afford.

'We'll find a way,' she says, untying some rope from a wooden pole.

That's when he notices that they're on ice and that ice caps are hitting the boat from the sides. Eva takes his hand, and he follows her down a ladder to walk on them.

'Keep looking down. This place is full of cracks.'

And it is full of them. Every time he takes a step a new one appears. Eva looks at them and takes notes in her IDEAS book. She says something about ice cracking in the direction of the currents underneath, but he's sure it's his own steps and the blasts from the fireworks, and so he stops walking and lets her carry on by herself.

'You alright?' she asks, bent over the ice.

'I don't think there's anything here,' he tells her, looking at a pelican falling to a stop-motion-neon-coloured death right in front of them.

'Then there isn't,' she says, her face a silhouette again. 'Let's get this boat out of here!'

.   .   .

He wakes up with a loud BANG and Fran shouts out his name and he hears her running in and out of his room. He doesn't get up. He doesn't get up because there's water coming down on his left from the table on top of him and it doesn't stop and there are still no chewing gum constellations.

'Up! Up! Quickly yes?!'

'What? What happened?'

'The house sky! The house, part above, roofs, fuck, I don't know how to say! Get up!' she shouts, pointing up. 'It all falling!'

He gets up from under the desk and looks at a large square piece of his ceiling that fell right on his desk. There's water coming down from the boiler and Fran is running naked between the bedroom and the hole in the roof.

'You have, plastic container yes?! Fuck! Like a bin, or rubbish. Something! Have a bucket or something?!'

'Nope. But try to calm down, it's really not a huge deal. It's probably some safety mechanism because water was, I don't know, maybe there was too much pressure in a pipe and...'

'You think? You think too much pressure and this safety? The rubbish, use thing for rubbish. Oh my God, Tomás!'

She looks at him holding her head with both hands but he's staring at the piece of ceiling, at his most likely dying computer, at the waterfall that splits on his desk, at the cheap cream-coloured carpet that now looks like moss. She opens the cupboard under the sink and takes the bin out. She turns it upside down and all his paper plates and straws and coffee packets land on Fran's feet.

'Oh my God, Jesus, Jesus.'

'I don't know how to cook,' he explains, pointing at the pile of trash.

'No, I don't care. And wait, you don't know recycle?! Fuck, put here, put here.'

'It's really—'

But she doesn't wait for him to answer and puts the bin on the piece of his ceiling on the desk. It starts to fill up and he looks up at the hole and sees black, nothing more, and he smiles because it reminds him of Jaime's coding, the way a waterfall can come out of nothing, ready for Tomás to have to justify with a story and the also...

'Your flat going smell to crazy bad.'

'I know, but it's OK. We can just light a candle or something.'

'You have will to throw this water the window down. If pour it down sink it all block with the dry paint.'

'Yeah, it's OK, I'll get it fixed tomorrow.'

'I scared,' she says, coming closer to him. 'I see you on floor and I think you dead, Jesus. Then I feel bad for talking of funeral at party, is very bad taste.'

'It's OK, it's OK.'

She kisses him and he hugs her and he touches her chest. He does it all because it's what he's meant to do, to let her see that he enjoys her despite the accidents. He wishes roofs fell more often and then Eva would have known it too.

He takes the bin to his smoking window and pours the water down and it splashes heavy with an echo on the parking spots downstairs. He lights a cigarette and Fran joins him to watch the snow.

'Crazy,' he says.

'What is?'

'The snow, at this time of year.'

'Yeah. I like. It like magic, it make city quieter, you know?'

'Yeah.'

He flicks the cigarette out and sees Fran looking from side to side, hugging herself.

'You probably should get a bed.'

'You know, I was just thinking about that. I'll do it tomorrow.'

He goes to his desk and puts the bin on it again. The water falling from the ceiling is slowing down and the stream becomes single drops and the rug's now a puddle of fur. Eva would have made a huge fucking scene. She would have told him that this was an example of why couples should sleep in separate beds, live in different rooms, even different houses, just like she read people do in France. His sister would have agreed, but would have clarified that it is just not the case in India. Angela once said Eva was more progressive than him because Eva hadn't laughed when Angela asked her whether or not it was possible for pet canaries to be gay. She asked this because her favourite male canary was trying to fuck another male and he was shouting so much and all, but she didn't want to break true love and when Tomás laughed and told her to shut up, Angela left saying Eva deserved better, someone who could understand the plight of women, the plight of birds and love, or at least the imbecility of men. Turns out the canaries ate each other. They really hated that dry feed.

Eva could not stop laughing. But Eva would have given him hell for the hole in the ceiling.

He lies down on the sofa and smokes, but then he hears a paper slide in under his front door. He gets up and picks it up.

> Are you OK? We heard some shouting and a lot of noise. If you need help let me know.
>
> Also, if anything in the house is broken, it might be a good chance for you to check out Abdul's vintage shop madness this weekend.
>
> Thanks!
>
> Your neighbours,
>
> Lucas and Jesús.

Tomás opens the door but there's no one there so he goes back to the couch and finishes his cigarette. He falls asleep and dreams about flying a small plane over the ocean. He sees a white island made of ice and tries to speed the plane up but he can't. He looks behind him and Jaime and his dad are smiling. His dad tells him he needs to get a flying license and starts singing the national anthem. In every pause he adds 'fuck them Argentines and shoot them good' and his teeth are shining. Jaime tells him that he's in a Flight Simulator videogame and apologises because he messed up the physics engine again, so it's impossible to land and his dad laughs and Jaime asks 'Can you write it in a story? Can you make us fly forever?' and they fly over the ice island and his dad shouts 'Finally! That's Argentina! Start shooting!' and then the chorus, *O la tuuumba seraaa de los liiibres,* and Tomás wakes up and it's Fran holding the French press.

'Eh, good morning.'

'Hi.'

'Where mugs, for coffee, you know? I can't find.'

'I just use straws,' he says miming using a straw with his fingertips. She frowns. 'Cupboard above the sink,' he adds. She stays looking at him so he sighs and gets up and grabs two straws. He lets her have the first drink. He looks at her, still naked, and he sees two red lines he hadn't noticed before on her left thigh.

'What's that? Did you get hurt yesterday? Did something fall on you? I'm sorry about that.'

'No, it's not worry. Not that. It nothing.' She turns her back to him and looks at the bin still filling up with water.

'No really, what is it? I'll pay for your doctor if you need it. I guess the ceiling is kind of my fault.'

'No, no. I mean. Yes, your place, um, fucking shit, you know? But no. Is just, OK. I tell. After sex, I get nervous.'

'Did you fall or something?'

'Eh, no. Is just I think Jesus watch me. Like God is angry. Hard to say. Don't know how to say.'

'I don't understand.'

'Like, if he watch me fuck, is very bad. I cut myself, you know? Like with knife. Cut make me calm down, pay for mistake, for you. Feel good, you know?'

'Oh.' If there was one other thing Eva left behind, it was a stack of Japanese knives that can cut through anything.

'Anyway, what you have to do, um, today?'

'Well, I think I'll—'

His phone rings and a beige couch appears on the screen. He looks at Fran and hugs her and walks her to the kitchen and then he takes the key from the inside.

'Sorry, I'm so sorry. I'll just be a few minutes.'

'Eh, what you doing?'

'Sorry, it'll be only a few minutes, I promise.'

He closes the kitchen door and locks her in.

'Eh, fuck! What you doing? Is cold! Come on!'

He takes Eva's photograph from under the piece of ceiling on his desk. The frame's cracked and he puts it on the coffee table next to the sofa before grabbing a T-shirt.

'Hey, I want to be out!'

'Two seconds. I'll just be two seconds.'

He answers the call and his mum and dad appear on the screen.

'Hello! Oh my God you look pale. Eat some vegetables. You know, I went to Aunt Marta's today. She's on a broccoli diet. She looks amazing. I'll tell her to call you, making a note of it right... now.'

'Hi. Please don't tell Aunt Marta to call.'

'Oh well, if you want to die young I suppose it's your call. How are you?'

'What's up? Why are you calling?'

'Just wanted to let you know I'm flying over Pichilemu beach tomorrow. Wondered if you wanted to come along,' his dad says behind his mum.

'Sorry Dad, I'm real busy right now, I really have to go.'

'I found chicken?!' Fran shouts from the kitchen. 'The head! Still has head! I scare now!'

'Who's that?' his mum asks. 'Is someone shouting? Is your flat safe? I knew you shouldn't have moved out there. Why not come back with us, save some money and move somewhere nicer later? Let me at least pay some metal bars for your windows. Santiago is really not what it used to be. Are you sure you're OK?'

'I'm OK. It's probably someone downstairs. I'm working on a new game. I think it's the best thing Jaime and I have ever done. I'm checking the sound at the moment.'

'Oh, well, it sounds very realistic,' his mum says.

'How's Eva?' his dad asks.

'She's good, real busy as always.'

'You know we saw her.'

'Yes we did,' his mum says with a clap.

'How? When?'

'She was on the news. How come you didn't tell us she's finally off on her trip? Isn't that what she always wanted?'

'Well, I wanted to keep it a surprise.'

'It's amazing, isn't it? She's so clever,' his mum says.

'Yeah, she is.'

'Did you see her too? On TV?'

'No. I'll make sure I get one.'

'Well, are you coming to fly with me? Come on, we'll fly over to Argentina, piss them off a little at the border.'

'I can't. I really have to go now. But have fun out there, I guess.'

'But you know you'll have to learn some day. Your grandfather, he—'

'Sorry, have to go. Bye.' He hangs up and opens the kitchen door. Fran is holding the frozen chicken wrapped in cling film from feet to head, and its eyes are wide open just like Fran's as they both look at him.

'What hell? Eh, fuck you, man,' she says pushing him.

'Sorry, sorry.'

'I thought you no cook,' she says, holding up the chicken.

'I try.'

She sighs and drops the chicken on the pile of trash and walks past him. He puts it back in the freezer. He goes to the bedroom and she's getting dressed real quick and he wishes she could stay for longer so that he won't have to shave for himself and try to work. But he doesn't say anything and she doesn't either, until they're at the front door and she's ready to leave. She kisses him and then smiles.

'I don't want see you again, we no fuck ever again in the world, OK?' she says, and he nods and his face feels hot and she leaves the door open. He can hear her take the stairs down and he hopes she'll be there in his next class because they're now ready to write the kind of adventure games people will remember.

He shuts the door, takes the French press and turns on the radio. He lights a cigarette by the smoking window.

(COUGH) (COUGH)
Tired of tissues that keep tearing when you blow your nose?
(Yes)
Tired of nosebleeds that just won't stop?
(Oh, God yes)
Well don't let them tell you that accidents just happen-ppen-ppen
Don't you know—

There's no snow but there are crowds and buses and noise and he smiles because his roof might fall, and his flat might flood, and Fran might hate him, and Eva might be far (so far) away and on TV, which makes her seem even further, but the sounds of the city always come back. Every day, they just appear right where they were before dark, the real accidents, the things no one understands at a distance, pure tone, bouncing aimless in echoes between mountains, between streets and tunnels, the creaking of an old house, their old house, its breathing, her breathing, the whole damn sky dropping in one cosmic sigh filled with rain, sometimes snow, just to be touched once more before it reaches the floor and becomes one of us, one of nothing. And no one, not a single person in a passing car or the white-lit crowd of mall workers driving past, can keep it from happening. Eva could not stop laughing about the dead birds that day. The noise woke him up that night. When he said it wasn't that funny, she stopped, turned to him and told him that people are stupid if they expect animals to act all normal and happy after putting them in cages. 'Accidents only happen to people because they believe in them,' she said.

He missed her on TV. He gets up, heads to the bathroom and starts to shave. He missed her and it's not his fault. He just doesn't have the space.

6

Namaste, asshole

IDEAS BOOK P. 30
4:53AM TV STREAM: *CHEF HANNIBAL JUNIOR FINALS*
Chef Hannibal presents the two kids. One of them is wearing black skinny jeans and a lumberjack shirt. The other's fat as hell and wearing what looks like a white bed sheet. But it doesn't matter because so is Chef Hannibal. The skinny jeans guy turns to his parents standing above and behind them on a platform. The parents are stuck behind a white picket fence and all they do is clap and then shout at the other group of parents behind the black picket fence. The fat kid's parents are also fat, and when they move they make the fence shake. The other kid's parents are also wearing skinny jeans. Chef Hannibal puts a whole chicken on each table. There's a cut to the parents, who are now in their backyards, in their kitchens filled with hanging copper pans and hanging garlic and hanging ham legs and a hanging meat pie calendar set on February – MINCEMANIA. And then they're in street markets looking at apples and pumpkins and jars of dried fruit that resemble skin, and something that looks like a papaya. Then, they walk off to an orchestral crescendo whilst not buying a thing.

'We made him cook from very early on,' they say, and then the show cuts to the kid helping his mum out with the pasta sauce by dropping specs of oregano on it.

'He's so talented. We've always told him that, haven't we always told you? That you're talented— Yes, yes… If you're talented, then it's your duty to win. You must win. Winning is everything. I have my own cardboard box company,' the father says, and the show cuts to him in a warehouse filled with empty boxes. 'I already won,' he says with a smirk. 'Now it's his turn.'

There's the skinny jeans kid holding a golden cup from some competition that was less important because they don't show it. There he is playing sports. He's good at basketball and swimming because he can throw a ball at a hoop and he doesn't drown. There he is talking to the lunch lady at school, taking notes as she says stuff we can't hear. There he is getting claps from his classmates because he solved a binomial theorem problem just for fun. There he is watching the fat kid work, and then in front of professional chefs looking all shocked because a kid his age cooked duck and oxtail consommé in the previous round.

The fat kid's parents shout less, but it's just as loud because they have bigger pipes. They keep cracking the picket fence. The dad is wearing his polo shirt inside his trousers, the most common of all fat-people mistakes. There's a cut to a sausage that the kid's making from scratch, filling it with a mixture that he assures is so good that he can't even wait to fill the sausage and he sweeps the bowl clean with his pinky instead. Then there's a cut to the mum feeding her dog the dregs of some potato soup that the dog refuses to eat at first.

'He always loved cooking. I'm terrible at cooking. But he's so talented,' the mum says, the dog almost biting her because she touched him while he licked up a potato.

'I always said,' his dad starts, a dart match playing in the TV behind him. 'I always said he was the one. I wanted to cook but I had a lot of debt to take care of. My dad cooked.' Another cut: black and white pictures of someone equally fat but without glasses. 'He was so talented. I'm sure, I'm sure,' the music stops, pictures of a newspaper about some accident. 'My dad died in a kitchen fire. He had problems breathing, you see, and had clogged arteries, which made him fall asleep while the gas hob was still on. He'd be so proud,' he says, and they blur a picture of the dead old man holding a cooking pot into the picture of the kid smiling in his school uniform. The music starts again and it's back to the fat kid on the platform facing the chicken, the parents clapping behind him, shouting at each other.

'This is a creation test,' Chef Hannibal says, who has no eyebrows and wears a purple scarf even in the kitchen.

The timer starts and both kids begin to chop. Onions and carrots and potatoes sliced to a dubstep tune that goes mental when they pull out the juicer. Then they chop the hell out of the chicken, bones snapping to claps and the sizzling of onions and garlic.

'What would you do with ten thousand euros?' Chef Hannibal asks the skinny jeans kid, who stops cooking to look right into the camera.

'I want to have my own food empire,' he says.

'But you're ten!' the presenter says with a smile.

'I hate waiting,' the kid says.

'I want to help my dad pay his debts,' the other kid says, even though no one asked him.

Action shots of everything: knives hitting chopping boards; Hannibal's face as the knives hit the chopping boards; the kids running from fridge to freezer to oven; Hannibal's face as they run; Hannibal checking his watch and smiling at the trophy on his table; the parents, the clapping, the shouting... And then the music stops and it happens. It happens and there are only fifteen minutes left.

There's a close-up of the fat kid on the floor, trying to pick himself up to the tune of a lonely bassoon. The parents have their hands on their heads. Silence. The kid fell, his soufflé dish has hit the ground with the dubbed soundbite of shattering glass, which gets repeated four times as the camera closes in on the kid's face and then the soufflé – it looks fucking terrible on the peach ceramic tiles. Violins start playing high notes. The other kid helps him up. The fat kid's palms are bleeding because he fell on the sharpest plate shards to the sharpest violin notes. He wipes the tears off his face but smudges his cheeks with blood, and it bothers the microphone on his chest until only the ambient mics can pick him up. He goes back to cutting more of the chicken with the muted knife. He can still do it. His parents still cheer. Blood's falling on the chicken and Hannibal comes in to look at his finger. He turns away from the camera so it looks like Hannibal's putting the kid's finger in his mouth to suck out all the blood. It's just a plaster in the end but the bleeding just won't stop. And Skinny Jeans is already adding the finishing touches to a plate of something perfect and small and he's smiling. And the fat kid's sweating so much he uses the napkin on himself, and the clock keeps going, Hannibal's face, the trophy, the shouting, the clock, and then it all stops.

Skinny Jeans is taking his plate up to Hannibal. Fat Kid stands in his way, red napkin on his hand. They stare at each other for a second, and then the fat kid takes a handful of the other kid's buttermilk potato mash and just sticks it in his mouth. Then another handful, and a third, and then Hannibal walks around the table to take him off the stage and Skinny Jeans starts to plate another…

'I'm so, s-s-sorry,' the fat kid says to the parents as he leaves, sobbing and choking on mash. 'I'm so sorry I disa-dis-disappointed you, that you'll be poor and fat for the rest of your fucking lives because of me.' And as he passes by his kitchen counter, he stabs the chicken one last time.

The show has been in French and with no subtitles and who knows what the hell was going on. Whatever happened though, Skinny Jeans got the ten thousand euros, the fat kid sobbed and stole some mash, and his parents just wouldn't look at him.

On his pre-work bench it now says 'How did you like the snow?' where Tomás's name used to be. He erases it and writes 'Tomás' on it again. There's no snow left, just a dark mush melting into gutters. Children still make snowballs out of it. There are people walking out with ski poles they never get to use. Others are stomping on ice puddles with boots made of plastic bags tied over at the knees. There are students flying drones to take pictures from heights in which what little snow is left would be invisible. Then there's the church procession.

—*Repent, Repent*

The news said it had snowed in the whole continent, every corner of Latin America, even the jungles, and all at the same time.

—*Repent, for the end is near*

Some people died up in the mountains. They'd never seen anything like it before. They weren't prepared to have something so familiar become suddenly so dangerous. They wanted less of it, and at a different time. Tomás can't see the mountains. If it's not the smog then it's fog. If the country weren't so thin, no one would even know the mountains were there. His coffee is too hot, so he removes its plastic lid and burns his hand with the drops.

On the news that morning, there had been people on TV saying that they were now seeing flowers in places where there had been nothing before. Animal protection agencies appeared too, clearing the roads of bird bodies and dumping them in already full trucks. There were stills of a white Amazonian forest, like a gigantic Christmas display, but with dead crocodiles spilling out onto beaches and monkeys gathering together for heat like penguins, their tails wrapped around themselves. 'Animals suffer in silence,' the scientist on TV had said, 'that's the saddest part of it all.' Then, an aerial take of Machu Picchu, which covered in snow looks like a regular hill. All the tourists gone. The churches have also been full this morning. There have been adverts for fallout shelters on the radio, the thickest doors, water recycling technology to drink your own piss, power to last you two years (and after that you're fucked, of course, and ice ages are longer, so you should consider upgrading). The Mapocho River almost burst its banks. His *sopaipilla* is as greasy as always, and he eats it in two bites to avoid the stains.

—*Even an ice age cannot cleanse the fires of Hell*

One of the news anchors cried as he read the news. His cat had frozen to death trying to eat all the frozen birds that were falling and sticking to tree branches. Pinpon, Pinpon, why did you always have to try and eat them? 'Don't eat the birds, don't eat the birds,' the Health Minister said when it was his turn to speak.

—*Repent, repent*

Tomás stands, lights a cigarette, and heads towards the office building. The Blue Peace people are out with their banners again, fencing off the religious procession by trying to outshout them. Their banners are now snowy mountains, but you can tell they just painted over the volcanoes because there's still some red on the edges, and mountains don't shoot out snow from the peaks. They also drew woollen hats on the poor brown kids who were riding tires before, now sledges, and facing storms of lava, now an avalanche.

—*Free our Futures, Free our Futures!*
Fear the snow for Satan cannot fool us!

A girl with a highway-worker overall hands him a mountain banner as he passes by. He thanks her and she calls him comrade and gives him a fist salute, so he does the same.

Inside, the elevator's still broken. He sighs, even though he expected it, and takes the stairs next to the healthiest man on Earth, who takes the stairs in twos and with a fucking smile and says hello as he passes by. And Tomás does a fist salute with a smile but the guy just rolls his eyes. By the time Tomás is on the third floor the other guy must have reached the sky. Thirty. If Tomás stops smoking before he turns thirty, he will also be able to climb things in twos and he will ask for his office to be the highest in the building.

Anna the secretary isn't at her desk, so Tomás comes out from where he's been hiding at the entrance and fast-walks into his office.

'Hey, right on time, check it out,' Jaime says. He's wearing the same clothes as the last time they met.

'What is it?' Tomás says, putting down the banner by the bin.

'Do you remember Bimbo?'

'The elephant?'

'Yeah, of course the elephant. Our elephant.'

'Yeah, sure, what about him?'

'I rendered him with the Unreal engine, man.'

'Does he come back down when he jumps this time?'

'Sometimes.'

'Well, at least Bimbo looks good.'

'I know.'

Jaime's moving a 3D elephant onscreen using the arrow keys. A three-dimensional failure is a failure no matter what angle you see it from. Even though the green field around the elephant is 3D too, Jaime's only made it possible for the elephant to move forward and backwards. And so the illusion of depth, the whole point of 3D graphics, is lost.

Jaime looks out the window. 'Really fucking weird, huh?'

'What is?'

'The snow. I was out power-walking but I had to stop. People started falling down and slipping over and shit.'

'Power-walking?'

'Yeah, it's for my core. Anyway, I have to tell you something,' Jaime starts.

'What is it?' He keeps moving 3D Bimbo and Tomás notices Jaime didn't render its tail.

'Had a meeting with the Head of School, with Pedro. They're cutting our budget.'

'Again? We're already sharing an office. What happened?'

'Don't know man, who knows? Just how it is. And Pedro said that if we don't finish a game that's publishable in four weeks we're getting fired.' He turns 3D Bimbo off.

'Fuck. Well, I guess Bimbo really doesn't look that bad anymore,' Tomás says.

'Exactly.'

Jaime picks up his coat from his desk and combs himself looking at his own reflection on the black of the computer screen.

'Come up with something. Please, man, anything,' Jaime says.

'But shouldn't you work out the gameplay mechanics first?'

'Well, no, I need a story first and then I'll just build around it. Please just make Bimbo do something. Anything will do.'

'Alright. How long have I got?'

'Two weeks, and that's pushing it.'

'Done.'

'OK?' Jaime points at Tomás, his hand emulating a gun – what Jaime does when he knows Tomás is lying.

'OK.'

Jaime walks to the door and turns around.

'Oh, I forgot to ask you.'

'What?'

'About Fran. How was it?'

'It didn't work out.'

'Ah, shame. Was it the language? I thought she spoke really good Sp—'

'It was the language.'

Jaime sighs with a smile.

'I'm off anyway. Get some work done man, please.'

Jaime puts his hat on and leaves. Tomás turns on the computer screen and looks at Bimbo. Two weeks for a story. He lies down under the desk. The chewing gum stars have moved, so he looks for the troll doll on the shelf and swears its hair wasn't always that bright a pink, and that it wasn't naked the last time he saw it.

What could he write about? Google says he should write about THE WORLD AROUND HIM. He should write about people, his people, their everyday lives, the walks in the park, the way they look forward to retirement by acting retired, the parties, last night's party, sleeping alone after said party, shaving for himself, getting into jogging because that will help at the next party, and then sharing mild party successes with a grin that says next time, next time it'll be his turn, despite the overwhelming evidence that luck always favours those who do not believe in turns. He should write about birds falling out of trees, write about frozen forests, suffering in silence, his comrades, suffering in silence, Bimbo, silence, pink dolls, silence, the hole in the roof, dripping and then, silent, the priests, hell, hoping for silence, Eva, himself, silence... It's useless, so useless, to try and write about the world around him when it keeps changing every night, the sky falling in snowflakes, the river of shit bursting its banks, almost out of the one place where it can flow ignored forever (and in silence). No one can write about that crap. Once, Tomás gave Eva a diary, her own IDEAS book, but she said writing her thoughts down made her uncomfortable. It made her realise she was never happy, that she was always far from who she thought she was. 'Let me be,' she said, giving the diary back to him, 'just let me be without having to know it.'

He gets up and closes Bimbo and goes on Amazon. He types in 'Antarctic equipment', but only books and documentaries show up: *Notes from a Cold Climate: Antarctic Symphony*, *Under Antarctic Ice: Photographs from the Depths*, *Frozen Planet: Full DVD Series*. They all sound like verses from a mediocre poem, but that's because no one really goes there unless they're dressed up like astronauts, and so they use words that could describe other planets. Tomás could go to that planet. He knows it's fucking crazy but he wants her to know it too. Although right now he needs to start working, and so he orders the *Frozen Planet* box set and opens his IDEAS book on the last page.

Eva gave him his IDEAS book on the wrong day. She had baked a cake, even made the candles, God knows how. But his birthday wasn't on that day. He hadn't remembered to tell her the truth after they met, when, as a joke, he said his birthday was the week after. It had been months away, and when no one called him, or gave him a card or some other stupid gesture people only do at birthdays, she made a big deal about it. She cooked some French cake that tasted like Chilean cake, and gave him a Moleskine pad wrapped in *Elle* pages with a tasteful photograph of a rusty tin of flowers and an anaemic model looking over the Paris skyline. She said it was the most important thing she'd ever give him, that she couldn't wait to see what he'd write, because that notebook is what writers and creative people use in Europe, where the best people write in the best way. It said so on the belly band. On the front page she wrote, 'So you can write about us'. When his family appeared at the door to take him out to dinner on his real birthday (which they didn't mention straight away), they asked what Eva had given him.

'We have guests,' Eva said to Angela, 'we were planning on going to an expat bar with my French class,' she said, and asked Tomás if he also thought that it was rude for them to all just appear uninvited. He agreed, but they wouldn't go. They just came in and sat down, the way cats do when you open any door ever.

Later, when the cake came out at the restaurant, and the waiters dimmed the lights, and the fucking mariachi came up with a guitar the size of a basketball player, and then strummed and hit it at the neck with the beat, Eva just stared at him through the flickering candles. She took the first slice of cake, which now tasted French or just foreign, because his sister had picked it and it was made of straw or bits of carpet or some other vegan shit. And his parents asked, again, as if it fucking mattered to them, what Eva had bought for him. She said she had given it to him already, to which the mariachi laughed and his dad laughed, and some waiters whistled and even tried high-fiving Tomás, because when fuckable people talk about fucking, everyone loses it. And it was just a notebook, but Tomás couldn't say it because he was already high-fiving a mariachi who had turned red with excitement. Eva stood up and left. His dad sighed and said something about women with attitudes being better than boring ones, and his mother asked if she was OK, and his sister looked at the straw cake, more than half of it still left, and she said 'Namaste bitch,' as Eva walked away, 'Namaste. You could at least have said thanks,' and…

He needs to work. WORK goddam it. He needs to write about THE WORLD AROUND HIM and… Before he does anything though, he YouTubes Radiohead's 'Let Down', which Yiyo and himself used to play in high school breaks, when they took their guitars so that people would know that they played guitar. This was the song they claimed inspired them the most, whatever that means. The guitars start out at a distance, layers intruding on other layers, getting louder and louder, as if Thom Yorke himself was walking around your house, and then the beat comes in and the mess is a riff, a loop, and when the beat comes in now, Tomás looks out the window where the crowds of Blue Peace activists are gathering with their banners and pamphlets about global warming because, like him, they're inspired by deadlines. Even they can look beautiful in a song, coordinated, all together marching in light steps, almost in slow motion, the angrier they are the better, and *Hysterically useless, hysterical, Let down and hanging around,* he writes at the top of the page, underlines it, and begins a new paragraph.

There's a plane and it's flying over the ocean. He has a limited supply of fuel and the objective is to reach a white island. The player has to choose whether to use the fuel to go as high as possible and then glide, or just fly straight on and… But why? What's on the island? And is it really a choice? If you were faced with this dilemma, wouldn't you fly as high as possible just to delay the fall? Wouldn't you wish to then pass out before touching water? And how would Bimbo fit all of this? It's useless. He turns off Thom Yorke, and all the Blue Peace anger is just anger, and the fake snowy peaks are just painted cardboard, and THE WORLD AROUND HIM is another smog-filled day in Santiago, another day at the office, another hour to pass before another night at the apartment. He lies under the desk again and checks his phone.

'All, uhuh, all this white powder's making me nervous,' @RealNicolasCage says on Twitter. On #Snowggedon, people are sharing pictures of Jesus crying blood and of crucified snowmen, of Amazonian tribes failing to make winter jackets out of snakeskin and tree leaves. #Repent is trending. Tomás starts watching a video of a guy reacting to a video of an avalanche off of Machu Picchu. 'Oh my God,' he says, 'oh my God, it could have been us, my God, it could have been us.'

Someone comes into the office and Tomás bangs his head on the desk trying to get up. It's Anna, standing by the door. He pretends to be looking for something on the rug and finds a staple and shows it to her. The guy on the video is still reacting.

> Oh – ma – God. Get out of there people,
> get out. Like, it's a fucking avalanche. My God, they've
> never seen an avalanche before.

'Found it,' Tomás says. 'Only one left. Have to use everything now, what with all the funding cuts and all…'

'I just came to tell you that your sister's on the line,' she says, looking at the staple. 'And yes, I'm still waiting for the papers.'

I'm shocked. Just too shocked. Oh my god,
not the parrots, please don't take the parrots.

'I was just grading the papers actually. You'll get them real soon.'
   'OK, but what should I tell your sister?' she asks.
   'Just put her through, I'll finish marking them right after,' he says,
still on the floor.
   Tomás looks at her but she just stares at the staple and sighs.

Look at them, they're so lost, My God, they don't know where
to fly to.
Like, so cruel. Why nature? Why?

He turns off the video and gets up to take the phone, line 2 blipping red.
   'Namaste,' she starts.
   'What?' he asks, even though he heard.
   'Namaste, asshole.'
   'Hi, what's—'
   'Dad's dead.'

7

Evasive Manoeuvres

When planes crash they do so in bulk. No one can fucking explain it. One goes down in the Atlantic. POOF. Another in the Pacific. POOF. In Russia, China. POOF POOF. Check online: planecrashinfo.com. The graphs will show spikes. The causes vary, sure, between military, weather, engine malfunction, a pigeon on the runway, a radar gone black. Like parts of a terrible orchestra, all the planes and airports in the world agree to throw melody out the window and the world nods, we nod, dead, we say, no survivors, they died quickly, without pain. But like the build-up of a strings arrangement, the fear of a key change lasts for fucking ages.

He wanted to be buried in Graneros. Out of all places, he chose the place that's already buried. Graneros, the town where people pay to see evangelical rappers go on about the power of faith, where people either work at the coffee and cereal factory or become junkies. His dad had been one of those kids once, and he had worked at the factory.

It's a warm sunny day, which makes going to a funeral feel wrong. There's a pleasant breeze rustling the leaves in the trees and the smell of coffee has taken over the plaza. This town never changes. People still play cards and stare at others who are doing the same while sitting on the threshold of their rotting doors. The abandoned houses (abandoned forever) look the same too, maybe a few more vines breaking out of their glassless windows. It snowed here last week, and despite the news last night mentioning sinkholes and mudslides and death and falling roofs in the southern tip of Chile, the short train in Central Valley between Santiago and Graneros worked as it always did (late, hot and overcrowded), and no one was even talking about the snow on the one-hour ride. Eva had once said that people in Chilean towns in the middle of nowhere (which is Santiago-speak for *not-Santiago*) were small-minded, unlike Parisians who had had to adapt to the great shifts in modern history. 'Having a little mind is not about knowledge,' she'd said when he'd told her she sounded like her friends at French book club. 'It's about understanding that everything we do has an impact on everyone else.' She didn't explain what 'everything' or 'impact' meant, but he's glad he didn't ask because, although she loved his mum and dad, she'd felt out of place in Graneros. 'I fucking hate it, she'd said, 'and I hate that fucking train.' And even with last week's snow, the narrow canals are as dry as they've ever been, and dust shines on the skin. His family always loved this place. 'It's simpler, much simpler over there,' his dad used to say, 'and there are no Argentinians.' Eva came with them on a daytrip once too. She said it was charming, which is what people say about old places where there's nothing to do. He agreed.

He's sweating. He can't wait to take off his fucking suit and tie but he's finally dressed for a funeral at an actual funeral. He lights up a cigarette that he knows he doesn't want. With the heat, the smoke makes him dizzy but he inhales it anyway. He can see the church, a crowd gathering in front and stray dogs barking and pissing on its walls. In the park facing the church, there are boy scouts putting up tents to the whistle of an old man dressed like a child. He shows them how to snap together metallic skeletons.

He looks up at the clear sky and wonders what it must be like to fall from it on a plane, to know that you'll die in just a few seconds, that your body will be suddenly crushed into impossible, unrecognisable shapes. His dad had been caught in the snowstorm. He must have… People on TV always go on about moments before death, the white light and the tunnel and the film reel of your life and all that bullshit, when it must be fear, pure fear, no deeper than the first time you speak out in public at school, but far shorter. Tomas hopes his dad didn't suffer, and he's real glad he never learnt to fly. Though considering how much safer planes are than cars, maybe he… The boy scout leader sounds the whistle and the kids destroy their tents, and start over.

He walks over to the church, which after the last earthquake is held up by a mere ten to fifteen wooden poles placed diagonally against the walls. Everyone who is attending the funeral appears to be wearing colourful Nepalese trousers, just like Angela's, and people he's never met before stare at him and shake their heads. And then there's his extended family; his cousins from Punta Arenas who dress like hippies anyway because they own a poncho stall in the Chilean Patagonia, and Aunt Memé-the-Deaf from San Fernando, who has refused to wear her hearing aid ever since Uncle Pato passed away, so she has no idea what's going on and just frowns at everyone because she – like Tomas – came dressed for a funeral. He hasn't seen any of them for years despite their invitations, so they now avoid Tomás in a corner, unsure of who should apologise first, and for whose loss. There's a cotton candy van giving out swirls of pink to one side next to a statue of a saint all white with bird shit on its head, and there's a shirtless man in swimming trunks sweeping pigeons away.

The one thing he and Eva indisputably shared (yes – everything else was relative) was their hatred of hippies, although they hated them for very different reasons. One of their first dates had been at a circus: The Nail Brothers, famous for using medieval objects (random objects with spikes) in their stunts. It started with one of the Nails jumping from a high-as-fuck trampoline into an open iron maiden (Iron Maiden playing in the background, of course). Fake blood splashed out once it was sealed shut. The front row ended up with red faces. The Splash Zone, they called it. The crowd cheered when the Nail Brother emerged from the chamber unharmed.

The four brothers all looked the same. Eva said she wouldn't have known if they actually sacrificed an artist at the start of every show and she laughed and held one of Tomás's thighs. A second Nail Brother jumped and she tightened her hand and Tomás got a half-boner as the blood splashed out. Anyway, why is he thinking about half-boners and blood and how does it all relate to hippies? Well, after the iron maiden jump and the magician who lynched and quartered his young assistant, a yellow Volkswagen van drove in through the curtains. Two hippies jumped out while it was still in motion. They had Indian feathers knotted to filthy dreadlocks, face paints, fake splifs in their mouths (probably real splifs), long loose trousers, sandals and they ended every clause with 'dude' or 'bro' (pronounced 'bra') and they were meant to be clowns. They ruined the whole medieval thing and no one gave a damn. Yes, it was Angela who got them the tickets and yes, these two assholes were her friends. After juggling knives and making each other jump through fiery spiky hoola hoops, they bowed and turned to the crowd. At which point, everyone started looking at each other. No one likes being picked. Ever. People secretly wished they didn't exist, that they were dead, that the Nail Brothers were all dead, that the circus would catch fire, that performance arts in general would catch fire – anything but get picked. The spotlight flicked through the audience.

Eva whispered into his ear. It was the first time she had done so. She would later do it again and again.

'Aren't these kinds of people the worst?' she said.

'Yes, but why do you say that?' he whispered back.

'It makes me uncomfortable, this whole hippie fashion thing, like wearing feathers and stuff. It's like disrespectful, you know, and it's not like we don't have our own indigenous people, who don't even dress like this at all, and...'

'I hate that it's a fashion, I've nothing against fashion but I hate, I don't know, I hate outfits. These douchebags are outfits. It's too perfect, perfectly 'crazy', perfectly 'random', perfectly 'peaceful' and 'loving',' he said, using both hands as quotation marks. 'But it's all so fucking fake.'

'Too perfect?' she asked and the spotlight stopped on them and perfectly lit their faces.

People clapped as one of the hippies came up to them. Eva downed the piscola she was not supposed to have. She was quite drunk by this point.

'Don't let them take me,' she joked, 'or I might fall down the stairs.' She grabbed him with both hands on his wrists, but the hippie arrived and took her hands away from Tomás. That bastard was handholding with Eva before Tomás ever did. Eva smiled and walked down (slowly) into the dirt pit. More clapping. Tomás didn't clap. That was his first failure. The fucking hippie just took her and put her in the van. He locked it. It was supposed to be funny that nothing happened, that they did nothing apart from lock her up, because trapping people, no, kidnapping people for no reason whatsoever is pointless and therefore hilarious because hippies too are pointless, so 'random', and therefore hilarious. The spotlight was still on him. They were waiting for him to react. He saw Eva looking at him from the driver's seat. They were too far from each other for him to be certain about it, but he swears there was eye contact. He just waited. For. Ages.

'Bra, dude, this guy sure is like a total bummer, man, a total bummer,' one of the Brothers said, and people laughed with him, and they let Eva out, and she came back to him and the spotlight moved away, thank fuck, and he was ready for her to walk out on him for not doing anything, but instead...

'Thank you,' she said, without a trace of sarcasm. 'It would have gone on for far longer.'

They fucked for the first time that night. After he had gone down on her she gave Tomás a blowjob, but he could not keep the image of the yellow van out of his head. She looked at him, gave him the pleasure of eye contact, the only way of communicating through a blowjob, the pleasure of communication, and despite all of this he could only think of her trapped eyes in that yellow Volkswagen and the ring of burning hoola hoops surrounding it. Fuck hippies. Fuck outfits. Help us, the Nail Brothers had pretty much said. Help us do our thing. He didn't help. But he came. He came hard in her mouth without telling her.

'I'm sorry,' he said, as she spit it out onto his belly. She didn't say anything but kept her eyes on him. 'I'm sorry,' he said again and then she looked away.

And that is what Tomás is thinking about when his sister comes out of the church wearing an orange poncho and sandals.

'Namaste, douche. Oh man, what's up with you?' she asks, looking over at the queue for cotton candy, where there are old people crying and fumbling with their rosaries and eating in silence.

'Um, why is it so full of hippies? Did I get the date wrong or something?'

'Didn't you get my message? I tried calling you, but as always, you wouldn't answer.'

'What message?'

She sighs. 'I sent you the dress code for the funeral, dumbass. It's what he would have wanted. Mum said he didn't want a dark funeral. He wanted a party.'

He looks at the people shaking their heads and whispering between themselves. Of course. Angela invited all her friends. All her fucking friends, and he'll have to hear all about their fucking travels, their journeys (as they call them), get a job already, travelling without any money, get a job, and still somehow meeting the right people, just the right person at the right time, a simple love story, not a job, that lasts for as long as it takes them to cross whatever forest these kinds of people want to cross. And he'll have to see them dance the hoola hoop just like they did when Lou Reed died, right in front of the Bellas Artes Museum. And there they are now, serving drinks to Aunt Memé who just stares back, and the Punta Arenas cousins are taking pictures of the hippies with their phones while the old people who aren't queueing for hot dogs are standing stiff by the church doors. Tomás doesn't know if he should talk to Angela's friends, make up cheap sentences about how despite Dad's death, and despite Mum now having to live alone until she dies too, Dad will always be present in his plastic toys and hell, he died doing something he loved. No one would say that. Even flying is really about coming back to ground. He can't say that either. His sister comments on stories for a living and so she would comment on this one too. She'd tell Mum he didn't mean it and she'd probably be right, but he isn't sure.

˙ Alejandro, who calls himself The World's Brother (if you really force the Spanish 'J' then you're pronouncing his name as he does), is probably the worst of them all. He's wearing aviator sunglasses and cargo shorts and his beard as a shirt. The beard has glitter on it. On the planet this guy's from, that's an acceptable thing. Angela used to date him because they had the same spirit animal, the rabbit, and because, according to her, his yellow Ferrari really did match the size of his cock (not the spirit animal). Tomás hates him, really fucking hates his guts, mainly because Eva liked him. She said that while Alejandro, Alejjjjjjjandro, is certainly too rich to be a hippie, he at least tries to make others happy, like he really did go to that orphanage in Thailand that summer (and probably created more orphans in time for the summer after that). And he really did earn the embarrassing pictures of himself hugging poor children on his Facebook wall, and he truly did believe his own bullshit. 'That's the thing,' Eva said, 'I like people who have the balls to believe in their own bullshit.

Even if they turn out to be hippies, though that makes it harder. If they really live their crap, if they are consistent, I like it. Do you?' She asked him that with a smile, and he put a hand up and another on his heart, a scout promise, just like the kids are doing right now, and he said, 'Yes, I really do believe in my own bullshit,' and then they fucked like rabbits, no, like birds, still and quiet, because this was during a holiday outing and they were sharing a flat with his sister and Alejandro, and before Tomás and Eva could even start, they heard Alejandro do his signature loud moan (OHMMM–OHMMM–Ohm...) as he came, most likely over his sister's ears (he said he loved HER EARS!) which, for a rabbit, are amazingly non-perceptive to the dangers of men out in the wild.

Anyway, Alejandro broke up with his sister because he wanted to follow a colony of pumas down South, PUMAS, a bit like that crazy American asshole who wanted to become a bear, and film himself and his growth ('internal growth,' he said), from being a cub to a full-grown puma. Unlike the American bear guy, Aleja-fucking-jandro did not get eaten, though Tomás has had that dream before, where Alejandro screams and screams that his skin is being ravaged and Tomás nods at the puma to continue and... His sister was so depressed she had to get Tomás to sit with her all day and night for a whole year. She said if he didn't she'd jump off the balcony. Alejandro appeared on TV. Angela was a mess of tears and envy. He appeared on the national news. 'Fuck him,' she said. He was on CNN stroking pumas. Jesus – the balcony – 'Please don't leave me alone.' And then, then he appeared one last time. He was on his way to the national tribunals for trying to sell puma cubs into an exotic animal black market ring in Valdivia. This time, his sister said nothing. Alejandro said he just wanted to give them better homes, you know? But the news added he was also on LSD. Angela turned off the TV. She made herself a cup of green tea. 'I guess we can still be friends,' she said, though everyone knows that a puma befriending a rabbit is only the stuff of YouTube legends.

But here he is, with his new Jaguar convertible double-parked at the edge of the plaza, and he passes Tomás a sausage on a plastic fork as he walks by.

'Thank you,' Tomás says as he takes the sausage.

'Brother, for you, any time,' Alejandro answers, and smiles at Angela. She smiles back and takes a sausage too, the largest of them all, and bites on it real hard. 'I'm sorry for your loss,' he adds with a bow that no one answers.

'You're serious,' Tomás then whispers to Angela. 'Isn't this all a bit too casual? And what the hell is he doing...'

'Yes. Well, it's not that serious,' she says with a big smile, 'it's a party, a party, a big party,' she repeats before covering her face and hugging him.

'I'm sorry. So, how have you been anyway?' Tomás asks, between bites that burn his lips. 'How's work?'

'Apart from Dad dying, you...' she pauses and looks at him from head to toes. She sighs. 'Sorry, that's just mean. I'm OK. You know me, I'm always OK,' she says, looking at her own shadow which is much larger than she is.

'Come on, you have a sweet life ahead of you. Screw that, you already have it,' he says, taking one of her hands, cold and tiny. Is he really doing this? Where was she when Eva left? What about him? Well, there is the fact that no one knows Eva left him apart from Jaime and Yiyo. There is that. But there is also anger, pure and irrational hate, HATE, for those who knew Eva and let her get away, and HATE for himself for even beginning to think like this. But Angela doesn't know. She doesn't know anything. No one does. So he continues without even knowing how he feels.

'You're OK because everything works out for you. I mean, I might not share your beliefs and all that but you get things done. That's what matters. You interview celebrities for God's sake. I'm lucky if a student even talks to me. And if they do, which they don't, it would be to ask about you and—'

'—Tomás.'

'But it's true, like—'

'—Tomás.'

'Yes?'

'I got fired.'

'What?'

'I got fired. And it was months ago. I know, I should have told you but I didn't want you to worry, what with your games not taking off and all. I'm back to, ugh, I can't even say it,' she puts one hand on her lips as if ready to puke, 'but it is what it is and the universe knows best. I'm back to blogging,' she says and throws the fork with the rest of her sausage into a clutter of bushes by the church gates. 'You had to wear black,' she says, now starting to cry.

'I'm sorry.'

'I know you are, little brother, you always are.'

He puts his arm around her. It lasts forever. The cold breeze straightens his back, almost aching, and he realises he isn't close to his sister, that he doesn't understand her. Eva once said she was growing closer to her family as years went by, and he agreed. When she asked him why he thought that was the case, he said it was because people get lonelier as they get older, and like other aspects of adult life, obligation becomes pleasurable, something to live for. She looked at him with a half-smile, turned her night table light off and turned to face the wall. 'Is that what's going to happen to us? Is that all there is?' He said it wasn't, but he couldn't touch her that night.

'Thank you,' Angela says, wiping her face. 'Let's try and keep the party going, alright?'

'OK but, what, how, what happened?' he asks.

'Look, Dad's dead, Tomás. Today, out of all days, I don't want to talk about it. Just don't tell mum or she'll worry about money even more than she already is.'

'Look, I'm sorry, I didn't know.'

'It is what it is. And I'll be taking Mum to India with me for a few months. She needs to get out of here so she can rekindle her love for the universe.'

'I'll help you pay it.'

'Alejandro is paying.'

'Come on.'

'Alejandro is coming,' she says, and she waves over at him – Alejandro – as she says it. Just hearing the words 'Alejandro' and 'coming' in one sentence makes Tomás a little sick to the stomach.

'And you should prepare the eulogy. I sorted out a stage for you already at the Golf Club.'

What? He has not done the...

'I'm ready,' he says with a nod.

'You better be. Mum will be upset if her only son has nothing to say about his father.'

He nods and watches her leave. She jogs over to the cotton candy kiosk, where a guy wearing something like a Peter Pan costume rolls her a perfect pink candy cloud. She then walks to his mother, leaving Tomas alone, with all the hippies. It's hard for him to see his mother this way. She's sitting alone, cross-legged on a bench wearing a purple toga with sunflowers on the knees. She looks like she's angry, a hard frown directed at no one in particular, and her toga hangs too large on her, like she's disappearing into her costume, and her shoulders are exposed and sunburnt and no one is even looking at her. Why is no one even looking at her, sitting with her? Even harder is knowing what to say to her. He lights another cigarette to the sound of the scout leader whistling the end of the tent session. As he watches the kids dismantling them, and as he sees them laughing at how easy it is to break things that you yourself have built, he realises why seeing his mother like this hurts him so much. He hadn't even thought that, just like him and Eva, his mum had lost her partner, her friend. And just like him, she couldn't do a thing about it. Is there really a difference between your girlfriend/boyfriend/wife/husband dying and going away far, so far that you'll never get to speak or see them again? Whatever the answers are, there is a comforting finality in all of this tragedy, and he finds himself getting dizzy with the smoke and, yes, he has to admit it, admit it despite his dizziness, that he feels envious of his mother. 'Fuck,' he whispers to himself, stepping on the unfinished cigarette. He is envious of his grieving mother.

He goes over to Alejandro to get another sausage.

'Your mum looks pretty rough there, dude,' Alejandro tells Tomás, handing him a napkin.

'I know. She needs some time off,' he says.

'We all need time off. I'm sure you could also—'

'—Take care of her in India.'

'She'll come back like new, just you remember.'

'No weird animal shit, alright?'

'I've done my time, dude,' Alejandro says; he holds both his hands up.

Maybe Alejandro isn't so bad after all. Could it be possible that it was all a mistake? Could it have been an LSD trip filled with visions of homeless pumas waiting to be rescued, and he, Alejandro, saving them all? Most likely not. Maybe Ale, fuck it, Alejjjjandro, The World's Brother, is his brother too. Maybe Tomás will go to India with him. Would Alejandro pay? He definitely would pay. And first class too. Maybe if Tomás went he'd come back like new, and some mentalist hippie will blow hallucinogens up his nose like those anthropologists on TV, and he'd forget Eva ever existed and then the universe will decide this and that and he laughs, he laughs because he actually said 'the universe' out loud, at his father's fucking funeral, he's dead, fuck he's dead here and now and in every universe and at the level of a person, no, the fucking atom, and he can't stop laughing, u-ni-verse, what nonsense, what utter nonsense. The V makes you bite your lips, just like E-Va, sexy nonsense, but still, the whole universe decides thing is such bullshit. Eva decided. He did not. But shit, his dad's dead… His mum's alone. Eva left him. He is alone. That's all that matters. And if the universe had anything to do with either, well then, fuck the universe.

Tomás flicks the new cigarette away and he watches the old orange circle burn out as he thinks about the Indian sunsets he has now decided he will never see.

So what can he say about his father? He hadn't even thought about the eulogy before Angela mentioned it. What can anyone say to the dead, to the gone, that can't be summed up in the things we say to the living: 'see you, bye!' But the obvious truth is these sorts of things, the funeral, the funeral 'party', the clothes, the tears, the speech… They're for those who still need to get up and go to work and sleep and get up again knowing that they got left behind. Tomás can say anything. It's a bit like the best kind of stand-up, where the comedian talks about people who aren't there as if they were there at their absent expense. But what does he say about his father? He realises he only knows a handful of things about him (do we ever know more than that about anyone?). He takes his IDEAS book and writes them down in bullet points.

- He HATED Argentinians (not a great way to start).
- He had high cholesterol and diabetes (Tomás should really eat better).
- He liked to fly (is it not too soon to say it?).
- He was a good pilot (he crashed!).
- He invented cereal boxes which kept toys hidden at the end of the box with a patented sticky tape system.

- He liked Eva. He believed in him and Eva.
- He loved Mum more than anything in the world.

And that is it. He wonders how long he's expected to talk for and almost walks over to his sister and mother to ask them but she just won't stop crying, which is probably the one thing he *is* expected to do but can't, because of all the colourful hippies surrounding him like a swarm of helium birthday balloons.

Tomás walks into the small chapel to the side of the church. There are women holding rosaries and no one says a thing. His dad's coffin is in the middle of the room (will it inspire him?), and there's a guy dressed as a clown, nose and all, spray-painting it with red flowers and glittering waves and a cartoon sun with a sad face. Tomás walks up to the coffin, stretches on his toes. Inside, his dad's wearing a purple suit, his cheeks bright red circles, his lips contorted into a forced smile that shows his teeth. He has a silver aeroplane pin on his chest.

'Any last words?' the clown asks him, spraying another layer of green onto a tree.

'I don't know,' Tomás answers.

The clown adds just that to the coffin: I DON'T KNOW.

'What the fuck are you doing?' Tomás asks him.

'Uh, making the last adjustments?' the artist says, as if spray-painting a coffin was the most obvious thing in the world.

'What adjustments could you possibly want to add?' Tomás asks, waving one hand over the mess of neon graffiti that now look like hieroglyphics, like they're going to bury a pharaoh who loved ecstasy raves and German electronica. What music did his father like? He has no fucking clue. Eva liked French retro which…

'Your dad is going out in style, dude.'

But didn't he already go out in 'style'? Could there possibly be a more sensational way to die? Spontaneous combustion. Maybe that. Though

Tomás doesn't believe in it despite all the documentaries he's watched, so no, plane crash remains number one.

Seeing the pin on his dad's chest makes Tomás feel a little guilty, perhaps even a lot guilty, about not wanting to learn to fly. Sure, he's alive because of it (he can't say that at the eulogy!) but it would have meant a lot to his father. In fact, if it had been Tomás who had crashed and died, his father would have written the proudest eulogy in the world because, well, old people like to see that what they've done is not a waste of time by having younger people want to do the same things as they have (he better not say that either). If Tomás were dead, his father's time would have remained an investment, with a shitty outcome sure, but an investment nonetheless. Now, as the artist begins to push the coffin towards the door, Tomás has nothing to think about except for wasted time, so much wasted time. Could that be the eulogy?

·   ·   ·

IDEAS BOOK P. 30:

An adventure game. A game ~~about looking, no,~~ searching for something which, as the game progresses, changes from being unimportant to the best thing in the world. ~~It's about the journey, man.~~ You, the protagonist, will have no eyes and no face, which will remain cloaked throughout the game with several colourful scarves (you will get to pick the colours). You will then travel through great expanses, the sandy peaks of the Atacama, the flower fields of the valleys, and then a vast ocean. You won't know what you need to look for until, while running around what seems like an infinite desert, you find the first *dream*: a floating painting of a coastal town made up of an island with a palm tree and a castle in the middle. There's a sound, a pleasant but sad sound bite when you pick up the item, maybe half a song, a verse, Serge's dead leaves on repeat, or Elliott Smith's 'Going Nowhere' loop.

And so now you know that these are the things that you're meant to chase after. You run farther and you will soon find a flower which buzzes red on top of a cliff in the desert. You are required to take a leap over a precipice to get to the flower. Everything around you darkens and a spotlight hits the flower. Do you jump? You have to. You take the flower and make a dizzying drop into the valleys, which are filled with life, animals and trees and fruit and no Serge at all, and Going Nowhere's perfectly fine now, and it's all so different and colourful that you can't stop running to take in specific details. You just run. ~~You live in the moment, man.~~ There are many *dreams* here, set in rows and columns and despite them showing the same image, the island with a castle, they shine less than they used to because the visual queues (due to there being so many) are so clear.

At the end of the last row of *dreams*, you find the island. The castle is only half-built but you will already know that the game is about ~~process, man, about~~ slow progress to something you didn't know you wanted and now you must, absolutely must see, no, must live to see, wholly realised.

So you run ahead, and in *the time it took a cigarette to burn* (Elliott Smith is still Going Nowhere) you board a boat that's anchored to a lonely buoy no one else has discovered but you – oh the good luck of it all! – and it takes you fast through a line of *dreams* which you collect, and then see the castle building itself right in front of you. You must sail, no, row by continually tapping the A button and collect every *dream* in the ocean. You are surprised at how easy it is, and how few *dreams* there are. You feel larger than the castle, than the ocean even, which is now to you more like a puddle. And then, white light, the spotlight hits the island, your island, and you get the keys to the castle, your castle, a French castle, and from the throne room, your throne, you can see the moon and you can see it clearly and full, its ragged craters, its vessels cracking it in parts stuck only by mystery and chance, and there you see it, a glow of red, the first flower, the first dream, back when they felt so special.

Now it is the memory that feels special. You want to feel the first jump, your hair in the tidal wavering of that dark drop Going Nowhere. You can never forget the valley, all that colour, all that life, and all the *echoes that drown the conversation out* (Elliott still playing) and you decide to do nothing. The castle is now more like a prison. The boat is entirely pointless. You had lived on the moon. Hours pass and you're still there and *the clock moves up a quarter of a turn*. You had the whole world to look at and there are no *dreams* left. The castle's bricks won't budge and there's only one thing you can think of before attempting your journey back Going Nowhere.

What have I done? What have I done? *I missed you a lot.*

.   .   .

Tomás is on the passenger seat of his sister's pickup truck trying to find something in his IDEAS book that he can use for the eulogy. They're on their way to the Golf Club burial ground and they're late. The 'clown from earlier' attached the coffin to a two-wheeled flat iron mount, and then adjusted a metallic cable between the mount and the truck. The hippies cheered as Angela tested the cable's tension by driving for about five seconds. The artist then gave them the thumbs up and off they went.

Tomás is the co-pilot. His mum decided to go with Aunt Memé because she didn't know how to get there, and wouldn't be able to hear any directions if she had to ask.

He looks at the coffin from the rear-view mirror. In some fucked up way, Tomás feels proud, as if he were finally paying his dad the debt of flying. And sure, it's Angela who's driving but it is he who knows where they're going and how to best get to the Golf Club.

'I can't believe it,' Angela starts.

'Take the next left and then into the highway again,' Tomás says, pointing left.

'Are you listening? I said I can't believe it.'

'There's nothing to believe Angela. People die, and—'

'No asshole, I meant I can't believe we're burying him there.'

'What, the Golf Club?'

'Yes the Golf Club,' she says, going on fifth.

'You're going too fast for...'

'Like I know why and all, I really do, but couldn't we...'

'You're going...'

'There's just no respect in it, you know? If it were up to me, we'd have him cremated or at least...'

'It's in the next...'

'It's like laughing at dead people. Imagine how Mum must feel. She'll have to ride a fucking golf cart to see her husband's grave. How would you...'

'We missed it.'

'What?'

'We missed the exit.'

'Jesus Christ, could you speak any quieter?'

Angela pulls off an illegal U-turn in the middle of the highway. Tomás can feel the thumping of his dad's body behind them.

'The next right,' Tomás says, looking back.

So why are they burying their father at the Golf Club anyway? Their father had never played golf, never even owned a golf club. But their grandfather Diego had. He played a lot. Was he good at it? He was, or at least he was told that he was by all of his golf friends, as they let themselves lose bets over fairly small amounts for people with that kind of money. $1.000.000. Diego won. $2.000.000. Diego won. $5.000.000, and so on. He must have felt like the fucking king of golf, because there's a picture of him playing with an actual golden crown. He kept it up until one day his friends decided that he should suck at golf and stopped letting Diego win, and they bet much larger sums, and Diego lost the car, an old Bentley convertible. And lost the washing machine (no one had them back then). And lost the German fridge. And the food in it. And then the money to buy the food out of it. And the house. The fucking colonial blue whale of a house with its long cold corridors and exposed terraces filled with servants wearing suits (yes, servants!), and so many flowers everywhere, down the interior balconies, lining swirling staircases, and petals just floating about like plankton in the ocean. And then there was the water fountain, which had a proud French cherub peeing in the full heat of summer. Tomás has seen the pictures. The house would have been his. But grandfather Diego lost it in a bet too. He could not believe that his luck had ran out, and he killed himself a day after he lost the house. Feeling guilty, or maybe it was all just a cruel joke, the same group of friends that left him penniless paid for his funeral and buried him next to the seventh hole in the Golf Club they all used to attend. Tomás's father has never played golf. And yet here he is, on his way to the green of hole number seven.

At the Golf Club, the same hippies from outside the church are now wearing suits. Alejandro looks the best, a magazine hipster, braces over his shirt, light tanned brogues and fitted tweed trousers. Angela goes straight to him and greets him with a kiss on the small mouth that's been recorded missing in action for years due to the curls of his disgusting fucking beard. Yiyo is here too and he waves at Tomás, holding up his acoustic guitar. Through high school, Yiyo missed every single one of Tomás's parties (which is to say, his birthday parties, where a maximum of eleven people once turned up – and that was because they thought Yiyo was coming). Tomás found that the only way to get Yiyo to come was to offer him a gig. Even then, he was always late. But he always apologised with a long hug that made it awkward to be angry about his absences.

Yiyo straps on his guitar, sits on the edge of the make-shift stage and does a little solo. It's the beginning of the solo for Metallica's 'Nothing Else Matters'.

Tomás heads over to the stage with a wave Yiyo doesn't see. 'Thanks for coming, man,' Tomás tells him.

'I'm sorry I didn't make it to church,' he says, and hangs his guitar to the side so he can hug Tomás.

'That's fine. Thanks for doing this.'

'That's cool, dude. A gig's a gig, right?' he says with a smile.

Tomás smiles too, and notices his sister frowning at him and shaking her head.

'How're you man?' Tomás asks Yiyo.

'Same old, same old, dude. Sold the ME-50 today at last. Seriously, it's the worst fucking guitar pedal ever made. Though no one wants to buy the blue drum kit. Seriously, it was fucking expensive and I can barely pay rent now. It's my life's mission to sell that thing now. But at least I got rid of the ME-50. Got to start somewhere, right?'

'Yeah, it's the worst.'

'Anyway man, like, I'm sorry for your loss. We'll talk later in the week, I'm sure. I'll just go say hi to your mum and sister.'

'Alright.'

Tomás has no idea what the ME-50 pedal is, but he wishes that he did. He wishes he too were gigging at other people's funerals and had a guitar on his shoulder. When did it happen? When did he decide that he could no longer believe in guitar equipment, in music? After their first date at San Cristóbal Hill, Eva went home with Tomás. She saw his guitar and asked him to play her a song. She said she loved Bob Dylan and Tomás didn't at all, but Bob Dylan is a great singer to cover because his voice always sounds like shit, and so it's easy to impress people just by knowing the words. He decided to play 'Wedding Song', and she kissed him for it and they even fucked because of it. But then again, it was she who later suggested, in front of all their friends (during a *foie gras* party one of her French-loving douche girlfriends organised), that he sell his guitar and music gear because their kitchen was basic, so basic, and she just couldn't live in a house with electric hobs forever and he said she was right. And so, whether it was her or not who was responsible for the fact that he'll never gig at other people's funerals (or even at normal parties) or sing about being young in Santiago, what he does know is that sometimes even dreams get tired. She said that too, but that was much later.

There are rows of white plastic seats with people Tomás has never seen before. Besides from a few of them and the hippies, there are mainly empty seats. The coffin is in the centre and at the front, on a block of black cement. The coffin's attached to a crane waiting to lift it and place it underground. To the side is a stand with a microphone, and next to that is the flag of the seventh hole. His dad had one request, his mother told the priest, and it's that as the crane lays him into the hole in the ground, the national anthem needs to be playing, and people need to be singing loud enough for Argentineans to hear. But Tomás's mother thought this was a bad idea, that songs about war have no place in cemeteries (or golf courses), and that she needed something softer. So Angela asked Yiyo to play an acoustic cover of it.

'Are you ready to read the eulogy?' Angela asks him.

'I think so,' Tomás says, his face getting hotter.

'Oh, I almost forgot to tell you. Mum said there was a box for you from Dad, a box the police found on the plane. She couldn't open it. I don't want it. Holding on to the past is not in line with my role in the universe. I mean, there's a cheque for each of us too. But we have to wait for the solicitor to cash it into our accounts. Just don't forget the box,' she says, and walks away to sit between his mother and Alejandro in the front row. Yiyo starts to play the national anthem.

A box? For a moment, a very sudden and unmemorable moment (Tomás will never think about these minutes again for the rest of his life), he ponders on whether his dad flew right into… Maybe he knew the snowstorm was coming. Maybe Tomás didn't know him at all. Maybe he was depressed, suicidal, had CANCER, or ALZHEIMER'S, or DEMENTIA or fuck it, all three of them, a holy trinity of doom, and how well do you know a person? If you think of the most embarrassing, the sickest thing you've ever done, would you tell your children? Would you be able to tell your friends? Would they still like you? And now think about the whole world finding out about these morbidities after you die, does it matter to you at all? Would you have spoken before it was too late to speak? And then the priest calls Tomás up onto the podium.

Tomás adjusts the microphone. Yiyo keeps playing but turns the guitar down and is now whispering the lyrics: *Puro Chile es tu cielo azulado...* Tomás takes out his IDEAS book and opens it on a random page. *Puras brisas te cruzan también...* It's the page which has the first notes about Bimbo the elephant, with the initial hand-drawn character sketch at the bottom.

- Must be heavy (jumping must feel 'weighty').
- Bimbo needs to be a hand-drawn cartoon, a bit like Babar (appeal to a younger or nostalgic demographic).
- His motivation is to save his cute little family from the evil Dr. Ratzenhower, a mouse who hates elephants ~~because they're fat and say that it's genetic when~~ because they stepped on his family. The doctor must wear a suit, must look like a politician or authority figure.
- The backgrounds in the game, the settings, will differ from a jungle plain to an icy peak, a woodland forest and then end in a factory, a cheese factory with giant pieces of moving cheese as platforms (add holes in the cheese for extra difficulty).
- Bimbo must remain gender-neutral (he must NOT have a penis).

'So, where to begin?' Tomás asks quietly into the mic as he stares at the words 'NOT have a penis' and Bimbo's face right next to it. And so he begins.

'Dad was, like, a big man with an even, um, larger, weightier heart. It was genetic. He sure as hell loved the younger demographic, um,' Tomás adjusts the mic again without needing to. 'I mean, he loved his children very much, and he was always nostalgic about the good old days (did he just say 'good old days'?). But more importantly, more importantly, like, to everyone here and myself as, um, his only, as his son, he was a motivated man. So motivated was he in fact, that he could have easily have been a (he sees the word, shit, he can think of nothing else) mouse, right Mum?' he looks at her with a smile and gets a long stare back. 'Anyway, jokes aside, jokes aside, my dad was someone who was loved by everyone who had the good luck of meeting him, and he could fit right in with any kind of crowd and any setting, be it the jungle plains, um, the icy peaks of the Andes, a woodland, like a forest, and even a factory. Yes, that's it, the Clover factory where he made cereal boxes which, as far as I recall were always gender neutral, which makes him...' The mic screeches out feedback. It wants it all to stop. 'Thank you,' he ends, and steps down from the podium to sit on the last, the very last chair he can find.

'OOOK,' the priest says, breathing heavily on the mic. Alejandro is the only one clapping. He places both his hands on his head and opens them to show everyone that the speech blew his figurative mind, but unfortunately not his literal head. 'You can lower the coffin now,' the priest says.

Yiyo starts the loud part of the anthem now, making his own mark on the song by needlessly changing notes at the end of every phrase in the chorus, *Duuuuulce Paaatria, reciiiibe los vo-u-otos* and the man on the orange crane pulls on a lever. As the coffin judders down, Angela looks around for Tomás.

'Goddam it man, the only thing you had to do right. Now Mum will have to…'

Suddenly the crane chain rattles and there's a collective wave of WHATs, SHITs, FUCKs and NOs as the coffin falls loose into the hole and Tomás's dad, for the second time, crashes into solid ground. Tomás's mother stands up and she points at the pile of dirt that will soon be on her husband. But she's laughing, laughing so hard that it makes others laugh too. Even Angela is laughing, so much that she has to pause for breath.

'Look everyone!' his mother says. 'It's Grandpa Diego's teeth!' and everyone sees the set of teeth on the earth pile and they even cry from laughter. 'He loved those teeth more than anything! It's the only thing he had left!' she adds.

Tomás walks over to the pickup truck to check the box Angela left for him. He finds it under the driver's seat. It's an old green metallic fishing tackle box (did his dad ever even go fishing?) and he opens the latch.

The first thing he finds is a sticky tape, but below is something far stranger than Tomás could have ever thought of: DVD cover sleeves featuring a famous Argentinian vedette, La Sole: 'La Sole in *Christmas Stuffing and Other Recipes*', 'La Sole in *Police Assodomy: Cavity Search*', 'La Sole in *Beethoven: The Genius of The Organ*', 'La Sole in *Assablanca: Director's Cut*' and 'La Sole in *Pulp Friction*'. On the back of the DVD sleeves Sole appears on all fours, wearing black lace lingerie, a sexy Santa costume, in full leather, with a cock in her pussy, Jesus Christ, his dad, young, no older than twenty, no older than Tomás, wearing the Argentina football team shirt, number 10, Maradona, and at the bottom of the pile there's a letter, and it starts *Dearest Sole, my love, I think this…*

Angela knocks on the window and Tomás quickly hides the box under his blazer.

'What are you doing? I need to talk to you.'

Tomás rolls down the window. 'Yes?'

'So what did he have on the plane? Mum said he never left without that box, but that it was a secret, and that no one was allowed to open it,' she says.

'A collection of sorts,' he says.

'Look, I just wanted to say goodbye properly. You should say bye to Mum too. We'll be off early next week to India.'

'Alright. Well, have a great trip, I guess.'

'Namaste douchebag,' she says, tapping on the door before turning to leave.

Tomás breathes in deep.

'Wait,' Angela says, 'how come Eva wasn't here?'

'She's busy.'

'Sure she is…' she rolls her eyes. 'It's OK, I won't tell Mum. She liked Eva a lot.'

Tomás sees Angela and Alejandro and his mother hugging it out. Eva would have been hugging it out too. His dad loved her, though right now Tomás is now finding it really hard to judge the nature of that love.

He sits in the van, rifling through the DVDs again, and he reads the end of the letter, because the middle is crossed out with thick black felt tip:

> *…everything that ends, ends badly. Your career has taken off, and I can't stand seeing you with that asshole McBone. I think*

125

*I'm going to go to college. I suppose I should thank you because
I can now afford it. I'll miss being onstage with you. I'm retiring.
Yours always,
Don Drillo*

And after going through the whole rubble of Argentinian porn once again, just as he tidies away the sleeve with La Sole tied up and getting spanked on the ass with a rather elegant silver candlestick, Tomás finds himself thinking – and yes, he feels guilty about it – about his inheritance money.

If all of a sudden you got more money than you could ever dream of having, how would you spend it? Would you go on a shopping spree to look just like you always thought you should look? Or would you quit your day job and pursue a dream (yes, dreams need money) of enlightenment or some other artistic bullshit that requires you to feel that it is truly better to be alone and at peace at all times? Whatever it is you would do, Tomás knows that there is only one thing he wants, only one, and that he now has the means to do it.

Tomás walks out of the truck and sits in the last row of seats.

'We're going,' his sister says.

'We're going to India,' his mother says.

'Where will you go now?' Angela asks.

But she leaves before he can answer, and if there was someone left in the Golf Club that could hear, they'd probably be too puzzled to advise him against it as he says this to himself…

'Not to India,' he says, 'not to India,' and he then shoves all the porno pictures out into the air, some of them getting dragged by the wind and landing on the coffin. He looks up at the sky because the sunlight is bright and just the right warmth at last, and when he closes his eyes he sees spots of colour that he can follow but never quite catch because they disappear at the edges.

8

The Jump

When was the last time you thought about the brightness of the moon? No, not only its brightness, but the size, the scope of a floating rock right next to everything you've ever cared about. It has a mass of seventy-four million million million tonnes, tonnes of dust which shine only because the sun wants it to. The moon is only a receiver. It itself is dead. And yet it talks to us, from behind mountain ranges, from the end of the ocean, halved, quartered, full of messages of light and darkness, which you think are for you and you alone. But you can never translate them, never speak back, never change or reword them. 'Look at the moon,' you might say, and there's nothing anyone can add to that.

Tomás is looking at the moon right now. Eva is watering a row of daisies in the front porch of their rented beach house. He's sitting on his *Zelda* Triforce beach towel and is trying to write a game about her using the scenery: the waves, the lighthouse, the faraway ship and its low whistle which sends seagulls and pelicans flying this way and that way and then the moon, a full moon which makes a glassy highway into the farthest end of the water.

Tomás feels, no, sees the moon getting larger and larger. The water soars, the tide changes, it's almost touching him now, almost touching their beach house too.

So Tomás picks up his things and runs into the house. Eva's in the kitchen with a glass of white wine and a wooden cooking spoon, stirring what could be her last *soup à l'oignon* in a large red Le Creuset pot, and he stops her from stirring.

'We have to go to bed,' he says, running out of breath.

'Tomás, later. Right now I'm making us some dinner,' she says with a smile, and then dips the spoon in the soup. She cups her hand under it to make Tomás try it and it's the best soup he's ever had, but from the window behind her the waves are taking over, they surround the beach house, their island, and the moon's only getting larger and larger, its mass gaining zeros, though its weight is still less than an apple's and then...

'We have to go now,' he says.

'Alright, alright. I'll set it to a slow cook. It's probably for the best anyway. It will taste even better in the end.'

Eva is in bed and she falls asleep almost instantly. The sea is in the house. It picks up the bed and drops Tomás to his knees, and the house creaks, the ground quakes, the roof flies off, weightless, a grain of sand to the immensity of the moon that is now right on top of them, so near he can almost touch it. And he looks at Eva who is now awake and trying to talk to him.

'I can't hear you!' he says. 'I can't hear you!' but neither can she.

She gestures for him to come closer to her, but as soon as he presses his face against hers, as soon as their cheeks touch, the moon drops into the ground with all the violence, seventy-four million million million tonnes of violence, that it had kept throughout its years of silence and solitude.

·   ·   ·

So say you wanted to kill yourself. No, wait, that wouldn't work. Say you wanted others to know that you were capable of killing... No, that wouldn't work either. One last try. Say you wanted someone to know that you were THINKING about your capacity to kill yourself. Now choose (only in your head, don't do anything stupid) how you would go about doing it. You arrange them by levels of pain. Jumping into a live volcano at the very top, and then you work your way down to walking into a room full of bullet ants while wearing nothing but a jacket of honey, then slit wrists, then hanging, med overdose and finally jumping off the balcony. You decide to go for the least physically painful way of showing psychological pain. Now imagine someone you despise, someone whose guts you can't stand for even a second, and just because throughout your life they've only ever proved you wrong, time and time again. When you thought your favourite band, the one you loved the most, did it all for the art, man, they said it was for money and BANG, they get a fucking Vevo YouTube channel a month later, and a cover appearance in *Vogue* soon after. When you said you preferred your shitty third-hand car with its plastic interior hardware, they said they could smell your envy as the red MINI Cooper convertible drove past you. And they were right, and you hated their smirk as you shook your head and thought how much you also needed, no, you DESERVED a red MINI Cooper convertible. Now imagine yourself living on the tenth floor, in a flat that you share with them because deep down you love it that they're always right, you envy that too, and they're perfect housemates. One night you tell them that you will jump. They tell you that you won't, and that you never will because you're a coward and you in fact love life, but you live it only to feel the approval of others, their approval, and so you'll never ever be able to kill yourself because you love the images of crowds gathering around your body, the news coverage it might cause, your crying mother and sister, all that noise, and you love it too much to not want to live it, to feel it. You will never jump. In fact, they'll say, I dare you to jump. So do you do it? Do you jump?

Tomás is thinking about whether he would jump or not, though he doesn't have a flatmate or despise someone that much (and Jaime is never right about anything), or even knows how he'd go about inviting said person to share a flat with him, let alone take them to a balcony he doesn't own.

He thought his dad had left him a lot of money. Tomás had called the bank that morning and realised he had miscounted the zeros, had missed a zero or two, and that he in fact got much, much more. Also, the bank clerk referred to his father as Don Drillo, and Tomás just nodded along with it, and finally understood the message in the fishing tackle box. His dad had given him all of his Argentinian porno money he made when he was younger acting with La Sole. He had literally fucked his way through life. And now Tomás will be able to rent, fuck it, buy a flat in Bellavista or Barrio Italia, a flat with green and purple walls, with black pencil marks at the kitchen entrance showing how hundreds of children grew up in it, a flat with real history and insulated walls so that you can shout and have dramatic arguments like artists do in movies, throwing expensive mismatched chinaware at each other with no one able to hear… And it will have a kitchen with six gas hobs that aren't even stuck to the wall because the oven's one of those old-world kinds, the ones that run on wood and are used not just for cooking but to heat the whole place, like in the old days… And a bedroom that overlooks La Chascona, Neruda's old house, so that every time Tomás gets up, he can say 'Big fucking deal' at it, and when it gets late it can inspire him to *write the saddest lines* whilst wearing a tweed suit that is now unsuitable for a funeral and then…

Tomás decides to take the bus to work today. He's been avoiding it because he knows Eva prefers the bus over the metro. He knows she isn't here, that it's irrational, that if she were here he'd like nothing more than to bump into her, but he just hasn't been able to shake off the feeling that… They'd even had arguments about it. She'd told him that she didn't understand why people prefer to travel underground, and he'd told her about the beauty of the sparks in the dark, the curious inclusion of full-sized windows to see absolutely nothing, and the way no one ever talks until they get off the train or even out of the station. But no, she liked the roads, the noise, the musicians, the city, the slow city, the one she could never lose, she said, her city, with all those timeless places and their timeless people. She once said that ice was interesting because it keeps matter that's as old as water intact. 'What is age to an ocean?' she asked him. 'But Santiago isn't frozen,' he said, and she just smiled back.

If he were honest, he'd admit that what he's been avoiding all this time isn't the illusion of Eva on her way to work, and it isn't the noise and colours of the city. What he hates is remembering how they met. It had been so casual and he had done nothing, had made no effort (and therefore spent no time), so that he had thought right then and there that he must have her, he must keep her, because if it had no cause to start then it couldn't have a cause to end. It was, again, irrational, and he'd always heard that love must be irrational and he'd never believed it until then.

He now looks at a couple of dudes laughing together and the way one guy leans his head on the other guy's shoulder. Back then he'd been writing notes for a game take on Moby Dick called *Ahab's Quest*; it would come with a web-page blog or forum where everyone would share the last sightings of a virtual whale. Whoever caught the whale would win a trip on a cruise ship he had no idea how he'd fund. At the time, he had so many ideas and at the time, he could sleep and at the time, he was dating Elisa (shit he had forgotten about Elisa), with whom he shared absolutely nothing apart from the fact that she never wore dresses and bras. But he'd known she was a good person. She was always talking about how family's the most important thing, and so his mum had once said, 'she's a good person, I like her,' and he'd agreed. He'd promised her a future with kids and a large house in the suburbs with gas hobs, real plates and tea mugs, and they were happy for two solid months.

But then, just like that, Eva had tapped his shoulder and laughed when he dropped his pen – and that was the end of Elisa. It was summer and Tomás remembers wanting to stop sweating and hoping she hadn't felt the moisture gathering on his back. He looked at her. She was wearing a black T-shirt and black shoes. It was an Elliot Smith T-shirt with the words 'Going Nowhere' in white on her chest, and she smiled at him. He closed his IDEAS book and she'd said…

'Can I sit here? I can't sit on the side with all the sun. I have a horrible headache.'

. . .

The couple on the bus now don't say a thing but that's OK because if everyone's always saying one thing to mean another, then silence is OK and really…

He'd called his mother this morning and she was silent too. His sister answered the phone and told him he was inconsiderate and self-centred because he hadn't instantly asked about their arrival in India. He'd told her his roof had collapsed, that he couldn't just leave it as it was, but she called it an excuse because she too had lots to do, juggling Mum and Alejandro and an important interview with some famous foreign writer he can't remember the name of, which might get her her old job back. He'd asked about his mum. Angela had told him she had locked herself in her hotel room for the first few days of the holiday.

The couple get off the bus, still in silence. A guy with three shopping bags sits next to Tomás and he sighs because he needs to get off the bus in a minute and will have to tell him to move.

After Eva had sat next to him, she pushed her sunglasses up to her forehead. He re-opened his IDEAS book because he wanted her to know that he lived his work, that he could write and concentrate anywhere, and that maybe, just then, he was writing about her in secret. And after she'd sat down with him, she asked him what he was doing and he said he was a writer because no one wants to know that you make mediocre videogames. He asked her what she did and she said her name, shook his hand, and told him she was a maritime biologist and that she was studying melting ice in the South Pacific. She gave him her card. It had a phone number. As she stood to leave the bus, she told him, 'Give me a call some time... If melting ice is your thing,' and he laughed and she left.

And now a guy comes into the bus and starts playing Victor Jara's 'The Tree of Forgetting', *so I didn't have to think about you under the tree. After waking from that dream, I thought about you again because I forgot to forget you, and then I quickly went to bed.* And the song ends and everyone on the bus claps.

He presses the button to stop the bus. He comes out in Plaza Italia, near the cathedral he's never been to, and near a *Fuente de Soda* restaurant he's heard on TV belongs to the local mafia.

Then he just sits on the same bench he always does and looks for today's written message. It says LUCKY SOD I HATE YOU, and Tomás smudges it (the messages are always written in ink so that he can smudge them), and he writes his name. He adds I HATE YOU TOO, which then reads TOMAS I HATE YOU TOO but he can't be bothered to change it.

The old people who take over the mornings in Santiago don't even look at him. Tomás finds himself getting annoyed that Angela and his mum went off to India so quickly and that they won't be able to see his new flat, his new car, his new job (OK that's pushing it), see him succeed. Their plane might as well have crashed, they might as well never see him again if they're to miss him winning at something, getting what he wants. They might as well all move to Antarctica... And then he shakes his head, closes his eyes, and agrees with the words on the bench – TOMAS I HATE YOU TOO – before making his way to class.

When he gets there, a few minutes late, he manages to hear his name spoken before the students spot him and shut up. He puts his bag on the only lonely chair (the room is a large square with tables that also make up a square along its walls, making the middle a bit like the sand pit at The Nail Brothers circus and…) and he breathes in deep and asks…

'So what do you all think about the Damsel in Distress trope in games today?' Everyone types and writes that (or some other doodle) down instead of thinking about an answer. They better fucking speak up though, because Tomás didn't prepare anything, not the reading, not the PowerPoint, *nada*, and he's counting on someone to please, please form a debate.

Debate
/dɪˈbeɪt/
Academic noun.

1. A form of discussion that never gets even remotely interesting before lunch is up.
2. A form of discussion which helps the teacher know that his/her students are wrong because the teacher has worked for years in that subject, and they have never even worked at all, and they never even do their reading but they just won't fucking stop talking back.
3. A form of discussion where a student that talks a lot also talks a lot of nonsense. But no one will stop them because they've gone on for too long to even care.
4. Academic lingo for 'I did not prepare the class but you are paying me to be here, sit here moving my neck from time to time like a fucking owl while I listen to your bullshit until the day, the holy day, that I retire or die young from a brain tumour that will most likely look a bit like the university's shield or logo'.

Synonym: 'Bullshit' /bʊlʃɪt/ vulgar academic noun.

Eva used to say that his students must love him. She said he was 'charming', that he made videogames (which she hated) sound like the most interesting things in the world, like they were always the newest and most exciting invention, and also that he wasn't handsome enough to make others lose focus when he spoke. She said that he just wasn't the type of guy to turn heads at the entrance of a bar. But she said she liked that, his 'invisibility', as she called it (attempting to make a games-related joke), though that was much, much later on in the relationship and she said it with far, far less appreciation.

'Anyone?' he adds. He finds that when he says 'anyone', the students with the biggest egos will always raise their hands because to them, being called 'anyone' is the worst insult ever and they just can't resist it. He might as well be insulting them for real, directly, swearing at them, and Tomás almost begins to mouth out F-U-C...

And the student with a T-shirt that says IT'S NOT ME, IT'S YOU raises his hand.

'Yes?' Tomás points at him with a smile.

'I think Damsels in Distress, the wording of it, is part of a liberal agenda to wipe out all of us men.'

Tomás wishes this were true, if only to wipe this fucker off the face of...

Another raises a hand.

'What are you talking about?' she asks the douche, her hands making fists on the table. 'The fact of the matter is that most games have guys saving women. Not all, but most do in some form or shape. And so you play and play and play and suddenly you feel it's OK that women are always the victims, and even worse, that they are victims whose only choice is often death or being with a man. When Bowser in *Super Mario* kidnaps Princess Peach, she will either spend her life in Bowser's fiery world, an actual hell, or live with Mario, who's only a fucking plumber! And Zelda has the option of either living her life as a prisoner to Ganon, some pig, literally a pig that travels through time, or getting saved by a dude who dresses up as Peter Pan, plays the flute, and looks like a cross-breeding experiment between a garden gnome and a Christmas elf. Like, a princess, a rich and beautiful woman, because of course they can't be fat or hairy either, I mean, who would want to save them? But they are rich and beautiful and powerful women, and they have to have their lives sorted out by a plumber and a garden gnome. It doesn't make any fucking sense! I mean just analyse the fucking words. Damsel. Why can't it be Punk? Or Writer? Or Doctor? Or just bloody Woman? Woman! Damsel is just a posh term for a mentally challenged, order-following woman-child sex object, and then… Distress. That one really gets to me. Why would distress be such a bad thing for this Damsel? Is it that she couldn't possibly deal with the complexity of human feelings, unless, they are, of course, to do with their desire for the plumber and the garden gnome? Is it that she has no possible way of overcoming stress unless there's some dude who wants to do it for her? I guess what I'm trying to say is that if we keep making games based on these old tropes, if we keep using the same language, the same codes, then there will be more Damsels, and there will be more Distress, even when both combined have never, and will never, be true.'

LEVEL SELECT:

† † † † † A----W----K----W----A----R----D † † † † †
S---------I-----------L------------E---------N------C--------E

Tomás nods and he loves her, he loves her so much, and he almost mouths that, I, I, I lo…

But the asshole's hand is up again. Why won't he just die? Why do people like him even exist? Have his parents not heard of condoms? Abortion? Cyanide?

'That is what I meant. Did you not see just how angry she was just now? What about women like Tifa in *Final Fantasy VII*? She's like a really good fighter and a total badass!'

'Have you not seen how big her tits are?' she answers back and then everyone starts to argue, on and on and loud and so Tomás leaves, he uses his 'invisibility', his real-life cheat code, because he needs to smoke, and he hopes that none of them notice because they're paying him to be there and listen to their bullshit and so on and he knows it couldn't possibly be true, but the bird that just flew by the window next to him looked a bit like an owl.

'Hey teacher, where are you going?' one of them asks (Tomás doesn't know any of their names).

'There's still an hour left of class!' another one says.

He gives them a thumbs up, gets his coat and heads out of the office building and the secretaries go all quiet for once when he passes by (they've been quieter since his father's death), and then there's the Blue Peace people and one of them gives Tomás a banner with an erupting volcano all red with lava. He starts running to get away from the crowd and suddenly someone takes his hand. He turns and it's Fran with a green plastic windmill on a stick and she gives it to him.

'Let walk, um, outs the ways,' she says and he nods.

'I'm teaching,' he says, out of breath.

'Let walk, um, yes?' she asks, and he nods.

They walk past the Providencia Avenue and into Balmaceda Park. Neither of them says a thing and she does what couples who have nothing to say to each other do, she takes his hand, and he does what an old man would do too, and presses his hard against hers.

'I so sorry. I hear what happen. It is in the news. I so sorry. I thought you no call back because you, um, you hated all of me, then but I see death parent and I feel so bad, yes?'

Tomás did see the news coverage of the crash the day after the funeral (only the first crash was newsworthy). Correction. He searched online

to see if there was any coverage of the accident. He found only two articles and they both came with the same video. Someone out there (how
is there always someone out there?), for some reason, was filming the
scenery from their car window and down went his father, wobbling to
one side of an otherwise perfect postcard view, and then to the other
side, as if it had been the plane that had had a stroke (Tomás only supposes this happened because he did not see the video) and BOOM
both articles sought the causes of the accident but neither of them had
any evidence of anything, so they both concluded that flying alone was
indeed very dangerous and they both had a 'Travel Danger Level' chart
and all, like a chart Tomás would make to explain videogame difficulty
levels to his students, and it showed spikes this month. His dad was on
the hardest level. They're on the rise, they said, and then hoped that his
dad didn't suffer. But their titles were very different: 1) Father of 2 DIES
in TRAGIC PLANE CRASH and 2) Be Careful What You Wish For:
Man DIES on his FIRST DAY in RETIREMENT. Tomás is glad his
mother is all the way out in India and hopes that she and Angela are in
some remote village, a stereotypically removed village that is far, far
from the internet.

'I want talk to you.'

'What about?'

'I want tell you, if even I angry at you, I really, forgive you.'

'Forgive me?'

'You lock me up, had terrible memories. My mum did used to do
this when I was child. I hate be closed in small spaces.'

'Right.'

They stop at Balmaceda's statue in front of a tall concrete pillar.
Balmaceda's wearing a toga and high boots, like a jedi. Eva once told
him the story of Balmaceda. It was strange, she said, how comfortable
Tomás felt with his own ignorance about the statues, the only people
that populate the city and will never move an inch, will never leave. 'How

can you go about your day ignoring them all? Does the fact that they'll always be there make it easier for you to ignore them? Or is it that you can always say, tomorrow, maybe tomorrow I'll read the plaque?' Tomás didn't answer and Eva smiled. She loved it when she asked things he couldn't answer. Don't we all? Even Balmaceda seemed to ask 'Who am I then?' and smile a little. And then she told him, which she loved even more. 'José Manuel Balmaceda was an aristocratic president at the end of the nineteenth century. Everyone disagreed with him and he started a civil war in 1891. When it ended, he shot himself. So now you know, don't start shit you don't know how to finish.'

'I'm sorry Fran, but I can't see you anymore,' he tells her.

'What is? Why can't?'

'I just can't. It's not right. You're a student after all.'

She takes the paper windmill from his hand.

'I'm sorry,' he says.

'I can't wait go to get to kitchen and cut myself.'

'Don't do that. Really, don't do that.'

'I will.'

'Look,' he says. She looks at him, tense and impatient. He can fix this. He should fix this. But… 'Alright,' is all he says.

'OK, then.'

She walks to the avenue and crosses it running despite all the cars and leaves Tomás in front of Balmaceda, the statue frowning at him all in grey and stone. Tomás can't look at him in the eyes.

He then walks to the metro and takes the line 1 home. The wagon is empty apart from this one large woman. She looks at him and smiles because he's looking at her.

When he gets to his flat, the smell of the wet rug makes him close his eyes. He needs to sleep. He needs to work. But instead, he smokes out his window and thinks that Eva would probably like to know about his dad because she liked him a lot. She had even once told Tomás she wished he were more like his father, although she never explained what that meant. But knowing what he knows now, he doubts that she would still like the idea.

He goes to the kitchen to start the kettle and suddenly there's a knock on his door. He doesn't go to open it and then a small note slips under it. Tomás runs to the door, ready to tell Lucas to stop junk-mailing his flat, and how could this day get any worse? So he opens and there are two people smiling at him and one of them points at the volcano banner by the cream-coloured couch.

'Cool poster, dude,' he says, 'can I have it?'

9

Iwantyoutoknowthatyoustillmatter

There are posters of Black Sabbath and Cannibal Corpse. There are no lights apart from a candle on a black coffee table inside a Jack Daniel's bottle. There's a skull in the middle of the dining table with the numbers 666 on its forehead, and there's a book about lizards, about Reptilians, alone on a shelf. They give him some coffee in a mug and Tomás had forgotten that steam rising from cups always makes him close his eyes.

They sit in front of him. One of them is wearing a black Goat Eater T-shirt and eyeliner and the other khakis and a tucked-in yellow polo. Tomás is sitting next to his volcano banner, and he looks at the metalhead and wonders how anyone could make so much effort, devote so much time (and time is, after all, always effort) in his make-up and clothing. And even though Eva had once told him that he shouldn't judge people he doesn't know, sometimes he looks at someone and he really can see the whole story.

'How's the coffee?'

'I like the mug.'

'Yeah.'

'So what do you do?'

'I'm not sure I got your names.'

'Lucas,' says the one with the polo shirt.

'Agreas,' says the guy with the Goat Eater T-shirt.

'Andrea?'

'Agreas.'

'His name is Jesús-María,' Lucas says with a sigh, taking a sip of coffee.

'Yes, but my friends call me Agreas.'

'No one calls you that.' Lucas shakes his head.

'What is it you do then?' Jesús asks.

'My name's Tomás.'

'Alright Tomás, what do you do?'

'I write stories for videogames at a university. I teach a games design narrative course.'

'Like *Final Fantasy VII* and *Zelda*? Those games are amazing. Man their stories are good.'

'Yeah, they are. And you guys?'

'I mostly work at Abdul's pawn shop,' Lucas says.

'He doesn't work. He just hopes to one day get into bed with Matilde, our boss's daughter,' Jesús says.

'But I like working there. It's better than the shit you do anyway.'

'What do you do?' Tomás asks, and Jesús puts his coffee mug next to the candle and takes the skull with both hands.

'I'm a Satanist.'

'Here we go,' Lucas sighs.

'What?'

'Nothing.'

'As I was saying, I'm a Satanist.'

'Is that like your job?' Tomás asks.

'Well, it's a lot of work at the moment. We do fundraisers mostly. But no, I also do part-time work at Abdul's.'

'Oh.'

'It's been hard.'

'He's not interested,' Lucas sighs.

'It's been hard,' Jesús continues. 'We thought the world would end in 2012. You remember all those movies that promised us the apocalypse? *The Rapture* and *The Horsemen of the Apocalypse*. Well, they fucked us over. It was horseshit. We had it all set up: the bonfires, the sacrificial goats and even Goat Eater were going to come and play a gig. But it didn't end. Nothing happened. And now we have to try to come up with a different story for The End Of The World because we're losing a lot of followers, like really fast and...'

'Just shut up Jesús,' Lucas sighs again.

'OK...' Tomás says, finishing his coffee. 'I hope you find your story.'

'Well,' Lucas says, 'we wanted to meet you and tell you that if you ever need anything, we're here. The hole in your ceiling looks awful.'

'I thought it looked pretty cool,' Jesús says.

'Thanks, that's nice of you.'

'Actually, the real reason is we want you to come with us to Abdul's shop. Business has been tough. So when we saw that hole in the ceiling, we thought maybe you'd find stuff you need and... How does this weekend sound? I'm pretty sure you'll find some useful replacements for your flat.'

'It's not that bad. I think I can live with it.'

'It looked pretty bad to me. Like, dangerous bad.'

'Alright.' Tomás stands and shakes their hands.

'Could I keep the volcano banner?' Jesús asks.

'Sure.'

Back inside his flat, there are still some drops falling from the hole. The trash Fran left is still on the kitchen floor but he doesn't clean it because it's not the weekend yet.

He looks through the pictures folder in his computer and notices he doesn't have pictures of his dad anywhere. Why did he have to fly? And what made the accident happen? He checks for more articles but the same two come up. They blame Antarctic winds. And to think he was meant to be there with him. Then again, was it the very worst that could have happened? Tomás knows he's being a complete asshole for wondering, but isn't it what everyone does? When you imagine yourself dying, is it not natural that you hope to die in the full glory of doing something you love? Wasn't that enough? And so maybe Jesús the Satanist has a point in being let down by The End Of The World. He also wants it to end while doing something that he loves.

And he looks at Eva's cracked photograph and he really should try calling his mother again but he lights a cigarette and turns the kettle on instead. And what if he went to meet Eva? What if he just appeared? Did he have that much to look forward to in Santiago? He can't work, he can't sleep and he doesn't even want to.

He will think more about this tomorrow. For now, he goes and sits by his window and drinks coffee from the French press and lights a cigarette.

Empty buses, empty streets, empty city. It's raining again, it's cold and it's dark and right now Tomás doesn't want a thing. Santiago, tonight, could be The End Of The World.

.   .   .

'Where the hell are we going?'

'Are you tired already?'

'I don't know. It's been too long. I can't remember what it is to feel any different. If this is what it is to be tired, then I've always been tired.'

'Stop with all the sulking already. Why can't you just enjoy the search? Doesn't it bug you a little to think of everything you'd miss out on if we did, in the end, find something?'

'But I don't even know what it is I'd miss out on, so I wouldn't miss it at all.'

'*Mais oui* you would. You might not want to, but the world is here and it is now and you have to, you must, discover it.'

144

'But why?'

She runs ahead of him without an answer.

After they left the boat on the lake, and then the ferry, they took a bus South to the wild plains of Chiloé. There, she said, there they would find a new boat, no, a ship to take them to the tips of Antarctic Chile.

They are by a harbour but there is no one there except from drunkards who spit out monosyllabic French grunts, '*pute, con, sot,*' and so on, while Tomás and Eva try hard not to step on them as they walk by. Tomás stops. What's the use of it all? There's no boat. There's probably nothing to find even if they did have a boat. Eva keeps on walking farther and farther across the monosyllabic drunkards and then, all of a sudden, makes a turn at the edge of a house, a pink and melon-coloured house which sits on a few unsteady wooden poles (they sway with the water) facing the sea. He can't see her anymore. And as he loses sight of her he remembers everything, tidied up in episodes of varying importance: HOW THEY MET, What She Loves, what she loves about him, what she thinks about politics, thewayshelikesherhairdone. And even though he likes these memories and their order, he can't stand having to remember them all. There's just too much under each section, essays with varying arguments and their own distinct conclusions and written by a mediocre writer. And he looks for her. He's scared. He steps on drunkard, *pute*, and another, *con*, and holds himself on the sidewall of the house, to breathe, no time for that, to breathe and then run to see her on the other side.

'BOO!'

He jumps, and then hugs her and kisses her on the forehead.

'I know how you like your hair done,' he says, 'and I know what you love, and I know how we met.' He tries not to cry as he says it.

'I have no clue what happened to you but look, *tu vois*? Look, here's the ship. And this one's ours.'

He holds her hand as they come on board. Still, she walks slightly ahead. He will never forget this or anything else about her again. But he still has no idea what they're trying to find or if they'll ever find it. Despite that, hewantshertoknowthatshestillmatters. And then the waves take them.

. . .

He's meeting Lucas and Jesús a block away in twenty minutes but he decides to see if Yiyo's at the guitar shop first.

He walks in to find Yiyo playing the guitar solo from Metallica's 'Battery' but he stops as soon as he sees Tomás.

'Man, you know, I've been thinking, I know you hate them and that Metallica are dumb as shit, but if I had to choose my dream band to join, it'd still be Metallica.'

Yiyo puts the Gibson LP on a stand. 'How are you dude?' Tomás asks him.

'Good, good. I sent our new demo to LittleShittyMonsters yesterday. They're always looking for good bands that they won't pay. But we need the exposure, you know?'

'Man, that sounds amazing. Good luck with that.'

'Thanks. And how are you? Really sorry about Eva, and much more about your dad. But who would have guessed? The fucking Antarctic, you know?'

'The fucking Antarctic,' Tomás repeats.

'So how is Bimbo going? You got a sequel planned or something?'

'OK, OK I guess. I mean, you know, just like with your songs, you think you're done with one of them but it—'

'—It never really ends.'

'I know, I know.'

'Yeah. But you have to finish some day, man. As your best friend I ask you, please, please just finish your shit. You used to be writing notes all the fucking time. You need to get over whatever's going on in your head. In the end, relationships are all just so temporary. Like, I know it's something your sister would say, but you should get into all this mindfulness crap, it really helps. Like all of my lyrics are about mindfulness now. And I get emails all the time from people saying that my songs have helped them through some tough times. Get into it, man. A girl's a girl. But there is no one like you right now, right here, having this conversation and feeling whatever you're feeling. Let stuff just happen to you. I'll lend you the book one day. It's called *Full of Mind*. The universe knows and all that bullocks.'

Tomás nods and turns to browse the guitars hanging on the wall. The ones they have on display are always either used guitars or cheap versions of classic Gibsons and Fenders. He touches the high E-string on a metallic blue Epi and it rattles hard on the bridge, so the note only lasts a few seconds before fading out.

'You want to try it dude? *Full of Mind* says that things always look worse than they really are before you actually try them.'

'No thanks man. I have to go meet some people in a bit. Just dropped in to say hi.'

'Girl?'

'Yes.'

'Good to know. You see? Things just sort themselves out, the universe really fucking knows.'

'Yeah whatever.'

'Drop by soon, man. I'll show you the demo when it's mixed and mastered. We sent it to New York to Open Meta-Creak, this big producer in Brooklyn. He only works with analogue machines and the natural sounds of animals. It's going to sound like heaven.'

'Awesome. Good for you man.'

'Thanks! See you around.'

'Bye.'

Tomás walks out and he can hear Yiyo's guitar feedbacking before he starts the Metallica solo again.

Why is it that Yiyo always feels the need to perform after meeting him? He always leaves to guitars exploding with feedback whenever Tomás tries to talk about Eva and he wonders if Yiyo has ever known him past the initial hum of his amplifier. But he'll think more about this when he gets home. For now, he crosses the street to Balmaceda Park and walks by the plastic windmill salesman. He's talking to a man pretending to be a statue in a suit and a top hat painted all in gold while sitting very still on nothing.

'Hi,' they both say, the man in gold not even moving his neck. The windmill salesman gives Tomás a windmill and Tomás pays him and walks away blowing on it.

He crosses the avenue again and gets to the Plaza Italia market. He can't see Lucas or Jesús at the entrance so he walks in to find them.

There are alpaca ponchos hanging from stalls, all red and black and orange. There are leather belts with carvings of horses and war, Chilean flags and Neruda's and Allende's face. There are coloured straw beach baskets and clay flowerpots and leather pouches so small they can only hold a single coin. He passes by a *charango* guitar salesman with an amazing beard (down to his chest, thick and stained red on both sides, and Tomás swears he sees a cigarette butt in the midst of all the hair) listening to a *cumbia* on the radio, and he can see Lucas playing a tambourine at the end of the corridor.

Tomás waves at him but he blanks him and a girl walking by Tomás lets out a quiet laugh and waves back. Tomás walks faster to Lucas and touches his shoulder and he stops playing the tambourine.

'You came! Hey, Jesús, he came!' he shouts towards the inside of the shop.

'Don't call me that in public!' Jesús shouts back. 'My people are everywhere!'

They're by the shop counter, a plank of wood with old Coke bottle caps encrusted around the edges, a cash register with an orange Virgin

Mary at the back, and a collection of *Gorditos*, those clay dolls of fat naked people striking yoga poses that *gringos* love to buy. Around the counter there are wooden shelves with old books, VHS tapes, records, speakers, wires, a Walkman, shirts and sweaters and hammers and tools Tomás can't even name. And under the shelves there are old car and bicycle tires.

Behind the counter, the shop extends into a mud hut whose inside Tomás can't see.

'So you work here?' Tomás asks.

'Yeah, it's a great place,' Lucas says, putting down the tambourine. 'How's it going? Fixed the roof yet?'

'No, I've been far too busy. So much work lately, you know?'

'Well, Abdul might have some stuff that you might find useful.'

Tomás laughs.

'Is his name really Abdul?' he asks Lucas.

'No one knows for certain,' Lucas says. 'But if I were you, I wouldn't ask him.'

Lucas does the cuckoo sign, drawing circles on his head with his index.

'How come?'

An old guy with long hair and a white beard comes out of the mud hut. He's wearing a *Super Mario Brothers* T-shirt, long white linen trousers and a pair of old leather sandals. He has a bunch of keys tied to his hair in a knot.

'This is Abdul,' Lucas says.

'You going to do any work today son?' he asks Lucas, who walks back into the hut.

'So, who're you?' Abdul asks with a frown.

'Tomás. I'm their neighbour.' Tomás stretches his hand for a handshake but Abdul doesn't even look at him, so Tomás pretends to scratch the back of his neck.

'No, no, I meant… Are you buying something or selling?' Abdul asks, looking around his shop as if he had so much to arrange.

149

'Neither yet, I'm just—'

'Browsing? Oh hell, that must be nice. The whole world in economic crisis and you, you're just brooowwwsing around. Kids today, I tell you...'

'No, I'm just—'

'Looking for work?'

'No, I've got a lot to do and—'

'Well, then I suggest you fuck off.'

Tomás looks at him but Abdul just turns to press buttons on the cash register and counts the notes, licking his fingertip after every single one. Abdul then starts laughing as he dusts the counter table with his own beard.

'I'm fucking with you, man, it's all cool,' he says, so Tomás laughs too. 'But really,' he adds, his smile fading again, 'are you buying or selling?'

'Buying,' Tomás answers. 'Is that OK?'

'Buying? Yes, good, good. Well, come in, come in, everything's inside. Just don't touch too many things you don't plan on buying. They might look like old scraps to you but some of us have to live on them.'

'Right, thanks.'

Tomás walks past the counter and he can hear Abdul starting to laugh to himself again.

Inside the hut there are thick black wooden rosaries hanging from the ceiling. There are more VHS tapes on shelves and bicycle wheels and seats under them. There are old suits and dresses on hangers, figurines of horses made of leather, old powdered milk pots with vintage pictures of vintage people in vintage seagull haircuts. Then, on one corner, there are machines Tomás can't recognise, like oversized cassette decks, with two circular belted motors but nothing in them, stacked up on one another. Some of them are about to touch the ceiling. There are also old skis and ski boots and poles leaning on them. Next to them are single bricks with single price tags and on top of the pile there are tea mugs and coffee cups.

Across the room, Tomás sees Lucas and Jesús. Lucas is brushing the floor with a wooden broom and Jesús is playing with one of the hanging rosaries, twisting it, letting go, and watching it spin.

Tomás walks to the coffee cups and checks the price under one with a picture of a naked woman.

'That's a nice cup.'

Tomás looks behind and there's a girl holding a typewriter. She's wearing a short summer dress with faded flowers on it. The dress is slightly too large for her.

'Thanks,' he says. 'I collect them.'

'You collect cups? Are you having a quarter-life crisis or something?' she asks, laughing.

'Never thought about it,' he says, putting the coffee cup back in its place.

'Well, hope you find more cups,' she says.

'Bye,' he says, and she turns and leaves with the typewriter and Tomás thinks that he should go out more often to these kinds of places. No, no more parties. No more clubs and booze (as if!). But no… He should go out to places where he can meet people like him. Now, he's not too sure what this means (and that doesn't matter), but what he does know is that he should join a reading or pottery club where bored and lonely people go to pretend they too can be passionate without love because there, the women he'd meet would probably hate men and he'd show them that he's different, that he's better, or at least just like them. Or he should frequent second hand shops because people there love the old and the broken and they buy typewriters in summer dresses and talk to strangers since everyone must notice, should notice them, because broken things should never break in silence and…

'Hey, Tomás, look! Maybe you could use this?'

Tomás walks up to Lucas and he shows him a large square of ridged tin. He shakes it and it sounds like cardboard.

'What for?'

'For your ceiling, man.'

'Oh, sure. I'll come and pick it up later.'

'I'll take it to your place after I'm done here.'

'OK.'

'I told you it was worth having a look.'

'Yeah.' Tomás looks over behind where Jesús is standing. There's a red door with a padlock on it. 'You mind if I use the toilet?' he asks.

'That's not a toilet.'

'What is it?'

Lucas shrugs and Jesús stops spinning rosaries.

'No one knows. We're not allowed to go in there,' he says.

'That's alright... Well, thanks for telling me about this place and the cover for the ceiling and all that.'

'No problem.'

'Before I forget...' Tomás starts.

'What is it?'

'Do you by any chance sell old kitchens?'

'What do you mean?'

'Something with gas hobs, at least four of them.'

'Oh, we had a few some time ago in the storage at the back. I'll let you know.'

'Thanks.'

'See you back at home.'

'See you.'

Tomás gets the coffee cup with the naked girl and takes it to the counter where Abdul's sitting and smoking a pipe.

'I'll take this, please,' Tomás starts, searching his pockets for money.

'Are you crazy? That's some damn ugly cup you got there,' Abdul says, raising his eyebrows.

'Well, I collect them.'

'Well, not this one you won't.'

Tomás puts the cup down on the counter with a sigh. They look at each other in silence for a few seconds until Abdul starts laughing real loud.

'Oh, don't be like that, man, I'm just fucking with you. Take it, it's a gift,' he says, and Tomás smiles and takes it back. But then Abdul's laughter disappears and he says, 'That's right, take it… you fucking pervert.'

Tomás comes out of the market and the sounds of the city come back. All the sirens, all the pedestrian crossing beeps, all the high heels against the pavement. He heads down to the bus stop. There's a homeless woman with a child on the steps of a bank and a small boy's playing a pan flute behind a baseball cap with coins in it. It starts to rain again and people use their briefcases and handbags as umbrellas. They all do it at the same time, like some coordinated dance they don't know they're a part of. Tomás decides to go to a *Fuente de Soda* because it's only six in the afternoon and that's still too early to start working.

He goes into a Fuente called Taca-Taca and sits by the window. The saltshaker is a Playmobile doll with holes on its head and Tomás laughs when he sees it. Is he really just having a quarter-life crisis? And worse even, is it visible that he is? He smiles at the saltshaker, the hollow doll, but he knows that no matter how much he laughs at it, some things just aren't funny. Is this the turning point to adulthood, to getting old, when a saltshaker makes a joke worth laughing at just because a doll is not meant to be a saltshaker? But no, surely quarter-life crises are an invention, a farce, a story for the weak who can't wait for a mid-life crisis because people keep living longer, and while blaming others for your misfortunes feels great, what is better still is to have no one to blame. If you're a victim of nothing, then you don't have to hate anyone, fight anything. It keeps you happy. Happy ☺. And so, no, Tomás isn't having a quarter-life crisis, because he thinks he could have done things very differently with Eva, and so he must blame himself and he must change. Also, he doesn't want to travel the world, or quit his job to be a barista in an indie café, or get a motorcycle license, or take some other douchy exit. He would, however, like to join Yiyo's band again because that... But he has way too much work. Maybe after the game's done he can...

A short guy with thick glasses and a hat that says 'The King of Chicken' comes up to him with a notepad. He's chewing on gum with his mouth open.

'What would you like, sir?'

'What do you have to drink? I just wanted to get away from the rain really.'

'Well, you still have to buy something, sir.'

'I know, that's what I was... Do you have coffee?'

'Yes, we do other drinks too, sir. Want to see the menu, sir?'

'Just coffee, thanks. What coffees have you got?'

'We got coffee, sir. Just coffee.'

'Alright, that then.'

'Big or small, sir?'

'Medium, please.'

'We don't have that, sir,' the guy says with a sigh. He makes a chewing gum balloon.

'Small, please.'

The balloon pops.

'OK, sir.'

'Oh, can I pay by card?'

'No, sir, that's not possible. Cash only.'

'Really?'

'I wouldn't tell you otherwise if it wasn't, sir. Not for a small coffee.'

'How about a large one then?'

'That could work, I guess.'

'Thanks.'

Tomás looks at people getting in and out of buses trying to avoid the rain. From inside, the rain and the dark look beautiful together. Even the crappy *cumbia* on the speakers above his table sounds a lot better just because it's dark on the other side of the glass.

When he got home with Eva's business card the day they met, he thought about calling her straight away. But he called Yiyo before instead because Yiyo is great with women. At least, even though he's always been single, he's good to them for a night. In high school he lost his virginity when they were still fourteen to a much older girl. Yiyo told him not to call Eva until he had something to say to her, something exciting, something he'd done in the week. Anything to avoid trivialities and formalities because 'attraction,' he said, 'is above all about the illusion that people can be anything other than trivial. You can be trivial later,' he said, 'because when you're old you'll have no choice.' Tomás still doesn't understand what he meant by this, but he'd understood the part about not calling Eva that same day and that he must lie to women at first, until he's old and unable to keep up with the lies.

And maybe that's what happened. Maybe that's what a quarter-life crisis is. It's about not being able to hide. It's about visibility. That girl at the shop, Fran, Jaime… Can everyone now see how trivial he knows his own life to be?

The waiter comes with a mug the size of a cereal bowl filled with boiling water, and he puts a tin of Nescafé on the side with a small teaspoon. Tomás sighs and puts in five spoons of coffee powder and stirs. He can't remember when he called Eva or what he said, but it was probably something about how happy he was writing stories at the time, and how all his friends, whom he would have named by their first names to increase the sense of familiarity, organised a birthday party for him and all the crazy things that happened there, like people in bathtubs together drinking champagne and… Being young in Santiago. He's sure he used the word 'crazy' for things that weren't crazy at all. But normality changed over time. And just like the ease he had in making jokes out of anything and anyone has been reduced to overthinking and shameful silences, so too has the way he had once felt alive by drinking champagne in bathtubs. Nothing, nothing is crazy, and nothing ever was. But whatever it was he said, they met shortly after in a café in Bellavista, and then climbed the San Cristóbal Hill on the cable cars. The city looked so small, tiny specks of light, and she said she was happy right then and there and he agreed. When she asked him if he had a girlfriend he remembered Yiyo's advice about lying to women and said that he didn't, and she kissed him in the cable car on their way back to the city. It was late and empty.

He drinks his coffee while looking out the window and notices that the girl with the typewriter is outside. She sees him. She smiles and comes into the *Fuente de Soda*.

'The usual?' the waiter asks her.

'No, thanks, I don't want anything. I'm just getting away from the rain,' she says, catching her breath.

'Well, stay for as long as you need to,' the waiter says with a smile.

'Thanks,' she says. She comes over and sits facing Tomás, her shoulders wet with rain and her summer dress with darkened flowers where raindrops have landed. She takes out a napkin from a wooden cone in the centre of the table and dries the typewriter.

'Cool typewriter,' he says.

'I know, right?' she answers without even looking at him.

'Yeah.'

She puts the typewriter to one side and looks through the window behind her. For a moment everything's just rain and they can only see distorted wet lights and the colours of the cars and buses and houses moving into and away from one another, like the mosaics of a kaleidoscope.

'So,' she turns, 'did you buy the mug?'

He shows it to her. 'Yup.'

'God, that's ugly.'

'Most collector items are.'

'Not this typewriter.'

'No, I guess not... So, what are you going to do with it?'

'What do you mean? It only does one thing.'

'I know, I know. I meant, what are you going to write with it?'

'We'll see, I'm not sure yet.'

'I know how that feels.'

She turns to face the window again and he finishes his coffee. Neither of them says a thing. Tomás understands that the silence is normal because strangers never have anything to say to each other. He should take the time and effort to elaborate on stories from simple observations: the rain, how once he was so wet the guards at the university wouldn't let him go inside to work, the lights of the city, how from space they look brighter than stars. Something. With Eva it had been too easy and maybe that's what he misses, the way she made effort seem so trivial, a thing for old and miserable people.

'What's your name?' he asks her.

She turns to look at him with a smile.

'Does it matter?' she asks him back, and he doesn't know if it does matter.

'What do you mean? You're asking me if names matter?'

'No, does my name matter to you?'

'I don't know.'

'Well then, it doesn't.'

Tomás gets up to pay and the girl leans towards him.

'What's that?'

'A windmill, they sell them at the park.'

'Can I have it?'

He gives her the windmill and she blows on it and it makes the sound of rain.

'Good luck with your writing,' he tells her.

'Thanks.'

Outside, he looks up at the rain. He's the only one in the street and he walks to the bus stop because when it's raining, when Santiago is dark and empty, when there are no birds or mountains or voices or anything at all that you could miss, then it's worth going home over ground. Trivial. The city makes everyone so trivial, just like rain, like buses, like age, like names.

He gets in the bus and smiles because all he can see are spots of light growing and shrinking, breathing, and he hopes that, even if his whole fucking cream-coloured flat gets flooded with its own interior waterfall, it will continue to rain through this crazy trivial night.

10

Items List

So forget about the whole *killing yourself and jumping off the balcony* thing. You have a 9–5 job and you've had it for a while now. It doesn't pay much but it covers your mortgage, your Sky TV Sports Pack subscription, the electric, gas and water bills and it even lets you save a little because you're a smart shopper, and you buy your groceries in bulk so that your freezer is full at all times. Why in hell would you want to die with a life like this? And so you tell your flatmate, the asshole who's always right, that you're taking a holiday to travel the world instead of committing suicide. And he tells you that you won't, that you're not the kind of person to just pick up your things and go. He reminds you that you've barely even left the flat this month unless it was to go to work. But now you're pissed off. You don't know if you're pissed off at the fact that your flatmate doesn't believe in a version of you that you like better, or the fact that you care so much about his approval, or that he attacked you after a week that you thought had been good, normal good (you even applied for a promotion!), but now seems like wasted time. So you really search some way in which to prove him wrong for once, and he reminds you that you didn't jump, just like he had predicted, and that this time it won't be any... I'll quit my job, you say. I'll quit it altogether. You've had the means to do it for a year or so and you will travel the world, travel light, so that whenever you feel hungry or get stung by some dangerous mosquito, your lack of preparation will only make you smile as you remember the asshole who never believed in you. And then he tells you again. He just doesn't think that you're the kind of... Fuck it, you pick up the phone but he takes it from you and hangs it up. He tells you people at work will need you at first and you'll feel free, freer than you've ever felt, whenever they call you up to reconsider. But then, the calls will stop, and you'll be at the top of Machu Picchu during low season, you won't even meet any tourists, and they'll already have a replacement for the job you now really want back, the life you'll really want back, in this flat, with him on your side. You see, he adds with a smile, the same fucking smile, everyone is replaceable, but there's no one out there exactly like you. And that kills you. But you want this guy dead. You should have jumped. He should jump instead. And you pick up the phone to call the office and you tell them you'll be a little late for the 9am presentation that you so well prepared.

Tomás thinks for a moment about quitting his job and travelling but stops the instant he crosses the threshold to the office building. He puts his hood on to walk past Anna and the secretaries. He walks fast and when he gets to his office door he notices the keyhole has been replaced by an electronic coded lock with two rows of numbers and some letters. He knocks but Jaime doesn't answer. He has no idea what the code is. He tries 000 in case but the doorknob won't move, and so he walks up to Anna's counter, hood still on, and he leans sideways on it, and he asks in a low voice, a bit like Batman does in the movies...

'What's the code for the doors?'

Anna doesn't look at him and keeps tidying piles of paper on her desk. 'It's with the marking you still haven't done,' she says with a sigh.

Tomás takes his hood off. 'It is done now, but I left it inside,' he says.

'Really?' Anna stops tidying papers and smiles back at him.

'Really,' he says trying to maintain the smile.

'Well, I never thought you'd say that. The world might actually end tonight.'

'So what's the code?'

'Four zeros.'

'Oh.'

'Bring them over as soon as possible, OK?'

'Will do.'

Tomás gets to his office, presses the four zeros and opens the door. He must finish something by the end of the week or Jaime won't have anything to start. And so he sits down and looks out the window but there are no Blue Peace people out with their banners today, and it must be because it's getting hotter and they're feeling defeated by global warming; by the way they couldn't stop anything from changing with their volcano signs and cheap megaphones.

He shakes the mouse and the computer screen turns on. Jaime left it on YouTube. He'd been listening to Phil Collins who Tomás thinks is the opposite of anything respectable because he wears gloves to drum and can't even sing (and with him it's not even about the lyrics) and he's overweight, has no hair, and his name is Phil Collins. Music for the old, the dying. And so he searches for Amusement Parks on Fire and listens to 'Vensosa' on repeat.

He could come up with a videogame story about Eva, about the Antarctic, about travelling and about unexplored ice holes in the middle of the frozen ocean. She could be waiting to be rescued (come on, Tomás, you know better than that). She could be waiting to see how much trouble he's willing to go through just to be with her (Jesus, man). And he would have to survive and fish with upgradable spears and make fires and meet animals, feminist polar bears who hate him for wanting to save someone who needs less saving than him (are there polar bears in the Antarctic?). And they'd give him stuff to do in exchange for information about climate change so they too can save each other with volcano banners and then, finally, Tomás would find the hole of ice and follow it down until he finds her at the very bottom of the ocean where it's all darkness and silence and the depths are infinite and…

It ends a mess. What's the point of the game anyway? Why would anyone want to play someone else's story? And isn't it too simple? Surely he needs to come up with a way of introducing drama to the whole thing. He needs villains and complications and obstacles, not simple objectives, because videogame stories are about playing the middle, even the beginning, but never the end. That's lesson number one.

And so he doesn't write a thing but keeps his IDEAS book open just in case, and he lies under his desk with it on his chest. He looks up to the chewing gum constellations, which have changed to groups of triangles bound by a circle at the centre, like a star. He looks at the troll doll on the shelf and it's wearing clothes again and facing out the window. Tomás sighs and shuts his eyes.

. . .

IDEAS BOOK P. 33:

Another game. A clone. A Pac-Man clone to sell for ~~cheap mobile platforms. Or maybe it will be~~ free, yes, free to download but with a crap-ton of adverts of anything from shoes to jewellery to watches and toilet paper. But before making any impulsive decisions as to the nature of the characters/story in the game, let's see what made Pac-Man such a big hit.

The game was an H-bomb in the digital world. And yet its premise is simple and elegant. You are Pac-Man, a yellow pizza circle without a slice (that's his mouth) and you travel through a maze (a 'board') eating white pellets. When you eat them all, you go to the next stage and so on. But here's the complication, the drama of it all. There are four ghosts: Blinky (red), Inky (blue), Pinky (yup, pink) and Clyde (orange) and they all behave differently. The programmers spent around eighteen months (that was long back then) on the AI alone. Blinky would chase you, Pinky and Inky would try and ambush you to take you on from the front, and Clyde, he would behave rather randomly and chase you but then change his course once he got too close to Pac-Man. This gave a whole new dimension to the game. You were now playing against characters with their own distinct personalities, with their own strategies. The game even included short animated cut scenes (revolutionary back then) between boards, where the ghosts chased Pac-Man.

If you knew how the ghosts behaved, you could outplay them, use their programmed weaknesses against them. Have you ever used someone else's weaknesses to your advantage? Have you ever found yourself saying or doing just the right thing to get what you want? If say, you hate vegetables and you smoke too much, but the girl you like is a vegan who has told you before that she sees smoking as part of the same exploitative economic industrial complex as the meat industry, would you change? Would you lie? And say you've changed, and you're eating more beans than you ever thought possible (and you eat even more because of nicotine withdrawal) but at least you get to fuck who you wanted… Then who won? And who used whom?

Anyway, this game will be different. The character will be a vegan mouse travelling through a a man or a woman travelling through a maze. Instead of eating pellets they will get shopping items, all of them real trademarks (advert issue solved) and once their shopping spree is finished, they go to the next stage (called 'malls' instead of 'boards') and shop for increasingly more expensive items: cars, European passports, houses, no, mansions and so on.

And what about the ghosts? How would you go about translating them? Well, Blinky, the ghost that chases you is now a Government Tax Agent. Inky and Pinky, who try to take you on from the front, will be a Worker's Union and Credit Card Debt. And finally Clyde, the terrified orange ghost, will now be a French hippy from the Elqui Valley.

But how will it end? There are, after all, a finite number of boards in Pac-Man. Billy Mitchell, the ultra-nerd, was the first to get a perfect score. Billy played the ghosts, not the pellets. And so in this version, the protagonist will go from mall to mall accumulating objects but there will be a limit too. What is there to own when you own the world? What would Billy say? Once you have every mansion, every car, every plane, every clothes line, every bottle of vintage wine, every dollar bill ever printed, every country, what then? In Pac-Man, the game ends because the hardware of the time, the memory available, was too limited to keep the game going any longer and so it just broke, bugged out, on the 256th board. You could be so good at it that you broke it! You beat not only the characters inside the game but the innards, the actual wiring of the arcade machine. A Kill Screen.

In this alternate version, once the player owns everything and there are no longer any participating sponsors to supply us with new objects to own, the game will not break (there are no hardware limitations for a game this size) but will instead automatically push you back to the first mall, back when your character was poor and terrified of the Tax Agent and the Worker's Union and Credit Card Debt and the French Hippie, back when you felt truly motivated to win at all costs, to beat them all and, well, to see the Kill Screen (massive bragging rights, just ask Billy). Only now you'll have to turn it off yourself to stop: Suicide Screen, *l'écran du suicide*, and you won't be able to tell anyone about it.

Presumably most players will turn it off when they're bored of collecting crap, but there will be a handful of people, there always is, the hard-core gamers, who will no matter how, want to risk losing all their progress to look for glitches in the code to keep the game going into infinity. Because of them, we won't be adding a PAUSE button, or we'll blast them with an annoying and short musical loop provided by a sponsor, or fuck it, invert the controls after every single stage. With all those difficulties in mind, would people still play? Would reaching the end now be a badge of shame, of wasted time? We'll have to see what happens on the forums post-launch.

Moi, je viens de finir, one of them will say, posting a GIF animation of the game restarting itself. *Imbécile*, another one will answer, *le jeu ne finit pas de recommencer*, and there will be no more related posts on that subject.

.   .   .

Can't he just leave? And hell, if he's not leaving anything he cares about, then can it really still be called 'leaving'? Surely him moving out of here and joining Eva would all be about arrivals, about coming back, an old first kiss and familiar laughter, the morning coffee out of cups he now has out of cafetières. Would it be possible? Can he really return anywhere but to Santiago?

And so he sits under the desk against the wall, opens his IDEAS book on a new page and writes...

Trip to the Antarctic 2013: Looking for Eva
Items list for a trip I won't regret.

- A coat.
- Metallic water bottle.
- French press and straws.
- Cigarettes.
- One hob (gas).
- Rope.
- Knife and snow axe (like in that movie *Vertical Limit*).
- GPS.
- Flare gun.
- Oil lamp.

- Snow glasses (or snorkelling mask, they're the same thing).
- Spiked boots (would football boots work in the snow? Google).
- Compass.
- Condoms (Eva might not be taking the pill).
- Find out if condoms freeze in backpacks and if they do, would they still work when defrosted in a pan on the gas hob? (Google).
- A pan.
- Single tent and single sleeping bag (I have to be careful not to appear to assume Eva will sleep with me. This is best left implied by the condoms).
- The frozen feathered chicken?

He gets up, moves the mouse and goes on Google. He types in 'Do condoms freeze and how to defrost them with a pan' but Jaime comes in before he can press the Enter key.

'Hey man,' Tomás says, turning off the computer monitor.

Jaime laughs. 'It's OK, I watch porn in here sometimes too but if I were you, I'd use my own laptop. They check your browsing history all the time here, and what with Fran sending the Head of School that letter about you, you have to be extra careful.'

'It wasn't porn. Just work. I don't want you to see it until it's done. Fran? What letter?'

'You're really working? Finally, man. No wonder Anna looks so happy today. Haven't seen her that happy for a while. Hey, remember I need something to work on by next week.'

'Sure. But what letter? What are you talking about?'

'I thought you knew.'

'No.'

'Well, you should probably talk to the Head.'

'You can't just tell me?'

'I have a class, man,' he says, picking up a folder by the keyboard, 'and then I'm off to meet my new girlfriend.'

'You have a girlfriend now?'

'Yeah, didn't I tell you?'

'No.'

'Oh. Well, OK, I will some other time. She's a writer too. Met her at a workshop I go to. It's a good place to hook up. You should... But it's not her writing that worries me. It's you, you have to keep writing, man.'

'OK.'

'Next week, man, deal?' Jaime points at Tomás.

'Deal.'

Jaime walks out and Tomás lies under the desk again. Why would she send the Head of School a letter? Is she totally fucking crazy? She knows that he locked her in the kitchen because he had to take that phone call. And not that he knew it at the time, but it was the last time he talked to his father too, and surely he can no longer apologise for that and everyone would understand. Had they not had a good time together as well? Had he not given her a plastic coloured windmill and coffee from the French press, his French press, and had he not even waited five minutes for it to brew before he'd done so? He still hasn't built the bed frame but he gets home so late and he has so much work to do and his ceiling fell and he understands that it probably wasn't the best first date but none of it is really his fault. She cuts herself for herself and now she's accusing him because really, there's no such thing as a cut, a mark, that is not meant for others to see.

But he will deal with this later. He looks at the troll doll smiling out the window and then at the chewing gum constellations one last time, and then he stands to turn the computer off. He looks out the window too and there's still no one outside asking for the world to cool down, for things to change for the better. And despite whatever that may involve, Tomás just misses the noise and the banners.

'Don't ever change. Though I like the circles better,' he whispers at the troll doll.

Then, he puts his IDEAS book in his bag and his hood on. He has to go home. He has to go and plan his way back to Eva and he has to finish writing up a story that others can play and he has to avoid the Head of School and Anna because what they want is his time (always an effort) and he needs it if he's to prepare for the Antarctic. He puts his bag on his shoulders and laughs, not because he just had a short conversation with a troll doll (and he hopes there are no cameras in his office), but because he knows this is all fucking crazy, but he'll do it, he'll do it, he'll do it, even if frozen places, in all their tranquillity, still demand so much movement, so much time, to be reached.

He'll start buying the stuff on his list when he gets home and he'll go to Abdul's shop to check for anything useful tomorrow. Now, he gets out of the office and runs along the corridor. Anna sees him and starts running after him.

'Hey, the grades, where are they?'

'Sorry, big plans tonight and I'm late,' he says, and runs down the steps and he doesn't feel like smoking, not between people and cars and buildings because he's too happy to smoke, and for once they will all have to miss him, and is there a better way of showing love? No, not missing, but being missed, being missed and knowing it, and tonight Tomás knows it. For the first time in a while he's looking forward to moving out and not having to be young in Santiago. And he might even buy a coffee cup and consider buying gas hobs although he knows that, like a good game plot, change should never appear forced. Rather, it should be a simple consequence of the gameplay and so the cups can wait, the hobs can wait, and the cars and people can all stay... Until, well, until he disappears. But for now, all he cares about is the list, the plan, the story, and running, just running and being missed by everyone and everything in Santiago.

11

Single Drops

He's smoking out the window in the dark.

Last night he was too excited to sleep and ordered a tent and a sleeping bag and some DVDs about the Antarctic, and he binned all his cigarettes (after splitting them in two at the filters) as well as all the lighters he could find around the house. But then Amazon sent him an email about the purchases not going through and Tomás remembered his dad's cheque still hasn't come through, and he was glad he hadn't gone to the mall instead and had his card rejected in public. Having said that, he still felt embarrassed by the email and so he went to the kitchen, opened the bin lid and dug out four cigarettes he found between the trash Fran had emptied on the floor.

Smoking without filters is so unpleasant to him and he knew he'd feel so rough later, so he thought he might as well smoke a couple instead of just the one.

So why is he smoking in the dark? Well, when Tomás got home after all the running, he was laughing real loud and he felt so young he punched the air boxing-style when he opened his apartment door, and then he flicked the lights on and there was a tiny explosion and then all of the lights in the apartment started to flicker. So he turned them off.

He used his phone to get to his room and noticed the ceiling was leaking. The leak must have screwed with the circuits or something but it was so late, or at least too late to fix, and so Tomás used his phone light to look for the cigarettes in the bin. He couldn't make new coffee, so he drank what was left in the French press. In the dark. By himself.

Now somehow it's 7am and Tomás doesn't shower, doesn't shave, and he gets dressed to go to work. But before work, he'll go see Yiyo and tell him about the trip he's planning. He wants him to know that despite him not being in a band, he still has dreams that take time, that take work and commitment and he wants Yiyo to wish him luck, just so he can then answer that it's not about luck but about time, work and... But does it matter? Does it make a difference to him if someone's watching? He doesn't know or care about the answer to this, but what he does know is that the more people he tells, the more he'll feel he has to do it, like when people tell their colleagues at work that they'll bungee jump or parachute out of a plane or do something extreme like that. As he once said in class, once the ending of a story is a possibility, then the beginning and middle become certainties. And so, as he buckles his belt, he also decides that he'll go to Abdul's shop and e-mail his dad's solicitor about that inheritance money on the way so he can start buying the things on his list.

He has a last cigarette by the window and it starts to rain. Since his flat is dark, the reds and yellows of the morning traffic and skyscrapers slide on the walls of his bedroom as if it were a metro wagon in its tunnel at full speed. And nothing is cream-coloured, nothing is still and nothing is boring and he, despite his collapsed ceiling, his wet carpet, his unbuilt bed frame, his lack of coffee cups and his two electric hobs, well, despite all that he's still part of Santiago and all its moving lights and shadows.

This makes him want to take the metro, but when he gets there he sighs because it's full of students dressed up as zombies carrying anti-government and free education banners. This one fat zombie sharing a metal pole with him isn't wearing a shirt and he painted his belly white and patched with black scars. He doesn't need the paint to scare anyone with that belly, but then a female zombie (much skinnier than him) is holding hands with him. Tomás lets out a quiet laugh, because he knows that militant people fall in love with other militant people just so they never have to think about how different they actually are. They stare at the sign with all the station names that they already know, and in the lapse of one hug they miss the sparks outside the metro windows, the silent hum of the doors sliding open, and the echoes of the steps of a leaving crowd.

But what really bothers him about the fat zombie is that he reminds Tomás about an argument he'd once had with Eva when the student protests began last year. He was getting ready to go to work and she asked him to go to a march with her and he had said that it was raining. She told him that for someone working at a university, she found it surprising how much of a shit he didn't give about education and he answered that either way, free or paid, his job would be the same. There was no French breakfast that day and she left to protest before work, without him. Now don't get him wrong – Tomás agrees with free education and all that stuff, but it had been raining that whole week, there had been endless crowds of douchebags shouting about a different world, and the only thing achieved was a full metro, a fight with Eva, and a day without breakfast. Still, he got hold of a banner on his way to work and left it by the door for her to see. When Eva came back she had sex with him and cooked *patates sautées* and some strange thing with duck liver he can't remember the French name of, and maybe the protests aren't so bad after all...

The metro gets to Baquedano and Tomás comes out and all the zombies come out behind him, and he walks quickly to the escalators to avoid any queues, and he can hear the echoes of their free education chants along the tunnels, their laughter and their insults against Piñera and the Right, and cheers for Marcel Claude and Allende and the Left. He turns right and left and walks up the stairs, and the echoes behind him disappear and are replaced by the same chants everywhere in the street in front of him, which is filled with other young zombies.

He walks between painted faces, riot police, banners and chanting on megaphones and he starts his way to Yiyo's shop. A zombie stops him and gives him a sign that says 'This is The End, My Only Friend' with a photograph of Piñera but with Jim Morrison's hair, and he takes it and the zombie cheers and takes a photograph of Tomás with his phone.

As he reaches Yiyo's street, the crowd stops and listens to a zombie leader on a podium, and she's wearing a green military jacket despite all the zombie cosplay, and she lifts her fist up and people cheer and play drums and then she says…

'We will march peacefully today! And to show them how organised we can be, how afraid of us they should be, we, we will dance!'

Everyone cheers and Tomás squeezes past more zombies and the rain gets heavier but zombies are immune to heavy rainfall, and he must get to Yiyo's shop before all the face paints start to melt because then the riot police won't be able to know who's a zombie and who isn't, and they'll beat everyone up like they always do. He can see the shop and then Michael Jackson's 'Thriller' starts playing real loud on the podium speakers, and the zombies make a line formation and start doing the dance from the video, and this fat zombie yells something at Tomás and pulls him into formation, and he stomps to their rhythm but he doesn't know how to do the dance at all and so he runs out of the crowd as soon as the bit with the sideways hip-shaking jiggle starts, and he pinballs between people and arrives at the shop, closing the door behind him.

Yiyo's bagging some drumsticks for a zombie. There are other kids trying out guitars and playing blues solos.

'Jesus, man, I can't stand this anymore,' Tomás says, rubbing the rain from his face.

'Hey dude, how're you?' Yiyo asks and comes to hug him. 'Dude,' Yiyo tells Tomás, holding his shoulders, 'if it's about fucking Fran, I didn't know you guys had dated. She told me after we did it.'

'You what?' Tomás asks, and then just shakes his head. 'No, man, I don't care.'

'OK, good. Well, how're you then?'

'I'm OK, just tired of all this shit outside.'

'Oh, come on man, don't be like that.'

'So now you're a protester too? You're a fucking cliché, man.'

'Nah, couldn't give less of a shit about it... But every time there's a protest I sell two or three guitars and a lot of gear, mainly bongos. Though who knows if I'll ever sell that fucking blue drum kit. It was the worst decision of my life, buying that piece of shit. I wish they made a much bigger protest. Maybe I should paint a peace sign on the bass drum skin.'

'You'll sell it man.'

'Yeah, whatevs dude. I can't complain today.'

A skinny zombie wearing a black Nirvana hoody takes some guitar picks and gives Yiyo the cash.

'Free education, fuck Piñera,' Yiyo sings, giving the zombie his change back.

'Yeah whatever, old man,' the kid tells him, leaving his change behind.

'You see?' Yiyo tells Tomás.

'Yeah, well, I hope it's the blue drum kit one day.'

'So, what's up? Come to get a guitar to start playing again dude? You know, you can always join me to texture my new songs. You probably can't be a member. I mean, we can't just kick out people who stuck around when things were bad. But you can definitely help at the studio.'

'No, I actually came to tell you that I'm leaving soon.'

'Where are you going to go, *huevón*? Did you sell your new game? Going to the US or something to promote it? We want to go to the US with the band too. Converse was interested in doing a deal with us, but

Chino, our new bassist after you left, you know him? Nah, you don't know him. Well, the guy has like, dactyl-something, or something-dactyl, who knows? Anyway, he like, can't wear normal shoes and won't wear fucking Converse, but man, me and the others, we're like going to chop his foot off if it means we get to the US with a sponsor. It's pretty cool isn't it?'

'Yeah, it sounds amazing… But no, I'm not going to the US. Although that might happen later. The game isn't finished yet.'

'Where then?'

'I'm going to go get back with Eva.'

'What? You got in touch with her? Did she tell you to go visit?'

'Well,' Tomás says, playing the strings of a guitar on a stand.

'Wait, does she, does she even know about it?'

'That I want her back? Of course she—'

'No *huevón*, does she know you're coming? Have you told her? And isn't she like really fucking far in the middle of nowhere?'

'I thought, you know, it'd be better to surprise her.'

'Dude, no, don't do—' Another kid comes to pay for a jack lead. 'Free education and fuck Piñera,' Yiyo sings quickly and the kid smiles. 'Dude,' he whispers to Tomás, 'don't do it. That's so fucking lame. I can't tell you how lame that is.'

'Come on, I think she'd really appreciate me just going, being impulsive and taking initiatives and all that crap. Didn't you once tell me to worry about stuff like that?'

'But you were together then. And dude, you don't even own coffee cups or a bed and you have the shittiest kitchen. Two electric hobs only. Jeez, what were you thinking?'

'What? How do you know that?'

'Fran told me.'

'Jesus.'

'It's a really bad idea, man.'

'I thought you'd be happy.'

'Let it go, dude.' The zombie playing blues calls Yiyo. 'I've got to work man. Hey, my band's playing a show tomorrow at Bar Loreto in Bellavista. Come and we'll talk about it some more. But don't like, do anything stupid.'

'Not sure I can make it to the show. I've got so much of my own work to do, man. Sorry.'

'Alright, whatevs, whatevs.'

'Alright.'

Tomás turns and leaves the store to the sound of guitars feedbacking and a bongo solo and why couldn't Yiyo just encourage him? Was it so difficult for him to appreciate the most important parts of Tomás's life when Tomás had always supported his music projects, his mediocre music projects, just because they were important to him? Friends or not friends, everyone just does and says whatever suits them better and this is why Tomás should go, must go, because it is what he wants, who he wants, and Eva will appreciate the impulse despite the absence of cups and kitchenware because doesn't the desire for one thing justify the lack of all other things?

. . .

IDEAS BOOK P. 40:

Pajitnov invented *Tetris* in 1984 at the Soviet Academy of Sciences, and it's still played today. It's so good that there are rumours online saying that Soviet officials had to lock up every single floppy disk they could find containing the game because it kept other officials from doing any work. Imagine something so addictive today, like meth, coke, *FarmVille*, but totally legal (*FarmVille* should be illegal), totally simple to play, suddenly getting locked up by police around the world. And he didn't even do it for the money (unlike the makers of meth and coke and *FarmVille*). Nope. Pajitnov didn't touch a cent until a decade later, when he claimed that all he really wanted was for people to have a good time. The man is pretty much virtual Jesus, and his lessons, much like those of real Jesus, have now been completely fucked over.

Anyway, the guy believed in fitting parts. He was OBSESSED with them. He even made a game called *Hatris*, where you fit hats into people's heads. But what is truly remarkable about it all is the fact that despite putting all his effort, all of his trust and artistry into every moving block, the game cannot be beaten! That's right, his vision was not only to manipulate virtual space but also to transcend actual time. The max. score is 999.999 but even then it does not end. Most people top out at far less and try again. The sense of victory you get when you line up the shapes ~~is a bit like when you line up the coke~~ is the satisfaction that you've won at everything in life, you beat the machine that fed you random shapes and limited possibilities. And, when you lose you know it's your own fault, your own doing, because you were not able to build anything resembling a simple straight line despite the machine feeding you random shapes and limited possibilities. The game is so fucking addictive and frustrating at the same time that a 1987 PC version included a 'boss button', which immediately left the game and changed your computer screen to display a generic spreadsheet so you could pretend to work.

So how can we build a *Tetris* clone? The main design choice here is SHAPES→SPEED/TIME→LIMITED SPACE. It will be for mobile platforms, and using the touchscreen ~~will move the shapes~~ you will form different shapes, as if you were using modelling clay or plasticine. Instead of landing perfect lines to keep the game going, there will be parts already missing from a line of ascending bricks and you will have to form said missing parts yourself for the bricks to descend. The choice will be about which shapes you'll spend your time forming first or, in other words, which shapes you will have to form just after and so on.

But just like *Tetris*, the max. score will be 999.999 and no one will be able to beat it, not even a computer playing itself. In fact, once, an advanced AI was left to play *Tetris* by itself. Because even it couldn't beat it, it decided to PAUSE indefinitely and never play again. It couldn't stand the thought of losing, and it was too clever to know it couldn't win. So it decided not to play at all. We will not be including a PAUSE function, though it's impossible not to wonder, what would that same AI do now?

. . .

He closes his IDEAS book and crosses the avenue to the park by the Mapocho River to walk to Plaza Italia. The river's full with rain but even with all the new water joining its flow, it still looks dark brown and smells like shit. But Tomás walks by the river anyway because the bad smell makes the zombie protesters gather up on the other side of the avenue.

He considers throwing the banner into the Mapocho but he doesn't because there's a beggar watching him from under a bench. He always feels judged by hobos because they can always take the moral high ground since they have it so bad owning fuck all. Someone should find them all social housing so that Tomás can walk free of judgement. But then he feels like a total cunt for thinking this way. And beggars can't even throw anything into rivers because that's the opposite of begging and he doesn't want to insult him with his own waste. He gives him some money and the beggar just gives him a dry grunt.

So he crosses the avenue again to get to the bank to ask about the inheritance cheque before heading to the market. It's closed because of the protests. For now, he'll have to just browse at Abdul's shop and he hopes he will agree to put things to one side for him so he can come for them later.

He gets to the market and heads straight through the open corridors and into Abdul's shop. There's no one at the counter but he can hear people talking inside so he walks in. Abdul's sticking price tags onto old tape recorders on a shelf at the other end of the hut and Jesús is sitting by the ski poles with a shoebox on his lap.

'Hey,' Tomás says, and they both look at him.

'Piss! You made me stick the price all wrong and now it's going to leave a glue mark when it comes off,' Abdul says.

'Sorry,' Tomás says, and Abdul sighs.

'Hey, man, how're you?' Jesús asks.

'OK, I guess. A bit annoyed with the protesting and all that.'

'I hear you bro. But the zombie costumes are pretty damn awesome. You got to give them that,' Jesús says with a smile.

'Zombie costumes. Awesome? You're all children,' Abdul says, sticking more prices. 'Children, fucking children, children,' he repeats after every tag.

Jesús shrugs and begins tidying things in the shoebox again.

Tomás starts to look at the shelves and he takes out his list. Under a shelf with old Thunder Cats action figures there are two kitchens with the oven doors open and all the hobs full of dirt.

'Interested in this kitchen? It's German. It cooks all your meals in half the time,' Abdul says with one hand on Tomás's shoulder.

'I don't think that's true.'

'You calling me a liar?' Abdul says, tightening his grip on his shoulder.

'No, but I'm not—'

'It's OK,' Abdul laughs, 'you're too easy to fuck with, you know that?'

Tomás laughs but he finds it hard to smile.

'So, you want the kitchen?'

'I'm looking for something smaller, portable even.'

'I have some electric ones that are good. They're really good actually. Not German though.'

'I need a gas one. It's for a trip.'

'Well, we only have electric.'

'OK.'

'Where are you going? If you go to Argentina I have things I want you to deliver for me.'

'Huh?'

'I'll pay you, I'll even give you a good price on our best kitchen. Come on, it's German.'

'I'm going to Antarctica.'

'Are you stupid?'

'No,' Tomás says, frowning at Abdul and stepping away from him.

'I'm just fucking with you,' he says. 'Antarctica sounds nice.'

'OK.'

'But why the hell would you go there?'

'Work, actually.'

'I see.'

'I have a list of things I need to buy.'

'Can I have a look?'

'No, sorry, it's a personal copy, I only have one.'

'Alright. Jesús,' Abdul says, waving at him, 'help him find what he needs. I don't have time for this. 'Going to Antarctica,' he says! Fucking children,' Abdul laughs, shaking his head.

Jesús walks up to Tomás. He's wearing a Cannibal Corpse T-shirt where a guy in black and white makeup is holding a shovel and is burying a priest alive who's crying inside a see-through coffin.

'How's the flat? Fixed your roof yet?'

'Getting there.'

'So, what are you looking for?'

'Anything that could be of any use in the Antarctic. Rope, snow axes, snow goggles, a compass, anything.'

'We do have an axe somewhere, actually. I'll get it for you.'

'That'd be great, thanks.'

'But it's just a regular axe.'

'I'll check it out anyway.'

'It's so cool that you're going there. I would love to go. I imagine there are no people there, as if the world were already ending. Maybe you can write about it. We really need a new theory as to how and when it's going to happen.'

'If I do I'll let you know.'

'Thanks. I'll go get the axe. I'll be two minutes.'

'Thanks.'

Tomás walks along the shelves and looks at the toys, the tools, the tiles, the kitchens and the pans and the postcards and photographs in old tins with tags for food that no longer exists. All these things once belonged to someone until they became a waste of space or something that people grew out of. But doesn't the fact that Abdul sells them mean that no matter how useless and how uselessly old a thing can be, they can always be rescued, always be put to some use in some room other than those they were intended for, without ever needing to be new again? Yes, this is what Tomás wants, to see Eva again in a new setting, to make new plans and new mistakes, without ever losing what made them so good to each other when they were still together. He knows their relationship never ended. When Eva said she knew she could do better he hadn't understood. She hadn't meant she could find someone better. She had tried to tell him that he, he could be better and that she knew it too. Things don't just end. They're put on hold, like the toys on the shelf, waiting to be wanted again and Tomás is sure he's never wanted anything so much in his whole life.

He pulls a pair of gardening gloves from a hook on the wall and tries them on. They feel warm enough and he keeps them on to buy them later. Lucas and the typewriter girl come into the hut laughing together. They both have black and white zombie face-paints but all smeared with the rain. She's wearing a tight black dress that stops just above the knees and black tights and a pair of black Vans and she reminds him about being young, when the women he knew would wear dresses and sneakers and he would wear jeans and sneakers too, before it all went to hell and everyone started to look like their parents, who no longer care about how they dress (even when they think that they do) because really, there's no fixing age and the bodies time creates.

She's carrying a flowerpot without any flowers and Lucas, wearing the same polo and khakis as always, is carrying one too. Tomás waves at him but Lucas doesn't see him and leaves through a door next to the ski poles.

'Hey again,' she says to him, coming closer.

'Hi,' he says, 'the protest?'

'Yeah, until the police started hitting people,' she says with a smile.

'Fuckers, fuck Piñera,' Tomás says.

'Yeah… Hey, nice gloves.'

'Thanks, nice flowerpot,' he answers, instantly wishing he hadn't said a thing.

'Hey, could you help me put this on top here?'

'Of course.'

She gives him the empty flowerpot and gets a chair to stand on. Tomás looks at her long thin legs and he wonders why there aren't more people with long thin legs like hers, and maybe she's a dancer and if she is, he'd like to see her dance.

'OK, give it to me,' she says, and Tomás hands her the pot and she puts it next to old tin boxes on top of the shelf.

'You come here often?' he asks her as she steps down from the chair.

'Yeah, most days.'

'You preparing for a trip too?'

'I guess you could say that.'

'I'm going to Antarctica.'

'Ah, so you're the one Lucas and Jesús talk about. The roof guy.'

'Oh…'

'I'm Matilde.' She shakes his hand and he wishes he wasn't wearing the gloves. 'Call me Maty. I hate my name.'

'Tomás.' He now hates his name too, but there's nothing he can do about it.

'Lucas told me you write stories.'

'Yeah.'

'Are you published?'

'One of them, sort of.'

'I write too, but I always hate what I write,' she says, looking up at the flowerpot.

'That's common.'

She nods and then there's silence. Abdul turns the radio on and it's Caravana playing that song he doesn't know the end of, and he wishes he could either meet women who talked nonstop or hated all conversation just so he didn't have to hate silences so much and didn't have to listen to the ending of a song he doesn't want to know because...

'So why do you come here so often?' he asks.

'I work here. He's my dad,' she says, looking at Abdul who's humming the tune.

'Oh, I'm sorry, I didn't—'

'You're sorry? Believe me, you're not the only one,' she says.

'No, I didn't mean—'

'Here's your axe, man,' Jesús says behind him. Matilde laughs so Lucas laughs too.

'I thought you wrote stories,' she says, smiling.

'I really get into character,' he answers with a smile, wishing again that he were dead, that he could shove the axe into his mouth and just end it all.

'It's for his trip,' Lucas says.

'Well, good luck,' she says, turning and walking to Abdul.

Jesús and Lucas are both smiling at him and Tomás hears the end of the song. He's disappointed to find that it ends on a fade-out of the chorus just looping over and over because it means the band love their song so much they couldn't or didn't want to decide on an ending. And as Yiyo says, that's just douchy as hell.

'She's amazing, isn't she?' Lucas says.

'You're obsessed,' Jesús starts. 'There are way more important things to think about,' he says, giving Tomás the axe.

'Like The End Of The World?' Lucas asks.

'For example,' Jesús answers.

'Jesús, come here and take this crap out of my desk!' Abdul shouts.

'Again?' Lucas sighs at Jesús. Tomás looks at them. 'The pamphlets for the gig tonight,' he tells Tomás, 'they actually think Satan will turn up.'

'Hey, I'm just trying to raise money,' Jesús says.

'Idiots,' Lucas says, shaking his head. Jesús just shrugs and goes to Abdul's desk.

'Hey, you're good with girls, right?' Lucas asks Tomás.

'No.'

'But you were talking to Maty. And you've had girlfriends before, right?'

'Why do you ask?'

'Well, it's just that Jesús is the worst wingman on Earth. I tell you, him and his Satanist group always talk about lust and bondage, but I'm not sure how because they're always single and anyway, it gets all a bit sour.'

'I don't think—'

'Wait. I just wanted to ask you if you could come to the gig tonight and put in a good word for me with Maty.'

'I don't know, why don't you just talk to her yourself? I hardly know any of you.'

'Are you crazy? I have nothing to say.'

'Me neither.'

'Bullshit. You're a writer.'

'For videogames.'

'Same thing.'

'Not really.'

'It is, come on. And tell you what, you help me and I'll gather up anything in the shop that could be useful for your trip.'

'Not sure this is a good idea, man.'

'Come on, show some commitment.'

Tomás looks at the axe and his gloves and then at Lucas's zombie face and he doesn't know what to say. Lucas is right, he should accept, but isn't this meant to be his own trip, all done in his own time and with his own effort and his own money? Why must he involve himself in the stories of others? Are people really that scared of being alone, that they ask others to join them just so that if they fail and lose it all they can still claim to have gained something, someone?

Still, Tomás did not bring any money with him and he should really be taking back home anything useful he can find here.

'Where's the gig?' Tomás asks.

'Amazing.'

'Where is it?'

'It's in Bar Loreto, have you heard of it? It's in Bellavista.'

'Wait, Yiyo, I mean, are Fármacos playing?'

'Yeah, they're amazing, huh?'

'Yeah, they are… Alright, could I take this then and pay for it later?'

'Yeah, just try not to let Abdul see you.'

'Cool, thanks.'

Jesús and Matilde walk up to them with a box full of old Minolta cameras.

'He's coming to the gig, dude,' Lucas tells Jesús.

'Great. It'll be good. Just remember the money, it's for a bad cause,' he laughs.

'OK,' Tomás answers.

'See you there,' Matilde says taking two cameras to the shelves.

Tomás nods and puts the axe and the gloves in his bag. Part of the blade is still showing so he puts his scarf on top of it.

'Don't worry, I'll distract him. See you tonight,' Lucas says.

'See you.'

'Hey Abdul, you coming to the gig too?' Lucas asks him.

'With those clowns you call your friends? No. Children, all of you are nothing but fucking children.'

Tomás walks out and it's still raining and he opens his mouth to the sky and catches a few drops. They feel cold and lucky because with all the fog, the skyscrapers disappear and the sky is infinite, enveloping the road and its people, all in grey and all of it, all of it coming down in drops. Tomás lights up an unfiltered cigarette and wraps his scarf round his neck just to see the end of the axe as he walks towards the metro. There are less zombies now and it's quiet and if the world ended tonight, the rain would fall in single drops and he'd be there to taste it next to Eva, just as he is right now, like always.

12

↑ ↑ ↓ ↓ ← → ← → *B* + *A* + *START*

In the Antarctic ship, Eva and Tomás are doing the Titanic joke. Eva spreads her arms and shakes her hair off her forehead. It is stupid, Tomás thinks, that he is taking so much pleasure in something so stupid. Does that make him… And then Eva turns to hug him and kiss him and then tells him that it's his turn. And so, whatever, he does it because she asked him to, and he opens his arms wide and he's surprised to see that from where he stands, his arms cover the whole expanse, the total width of the ocean.

'Shout something,' Eva says.

'Like what?' he asks, turning over to look at her.

'Anything, something nice… No, something honest. Whatever you're feeling right now.'

He has no idea how he feels right now. If you stand in front of an ocean, and there's nothing to see but water and foam and the occasional porpoise and whale, then all you can say is OCEAN.

He takes a deep breath, opens his arms again and closes his eyes…

'Come on,' she says, 'just shout it out already.'

'GAS HOBS!' he shouts.

'More!' she presses him on the ribs.

'BILLS! GAS BILLS!'

'Yes!'

'CHEWING GUM CONSTELLATIONS!'

'Wow!'

'I HATE FUCKING HIPPIES!'

'Me too! We have so much in…'

'I MISS YOU! WHY DID YOU…'

But now he turns between breaths and Eva isn't holding him anymore. She almost let him fall into the water, he could have drowned and disappeared and she would have never known where to look for him (would she have looked for him?), though she does understand aquatic life beyond simple waves so there is that, maybe she…

He notices that Eva is talking French to one of the crewmembers. He's wearing a beret and a striped black and white fitted shirt. His jeans are rolled up to ankle length and he's not wearing any socks under his brown leather moccasins. He talks in a low deep voice with a cigarette hanging off the side of his mouth and fuck, Tomás is truly fucked this time, because it's Serge Gainsbourg.

'*Oui, oui, eh bah… J'sais pas, quoi. Tu sais, avec tout ce vent, on ne sait jamais.*'

'*Ah, oui! C'est trop vrai,*' Eva says with a big smile.

'What's up?' Tomás asks. Eva turns to him and loses the smile.

'Serge here was just telling me that he's not sure where the wind will lead us.'

He looks at Serge calmly smoking his cigarette that never even drops any ash.

'But isn't that, like, his job? Isn't it dangerous?' Tomás asks, and Eva and Serge do a little giggle. 'What?' he asks with a frown.

'That's half the trip,' she says, 'half of it is in the discovery, in not knowing where you're really going.'

'*Oui,*' Serge says, '*ça.*'

'And what's the other half?' Tomás asks.

A whale appears right below them, spraying the side of the ship and making a tiny rainbow, which lasts only until the whale decides to dive back down into the water.

'So what's the other half then? Tomás asks again.

'It's what you do when you get there,' she says.

'*Oui*,' Serge the total cunt adds, '*ça*.'

Tomás takes Eva's hand and leads her into a bedroom downstairs that looks exactly like their bedroom did back in their flat in Santiago. Her mother's mediocre attempts at still life painting line the walls. There are French books about French cooking on the shelves that she made him pick up from a hip little bookshop in Barrio Italia. There's an umbrella pot, an art nouveau vase with a transparent umbrella inside that's big enough for two. And then there are pictures of their one intense holiday to the South of France where they're picking grapes at a local vineyard and putting on life-vests on each other before daring to go down a river whilst on an old lorry tire, which did not go so well because they got stuck on a... Now there's a photo of them stuck on that pebble island, where they looked around and then at each other and she took off her life-vest and then his, and then her top and then his, and they had sex to the foam of the rapids and now...

They're having sex on a bed that she built as soon as she got on the ship and Serge is watching them, still smoking the same cigarette, and he smiles at her whenever she tenses up out of pain or pleasure or both and she invites Serge over as Tomás fucks her from behind, which he knows is not her favourite way to fuck but now it's too late, she's going down on Serge and now she's moaning, now she looks back at Tomás with someone else's cock in her hands and she smiles, she smiles at God knows what and Serge smiles too, and he looks at Tomás right in the eyes.

'*Oui*,' he says, '*ça*.'

And Tomás just keeps it going. Why? Why? WHY? But he does, and the worst part is they both come at the same time, Tomás and Serge, and then Eva is fully clothed and watching both men making out, Serge somehow still holding the cigarette on the side of his mouth and she leaves them both in her room to kiss in kisses that leave ash trails on the lips.

'Look!' Eva shouts from upstairs. 'Come up and look!'

Tomás runs up to see her and she's holding an antique telescope to her face.

'Look,' she says, passing it to him.

'It's an island,' he says. 'We found an island.'

'*Oui*,' Serge adds, still naked, hugging them both from behind, '*ça*.'

From the magnified circle of the telescope, Tomás can see a house by the beach and he knows, and knows that she knows too, that this is where their search will end.

.   .   .

He's on the bus on his way to Baquedano again and from there he'll walk on to Bellavista. The streets are covered in protest banners creased with rain. He rubs the window to look outside because he doesn't want to miss his stop, even though he knows the road and the time it takes to reach it by heart.

The bus driver's listening to a *cumbia* about people having sex in different Kama Sutra positions in a kitchen, and he's singing along real loud because he's old and fat as hell and really needs to consider the exercise, though the kitchen is probably the worst place for... But Tomás is young and Lucas even thinks he's good with girls (what does that even mean?) and so he turns on his iPod and listens to Amusement Parks on Fire's debut album, 'Amusement Parks on Fire', and there's this song on it called 'Venus in Cancer', and he has no idea what it's really about (it can't be about cancer) but at least, unlike Bob Dylan, the guy can really sing and it's all about the sad textures behind the voice, overlapping and disappearing, just like the fog condensing on the bus windows.

When he had got home after Abdul's shop, he received an email from Facebook telling him Lucas had added him as a friend. He had kept away from Facebook since the breakup because Eva hadn't deleted him from her Friends list, and so he was still getting the music she was sharing. Although he enjoyed discovering new bands like Amusement Parks on Fire, he hated having to imagine what moods she was in and who she was really sharing music with. He hadn't even been able to go through the options to disable his account in case a photograph of her, or a name he couldn't recognise, or a mood he didn't suspect, came up on his Homescreen or Wall. But maybe he was wrong. Maybe the Wall is there to show that despite the little you've done and grown, you are still there, that there is no distance further removed than the Wall. It's your lowest point, and he is still there on her Wall. And so he decided to log in and accept Lucas, and he quickly clicked on Lucas's profile to avoid his own Wall and to look at his pictures. You can tell who's single on Facebook because single people never appear on any pictures, and it's all mostly landscapes or their non-single friends having non-single fun (because single people are always the ones holding the camera), or black and white pictures of their own feet or a celebrity they like, because they have so little worth sharing, so little anyone would ever want, that they have to convince themselves that it's their choice, that they belong to the open spaces, to the fields and the volcanoes and their friends, and that they can even find beauty in their shoes, and that they're alone not because no one loves them, but because no one else would understand that they belong to the open spaces and…

Lucas's profile pic is a geyser exploding into a stream of water surrounded by thick steam clouds pierced by sunlight. His cover pic is a set of black and white Converse. Most other pics are of Abdul's shop.

Tomás Googled 'Antarctica' and downloaded a photograph of a hill all in white with the sun coming down at the peak. He put it as both his profile and cover photo, because not only is he still single (and he wants Eva to know that he is), but he's also an exception to his own rule. His pictures, unlike the dead landscapes and shoe stills, show intent, they show desire, and he doesn't belong to the Antarctic or his friends, but her. And she would know that and contact him, and he'd tell her that he's no longer boring and that he'd be arriving back to her soon and she'll say that she knew it, and he'll say he knew it too, that it was all just meant to happen, that it wasn't a mistake.

A guy with a guitar gets into the bus and Tomás takes one earphone off to listen. It's the same bus singer as last time and he starts playing Victor Jara's 'Canción Del Arbol del Olvido' again, but this time it's as if Bob Dylan was covering it because he really can't sing and he's wearing dark sunglasses. Everyone just looks at him in silence. When he's done with the song, people still give him money and Tomás remembers what his sister told him about the artists she once interviewed at work. She said that most of them are douchebags and their work often sucks real bad, but they suck with such conviction that every criticism justifies their egos and their stories and their dark sunglasses even when it rains, and he must remember this, that his loss is nothing compared to what he's about to gain, and all of this is just part of an ending he... His whole situation sucks. But it sucks with conviction.

He gives money to the singer and gets off the bus. He walks past the bridge over the Mapocho River and towards Bellavista. Despite the rain, it's as busy as always and it's full of people eating and drinking and shouting and listening to music. If the world ended, Bellavista would still be there, unchanged, with ceviche restaurants and expensive ponchos for *gringos*, red, yellow and orange walls filled with graffiti and cheap attempts at poetry, retro music nightclubs and signposts to Neruda's house by the San Cristóbal Hill.

He walks past people selling cigarettes on carpets, and around *gringo* couples eating ceviche on open terraces, and past waiters waving at him to their restaurants, and some old dude wearing a poncho and hair beads playing the accordion with one foot strapped to a bass drum to keep the beat and look impressive despite his age, and some people clapping around him, and then Tomás finally gets to Bar Loreto. He decides to get a coffee and watch the accordion player finish his song first. He opens his IDEAS book.

· · ·

IDEAS BOOK P. 45:
Another game. A relationship simulator, like the ones in Japan, like that one game where you're a pigeon (literally) trying to get hot schoolgirls to go out with you. So how will this one be any different? If a pigeon can date, then maybe the dating simulator format has already doomed itself to bargain bins around the world. There are, after all, very finite ways to play a relationship. And like all games, you win and it's over, or you lose and try again.

But no, this dating simulator won't be about love or even making people like you. The game will be quite the opposite. You'll be a guy or a girl in high school, and the objective will be to cheat on as many partners as you possibly can without any of them ever finding out. It will have to be an *indie* game so that its sheer immorality can pass up as social commentary.

You will start on the first day of school. It's still hot from the summer you've just left behind. You've been in the hospital and you've no recollection of who you are, the things you like and those you don't, and it's here that you create your avatar, which will either be a hotter version of yourself or the person (or pigeon) you'd like to one day get to fuck.

So you arrive and the girl on the desk next to yours asks you if you'd like to go to her birthday party. You say yes, but only because you've no idea who anyone in your class is yet, and you think that making friends will let you find out who you really are, what really happened to you.

And so you go to this birthday party (which is in a mansion), and you go to the girl who invited you.

'You're so rich,' you say. 'Nice house.'

'I inherited the world,' the hot douchebag says, and then kisses you on the lips.

Suddenly you remember that you like kissing, no, you love it, and will speedily press L and R, alternating them until your thumbs go numb just so you can wiggle your tongue a little.

She takes you to a room upstairs. A private room. And she talks to you but you don't give a shit. Please shut up. L,R,L,R,L,R and so on until...

You fuck, in real time, with strategy, and you get points every time you make her flinch out of pleasure. She says *oui, oh oui, continue, plus fort* and L,R,L,R,L,R, *oui, là, comme ça, continue* and then you remember there's a party, a whole world out there and you can do better, you always can, but you don't say it. You count the points, you rest your thumbs, and you get dressed in silence.

Outside, by the white stone water fountain, there's a multitude of couples (they have to be already coupled so as to stimulate competition) and you will interrupt their conversations.

'Nice shoes,' you say.

'I bought them myself. I am the independent type,' a new girl answers.

And you will love that. You will almost have an orgasm out of hearing such an infinitely freeing possibility. IN-DE-PEN-DENT you say to yourself, unsure of which syllable sounds the sexiest.

And then, the same room again. But this girl fucks different. Now it's A and B. They like it slow and deep. They like dirty talk. Dialogue options come up onscreen, options you're sure you've never had before. Take me hard. Fuck me like you own me. I want it to hurt. Choke me. Finger my ass. And then, then it's *oui, oh oui, encore, comme ça, continue,* and you rest your thumbs, maybe even blow on them a little, and dress in silence, gaining extra points for guilt.

Back out at the water fountain you spot someone in a couple that look like they're from another planet. They have orange mohawks and their jeans are filled with rips and tears and chains. You're now bored of talking about money and shoes. You want deep conversations about real issues, like, what got you into the hospital and made you lose your memory. This couple is at the very edge of the patio and you interrupt their conversation.

'Who am I? What happened to me?' you ask.

'Let me show you. I'm the kind of person who hates everyone because I can see right through their bullshit. I can help you.'

FINAL STAGE: The Room. This girl fucks harder than anyone in the world. She doesn't have time for varying positions or dirty talk: all of it a waste of time. You remember that you were also the kind of person who hated wasting time, and so you fuck harder than you ever have X,X,X,X,X,X,X, you are still fully clothed, there's no time X,X,X,X,X,X,X, you hurt her and they hurt you, you know you're both doing it too hard but who gives a shit? Points for guilt and points for strength and speed and violence and blood, bonus blood X,X,X,X,X,X,X, she comes, you come, she goes down on you, you go down on her, you both come again, and then you want to talk but she has nothing new to tell you. You press X and – nothing. L and R – nothing. A and B just in case but nope, nothing works. You see yourself going over the old cheat codes: ↑ ↑ ↓ ↓ ← → ← → B + A + START and you remember how invincible you used to feel playing a game. Now the game plays you. When did this happen?

Now a cut scene shows you that all the characters you fucked were actually friends and they had planned out everything. They fucked YOU. You hear them laughing, and their laughter reminds you that before any of this happened, they had fucked you so hard and all at the same time, *oh oui, encore, oh non!* that they had to take you to hospital in a wheelchair.

And so back at the fountain you make it your objective ~~to fuck them all,~~ to screw with their heads, their friendships and families, but before you can even make a move, a couple interrupts you.

'*Bonjour,*' they both say. 'We love your shoes.'

Suddenly you notice a line of pigeons looking down on you from the tiled rooftops.

'*Oui,*' you say, staring at the birds, 'I bought them myself.'

· · ·

Outside the club there's a group of guys all in black, all of them smoking. They all have beards and long hair and T-shirts of obscure bands with fonts that Tomás can't decipher. He can hear electro playing inside and when he gets closer to the door he sees a poster:

'We are THE END!'
Beast Beat Records presents:

Miss Garrison
Kamel Toe (Feat. Dr. PingPong)

and...

FÁRMACOS
($5.000)

DJ sets:
IHATECOMMAS
DJ Kuntzz
DJ Propane Milk

Santiago 666 Society:
Funding the End of the World

He pays at the door and gets his hand stamped with a sad smiley in black before walking past the cloakroom, where there's a girl with four lip piercings tidying coats.

He shows the ☹ stamp to a bald bouncer and he opens a door with a glass circle for a window by turning a hard metal wheel, like in a submarine. Inside it's pitch black, but streams of bright neon greens and reds move along silhouettes all dancing and shouting and standing in the dark. Tomás goes straight to the bar and asks for a coffee, but the bar guy tells him they don't have any mugs and asks him if a normal glass is OK. Tomás says that it is and gets a straw from the counter.

He turns to look for Yiyo and Lucas and goes to the tables on the edges of the club. All the goths are in couples and Tomás thinks that it must be great to have fewer options to settle for but he could never invest so much effort in growing his hair and buying black clothes with obscure band names just to create a version of himself that excludes all other versions and their outcomes and… Still, the thought that all these dudes are getting laid tonight, unlike him, despite being total freaks, really gets to him and he forgets his coffee's still too hot and burns his tongue.

He finds Lucas and Jesús and Matilde sitting around a table full of empty Corona bottles. He waves at them but no one sees him and so he pretends to comb his hair and takes another sip of coffee despite the heat.

'Hi,' Tomás says, putting down the glass on their table.

'Dude, you made it!' Lucas says.

'Hey man, thanks for coming,' Jesús says.

'Hi,' Matilde says.

The only free chair is by Matilde so he moves it away from her and sits down.

'Kamel Toe just finished,' Lucas says.

'They were amazing. And Dr. PingPong, man, you should have seen him, like, what a voice! He's mental. He looped a burp for a whole song and somehow made it beautiful,' Jesús says with a smile.

'I'm sorry I missed that,' Tomás says.

Matilde laughs and so Lucas laughs too.

'It's pretty packed in here,' Tomás says. 'Must be good money.'

'Yeah. I mean, I don't want to get ahead of myself, but a few more of these fundraisers and we'll have a new End Of The World to look forward to. Maybe in the next few years, who knows? We're paying a *gringo* astronomer up in Vicuña to find out.'

'About what?' Tomás asks, and Matilde shakes her head smiling.

'Well, apparently there's a 1% chance a comet will hit us in 2018.'

'And that would end the world?'

'That's the thing, we hope so, but at the moment all we know is that it would wipe out civilisation… But the planet would still stand. So we're hoping to confirm that it all goes to hell.'

'But isn't it the same?'

'Well, not really. We're hoping that there isn't a chance life could ever return.'

'It's 1%, it's not going to happen and you know it,' Lucas says, looking at Matilde, shaking his head just like her.

'Might be so, but we need to know so we can prepare for it if it happens.'

'It's stupid, you'd die either way,' Lucas says.

'Well, I hope so. But the three years before it will be the best years of my life. And then, when it hits, I'll knock on your door and say I told you so.'

Tomás drinks his coffee, lights up a cigarette and hides it under the table between puffs. He looks at the stage where people in black are setting up a drum kit and tuning guitars for Fármacos. He sees Yiyo talking to a metalhead nearby and Tomás waves at him and Yiyo waves back and comes to their table.

'Hey dude, I thought you weren't coming,' he tells Tomás.

'Well, my plans fell through so…'

'But you never have any plans,' Yiyo laughs and Matilde laughs too.

'Work plans, I mean. I'm done, finally.'

'You're done with your game?'

'Yeah, so done, with the story at least.'

'Oh, dude, so glad. Congratulations. Thought you'd never finish.'

'Yeah, me neither.'

'Well, we'll celebrate tonight then. I'll dedicate a song for you.'

'Wait, you're the guitarist from Fármacos?' Matilde asks him. 'You're the crazy guy from that meme with the monkey and the—'

'Yeah, I'm Yiyo, what's your name?'

'Matilde,' she answers, tidying her hair behind her ears.

'Tell you what,' he tells Tomás, 'you and your friend could come backstage and grab a beer or something if you want.'

'Sounds great,' Lucas says, smiling at Tomás.

'Not sure man, I—'

'Let's go!' Matilde says.

'Go,' Lucas says too, and Jesús just shakes his head.

'Alright, let's go.'

He gets up and Yiyo leads the way with Matilde behind him and Tomás wonders how the hell Yiyo does it, how he can say anything, do anything, and always have girls follow him. And he DOESN'T GIVE A SHIT. He's thin as hell and dresses like a teenager but somehow that never matters. Maybe girls feel young around him too, or maybe they feel they can change him, like he's a project or something, like when hippies on TV clean up and become hot normal people. Or were those homeless people? Whatever it is, it makes Tomás want to still be in Fármacos. Not that it would really change the fact that Eva left him, but wouldn't it make him feel younger too? Maybe he could be a hot normal... Wouldn't holding a guitar and playing songs about Santiago at night make it easier for him (and her) to believe that maybe it's... No, no, even better, wouldn't it show her that there is still so much future left for him to give?

They walk past the crowd and get to a door by the stage and Yiyo waves at the bouncer and he lets them through. They climb a narrow staircase and the walls are filled with graffiti of band names and dates and Che Guevara and upside down USA flags and pictures of dicks and insults against Piñera. None of them say a thing as they climb up the stairs, where suddenly the club's music becomes a vibration on the steps and a hum on the walls. When they get to the top, they go through another door that says 'Artists' on a scratched golden star.

Inside is a small square room with a fridge, a sofa, graffitied walls and a sink. Yiyo takes three beers from the fridge and opens two of them WITH HIS FUCKING LIGHTER and another AGAINST THE BLOODY TABLE because it's what cool people do, and he gives one to Tomás and Matilde.

'To your game,' Yiyo says, raising his bottle.

'Thanks,' Tomás says, and they drink and then Tomás sits on the sofa while Yiyo and Matilde talk. He looks at the graffiti, all those bands who at least for one night knew that they were artists, that whatever they didn't do at work, or how many people screwed them over, it was all worth it for a name on the wall. But most names are written on top of other names. Tomás tries to think what it'd be like trying to find your own band name 20 years later. Fucking impossible. And so while they might not forget that their fuckups were worth it, everyone else will because no single wall can hold that many memories and no one can make their own name timeless in such... But does it matter? If it disappears behind other names, does it make it less present? Plus, with enough layers it would become random lines and scribbles and anyone would be able to see their own name somewhere, even the names of bands that don't yet exist.

Tomás takes a pen from his pocket and writes his name on the wall because it will last forever, just like Bellavista, overwritten by time, but impossible to erase in his own memory.

'Hey, no use writing your name there, dude. Didn't you hear? The world will end in 2018. No one will be here to remember any of us,' Yiyo says laughing and so Matilde laughs too.

Tomás smiles and has a sip of beer.

'They're nuts,' Tomás says, but when Yiyo turns back to Matilde he crosses out his name.

'Hey *huevones*, I have to go play. They must be waiting for me. Stay here for as long as you want. Beer's in the fridge,' Yiyo says, winking at Tomás.

Matilde nods and watches Yiyo stretch his arms up over his head and then touch his feet. He's SO FLEXIBLE, of course he's bloody flexible. He must remind women about themselves and how they'd like to be too, or just how they think they are. But who knows? Maybe it's something else, something without any rational explanation.

'Good luck man,' he tells Yiyo.

'I'll fuck up as always, I'm sure,' Yiyo says with a shrug. 'I just hope they don't notice.'

He says 'they', as if we're all so fucking…

'Don't worry, no one will remember,' Tomás says smiling.

Yiyo laughs and so does Matilde, and he leaves them both in the room and the hum of the club gets louder. She sits by Tomás on the sofa and he thinks she's looking at him so he takes a big gulp of his beer but then, when he turns to her, she's looking at the graffiti all over the ceiling.

'I can't believe you're friends with the people from Fármacos. That's so cool,' she says.

'How come?'

'Well, I thought you were pretty lame at first, what with the gardening gloves and all.'

'No,' he sighs, 'I meant, how come you like Fármacos so much?'

'Oh… Sorry. I don't know. Their music is just beautiful. I don't really like the guy's voice but it's all about the lyrics. They remind me of being young in Santiago.'

'I know what you mean.'

The music downstairs goes quiet. They can hear people clapping and it sounds like raindrops and Tomás wishes he could just stay here looking over the names of people he doesn't know because, like rain, crowds are only beautiful at a distance, when you don't have to be in the middle of it all.

'So, your trip... Is it for your writing?' she asks him.

She's facing him but she's looking over him, and he wants to tell her that it's OK not to talk to him, that when he was younger, silence made him uncomfortable too, and that at her age he enjoyed the rain.

'Sort of, why?'

'Well, I want to be a writer too.'

'Great.'

'I applied to do a Masters in Creative Writing at NYU. I've only ever written short stories though. I'd love to try out a novel. I've been going to this workshop in Providencia which—'

'Sounds good.'

'I don't think I'll get it in the MA though. I haven't published anything like you.'

'Well, good luck.'

She looks at him and they share the raindrops and the crowds with all their forgotten names dispersed across the ceiling. They drink and he looks at her dress, at her shoulders and her neck and when does it happen? When do bodies stop standing so straight? When does skin suddenly decide to let go of its perfect shoulder? When do dreams stop becoming plans and instead turn into impossibilities, into stories? He wants her to wish him luck too, because it would mean that, like her, he has something to fail at, something to lose. He wants to know that, unlike the names on the wall, these things haven't happened yet and so their consequences (in his life, on Eva's life) can still be infinite and timeless.

A beat starts downstairs and people cheer.

'Aren't you going to wish me luck too?' he asks her.

'On your trip?'

'Yeah.'

'Things don't just happen. I don't believe in luck,' she says. 'You can prepare for stuff, you can look for opportunities and then succeed or fail. It's never just luck. You're doing both so you'll be fine.'

'Thanks.'

The singer from Fármacos starts the verse to 'Abril' and people cheer.

'I love this song. You want to come with me?' she asks him.

'Sure. Hey... I forgot to ask you...' She turns at the door and doesn't open it.

'What's up?'

'I think Lucas has a crush on you.'

'I know, poor dude, we're friends though, you know?'

'Yeah.'

'Let's just go. This is a short song.'

He nods and they go down the stairs in the dark. He imagines her breathing in synch with her heels, letting herself drop farther and farther down in perfect balance. She doesn't believe in luck because she doesn't yet believe that some things are just impossible. And even when you can trace every single one of your choices to a particular moment and desire, no one really shares them with you. We're all listening in for signs, watching graffitied walls and believing we're special for picking out single details. We're hearing each others' heels tapping on the steps of a staircase in the dark, at a concert hall full of music drowned out by rain. He spends so much time trying to come up with a story for a game for others to play, but he knows everyone just wants to play their own stories and not even... They want to play their own mechanics.

'Ouch,' she says, stopping at one step.

'Are you OK?'

'I think I hurt my foot,' she says, laughing.

'Wait, I'll try and turn the lights on.'

Tomás tries to squeeze past her and she grabs him from the shoulder so he doesn't trip and instead of stepping down he turns to her and 'Abril' hasn't ended yet, although it's on the last verse and he feels her breath *We've never seen April* on his neck and he can't see her eyes *The weak hand wasn't drawing* and he kisses her *You never, never* and she stands still and kisses him back barely opening her mouth at the guitar solo *Search later, search later, search never* and their tongues don't touch, their hands don't touch, and the stairs aren't there and the painted walls disappear and he wishes he were absent too, fucking gone, silenced like the rain, just so that he didn't have to know once it was over, that he's really kissing someone else because nothing in the world can just change the outcome of such a simple fucking mechanic.

'Sorry,' he tells her but she doesn't answer. The song is over.

When they leave the staircase and head back into the crowd, will they talk about it? He fucking hopes not, if he's to ever get to Eva. Just like the names on the wall, the kiss will be lived over, forgotten, and he's not really sorry for kissing her, but he is for the fact that he's already started to forget her, and that it's easier to do so in the dark.

'I'm sorry,' he says.

'Don't worry,' she says with one hand on his cheek. 'I do have a boyfriend though.'

'Don't worry, I have someone too.'

'Let's go. They're going to play "Other",' she says, taking her hand away.

He takes his phone out and lights the staircase as the sad acoustic strum starts, but the light lasts only a few seconds and the strobes make the graffiti look as if they're moving.

They open the door and the crowd is all lights and noise and Lucas and Jesús see them and cheer things they can't hear. *I believe in other worlds.* Matilde stands in front of Tomás shouting the lyrics to the chorus. *The one I hear when I feel you.* Yiyo is crouching with his guitar next to the amp, making it feedback and some people cover their ears but they're still smiling because electric noise behind a clean sad chord makes the lyrics even sadder. *You can make feel alright* the singer keeps repeating, and although everyone there feels alright, no one's felt it like that, just like that, and Tomás wishes he could do that in his games too, *We can meet somewhere, will you remember where?* to make people see that what they know could always be different, sadder, much sadder despite all the noise. *You can solve my life with yours.*

Lucas looks at him and mouths 'so?' and Tomás smiles back at him and nods, and he wishes the song never ended so he didn't have to speak to him, but it does end and everyone claps at the wall of feedback and the singer announces that their last song is coming and that it's called 'A Great Ending' and that it's a new song. Tomás sighs because he wrote the bass line for it and had complained about not liking it. But when others are playing it, it always sounds so good. *I can inveeeent, a great ending when you're hiding. I can imaaaagine a great ending.*

They finish their set and the electro starts again and Lucas and Jesús walk up to Tomás.

'Awesome set, huh?' Jesús says.

'Yeah, amazing,' Matilde says.

'It was amazing,' Lucas says.

'You said you didn't like them,' Jesús tells Lucas, laughing.

'Come on, I said the bass was a little off. And I had only listened to their latest stuff. I prefer their first EP,' Lucas says, also laughing.

'Hey man, I have to ask you for a favour,' Jesús tells Tomás.

'What is it?'

'We're meant to have six people talking onstage tonight about The End Of The World. One of them is a writer, just like you.'

'OK.'

'And he didn't turn up.'

'OK.'

'So I signed you up to talk instead.'

'No way.'

'It's just for fun.'

'No.'

'You're a writer, make something up!' Lucas says.

'It would be hilarious,' Matilde says, laughing.

Yiyo turns up to meet them sweating like hell but somehow still looking cool and Matilde still staring at him.

'That went well,' Yiyo says with a big smile.

'Totally,' Matilde says.

'Yeah,' Tomás says.

'So, what you up to next?' Yiyo asks Matilde.

'We're trying to convince Tomás to go onstage and talk about The End Of The World but he doesn't want to,' she says, and Yiyo laughs and pats Tomás's shoulder.

'Come on, man, when was the last time you were on a stage?'

They all look at Tomás but he has no idea what he'd say or why a story would matter if The End Of The World will indeed happen any time soon. And so he thinks about his games filled with computer bugs, with mistakes that don't allow anyone to finish them, and how fucking ironic it is that he has spent so much time trying to write a story for something that can't end, and now he has to improvise a story for the end of everything. And just as he's laughing and shaking his head to leave (because he really should get back to work), a goth chick in red platforms walks onstage and taps the microphone and the music goes quiet.

'The end is coming,' she says and people cheer. 'But before it does, I'd like to invite a few people up onto the stage who will tell us what we can expect to see.' She takes out a paper from her pocket. 'First up, Tomás.'

People cheer even louder as she steps away from the mic and Tomás just shakes his head and Yiyo lifts Tomás's arm and everyone claps and a goth starts pulling him towards the stage and then more people pull him and cheer for him until he's onstage and then it's all silence again. He squints his eyes trying to look for Yiyo, but with the stage lights on him everyone turns into silhouettes.

The host goth adjusts the mic up to his height and he has still no idea what to tell them because endings just spoil everything. And no matter how much you may want it to be a beginning of something else you can't, because from then on you can't be new again, and you can't just choose what to forget or how to remember and... And so Tomás comes closer to the microphone and he shuts his eyes and he figures that what they want to hear is not an ending but a story told backwards, all life coming to a halt and then, then all the explosions, all the causes and then at the end, or beginning, Tomás meeting Eva and smoking out the window.

'Come on!' someone shouts in the crowd and people laugh.

'The world will end,' Tomás says and people cheer.

'How?!' another silhouette shouts.

'With an explosion.'

'Of what?!'

'We won't know, we won't find out, because it will end us completely.'

'Is that all?!'

'No.'

'What else, where is Satan?!'

'I don't know, but if I had to guess, then he's smoking out the window right now, your window, and he wants to go to the Antarctic.' He knows he can tell them anything so long as he keeps the promise of an ending.

'The Antarctic?!'

'Come on, man!'

'This what we paid for?!'

'Where are the explosions?!'

The host goth takes the microphone and Tomás is behind her and looks at the blue and red dragonfly tattoo behind her neck and she says someone else's name and then…

'Guys, remember to buy some merch at our table. We got a ton of sponsors endorsing us for The End Of The World.'

People cheer and Tomás walks off the stage and back to Yiyo and the others but he just wants to go home to work.

'That was hilarious,' Yiyo says and Matilde laughs.

'Hardly,' Jesús says. 'I expected more… Well, it's why we're fund-raising I guess.'

'I'm getting out of here,' Tomás says.

'Wait,' Lucas says, pulling him to one side from his sleeve.

'What did she say?'

'About what?'

'Maty, about me,' he whispers.

'She said,' Tomás starts, but who is he to end someone else's story? He's tired of doing it. It's enough. And, at the same time, who is Lucas to stop him from living his own, from getting the things he needs and going to Eva?

'She said she likes you. She likes you most of the time,' Tomás says.

'What does that even mean?' Lucas asks.

'Women are strange, man. I have no idea.' Tomás feels a little sick in his mouth.

'They are strange,' he laughs. 'Thank you, thank you, thank you. I didn't think she liked me. I would have put things to one side for you at the shop either way.'

'Thanks.'

Tomás waves bye and leaves the silhouettes to the next speaker who's setting up a PowerPoint presentation with a picture of a comet with an upside down cross stamped on its surface.

He walks past the cloakroom at the entrance and someone pulls his jacket from behind and it's Matilde.

'About the kiss,' she starts.

'Don't worry.'

'Yeah, it's just—'

'Is your boyfriend here?'

'No.'

'Then don't tell him. If he doesn't know, nothing will happen.'

'The thing is you might know him. He works at university and he makes games too. I met him at that writing workshop. He actually, like, told...'

'What his name?' he asks her.

'Jaime.'

'Small world.'

'I know. But come on, just don't tell him.'

'He won't know.'

'Thanks.'

They smile at each other and he leaves the club and outside it's still raining and still full of people and noise. He puts his headphones on, heads to the park and looks down the bridge at the Mapocho River with its waves swirling in foam in all directions, but he knows that it will always only flow in one of those directions, with the current it cannot ever go against.

Tomás decides to walk home and tonight, thinking about the end of the everything, the names on the wall and the river waves against the concrete tunnels of a city that is his and Eva's, always Eva... Thinking about all of this, he realises he has an idea, a real idea, and he'll finish a story that others will want to play despite all its broken mechanics.

13

The Box

He sits under his desk against the wall. It's 2am and he's ready to start working. He has to sit on his coat because the rug's still wet and a piece of his ceiling is still on his desk, and even though it drips from time to time, he has decided that none of these things matter when there's an idea and who knows (he thinks he does)... This might be 'the' idea, the one story he's been waiting to come up with all this time.

So he opens his IDEAS book, has a sip of cold coffee and turns to a blank page. He starts with a list:

What makes a good game?	*What makes a shit game?*
– Realism: real consequences to every action	– Realism and real consequences.
– A recognisable story structure. Tropes like Damsels in Distress (fuck my own lessons), being the victim and overcoming injustices, going from imprisonment to freedom, from poverty to wealth.	– A story that relies only on tropes and therefore becomes predictable.

– One main clear objective.	– Too many side-quests and minor plots.
– A dog, a child or any made-up creature that the protagonist has to care for so as to give the illusion that his/her choices have an impact on those he/she loves. Make a reward system so as to encourage the player to always think that he's not alone or free.	– A system that rewards care for others too much, because it would mean the player would feel like they are playing someone else's game. Excessive responsibility is the OPPOSITE of fun.
– To make it so that everything the protagonist does seems to draw him closer to the end but there will always be an obstacle…	– Obstacles that are predictable, because since the desired end is revealed from the start, the middle will just become unnecessary clutter, like cleaning plates before a dinner party only to have to then clean them again.
– A game that takes into account Jaime's lack of talent and then justifies it.	– Jaime, everything about him.
– What if the game has no ending? What if it randomly generates content and there's nothing at the end? What if you make a game about an empty promise?	– The lack of an ending would make people stop playing the middle because nothing in this world is more motivating than being able to get what you believe you're entitled to. That's what a story must do, entitle you to desire, to accept an ending.
– There always needs to be something to lose. This can be the pet mentioned above, your life, anything…	– There's always something to lose. Your life…

But is it enough to simply make a list about it all? Sure, all these elements would make a good game but without a story they're just independent pieces that trace back to nothing, drive towards nothing. Plus, if he can give examples about every point he makes, doesn't it mean that these perfect parts already exist, that they're everywhere and never his own? And so he decides to tear off the list from his IDEAS book because really, they're not his ideas. And so, how should he start a story? Since he can't figure it out he decides to start with the ending.

The protagonist's pet dies whilst looking for his lost love and when he finds her he's still carrying the pet's body around in his camping bag (or in his arms, to increase drama), and she understands his devotion to dead things and helps him bury it under the ice, or they send it off to sea on a wooden rowing boat before they can finally go back to her campsite, where she'd been living all this time with a grumpy walrus that told her she would never leave. And then he checks if his items are frozen (and they aren't because they had kept warm with the pet's body) before he starts to undress her and then…

Tomás's flickering lights die out and it's all darkness and silence and he can hear himself swallow.

· · ·

IDEAS BOOK P. 56:

~~Eva Eva Eva Eva Eva Eva Eva Eva Eva Eva Eva Eva Eva Eva Eva Eva Eva~~
~~Eva Eva Eva Eva Eva Eva Eva Eva Eva Eva Eva Eva Eva Eva Eva Eva Eva~~
~~Eva Eva Eva Eva Eva Eva Eva Eva Eva Eva Eva Eva Eva Eva Eva Eva Eva~~
~~Eva Eva Eva Eva Eva Eva~~

~~Eva Eva Eva Eva Eva Eva Eva Eva Eva Eva Eva Eva Eva Eva Eva Eva~~
~~Eva Eva Eva Eva Eva Eva Eva Eva Eva Eva Eva Eva Eva Eva Eva Eva~~
~~Eva Eva Eva Eva Eva Eva Eva Eva Eva Eva Eva Eva Eva Eva Eva Eva~~
~~Eva Eva Eva Eva Eva Eva Eva Eva Eva Eva Eva Eva Eva Eva Eva Eva~~

~~Eva Eva Eva Eva Eva Eva Eva Eva Eva Eva Eva Eva Eva Eva Eva~~
~~Eva Eva Eva Eva Eva Eva Eva Eva Eva Eva Eva Eva Eva Eva Eva~~
~~Eva Eva Eva Eva Eva Eva Eva Eva Eva Eva Eva Eva Eva Eva Eva~~
~~Eva Eva Eva Eva Eva Eva Eva Eva Eva Eva Eva Eva Eva Eva Eva~~
~~Eva Eva Eva Eva Eva Eva Eva Eva Eva Eva Eva Eva Eva Eva Eva~~
~~Eva Eva Eva Eva Eva Eva Eva Eva Eva Eva Eva Eva Eva Eva Eva~~
~~Eva Eva Eva Eva Eva Eva Eva Eva Eva Eva Eva Eva Eva Eva Eva~~
~~Eva Eva Eva Eva Eva Eva Eva Eva Eva Eva Eva Eva Eva Eva Eva~~
~~Eva Eva Eva Eva Eva Eva Eva Eva Eva Eva Eva Eva Eva Eva Eva~~
~~Eva Eva Eva Eva Eva Eva Eva Eva Eva Eva Eva Eva Eva Eva Eva~~
~~Eva Eva Eva Eva Eva Eva Eva Eva Eva Eva Eva Eva Eva Eva Eva~~
~~Eva Eva Eva Eva Eva Eva Eva Eva Eva Eva Eva Eva Eva Eva Eva~~
~~Eva Eva Eva Eva Eva Eva Eva Eva Eva Eva Eva Eva Eva Eva Eva~~
~~Eva Eva Eva Eva Eva Eva Eva Eva Eva Eva Eva Eva Eva Eva Eva~~
~~Eva Eva Eva Eva Eva Eva Eva Eva Eva Eva Eva Eva Eva Eva Eva~~
~~Eva Eva Eva Eva Eva Eva Eva Eva Eva Eva Eva Eva Eva Eva Eva~~
~~Eva Eva Eva Eva Eva Eva Eva Eva Eva Eva Eva Eva Eva Eva Eva~~
~~Eva Eva Eva Eva Eva Eva Eva Eva Eva Eva Eva Eva Eva Eva Eva~~
~~Eva Eva Eva Eva Eva Eva Eva Eva Eva Eva Eva Eva Eva Eva Eva~~
~~Eva Eva Eva Eva Eva Eva Eva Eva Eva Eva Eva Eva Eva Eva Eva~~
~~Eva Eva Eva Eva Eva Eva Eva Eva Eva Eva Eva Eva Eva Eva Eva~~
~~Eva Eva Eva Eva Eva Eva Eva Eva Eva Eva Eva Eva Eva Eva Eva~~
~~Eva Eva Eva Eva.~~ And then the game is fucking over.

·   ·   ·

He stays under his desk and finishes his coffee. It will have to do for now.
He'll improvise a beginning and a middle tomorrow morning before his
class and take it to Jaime to check. He should prepare his lesson too, but
it's definitely not his fault that he's always under such tight deadlines.
After all, he does tell his students that real stories sometimes take years
to complete, even when the idea might come all at once.

The class is about justifying gameplay mechanics with story elements.

He will ask his students basic questions, like 'what if your game only involves a physics engine and animated particles? What kind of game could you make then?' Or 'if the only thing you can program is an 8-bit sprite, one simple character, no backgrounds or added scenery, and they can only move right and left, what could you make?' Most students come up with, frankly, the most outlandish things, like there's a competition to see who's the sickest mentalist in the world. Most years he hears the same ideas too, as if there was an ancient jackass passing down the same shitty ideas. The 8-bit man is a rapist. He is a burglar who eats children. No, he kills the children, then burns their pets in the oven to make a perfume bottle he then sells to the dead children's families. He's a dentist gone mad with power and he's performing non-consensual surgeries. And Tomás has to pretend that these ideas have some value, something worth talking about. And always, ALWAYS, every single time, everyone dies at the end. No matter how many times Tomás explains what a story arc looks like in most games, either $\bigcup$ or $\diagup$, they always find a way to make it $\sim$

Tomás used to think that he'd learn by teaching. That's what all the old teachers who would rather be dead tell you when you start. If he were being honest with himself, he'd go so far as to admit that he thought he'd be able to steal game ideas from his students while teaching. But it never happened. The only question they go bananas for is 'Re-write the ending of a *Super Mario Brothers* game', where they discuss it for forty minutes before concluding: 'Bowser kills Princess Peach. And then Super Mario. And then himself.'

Tomás pulls himself out from under his desk, watching for his head. He uses his phone light to look for his sofa and lies on it. He wishes he had pillows but she took them too, even though one of them had a T and the other an E embroidered on them in red. Yes, they were the sort of couple who do those shitty things, shitty things that become more valuable as time passes and you still don't have other shitty things to replace them with. It also means that Eva has been literally sleeping on his initial, on his name made secret, on things only they could understand, on their inside jokes. And so when he gets to the Antarctic and he tells her he's been sleeping on their decisions and on their mistakes, she will say she has done the same.

Tomás falls asleep, and it might be because of the stories he's been trying to come up with or the fact that the mixture of coffee and the cold dampness of his flat from the leaking cracks on the ceiling have by now become comfortable, but Tomás snores and smiles and he dreams.

He dreams he's piloting a small aeroplane and his dad and a walrus are playing cards behind him. Tomás is happy because the walrus is smoking and his dad isn't telling him that smoking will kill him. But then his dad tells Tomás not to light up because it only kills people.

'Where are we going?' Tomás asks them. The walrus laughs and Tomás laughs too because the animal sounds just like Yiyo.

'Son, for once I have a good hand, could you talk to us later? Your flying is great by the way,' his dad says.

'Dude, you're so dead,' walrus-Yiyo tells his dad.

'I am dead.'

'I meant I have a better hand.'

'You have no hands.'

'Well, at least I'm not dead, dude.'

Tomás looks below him and everything's frozen white. Shouldn't he be able to see what's frozen underneath? Why must water lose its transparency and why must everything inside lose its colour, its particular shade, and instead become a consistent sheet of white whose only distinctive features are the cracks? But even they lead to nothing. And he feels real bad about it, but maybe, just this once, Tomás thinks Eva is the one who's boring as hell for wanting all of this. But then again, if she left him for such epic miles of white frozen boredom, then what does that say about him? Clearly he should have never been content with less than four gas hobs. She's right. She's always right.

And it is at that moment, when Tomás feels the urge to take his hands away from the Xbox controller with which he's manoeuvring the plane, that he feels a pat on the shoulder.

'Hey, don't be such a pussy.'

He looks to his right and sees a life-sized troll doll smiling at him.

'I hate this. I hate this,' Tomás tells him, looking out the window.

'Come on, keep flying, don't be such a pussy.'

'Stop saying that. It's my dream. Why can't I see her? What's the point of all this if I can't see her?'

'I'm not trying to troll you. Just stop being such a whiney little bitch,' the troll doll says, lighting up a cigarette.

'Can I have one?' Tomás asks him.

'Nah, smoking will kill you.'

'You've got to be kidding…'

'Look at the stars,' the troll doll says with a puff of smoke.

Tomás is flying in the dark and the stars made of chewing gum are moving around and forming shapes. Coffee cups, squares and triangles and the frozen feathered chicken and light bulbs that flicker shapes and colours, tiny pieces of gum like a pink firework display.

'I knew it. I knew it was you,' Tomás tells the troll doll.

'You know a lot of things,' he answers, 'but I'm not one of them.'

'Can you make her appear then?'

'My mum used to say there are plenty of fish in the sea and even more sea in the fish.'

'But it's all frozen.'

'Sure it is. And so are the fish. Now I'm just trolling with you.'

'So what do I do?'

But the troll doll turns to Tomás's dad and the walrus and they start singing, *vamos llegando, chuvai chuvai, we're arriving* and the chewing gum disappears and Tomás sees a stone clock tower on a hill made of ice and the bell rings to the rhythm of the song and Tomás drops the Xbox controller between his feet and he feels the aeroplane dropping.

'What do I do?' he asks, looking at a map in front of him that looks like his students' story arcs.

Chuvai, chuvai, they sing to the ringing of the bell.

'What do I do?'

And before Tomás flies into the clock tower everything goes dark and everyone stops singing and he can hear himself breathe and he's cold and Eva appears in front of him and they look at each other and...

'You get out of here, and you get yourself a new hob.'

And at that moment Tomás wakes up and falls off the couch. He doesn't remember what he dreamt about or even that he dreamt at all, and all he can think about is that the pain on his neck could have been avoided if she'd let him keep the pillows. At least the E. But he can't stay lying down on the floor because the doorbell's ringing and he hopes he hasn't overslept for work, although he knows all too well that he forgot to set an alarm to start with.

'Coming!' he shouts, his voice quieter than he thought it would be.

He gets up and bends his neck to both sides and he tidies his hair and opens the front door.

'Hey,' Matilde says, holding out a cardboard box. Her hair's tied into a bun with a pencil that has a rubber at the end. Tomás hasn't seen one of those in years.

'Hi,' she repeats. 'Are you OK?'

He wipes his eyes with his hands.

'What time is it?'

'Just turned one.'

'Fuck, fuck...'

Tomás goes back inside without shutting the door and heads straight into his room to put a shirt on and look for his shoes. Matilde comes in and leaves the box on the desk on top of the piece of ceiling and drops her backpack against the couch.

'You really are preparing to go into the wild,' she says, looking around his flat.

'I can't find my fucking shoes,' he says from his room.

'They're here,' she says, picking them up from one of the gaps in his sofa (those gaps with infinite capacity, portals to fucking Narnia) which he knows is where most of the things he loses end up.

'Why are there so many straws in between the gaps of your couch?' she asks.

'Thanks,' he says, taking his shoes from her and bending down to put them on. 'Um… Not sure, probably left from the previous tenant or something.'

'Oh, OK,' she says, looking at the piece of broken ceiling on his desk.

'It's being refurbished,' he says.

'It better be,' she says with a smile.

'Yeah.'

'Going to work then?'

'Yeah. Why are you here?' he asks her, and this time he notices his voice came out much louder than he'd hoped. She stops smiling and looks at the box.

'Lucas is working late at the shop and he'd been collecting some stuff for you and I told him I'd bring it over.'

'Oh.'

'It's fine, I'm going now.'

'I'm sorry,' he says, 'I didn't mean it like that.'

'It's fine, it looks like you have a lot to deal with right now,' she says, looking at the trash pile on his kitchen floor.

'Sorry, I have to go.'

'Well, I also wanted to tell you, I got a short story published in the *Paula* magazine. It was good timing because it meant I just got accepted into NYU. I'm leaving in a few weeks.'

'Why would I want to know?' Again, his voice is too loud. He wants to apologise but he doesn't since he's always thought that the apologies of the ugly are annoying and pathetic because they make it seem as if their misfortunes were not their fault.

'Well, I'll see you around then,' she says, turning to leave.

'What's in the box?' he asks.

'Why would I want to know?' she says, imitating him.

'Thanks.'

She turns to leave again but faces Tomás at the door.

'You know, it doesn't always mean you have to forget it, even if it doesn't really lead anywhere. You never know,' she says, and then she closes the door behind her and Tomás can hear the rain outside.

What does she know about forgetting and leading anywhere and all that bollocks? What does she know about anything? A story in *Paula* and New York! He wishes he didn't look so fucking ugly when he wakes up just so he could tell her he's sorry for her for achieving something so early, because all she will ever do for the rest of her life is try to keep up with her previous achievements. And what did she mean by 'always'? Does it mean she believes herself to have the ability to pick out what she remembers and forgets? And while Tomás would like to know more about how selective memory works, if it works at all, he is certain that only the young could pull it off, that the 'always' is just some word to her because she's never had to face a 'never again' like he has. It is not a game, he mumbles, it is not just some game, and sometimes you can't just start over.

Outside, he wonders whether he should go and get his coat but he doesn't because he's late and in the movies people who have real problems are always drenched when it rains.

Taking the stairs down, he thinks that when he asked her what was in the box she should have answered that inside is everything he needs, just so he could have then asked her how she knew what to get and have her say that just by looking at him, at his flat, it was clear from the start. But then again, Tomás knows that no one ever says what they should at the time when it is most needed.

14

Star Signs

He passes by a small kiosk on his way to the office.

'Hey Matías,' he says, rubbing his face– which ends up spreading the raindrops even more.

'Hey *huevón*, pack of twenty Camels?' Matías turns to fetch the packet without waiting for an answer.

'No, no. Can I just have ten?'

'You OK *huevón*? I know the weather's been bad but come on.'

'Yeah, yeah… Just been a bit stressed out lately. I forgot my coat.'

'No, I meant, you OK? How come you don't want to smoke your usual twenty? Everyone's quitting, right? I heard they're passing a new law to stop people smoking inside. No one asked me anything though, right? Fucking typical. Let's see if they pass a law to give me back my money. Why don't you smoke twenty? You're the only *huevón* who buys twenty. Come on…' He says all this with his back to Tomás and a hand ready to pick out the Camels from the plastic dispenser that goes up to the tin ceiling. The column of twenties is full and Tomás sighs because things have changed in Santiago. The once-empty cigarette cases are full. Everyone will outlive him and no one asked him either. Matías and his wooden stand, the empty avenues surrounding it, the pigeons fighting for scraps in the riverbank, the ancient skyline dwarfed by the flashing lights of skyscrapers veiled in the morning fog, all of this, all of it without asking him. The river of shit passes without a sound, or maybe Tomás just can't hear it anymore, having always sounded the same, always ageing, the city with its many silences. Now Matías offers him things no one else wants from the full plastic columns just so at the end of the day it can look more like the empty ones. Tomás looks at the river and doesn't understand why he can't hear it.

'I'm just trying to stop smoking,' Tomás says.

'Don't stop. It's all bullshit. I wish it weren't *huevón*, I really do. It'd be a miracle. But it's really just bullshit. My mother in law, been smoking all her life and is still the same healthy annoying old bitch she's always been. My God take her, I say, please just take her, but no, she—'

'I'm late.'

'So, will it be twenty?'

'Alright, a pack of twenties please.'

'Ah, and that's why I'm still here. You see any more kiosks? They're all fucked. But not me. It's because I know what you want even when you have no idea.'

'Thanks.'

'And get a coat *huevón*,' Matías tells him, taking the money and giving him the cigarettes. 'You look like you just jumped into the Mapocho.'

'Thanks, I will.'

He walks into the alley and it's full of Blue Peace people with banners about the excess of rain and flood warnings with pictures of poor kids in school uniforms navigating a canoe made of truck tires on their way to school. One of the hippies is selling vegan empanadas (what the hell is in a vegan empanada?) for two thousand pesos each and yes, Santiago is changing, but not for him. The banners all say 'Global Warming: RIP Civilisation' and Tomás sighs, not because he disagrees with them but because they, as nature lovers, should really appreciate the beauty of the mountains after it rains and the smog clears out of the city. Still, he feels like a jerk for thinking like that when the streets are rivers and there are people getting to work by punting on flat tires. And he should really be getting to work himself, rain or no rain.

He runs up the stairs to his office and Anna sees him when he comes into the lobby.

'Hey, you! Come on, I need those marks, like right now,' she says, getting up and holding her belly with one hand and her back with the other.

'But I'm really late,' he says to her.

'I know you are, you are so late! So please, please just give them to me now,' she says standing between him and the door to his corridor. 'I'll get into trouble.'

She's too big for him to simply pass beside her, and Tomás's mum had once said that she knew of a pregnant woman who had been able to summon freak strength out of nowhere to save one of her kids. She lifted a whole truck to prevent him from getting run over. So Tomás just stands there and looks at Anna.

'I meant I'm late for class.'

She doesn't answer anything but she takes in a deep breath and crosses her arms above her belly and Tomás thinks she's going to slap him so he shuts his eyes but nothing happens. When he opens them he sees Anna starting to cry.

'Come on,' Tomás says, but he doesn't have a follow-up.

'Please, just do it, I'm so fucking pregnant, and I still do my work, I still have to work, and you and your marks, your marks are the only missing ones and I can't finish and I'm so fucking pregnant and I hate it, I fucking hate it, I can't, I just—'

'I'll try my best,' he says, looking at his watch, but she lets out a loud cry just as one of the cleaners comes out of the staff toilets and Tomás smiles at him but the cleaner just stares at them and puts his bucket down on the floor.

'I'll mark them,' he whispers to Anna. 'I'll mark them, OK?' he says, touching her on the shoulder. 'OK?'

'OK,' she repeats, rubbing her eyes and taking in deep breaths. 'Thank you.'

'OK,' Tomás says loud and looking at the cleaner guy who takes up his bucket again.

He runs into his office and it's already past two in the afternoon and who is he kidding? He's an hour late and most students must have gone home by now. He'll just write an email to them later, telling them the streets were all flooded. What he has to do is wait for Jaime to get back from his class and tell him all about his ideas.

And so he lies under the desk and looks up but the chewing gum constellations have all disappeared and so has the troll doll on the shelf and, hearing the protesters outside crying out that they miss simpler and cleaner times, Tomás is comforted by the fact that he too is capable of missing simple things: a doll on a shelf and the ever-changing pieces of gum that, thanks to their new absence, Tomás can finally be certain never actually moved.

He gets his IDEAS book out and checks what he wrote last night. Tomás is in trouble.

.   .   .

IDEAS BOOK P. 60:
Idle Games are all the fucking rage right now. An Idle Game is a type of videogame that has you do the simplest possible task to gain the right to do the next simplest task and so no. Click on a cookie. Check. Now get two pies. Click on them too. By tomorrow you'll be clicking on a bento box, only to feel rewarded with newer and sexier scenery.

~~In a way these aren't games at all. They're brackets of time, kind of like smoking, but not even as fun~~ Jaime proposed we make one where you need to click on your character for him or her to get up every morning, and then again to fall asleep at night. During the day they'll be as bored as you are, eating always the same breakfasts, and then bored at the office as they try hard to read a spreadsheet that is beginning to look like a bullet through their younger self's head, and then bored on the journey home, where they always hit every single fucking red traffic light in the world, and then bored when they get home and watch a French fantasy TV show that is all talk and no sex and fucking boring, and bored then when they have to fuck their husband or wife who moves so little they may as well be fucking one of their boring china ornaments they keep on their coffee table, maybe the boring elephant, and then they'll have boring dreams with boring characters who have the same boring days as they do.

Two clicks.

Click. Click.

But what if there were more? And what if there were none?

· · ·

Tomás is in deep shit. He never quite got to writing a story and he begins to breathe hard trying to look in his IDEAS book for what he knows isn't there and he feels his back still wet with rain and he wishes all those assholes outside would just be quiet for once and understand that there are people here who actually have to work and… He will have to improvise. He will have to fucking improvise and God knows how much he hates improvising (most of *Bimbo: The Elephant* had been pure improvisation and the damn thing wouldn't drop back down after jumping) and all he can think about is his wet back, Bimbo, and the fact that he made a pregnant woman cry and none of it would make a decent story.

He could just leave. He should pack his stuff and go to Abdul's and buy things from his list and just book tickets to see Eva. He stands and just as he's closing up his IDEAS book, Jaime comes in.

Jaime hangs his coat and leaves his umbrella by the door.

'You look like you just jumped into the Mapocho, *huevón*,' he says and Tomás laughs but Jaime doesn't.

'I finished. I have your story,' Tomás tells him, instantly realising that the only possible outcome is…

'So, let's hear about it,' Jaime tells him, sitting on his office chair with both hands on his knees.

'OK.' Tomás looks at the shelf and listens to the protesters shouting out louder than ever.

'So?'

'Yes… So stupid, these Blue Peace hippies, huh? Did you know how soon we won't even be able to smoke inside?'

Jaime sighs. 'I don't smoke. So what's with the story?'

'Yeah, well,' he starts, and could Jaime just die? Like right now, could he die? Could he have a heart attack? Catch fire. Tomás does have a lighter. 'Well, it's about lots of things. Different things.'

'Great work.'

'No, wait, I'm getting to it, to the good bits, just wait.'

'I'm listening.'

'OK, well, it's about a dude who has to save his girlfriend from freezing to death in the Antarctic and he befriends this animal, a penguin or a walrus or something, and they have to get to her before… Well, before—'

'Before what?'

'There's this iceberg heading towards the ice block she's frozen in, and it's going to smash it all to pieces. Thing is, the pillar she's inside also holds the world together, and once the iceberg hits it, the whole world will end.'

'So how does he save her?'

'Well, he rescues her, I suppose.'

'Yes, but how?'

225

'He goes up there and dives or something. I don't know. Maybe he needs to get some power-up before that lets him breathe indefinitely underwater.'

'But wouldn't the iceberg still hit the pillar? And wouldn't he need to break the pillar to save her anyway? Wouldn't the world still end?'

'Yeah, I guess.'

'Yeah.'

'But at least he rescues her, even if for a moment. I guess you could just roll on the end-screen after that... The credits or something.'

'Look,' Jaime says with a sigh, looking out the window. 'That all sounds alright and I wish you the best of luck.'

'What do you mean? I have the script here somewhere,' Tomás says opening the bag looking for the pages he knows he doesn't have, but he takes out his IDEAS book anyway and opens it on the list of Antarctic equipment.

'Stop, man,' Jaime says, turning to him.

'What?' Tomás looks back at him and closes his book.

'It's done, it's all done now.'

'What is?'

'You were taking so long. You were never here.'

'Hey, you know why, you know it's not been easy and—'

'It hasn't. But I have to give them a game next week or I'm out too. It's done, I finished it.'

'You finished it.'

'I finished it. I tried to tell you but, well, you were never here.'

Tomás doesn't know what to say or do. If he had the script for a story he'd do something dramatic, like he'd take it out of his bag and slam it on Jaime's desk, no, his fucking fucked up fucker face fuck and tear up a couple of pages in front of him and maybe even eat the first page while staring at him like the deranged do in movies, just so he thinks he's capable of anything. But he doesn't. Instead, Tomás grabs Jaime's umbrella and Jaime stands in front of him but Tomás doesn't care and he looks for the tip where the metallic bars join with the fabric and he pulls them all apart. It is, however, way harder than he thought it'd be and he keeps pulling but nothing comes off.

'Come on,' Jaime says, but Tomás keeps trying and a minute passes by in silence with Tomás trying to break an umbrella.

When he gives up, he takes it under his arm and looks at Jaime one last time before opening the door to leave and when he does, he notices that Pedro, the Head of School, is there with his arms crossed and to his side is Fran, smiling at Tomás.

'Dear Lord, did you just go for a swim in the Mapocho?' Pedro says, inspecting him from head to shoes.

'Are you kidding me?' Tomás says.

'No, not at all. We have to talk in my office. Now.'

Tomás nods and when he's behind Pedro, he notices Fran at the end of the corridor, looking at him and unfolding her right shirt sleeve and it's full of red lines in all directions, full of cuts, and she pulls the sleeve back down before Pedro turns to her with a quick wave.

They go into the office and inside everything looks like it was taken from the set of a nineteenth century TV drama: the old green leather chairs with carved armrests, faded paintings of flowerpots and people with hats smoking through long cigarette holders, a skull, a miniature ballet dancer inside a bell jar, and am embalmed owl looking out the window at the protesters still shouting downstairs. There are rows of embalmed birds in bell jars to both sides of the owl.

Pedro sits behind his desk and turns to look at the owl. Tomás sits facing him.

'Franziska told me you didn't come to class today. Is this true?'

'I tried, but I had been—'

'And Jaime says he's been doing your work for you.'

'That's not entirely true but—'

227

'Tomás, how has this gone on the way it has? Why has it gone on the way it has?' he asks, scratching his chin. 'You do know that I must, above all, I must follow procedure. You do know that, right?'

'Yes.'

'What do I have to follow?'

'Procedure.'

'That's right. And you know what happens when I don't follow procedure?'

'Well—'

'Let me explain to you what happens when I overlook procedure. What is a university Tomás?'

'A place where you get degrees?'

'No. It is a universe. It is a system. It is, above all, a set of connected procedures, just like computer code. And what happens when one line of code fails?'

'Ask Jaime.'

'The whole system crashes.'

'Like Bimbo.'

'Like Bimbo. I'm so sorry Tomás. How I wish the elephant had been a hit. How I wish you had been on time for your classes. And how I wish you were the games designer you had the potential to be. Don't take it personally, please don't do that. This has not been an easy decision. It's just procedure.'

Tomás doesn't say anything but he opens his bag, and since he doesn't know what to do he opens his IDEAS book on a blank page and takes out a pen, because Pedro has to at least see that despite all these mistakes and misfortunes, he's still trying. And so he pretends to take notes but only writes his name over and over, like his own students do in his classes. There it is, he did learn something from...

'And I got a call from my PA saying some students had mentioned something about you harassing some of our students. Tomás, how long has this been going on for? I'm so sorry, I really am. I wish I could help you, but can you even imagine the stack of procedures this whole thing will entail if it becomes public?'

'What?' Tomás says looking up from his IDEAS book. 'That's just plain untrue,' he says.

'Well, so you haven't done that either. What have you done? What do you do with your time Tomás? If there was something on paper, something to show, some publication, something… I could help you out. I mean, that would make it easier on the—'

'Procedure.'

'Exactly. I'm glad you understand. I mean, it is really awful. I don't know what to do.'

'I've been working, trying to work, but—'

'I don't think so. Look, I just can't have this place running like this. We talked about it with the Dean and you know what she said? Do you want to know what she said about you?'

Tomás shakes his head.

'She said you were "unnecessary", that whether you are here or not, everything can happen without you and no one would notice, that you are an unnecessary budget to consider. And Anna says you haven't done your marking. Your marking, Tomás, the most basic thing… Why didn't you ask for help? You could have even asked me. There are procedures for late marking too. So, well, there's no easy way to say this, but, well, you're fired, as dictated by article 659 on page 442 on the Staff Manual.'

'Fired?'

'I'll ask you this, would you employ yourself?'

'Yes.'

'Would you, really?' Pedro says.

'Yes, I think so.'

'No, no. Let me ask you again. Would you employ yourself?'

'No,' he says, and Pedro just shakes his head.

Tomás looks at the skull. Unnecessary? He knows that this is the sort of moment he'll be replaying in his head for the rest of his life, coming up with edgy answers, maybe even a quotation from some famous civil rights activist who also endured a great injustice. But right now the skull and the protesters outside are all he can think about, how unnecessary they are, all of them, and then he thinks of Eva and he must remember to tell her how necessary she is, how necessary she's always been, and how necessary all the little details she wished for him to change also were: the hobs in the kitchen, the French dinners, the Trans-Siberian train… Those are the things that matter and he knows he can change it all in a day, in one decision.

'Do you have any other comments to add?'

'No,' he says.

'You have until the end of the month to empty your office.'

Tomás nods and gets up and waits in silence for a handshake or a goodbye and when he realises it isn't coming (because that would be unnecessary), he turns and leaves.

He passes by Anna who, for the first time in his life, pretends not to see him and instead fiddles with a bunch of forms on her desk as Tomás heads onto the stairs.

Outside, the protest against the rain is still going on and Tomás briefly considers joining them just because he feels like shouting too, and he knows all these people also gather because they all feel like shouting but really, is there anything more unnecessary than shouting for the rain to stop?

He walks past them and heads towards the river. He leans on the edges of the bridge and he looks down at the waves and he wants to cry and think about Eva but with the noise of the traffic and couples walking by, and business men and women talking on their phones, his sadness would never be authentic.

Instead, he opens Jaime's umbrella and thinks about jumping into the Mapocho. He lights a cigarette and trembles with the cool rain still touching him behind the neck. And when he closes his eyes there's a moment where everything is quiet and it's just him and the river, the river and him, and the wind picks up and lifts the umbrella and breaks it at the joints.

Remember the story of grandfather Diego buried under the seventh hole at the Golf Club? Well, now, looking down from the bridge at the river of shit, at the shitty ocean passing under him, Tomás remembers his grandmother. Yes, she had irritable bowel syndrome and would often burp out loud at dinner parties and yes, that began shortly after her husband's death. But no, this isn't why Tomás is thinking about her over all this moving shit. He's thinking about her because he lights another cigarette.

His grandmother Andrea would often tell him she wanted to die. Even as a child. 'I wish I were dead,' she would say after telling him about the horses she used to ride in the stables she used to own. She told him she was tired, and smoked as much as she could. 'I want cancer,' she said, 'I want it to be my star sign that takes me to the next world.' Tomás remembers the stars that night because they were the same as on any other night. And he remembers even better that two years later, cancer came. The stars hadn't moved but she said, with a quiet laugh and pointing at the sky, 'I told you they would take me back,' and Tomás didn't know whether to cry or laugh so he did both.

Anyway, that same weekend his grandmother died in a bus. The driver was drunk. Chile had beaten Argentina 2-1 in a friendly match, and he was wasted. Grandma Andrea had been out in town getting her favourite tobacco, Blue Drums, and was on her way back home to die a little slower, predictably, and with her family, but BANG and the sky had nothing to do with it.

Tomás sighs and drops the umbrella into the river and it doesn't even splash. Neither would he. It's at that moment that the plastic windmill salesman walks up to him pulling his cart full of windmills now covered by a sheet of plastic that rustles in the wind.

'Windmill?' he asks Tomás, holding onto his beret.

'No thanks, not today.'

'Can I have a cigarette then?'

'Yeah,' Tomás says, handing him the packet.

'Amazing *huevón*, you bought a packet of twenties, no one does that anymore. Can I take two?'

'Yes, sure.'

'It's a shitty river isn't it?' the salesman says lighting his cigarette.

'The shittiest.'

'Here,' the salesman says, picking out a windmill from his cart. 'Free of charge.'

'No, don't worry, that's not necessary.'

'Nonsense, when you're as old as I am, you understand that only unnecessary things can make you happy.'

In the metro, he tries to imagine all the unnecessary things inside the box Matilde left in his flat.

15

8 minutes and 20 seconds

IDEAS BOOK P. 64:

~~Today it'll be a game about… No,~~ fuck it, today I can't write a game. My. God. I'm writing a fucking diary: quarter-life crisis UNLOCKED. Now I have truly become *it* (*it* = terrible megadouche). I didn't mean to start being *it*, promise. Then again that's what *it* would say. It's just I can't stop thinking about my first job, back when jobs seemed exciting, and every shitty little thing that you knew you were too good to do seemed like an exciting possibility to show it (regular 'it').

I got my first job through my dad with Clover, age 16. I was to work for a month in the summer (that felt like a year) at the Paper Cutting Department. Yup, they have a Paper Cutting Department, and my job was to cut up ice-cream ads to place outside street kiosks. But that isn't why I'm thinking about all of this. The reason is Bernardo, Bernardo the veteran paper cutter.

I got an email telling me where to meet him. I was to go to the basement. Then the guy who took me to the stairs told me not to worry if Bernardo seemed a little off, which is what someone who does worry about how off he was would say. And so I worried.

He left me in front of a broad blue plastic-coated door, a constant

SHIN-SHIN-SHAN-SHAN-BIP-BIP-BIP inside. I waited there for a few minutes. I opened the door. Bernardo had his back to me as he tended a machine where he was cutting the edges of a giant chocolate cornetto. Damn was he good at cutting those little corners on the chocolate flakes.

'Hello,' I said, still in the doorway.

'Hurry, hurry. Get your apron and you can help me with this. My name's Bernardo. I cut things.'

He said that. I shit you not. He said he cut things.

'I'm Tomás, I've never cut anything,' I should have said.

'You'll learn, though it's not easy,' he said with a sigh.

'That's what I want. I want to learn. I'm ready for anything,' I definitely did not say.

And this is when Bernardo turned to me and I could see him full. Well, full isn't quite right. His right hand was missing and he had made a knot on it with the extra sleeve length over it.

'I learnt the hard way kid,' he said, and all I thought was, shit, this guy works in a basement, in a FUCKING BASEMENT and HE LOST A HAND to a chocolate cornetto, the worst way to lose a hand (I could never eat a chocolate cornetto ever again), and shit, shit the world is unfair, and shit the knot is disgusting to look at, and the knot only makes it MORE VISIBLE. That's right. A naked stump would have remained hidden given the appropriate lighting conditions but… A knot. A basement. Ice-cream. No hand. Fuck.

'Be careful with that machine,' he told me. 'It's French and it's expensive,' he added, and he pointed at it WITH THE KNOTTED ARM. By that time I just wanted out of it all. I never touched the machine. I was careful. I quit. Dad shouted about quitters. He called me 'a quitter, just like Argentinians.' But Bernardo just shrugged a disfigured shrug, an asymmetrical shrug, and what he told me I will never forget.

'It's not worth it kid.'

·   ·   ·

It's just past midnight and Tomás is wondering if the rain will ever stop. When he got home he lay down on the sofa and stared at the hole in the ceiling for so long he's not sure if time went by too quickly or if he fell into a sleep too light to notice. Then he got up, and lighting his way with his phone he made himself some coffee. But since the kettle has burnt out, he had to just fill the French press with hot water from the tap. It still tasted the same though, because he waited even more than five minutes for it to brew. He went to his window to smoke and got angry at himself for not being able to quit and briefly considered how clean his apartment would be if he didn't waste so much time smoking. He'd probably be in the Antarctic by now! And so he decided to chain-smoke so as to only have ten cigarettes left by the end of the night and from tomorrow he'll make sure to buy only packs of ten.

And because he's been smoking ever since he got up, he hasn't had time to do anything else, even less to open the box, which still remains untouched by the front door. Now that he's on the last cigarette, he's dreading its contents because whatever Lucas decided to include inside would reveal what others think about his plans and how badly they think he wants Eva back. What if they thought he was joking? What if they thought that he was a joke? And even worse, what if they thought that he's been doing all of this to make himself seem less of a bore, or as an attempt to intimidate them with eccentric claims of an impossible journey? He just hadn't considered that what may be easily believable to one person does not always make it so for everyone else.

And so he sits by the box and wonders whether he should open it at all or just return it and start over by himself. But then again, don't long journeys always constitute a certain degree of madness to those who stay behind? Weren't the Spaniards he learnt about in school, those explorers who set out to unknown places, considered nuts by the rest who were too afraid to go with them? Plus, he knows Eva very well, too well, and as he once told her after sex (when, if you perform well it's OK to lie about your feelings for dramatic effect), if there's anything, anything he could be crazy for, it was... Ugh...

Fuck it. He gets the knife Fran left by the hobs and cuts the tape around the box to open it. Inside there's a lot more than he expected, all piled up like *Tetris* bricks from the bottom up: a tent, a sleeping, an old gas lamp, packs of gas, a ski mask, two tennis rackets, a few DVDs without a cover and a compass with a neck chain.

He puts the compass chain around his neck and turns around on the spot but the compass needles stay still. He hits it a couple of times and they start moving and Tomás can't help himself and says 'Yes' out loud, but the needles move slowly and then get stuck right where they started. He sighs but then wonders if maybe the rain has something to do with it and maybe the Blue Peace people were right to protest against it, the lack of direction it pours down in every drop. They should try harder. It's OK, he thinks, it will work in Antarctica.

He takes out the sleeping bag and the tent. He opens the tent bag first. It must be from the 80s because it's pink and grey but this is better in case he ever gets lost, since even in the darkness of his flat it looks bright as hell. He moves his couch against the wall and spreads the tent on the living room floor. He then takes the smaller bag full of fine metal sticks and starts building the arcs.

Once it's up, he crawls inside and he can't hear the rain and he likes how it makes all the light coming from outside shine pink. He wishes it were colder though, just so he could see how effective it is for the conditions he imagines himself under. His freezer still works, and if he didn't have the frozen chicken inside, he would leave it open and camp nearer to it. But he's had it for so long he just can't get himself... So he starts taking off his clothes instead until he's fully naked and only wearing the compass around his neck.

Next, he takes the sleeping bag out and spreads it inside the tent, before reaching down into the box for the ski goggles to put them on.

'Hi Eva,' he practises in front of his tent. 'Remember me Eva? It's been a while but… Hi Eva…' he starts again in different tones before deciding that tones don't matter because he sounds fucking mental, and actions reveal way more than words can ever do.

He goes inside the tent and as he lies there on the sleeping bag, he thinks about the job he no longer has and how the hell his mother and sister will react to the news. His mother will tell him that he needs to seriously consider his future, that despite him always being *her* child, he is not *a* child anymore, and that what he wants out of life should not be more important than what he ought to be doing with it. But she won't tell him what any of that involves just to make him understand how clueless she thinks he is. Then, his sister will just let out a quiet laugh and say that none of it surprises her, and that he should go and live with his mother because she's lonely but really, she would just enjoy seeing him in his childhood room so he can admire how far she's moved on with everything he still doesn't have, and with Alejjjjandro on her side to boot. And his father, well, at least he's not going to… And so he decides to keep it all a secret for now. He'll send them a postcard (do they have postcards in Antarctica?) when he's there and it will also have Eva's signature on it, and they will finally realise that he too was destined to a remarkable future, where all his failures will turn out to be life lessons for everyone else.

. . .

Tomás is in a beach house with Eva. She's just finished watering a row of tiny daisy pots she keeps by the front porch. She's going to start cooking. She waves at Tomás. Take your time, she says, take your time, it will be a while. So Tomás stays on the sand, on his old *Zelda* beach towel writing up games, which are just as good, no, better than *Zelda*.

As he gets closer to the end of the story, he realises it's getting dark and he can't keep writing and Eva has still not called him in. The lights in the house are on.

'Eva?' he asks, still sitting.

No answer. Have you ever been in a beach in the dark all by yourself? Did you ever feel like what made the ocean beautiful (the power of the waves, the foam, the washed up knots of algae, the sound, the noise) suddenly became terrifying?

'Eva?' he asks again, standing and tidying his notes and towel and he faces the ocean and then, then it begins.

At the end of the ocean, Tomás sees the sun, still lit but lighting nothing, and suddenly, it turns black, a shadow, a sphere of ash that slowly falls into the waves and just disappears. Tomás drops his towel and his notes.

It takes roughly eight minutes and twenty seconds for the sun's light to reach the Earth. It takes far less to end someone else's suffering. A few seconds in fact, the time it takes you to say whatever it is that you know people want to hear, the three perfect seconds in I-love-you, the longer four in I-still-love-you or the immediacy of a smile. And yet you can't do any of it. The sun has stopped working and every second is a second nearer to the – very imminent – end.

Tomás runs into the house. He can hear Eva in the kitchen. He wants to kiss her, no, fuck her, no, just look at her. She turns to him with a smile, a white wine glass on one hand, a wooden spoon on the other.

'You want some?' she asks, holding up her glass.

He shakes his head. Two minutes have gone by.

'We have to go to bed,' he says. 'We have to go to sleep.'

'What?' she asks. 'We can fuck after we have the *canard à l'orange*, Tomás. But nice try,' she says, still smiling.

'No, you don't understand,' he puts her glass down. Three minutes. 'We have to go now.'

She frowns at him, rests the spoon on an unlit gas hob. There are eight of them. Four minutes. Tomás takes her hand and pulls her towards him. She resists, shakes him off.

'What's up with you?' she says, pissed off.

'We don't have time to argue.'

'No one has time to argue, Tomás. That is why it's unpleasant.'

'No, I mean...'

He takes her from the waist and pulls her even harder. Five minutes. She almost trips. Almost. And he takes her hand and runs into the bedroom. It's dark, so dark, and she's not resisting anymore, six minutes, and all he wants her to do is sleep, just sleep for God's sake, the one thing people must do every single day, the one thing that gets harder the more you do it as years go by, and another minute goes by. Seven.

And she does fall asleep. She's breathing deep. He sits besides her and looks outside from the wide-open windows of the room. It's too late for him. You can only save one person, he thinks, there's never enough time.

Eight minutes. Tomás hears the soaring waves of the ocean, the last cries of the seagulls, the low whistle of a faraway ship and he stands to the sound of a waterfall... Only it's not a waterfall, but the air which has began to fall in liquid form, liquid doom, and the windows cloud over with water, so much water, so little air, and he coughs, and time's almost up, and he looks at Eva under all this unbearable noise and she's awake, she's awake, she's awake and five, four...

'*Je t'aime*,' she says, and there's nothing he can do about it.

·   ·   ·

He closes his eyes and then there's a loud knock at the door and so he gets out of the tent and covers his crotch with his shirt and opens it. There's a guy with a motorcycle helmet and a pizza box in both hands. They look at each other in silence for a few seconds and then the guy quickly gives Tomás the pizza and Tomás has to catch it with both hands so his shirt falls and the guy pulls down the shade of his helmet.

'I didn't, I didn't, or... It's a mistake.'

'No problem sir,' he says.

'Would you like a coffee or something?' Tomás says just to say something to stop the guy from looking at him.

'Enjoy your pizza. Here's a coupon,' the guy says, putting a coupon on top of the pizza and then he just leaves.

'I didn't order any!' Tomás shouts as the deliveryman leaves. He sighs. Then again he hasn't eaten and he's happy to find it's a thin crust Hawaiian pizza, even if it doesn't fit in with the whole Antarctic thing. He eats someone else's mistake inside the tent and decides not to brush his teeth to make it part of the authentic experience of camping out in the wild.

He stretches on the sleeping bag. Tomorrow he'll make sure he thanks Lucas for all the stuff and he should really apologise to Matilde because, after all, just like his new equipment, who is to say what's necessary and what isn't, and who one day might or might not have a role in this whole story? Plus, there are no hobs in the box and he will have to go back to the shop for them, two of them at the very least.

He looks at the compass one last time and he's sure that now the needles are moving just like they're meant to. Maybe the rain has finally stopped.

16

The Oxygen Tank

IDEAS BOOK P. 70:

Another game. A game about strategy, an RTS: Real Time Strategy. And like all strategy games, it will be about earning the power to destroy ~~other nations, no,~~ the whole world at the press of a button.

But most games of this type have too many countries, cultures, tribes, factions, or whatever you want to call them and Jaime cannot, will not, create more than one, because he said one is enough, and that it only takes one of these groups to destroy itself and everything with it. He's still going to make it a two-player game though, so really it's his laziness which will direct the fate of this virtual world.

But how can you make an original RTS nowadays, what with all *The Lord of The Rings*'s bullshit collateral residue of green mean people and wizards and all that fucking fantasy nonsense? How much of a format can you change before you ruin it completely? When does it become something else, something unintended?

This game will feature only France. It will start you off as French cavemen and women (they grunt with throaty Rs) and well, in caves, and you will be hunter-gatherers. You skin animals, make pelts, and weapons made from bones and have tons of off-screen sex in tiny mud huts, which release chimney smoke whenever they are being used. You will feel so productive, so reproductive, that you will ignore the fact that the objective of the game is to destroy yourself.

When you've farmed enough animals, collected enough grain and built irrigation canals, the resources counter at the top of the screen will shine green. You click on it...

And in comes the Bronze Age. The huts are now mud houses (did they already... who cares!) and you are building daggers and swords and bronze-pointed arrows so what used to take ages, killing animals and gathering wood and so on, is now a matter of seconds. You keep making weapons and the blacksmith will shine blue and you click him and he says '*Oui?*' and...

The Iron Age happens, and you keep making weapons, an army that would guard all you've ever built, and more babies, always more babies, and for every baby a sword to guard their babies, and so on until the first gun arrives (somehow, in the game the French invented guns too – remember to Google) and now, now you're so fucking safe no one would ever dare...

Revolt! You've taken over the Bastille, you've decapitated your way to democracy, *Vive La France*, and now you can finally rest but...

Industrial times ahead. The train, the plane, shopping, a 9-5pm job the title of which none of your friends can understand, and modern babies, and for every single one of those features, those UPGRADES, you now have five guns, two jet planes with eight missiles each, and even a nuclear bomb. No one will ever dare stand against you now. You've even conquered the moon and Mars. That's right, and on each you have more nukes and babies. And now you've no idea what to do. You explore into space but most of it is plain rocks floating about and they are barren. They remind you of how little there was to worry about in your hunter-gatherer days. You envy the microorganisms probably living under those rocks. You wish you could de-evolve whilst keeping the knowledge you've accumulated over the years, your pride, your history, you.

So now the game offers you nothing. No one needs you because it plays itself. That's how good you were at it. The guy who used to be the blacksmith is now a nuclear researcher and he shines red. You click on him. '*Oui?*' he asks you, and gives you two options: 1) Nuke yourself back to the Stone Age and b) Sit back and let the days and nights cycle on and on in autopilot with babies and bombs coming out of every fucking building you ever built.

'*Oui mon seigneur,*' the man will say to either option. You take a deep breath and you consider how long it took you to get to this stage. Now what would you choose?

.   .   .

Tomás's mouth is so dry from all the pizza. He wriggles out of the tent and takes off the goggles and his face hurts around his eyes. He drinks water from the tap and puts his clothes back on. He has a cigarette by the window and laughs to himself thinking about the stories the pizza delivery guy must be telling his friends and the way in which someone's greatest misfortune can be someone else's comedy for a day.

He leaves his flat and outside it's raining very thin drops so he decides not to take his coat again. Walking to the metro, he notices that the streets look more crowded and much larger than they usually do. He wonders if this is a side effect of being jobless, the way the city can expand and contract, breathe, depending on where you go and what you have to do in it. And with the new crowd in mind, he decides not to wear his headphones for the first time in years, because if he's still a part of the noise, he needs to learn to accept it.

But in the metro he remembers how quiet everyone always is and he finds himself tapping the rhythm of a song that doesn't exist and no one even looks at him, so he puts his headphones back on and the sounds of the scratching train tracks fade to the ambient keyboards of Yiyo's music.

Tomás dislikes watching people all silent and alone because if he looks for long enough, there is a moment in which everything they own, all their clothes and all their gestures, they all seem to have a reason, a hidden purpose and very specific projections. The summer dress is there to impress, the beards and the tattoos to show others how alternative they are and that they can take the pain, and the dude with nothing worth anyone's attention wants to fit in by being invisible. What really gets to Tomás (and he'd never admit to this) is that in this moment where everything is part of a lie, he must assume that there are also hidden truths that no one's sharing or even... And how can anyone live in a city with thousands of people and always be hiding, taking trains and walking and fucking but never sharing a thing? But he also knows that these moments don't last and soon he's looking out the metro window again and waiting for the brakes to spark and announce that the noise of the world will be back as it always does all around him.

When he gets to Abdul's shop, Tomás realises he still hasn't got the inheritance money and he hopes Lucas will still let him take some things again. After all, it is really not his fault Matilde doesn't want anything to do with Lucas, that she friendzoned him. Abdul is shelving a pile of books with Jesús. Lucas and Matilde are reading next to them.

'Hi,' Tomás says, but no one answers, so he picks up an old music box next to him and pretends to look for the key and then 'Hi,' he repeats, louder than before.

'Did you know that birds sing to have sex and people just copied birds and started singing to get laid too?' Lucas tells everyone, pointing at the book on his lap.

'You should get a bird then,' Abdul tells him. 'You could use the advice.'

They laugh at Lucas and then see Tomás. Matilde doesn't look at him and instead just continues reading a book called *The End of Mr. Y.*

'Hey, about the other day,' Tomás says to Matilde, opening a book from the shelf and paging through it. 'That was out of line. I'm sorry.' His book is called *Understanding Football: Beyond Boredom.*

'And I'm reading.'

'You're not... What is it about?'

'I am. I'm at the beginning so I've no idea yet. It's a very weird book though... Did you come here just to piss me off?'

'No, no, sorry. I came to thank you for the box. It's all very useful. So... Thanks.'

'You should thank Lucas.'

'I will.'

'But be careful. I told him we made out.'

'Why would you do that?'

'Because it tires me to keep on encouraging the egotistical delusions of young men.'

Tomás closes the book and picks another. He notices it's one of the few books he's actually read from start to end. It's an old copy of *Don Quixote.* He had to read parts of it at school every week for a whole year and remembers hating it because he didn't believe (and still doesn't now) that a conviction could be so strong as to render a man's constant failures absent from his mind when they're so clearly damaging to him. And how could Matilde call anyone deluded? Isn't she the one going to New York? Isn't that whole city one big delusion, the biggest windmill in the world? He places the book back in the shelf and decides to let the whole thing go because Lucas is watching him and because he figures that without a job, he might need to start worrying a little more about making and keeping friends.

He doesn't know what to say so he goes to Abdul and helps him shelf the pile of books.

'I'm not that old, I can do it by myself you know?'

'What's the order?'

'I said, I'm not that old, damn it,' he says, slapping the back of the book he's holding.

'Fine, fine.'

'Hey, I'm just fucking with you,' he laughs, looking at the others to see if they're laughing too but they aren't.

'Really?'

'Yeah, just put them anywhere.'

Tomás picks up a pair and starts helping out, and as he presses on the row of books on the shelf to make space for the new ones, he thinks about how crap it would be to do this for a living, how boring life can be, and how lucky he was in his job. Sure, he always had so much to do but it always seemed so important, something that couldn't end after an hour or even a day and he knows it's because important things must always last. The most important things do so forever.

He presses on the books on the shelf even harder but the new ones still don't fit, which annoys Tomás because he doesn't want to show that he's incapable of simple tasks. Surely doing things that are below him means he just isn't that boring. So he stands facing the shelf in silence.

'Here,' Matilde comes over and takes Tomás's books and puts them lying sideways on top of the shelved ones.

'Thanks,' he says, but she stays quiet. 'Congratulations on the whole New York thing.'

'Oh, thanks.'

'You must be excited.'

'I don't do 'excited',' she says with a grin.

'What do you mean?'

'How can I be excited over things I don't know or haven't lived yet?'

'Well, because you don't know them and you haven't lived them yet.'

'We're not children, Tomás, we're not children. Could you pass me those books over there?' she says, pointing at one of the piles.

'Listen,' he starts, 'I just wanted to apologise and thank you. It's been a rough day.'

'I don't do apologies either.'

'Oh.' She's just being cruel now. When he was younger he also felt entitled to only accept certain forms of love that could show others who he wanted to be. He doesn't really know what that means but Eva constantly reproached the way he had always been so dismissive of her friends when they came round to eat. Once, she even made him sleep on the couch because this one guy kept talking about his issues with women and referring to himself and Tomás as 'us men' and so Tomás just had to lie about not having a Facebook account when he asked. Would he add him now? He would like to believe that he would because things have changed, he has changed, and no asshole in the world would be able to turn him from the things he really loves. That's why old people very rarely argue with strangers. No one can fucking change them. That, and also because they're alone and well, they're old.

'It's OK,' she says, just as he was about to ask her if he could add her on Facebook.

'They fired me at work.'

'Ouch, what did you do?' she asks with a quiet laugh. He finds the question funny too because he hadn't thought about it up to now.

'I'm not sure.'

'Early mid-life crisis, huh?'

'How do I know if it is?' he smiles at her, giving her a book from the pile.

'I don't think you'd be able to notice, unless you bought a motorcycle or something.'

'Maybe I will,' he says, knowing all too well that his mid-life crisis will be a quiet one, and full of quiet habits and quiet friends: a bench in the park, small-talk at the kiosk, reading one book over and over in a university library and telling on students who decide they can work in groups in the non-group study areas. But then again, if he can think about all of this, maybe he's already there. Eva did once say that his projections for the future said more about his present than his future; this was when he told her one night that he had no idea where he was going with his life, that he was lost about his future. 'That's your problem,' she said, 'you're always so absent now. You should try to come back to us some day, try to reappear.'

'Anyway, aren't you leaving soon too?' Matilde asks him, shelving the last book of the pile and turning to him.

'Sorry, what?' he answers, even though he heard the question.

'Are you leaving soon too?'

'Yeah, just need to prepare a few more things and then I'm off,' he says looking around the shop to find anything that might be useful.

'I have an idea,' she says.

'What is it?'

'I don't know you. You don't know me, right?'

'Right.'

'Well, if we're both leaving it's because we don't like what we do now, our lives right now. Right?'

'Yes,' he says, but surely that's a lie. It has to be a lie because he has no fucking life to dislike right now. Unless you count drinking rain, smoking way too much, browsing at a second-hand store, camping at home, and planning a trip. That could work, planning a trip is his life now, but he likes that part, so it's still a lie, and he has no job and he is going to die young and alone if he just doesn't...

'Well, I was thinking... We could try and spend the best week either of us has ever had in Santiago. Together, I mean. I would hate to spend my last days here with the same people I always see.'

'Isn't that what most people do though?'

248

'Sure, but it's such a waste of time, and so stressful, everyone trying to make memorable moments out of familiar situations. It's impossible and depressing.'

'Are you asking me out on a date? Aren't you still pissed off at me? I don't think it's a very good—'

'Get over yourself. I'm just saying we can make the last days here something new, enjoy it one last time, and then we can forget about it. And it won't matter because... I guess because I don't know you.'

Tomás thinks it's a terrible idea, that this is exactly what he hates about young people today, the new-age conviction that all things must pass so that they no longer feel accountable for their own mistakes. And then there's the value they place on forgetting, on letting go, on getting over things, and all those other expressions people use to feel better about loss and being irresponsible. Because isn't that what she's asking him to do, to be irresponsible? She's right about one thing though. She doesn't know him at all.

'Well, I'm not too—' But before Tomás can make up an excuse to explain how responsible he still is for everything in his life, Abdul comes to them and slams a round metallic container on the table next to them and they both take a step away from each other.

'You're going to the Antarctic, yeah?' he asks Tomás.

'Yeah,' Tomás says.

'How serious are you?'

'What?'

'If you're serious about going somewhere like that, you're going to need to be able to breathe,' he laughs.

'What are you talking about?'

'He's a slow one,' Abdul says, smiling at Matilde and rubbing his beard. 'It's an oxygen tank, you tool. Buy it. Is that simple enough for you?'

'I guess I might need it.'

'You will. Let me show you how it works.'

Abdul turns a valve and the rubber straw attached to the tank makes a high-pitched whistle. Abdul then puts his hand at the end of the straw to feel the air pass through his fingertips.

'Look,' he says, taking Tomás's hand and moving it under the straw. Tomás smiles because Eva would be so impressed that he thought of everything, even breathing, and if they ever faced a snowstorm and had to camp out somewhere, they'd share everything again, even their oxygen.

'It comes with a mask too. I think it belonged to a dentist. It works,' Abdul says.

'Cool,' Tomás says. But at soon as he takes his hand away from the straw, the air stops coming out and the whistling disappears.

'Oh, I guess it's empty.'

'Yeah.'

'Good thing you didn't buy it, huh? Horrible, horrible way to die,' he says with a smile. Then, he turns to Lucas and Jesús and Matilde. 'Never try things out before you sell them, understood? Do you want to buy it anyway? Half price. You can refill it yourself.'

'Alright.'

Abdul gives Tomás the tank without any oxygen and it's much heavier than he thought, but he will have to figure out a way to take it on his trip, not only because he finds it so hard to return things at shops (he finds indecision the worst of all human afflictions, although mainly it's just that he hates bothering people) but also because the thought of sharing air, breathing, his tank of oxygen with Eva is just too much to pass on. It could, after all, if they ever needed it, save her life.

'Can I pay later? I'll be back during the week,' Tomás says.

'I've heard that one before!'

'Dad, I know him, just let him pay later,' Matilde says, looking at Tomás.

'Alright, alright… Lucas, *huevón*, make a note of it. Oxygen tank, no oxygen, twenty-five thousand.' Lucas nods with a frown and goes to the front desk to write it up.

Abdul walks off with a price-tagging gun, leaving Tomás with Matilde. They look at each other in silence for a few seconds.

'So?' she asks.

'So what?' he asks back. She sighs. He wants her to tell him about her plans for them on their last days in the city just so he can refuse and show her and himself that oxygen is now far more important than forgetting Santiago with her.

'Nothing. I'll keep things on the side for you until you go.'

'San Cristóbal Hill,' he says, turning red because it comes out much louder than he'd anticipated. It's not that he changed his mind. It's not that he needs anyone new. But if she's willing to help him (help him breathe even!), the least he can do for her is help her get over this fucking city before she leaves.

'What?' she asks.

'If you want to go somewhere, we can start with the hill.'

She nods with a smile. 'When?'

'Tonight? At eight.'

'Alright.'

Tomás walks out of the shop and he smiles at Lucas who doesn't smile back at him. He starts walking home and Matilde is right about another thing. A week doesn't have to change your life. In the Great Narratives of the games he admires, everything is always changing as you near the end: characters die, you are in danger of dying, and you get the last power-ups before the last boss, and you still feel anything could go wrong... But that's a lie, a limitation that exists only because in games you can't experience anything outside of a world that's been programmed and coded to end. But they are just games. In real life you never stop forgetting. Once Tomás is back with Eva, the whole time she's been away will be but a blur and if so, why not start tonight, with Matilde, at the hill that started it all?

He waits for a bus to pull over and watches a clown failing to make a child laugh by blowing on one of those whistles that make people sound like birds. He remembers the whole thing about birds only singing to get laid and he's glad the kid's mum comes to take him away from the clown. But the clown gets on the bus too and after whistling his jokes away, Tomás gives him some change because if he doesn't, the clown might stand by him whistling about his empty oxygen tank sticking out of his bag the whole way back to his flat.

17

It's Just Water

Of course it's not cheating. Isn't cheating about giving away moments and words and memories that should belong to someone else? Or is it simply about fucking? No, no, either way, what he's doing has always been for her. If anyone's cheating, it's the world, the city. And he isn't just thinking this to make himself feel less guilty. No way. He really fucking means it, somehow, but he's not too sure how it would... And in the end, does Eva really have to know about it anyway? He messed up with Fran, but that was because he'd tried to convince himself that it was what Eva would have wanted. How in the world could that possibly... Yes, that Eva wanted him to move on, at least a little, and it had been so... But he always knew it couldn't be that simple. And won't she also hide the months, the faces and the names that don't relate to him when they meet up? And he's sure as hell that she would never cheat on him either. How? He doesn't even... She had told him so in one of their weekend walks up the San Cristóbal Hill, when he had asked her if she had ever cheated on someone. 'I don't cheat,' she said, 'I get cheated on though,' and he said he would never, never ever, ever, ever, ever...

And here he is again, walking past the bars and the lights and the ceviche restaurants in Bellavista on his way to the foot of the hill. He forgot to set a specific meeting place with Matilde and he hopes she hasn't taken the cable car lifts up already, because there are so many people and so much noise that they could spend the whole night looking for one another. But he reassures himself that it'll be fine, because what two people would decide to meet at a hill and not want to climb it together?

He turns away from the main street with all the bars and passes by Neruda's house because it's always quiet there, and he likes to see if anyone's painted new graffiti on the wall opposite. But when he gets there he remembers that new graffiti appearing and disappearing on these walls are a thing of the past. It really fucking gets to him. For the last couple of years it's mostly just been filled with gig posters on top of other posters and behind them, hidden, the last fading traces of painted faces and gang signs and crosses and dicks and angry sentences written with intentional spelling mistakes. In front of this wall he wonders what happened to the city he arrived to so many years ago, when did it stop feeling like home? Was it ever? But he knows that what really bothers him is the way a wall can be there for centuries and still be unrecognisable in a matter of weeks. And so he keeps walking until he reaches the lifts. Eva had once told him, when they were together in the lift, that she hated the bit on the way up where she couldn't see the buildings below or the top of the hill because, she had said, she disliked being nowhere, that it made her feel as if she had disappeared.

Matilde isn't there and there's a short queue of *gringos* with big cameras waiting to buy tickets. Years ago, when they were still in high school, Yiyo told Tomás that you can tell who the *gringos* are because at least one in the group would be wearing a visor or a money pouch. Even though Tomás had disagreed, he is yet to prove Yiyo wrong. He leans by the railings at the beginning of the queue to wait for Matilde. The *gringos* make gestures at the ticket man inside a booth who looks all angry at them in silence. Tomás could help them. Eva would have helped them. She would have introduced herself and even asked them their names, and she would have had something to small-talk about, and then would have wished them all luck using their first names, and even in all her broken English the *gringos* would have felt important and even better, welcome. She was always saying that when you meet foreigners you represent the place you're from but the truth is that Tomás isn't sure what he'd represent and why he would even have to, since there's no one representing him back. And so he decides not to help them.

He looks up at the clouds starting to gather and he listens to the crowds on top of the hill. Crowds at a distance always sound like everyone in them is shouting real loud but when you get to them they're quiet as hell and most people are alone. Anyway, it looks like it might rain and Tomás wonders if he should just leave because, like the crowds, Matilde's idea is starting to sound better at a distance.

He lights a cigarette and decides to wait until it dies out before leaving. The *gringos* go into the cable car and when it lifts up from the ground they laugh all excited although it's a pretty slow lift. The man wearing overalls inside the ticket booth is looking at Tomás, still frowning, and Tomás avoids him by looking back at the poster-covered wall but when he turns, the man is still staring and Tomás sighs because he always does the same thing, he always looks somewhere else, the sky, his sleeves, his shoes, anything... As if that could make him suddenly invisible to all those he dislikes, those he'd like to see disappear, dead, dying and...

Just as he's stepping on his dead cigarette he sees Matilde running towards him and he waves.

'Hey, so sorry I'm late,' she says with a smile.

'That's fine.' He bends down to kiss her cheek but she doesn't look at him because she's putting her motorcycle helmet inside her backpack, and so he finds himself bent over for nothing.

'There,' she says and leans to kiss him. 'The traffic is crazy. I think there's a student protest coming over to Plaza Italia tonight.'

'They will never be happy,' Tomás says, realising in an instant that since Matilde is younger, she might still believe that no one must ever be happy with what they have, and so he looks back at the man in the booth and then at the wall because he's still there and why hasn't he died, why isn't he…

'I hope not,' she says. 'Not like this at least.'

For a moment neither of them say a thing because both lifts are in the middle of their trip up and down the hill, and they can't even see them with all the clouds and the thick layer of smog that always shrouds the city. Tomás notices the man on the booth is now smiling and staring at Matilde's ass. He lights another cigarette.

'Should we get the tickets?' she asks him.

'It might rain.'

'It doesn't matter.'

'You'll be drenched. The queue down will be so long if it starts raining.'

'I brought my raincoat.'

'I didn't.'

'Come on.' She walks over to the booth and gestures for two tickets and she pays for him and he's glad because he still hasn't remembered to call about that inheritance cash. Tomorrow, he'll do it tomorrow if there are no protests.

'I'll pay you back tomorrow,' he tells her as she gets her change back.

'Who told you I'd see you tomorrow?'

Tomás doesn't know what to say so he steps on the cigarette even though he hasn't finished it.

'I'm messing with you,' she says laughing, and the guy in the booth laughs too and when Tomás looks at him he shrugs with a smile.

The lift is coming down all empty even though it's still real noisy at the top of the hill.

'Awesome, we get to have it all to ourselves. It's been ages since I last took one of these,' Matilde says.

'Yeah, I used to come here a lot.'

'Let's go,' she says as the lift doors open to the sound of the chain pulleys coming to a halt.

They get on and sit down facing each other from opposite sides of the lift. The wooden boards on the floor and the ceiling, the small cracks and the netted windows... The lift, Tomás thinks, the lift does make him feel welcome because it's just as he remembers it.

Tomás looks out the window to the side of the rising hill and Matilde does the same on her side facing the city.

'This side is much better,' she says. 'The buildings will look like stars from here.'

'Maybe, but I can't see much with all the fog.'

'Yeah, I'm pretty sure it'll start raining again soon... Chewing gum?' she asks him, holding out a piece towards him.

'Thanks,' he says, surprised by the fact that it isn't mint-flavoured. But then again, she's so young.

The lift starts to pull and vibrate and then slowly begins to rise. They don't talk and Tomás watches Matilde all still and focused, looking at everything outside turn small as they move up and Tomás wishes he could get closer to Matilde, share the exact frame of the view before her. There's a moment in the lifts where the whole of Santiago becomes visible and he always thought it was sad and beautiful, the way you can only see the whole when you're that far away, because didn't it also mean that being close to something is only knowing a part? Yes, maybe this is why Eva said she knew she could do better, this is why she needed the distance. She did it not in order to lose him but out of love, so that she too could then look at him from afar and see him whole. And he is sure that this must be love. No, not that Hollywood rom-com need to merely know the defects and the mistakes just so characters can then claim to have accepted them. Those are just the parts. It is about knowing and loving even what you reject and could never forgive which is really not the...

But just as they're coming to the middle of the line it starts showering with rain and the pulleys on the ceiling start to creak as the wind hits the lift walls. And then the lift comes to a halt and begins a gentle swing.

'Ah, fuck,' she says smiling at him.

'Best days in Santiago, huh?'

'Yeah… If there's one thing I'll miss in this city it's the way you can't plan anything because nothing ever works like it's supposed to.'

'I know what you mean.'

They can't see the top of the hill or the city from here so they have to look at each other instead.

'The Virgin Mary on top of the hill, they say it's the only virgin in town,' he says, 'what do you think?'

She laughs. 'Probably true, though the fact that there isn't a male virgin statue says something that's way more accurate than that.'

He laughs too. He had never even thought…

'Those are some pretty badass clouds,' she says.

'Yeah.'

'Once, I went on a trip to see a cousin down in Punta Arenas, and he said it rains so much there that he sometimes stops believing the sky's actually blue, you know?'

'I've never been there.'

'It was a joke and all but I think there might be some truth to it, the way you can just forget how things were, or forget how things are behind what you can see. We've had such a long winter. Haven't you ever thought, I mean… When you can't see the sky, that it is not blue, that there is no sun, that they've disappeared and you will never see them again?'

'No, because you know it isn't true.'

'Yeah, I know, but…' she takes the chewing gum out of her mouth and sticks it under her seat and Tomás finds it too disgusting to watch.

'I don't like this middle part in the lifts,' he says.

'It's OK, I've been stuck here once before. There's nothing to be scared of.'

'Yeah,' he says, thinking that, as always, Eva was right. Being here is like disappearing. But even worse, it makes everything around the lift disappear with them too. They can't see anything with all this...

'So when exactly are you leaving?' she asks.

'Soon. I still haven't booked my tickets. I should really book my tickets. You?'

'Next week. I'm pretty nervous about it now. I'm at the stage where I keep adding extra things to my checklist just to cross them out, you know? Like to feel prepared or something. I figured, the more I write down, the less I'll miss, but I'm not sure that's how forgetting stuff works... Apart from that, I've been translating what I write too, so I can use it over there. You know, E.L. Doctorow taught where I'll be in New York.'

'Who's Doctorow?'

'And you call yourself a writer?'

'I write videogames.'

'Oh. Well, you take them pretty seriously if you're going all the way to the Antarctic to do your research. Can't you just Wikipedia the hell out of everything nowadays?'

'I'm actually going to see my girlfriend.'

'She lives there? You meet online or something? Didn't know Tinder had such a large radius.'

'She's working there.'

'Amazing. How long have you two been together?'

'Quite long. Long enough,' he says, and feels his face turn hot so he looks out the window at nothing.

She laughs. 'It's OK, a kiss isn't cheating in my books. It was a pretty shabby kiss too. It really doesn't count.'

'No, no, she's kind of my ex for the time being,' he says, and he notices he's swallowed his chewing gum. 'But it'll be fine.'

'Shit, man, that's tragic… I could write a story about you.'

'Didn't you have a boyfriend too?'

'Yeah, but we broke up. I mean, I'm leaving. There's just no point keeping anything like that,' she says with a sigh. 'It'll just be extra baggage.'

The rain softens and he can hear the crowds on top of the hill again.

'How would you end it?' he asks.

'End what?'

'The story about me.'

'Not sure. However you want me to, I suppose,' she says, and the lift begins to rise again. 'I'd ask you.'

Tomás notices that the ceiling is leaking when a few drops hit his head but he doesn't move because he wants her to know that little things don't bother him and also because it reminds him of his flat. He must get home and fix it before he leaves. His dad had once told him that the problem with his generation is that no one wants to suffer for what they want, that they expect everything to be done by someone else. But he was wrong because Tomás is willing to put up with a wet head just to remind himself of what he needs to fix and this makes him happy.

'You should have brought a coat,' she says, putting hers on. 'It's even raining inside now.'

'I'll be fine.'

'Hey,' she says, coming over to his window and kneeling on his bench, her arms against his. And she doesn't even look at him and it's as if he weren't there at all, until she smiles and… 'We're here.'

· · ·

IDEAS BOOK P. 76:

Another game. A Survival Horror game like *Silent Hill* or *Resident Evil*. We will keep fixed-camera angles, the twisting and turning of straight long corridors with nothing but a few spaced out dissonant keys or a piano with full-on reverb. We will also keep the fact that it is always night, no matter how long you play for. ~~But what we won't keep are the zombies and monsters and no~~ We'll create Freudian monstrosities, literally, like actual cocks trying to eat your actual cock, or round ovaries that scream your mother's name as they get nearer to you, where they will then spew out undead babies with your own face and voice (we'll need to use camera functionality for this). The corridors in the game will be mazes of twisted mirrors, and we will succeed if you try to quit the game out of fear, which won't be easy, because quitting will show you a cut scene of your mother going down on you and biting hard and then you'll bleed out and turn into one of the undead babies and wait, no...

Jaime could not possibly program something so complicated. He just can't get liquids to not look like solids, so blood and spunk are out of the picture. Let's start again.

You are a massive penis and you are the bad guy. It is not Survival Horror but the Horror of Survival, because you need people's lifeblood to keep yourself erect or you'll shrink to public shame and you'll wander the dark cities, a lonely dick, getting numbers at the night club, getting hits on Tinder with Photoshopped pictures of your best angles, updating your Facebook profile with photographs of yourself next to expensive things and expensive people because being a dick needs to remain hidden... And you're good at it, it's in your DNA to hide amongst the crowd you secretly wish were dead or dying by your own doing, just so you can see yourself grow and tense up and almost come out of the joy of winning. You might meet other dicks along the way. They drive sports cars and segways and call themselves 'entrepreneurs' and will give you business cards when all you asked them for was to serve you a dry martini at the bar. And then you'll go to a jazz café and you have no idea what jazz is all about, but there will be plenty of other dicks there who will tell you 'it's about feeling, man, it's about breaking time and melody, it's just so hard to explain it. It's something you either have or you don't. It's about sadness, sadness, sadness and depth of character.' But then you get bored of those dicks too. They're too small and all you want is to meet a dick that can at least challenge you, send you to hell, think that you're lame and crooked, because now you miss not being the largest dick in the room.

So you get a tip from one of the little dicks at the jazz café. 'Go to a math-rock gig,' he says, 'that's the real underground music scene nowadays, and there you'll meet much larger dicks.' After saying this, he thanks you because you made him grow a little. Though because he thanked you, he shrinks back in an instant.

So now you're at the math-rock gig and it's full of amazing cock pillars wearing hoodies and skinny jeans, dicks pretending to love the broken assonance of songs that start and stop for no reason at all, and you feel yourself grow just by being here. But no one here talks to you. They would shrink if they did. No one here even looks at you. Everyone's about your size. You now wish you hadn't taken the tip. You wish you weren't as big. You wish you'd never been on Facebook and Tinder or met with the French bartenders pretending to be entrepreneurs. But you stay despite all this because you know, just as everyone at the gig knows, that leaving will have you shrink to your starting size, and then no one will even notice you at work or on your way home, the only two activities you'll be able to do.

And then, a depressed and lonely dick, you start to go to bars on your own, to nightclubs, and then Facebook, Tinder, but nothing works. It's just not the same the second time round. You're older. There's no one like you. And now the bars and concert halls are filled with assholes.

.   .   .   .

When they get off the lift they pass by a long queue of people waiting to go back down. A guy in blue overalls has organised them by height, like a poster of human evolution. And the woman in the booth shakes her head, and the people in the queue look all mad at Tomás as if it were his fault the lifts had stopped for so long or that it had started to rain, and he whispers 'Sorry' to an older woman whose oversized handbag is in *his* way, but she doesn't move or answer so he pushes against her and she curses something at him that he doesn't hear.

They walk over to the souvenir shop and Matilde tightens the hood of her coat. People are running around with their handbags and backpacks and even plastic supermarket bags on their heads to avoid the rain. In Santiago no one knows what to do when it rains and there are no roofs to shelter under, and everyone suddenly forgets it's just water that's pouring down from the sky and that's it's only there for a moment.

Matilde starts to walk towards the steps that lead to the top of the hill. A group of young people run past them wearing masks of Piñera's face with little holes instead of eyes. Matilde turns to them as they pass by.

'I told you there would be protests today,' she says, and Tomás nods and lights up a cigarette.

They walk up the stone steps and when they're at the top, they lean against the metal railing that encircles the summit. She holds the magnifying telescope beside them up against her face, knowing that without a coin it will all be darkness.

'I can't believe I'm finally leaving this place,' she says, letting the telescope fall back in its place. Tomás nods with a smile because all they can see across the fog are the faded lights from the skyscrapers.

'Although my dad says you never really leave home,' she adds. 'Come,' she says, walking back to the last stone step.

She takes her coat off and she places it flat on the step and then sits on it.

'Let's watch the lights one last time,' she says.

'We can't really see any though,' he says, sitting down anyway.

'Well, we can imagine them then. It's not like we don't know where they're meant to be.'

And then there's silence. No crowds, no kids with masks, not even the hum of the lifts and it's all just rain and Matilde's foot lightly tapping on the steps to no particular rhythm. Or at least nothing that Tomás can follow.

'Are you sure you don't want to put your coat back on?' he asks, flicking down his cigarette.

'It's just water,' she says, looking down at the missing city, 'it's just water and it doesn't last.' And then he holds her hand.

18

I Do Not Regret This Journey

She said she'd come and pick him up on her motorbike in the evening. Tomás said that he'd rather take the metro or the bus, that he's used to it, but she just answered that it wouldn't bother her. And after holding hands for so long on the hill, Tomás thought it best to just keep quiet and accept, because she said 'This is nice' even though they had been soaking with rain and Tomás didn't want to spoil the moment for her.

But now, inside the tent and wearing his ski goggles and gardening gloves, he's not too sure it's such a good idea. No one can look manly sitting behind a girl on a motorcycle, grabbing her with your legs spread out just under hers. He knows it's macho bullshit and he knows that's such a dickish thing to worry about and Eva would give him hell (and he'd have another frozen feathered chicken in his freezer) for thinking like this but in a way he likes to know that he's still young and stupid enough to care about stuff like that, which he calls his 'dignity' but in fact is something much, much less...

He should probably put on some trousers or at least check the time but the sleeping bag's comfortable and every time he moves, it makes a long 'shhh...' as if he were telling someone to be quiet. And then he stops moving and everything does go quiet, and he thinks it funny that even when Eva's not with him, and even without a job, he still finds a way to order himself around. Again, such a dickish...

The trousers can wait. He gets up and phone-lights his way into his smoking window, where he now decided to keep his cigarettes loose and in a line. Spreading them out will make him notice how much he smokes and make him feel guilty, so that he can then find it easier to want to stop. He takes his gloves off, turns the radio on and opens the window, hoping it's still raining as hard as it had been last night. It isn't, but then again rain is never hard, there's just either a lot or very little of it. It's all the same really, and the streets are just as empty.

He smokes and leans out so that his goggles can catch a few raindrops in order to test them. They work, nothing touches his face and all the lights outside become circles of gold blurring into each other and it reminds him of last night, when the sky cleared away for a few minutes, and from the hill Santiago became dots of wet colour, dispersed and untidy like a teenager's bedroom, before disappearing again behind the fog.

He looks behind him at his room, still without a bed and the clothes just piling up but he won't start tidying now because Matilde might arrive at any moment. Still, when did he stop caring about himself like this? People always say that when you're single you should enjoy having your own time again, to do all the things you lost touch with over the years: videogames, clubbing, getting hammered, seeing old friends you no longer care about so you can care about them again, learning to cook, achieving something at work, shaving for yourself. But he knows he stopped doing these things because he never really loved them anyway and Eva was the way out. Then again, he might not want to start any of these activities because he's not really single and that is just yet another...

On the radio, the speaker is introducing Fármacos's new album, and Tomás lights up a new cigarette. Yiyo's on the radio. Yiyo's on the fucking radio.

'What are your influences?' the radio woman asks him.

'I don't really believe in influences,' Yiyo starts. 'I wanted to add,' he continues, 'that I'm selling a great drum kit, if anyone's…'

Tomás rolls his eyes and turns off the radio. He should have known this would happen. He should have kept playing music with Yiyo. Then maybe he too could have stopped believing in influences.

As he flicks his cigarette out the window someone knocks at the door. Tomás pulls out a pair of black jeans from the pile and when he puts them on he fills his right pocket with loose cigarettes. He opens the door and Matilde is standing there, wearing a black dress and an open motorcycle helmet.

'Hi,' she laughs.

'Hi,' he says.

'I brought you a helmet but it looks like you have that covered.'

'Oh,' he says, taking his ski goggles off and throwing them behind him.

'Your flat's still a mess,' she says looking in.

'I've been packing, getting things ready,' he says grabbing his wallet and stepping into the doorway. 'Let's go.'

Downstairs, Matilde gets on her bike and hands Tomás a helmet hanging from one of the handles. It's pink with green lightning bolts on the sides. Her motorcycle's an old blue Vespa and it only has one mirror, the left one, and a pretty small space for him to sit on.

'How do I sit here? Both legs to one side?' he asks, putting on his helmet.

'No, just spread your legs around me and hold on.'

'Really? Are you sure? I've seen some people—'

'Yeah, come on, just get on.'

He gets up on it and grabs her from the belly. She starts the bike and it begins to vibrate and sound like machineguns do in movies and he holds on harder as he slides down to the sides.

267

'Shouldn't you have two mirrors?' he asks her.

'Nah, don't worry, that was the car's fault, not mine. You can tell me if anything comes up from the right. Hold on!'

They start their way into the Kennedy Avenue where Matilde speeds her way, despite all the rain, between cars and lorries and buses.

'Where are we going?' he shouts.

'We're going to say goodbye.'

'What? Who to?'

'It's a surprise! Hold on and be quiet or you'll make us crash,' she says, before passing between two taxis.

They hadn't talked as they held hands last night, not about the rain, not about their upcoming plans, not about other people, not even about their hands. In fact, she had broken off the handholding as easily as she had grabbed onto him, and maybe things have changed beyond recognition here in Santiago, since touching someone, holding onto them, had always meant to Tomás some kind of promise, a lead up to going home and... But come on, none of that was ever true. She stood up and wiped her face with a smile and started her way back down to the lifts. Tomás stayed sitting down to see if she would wait but she didn't. And maybe it was the noise of the rain taking hold of everything around them, making the scenery an indistinct late night TV static screen, or maybe she just wanted to be alone, but from there all the way down back to the town, it was as if he hadn't been there at all.

From the motorbike the city is one large dimmer lamp, and it might be the helmet or the speed but all the lights look the same, faint and stretched all the way to the sky, red and purple amber rising up like thin and tall concrete trees that end in complete darkness. It's funny that all it takes is the small engine from a Vespa bike, one girl, and the whole city just dies out.

Matilde turns away from the avenue and into little streets, and she cuts through traffic jams, people on pavements, even an old lady walking her dog. This is why Tomás will never drive. Eva said it would make him feel independent, just like her, and he told her that it wasn't environmentally friendly and that for someone who claimed to care so much about global warming, she should have known better. But he knows better too, that the real reason for never learning to drive is that he'd feel like he's bothering everyone he overtakes, that he'd always drive behind other people, that he'd always be so fucking boring.

'You should be careful,' he shouts to her.

'Don't worry, I've done this hundreds of times. Hold on!'

On the pavement she drives past kiosks and large crowds of people having dinner on small tables with umbrellas, old people playing chess with oversized pieces on black and white floor tiles, and a fried *sopaipilla* salesman with his trolley, and a guy taking a piss right in front of him. How does she do it? How do others do it to care so little, to just speed past everything? His problem, he thinks, has always been that he cares too much. Jesus, did he just think that out... But then again, he has so much to lose. He holds on tight and Matilde's belly goes hard.

She turns and the little street opens to a broader one with stone tiles and the bike rattles until they stop at a traffic light.

'We're nearly there,' she says.

'OK,' he answers, and he notices that there's a moth standing still on Matilde's back. How annoying it must be to be attracted to all the lights, to sit there and then wake up somewhere different, all because of a light. But then again, at night and at a distance everyone can look like a tree branch and he imagines her full of butterflies, none of them ever coming back home.

A young guy and girl at the traffic lights start throwing each other fire-lit torches and juggling them under their legs and behind their backs. Then, they walk up to car windows for change and when they get to Tomás, he says he's sorry but the guy just stands there looking at him as if he'd said nothing at all so Tomás pretends to look for money in his pocket until the light turns green.

Tomás closes his eyes and a few minutes of driving pass and then, suddenly, they come to a stop and all the noise comes back.

'We're here,' she says.

He takes his helmet off but they are nowhere in particular, just another side street in Santiago centre, and Tomás wonders whether, maybe, just maybe, she is as boring as he is.

She chains her bike to a lamppost, takes his helmet and puts it inside a box at the back. Walking to the end of the street, Tomás starts to hear someone playing a *cueca*, people shouting and laughing and he hopes her surprise, the whole reason they crossed half of Santiago, isn't just another party.

But, as always, he's right about the wrong things. They stand outside a large black double-door and Matilde rings the bell and it buzzes open. Inside, the music's real loud and the tapping noises upstairs sound like microwave popcorn. They walk up a staircase, the handle lined with miniature plastic Chilean flags, upside down crosses and signs that say 'Happy 18th of September' even though it's still only August. It's dark upstairs, but Matilde walks into a corridor just as fast and stops at the end by another door.

'Sounds busy,' she tells Tomás.

'Yeah, what is it?'

'It's a *fonda* party. I know it's early but…'

She opens the door and it's full of people and noise. Most in the crowd are goths all in black but there are also a few hipsters with black-framed glasses, beards and Nazi-youth haircuts. In the middle of the room, couples are dancing *cueca*, waving handkerchiefs and all (some even have their ponchos on), and they stomp on the floor and the crowd around them clap to the rhythm directed by an old dude playing guitar and singing on a stool on the stage in the corner, and another guy slapping a wooden box in between his legs. There's also an older man with an accordion hanging from his neck, but he's waving a glass of wine and shouting the song instead of playing.

In the middle, there's a table with bottles of wine and *pisco* and *chicha* and Coke and plates of fried empanadas. Matilde walks up to the table and Tomás follows her. In all the parties of his youth, Tomás always somehow ended up alone by the drinks table. This is why he can now make perfect *piscolas* and even mojitos. Or at least he could, until he discovered that he had to pretend, like he's sure most men do, to enjoy dancing and talking to strangers just so he could get laid, because people like to see that everyone likes the same things, that they are willing to give up their desires for the greater desire to have them. And so when Eva said they should dance at a party, that all her friends and their boyfriends were dancing, he just said 'after you.'

He serves himself a heavy *piscola* and then makes one for Matilde but with less *pisco*.

'Here, a light one for you, since you're driving and all,' he says.

'Thanks,' she says smiling, taking the bottle of *pisco* and pouring herself more until the Coke becomes almost transparent.

Tomás looks around to see if anyone's smoking but no one is.

'Can I smoke here?' he asks Matilde.

'Hm?' she looks at him and then behind him where Jesús is standing and drinking Cristal from the bottle. She puts her drink on the table. 'Hey Jesús! This looks awesome,' she says, hugging him.

'Thanks,' he says, adjusting his Tarot card-inspired rings on his right hand.

'Hey man,' Jesús says to Tomás. 'Didn't know you'd come.' He laughs and grabs his shoulder, balancing himself against him.

'Hi, hi,' Tomás says. 'Can I smoke in here?'

'Dude, it's a Satanist party,' Jesús says to him, taking Tomás's *piscola* and downing it.

'Does that mean yes?'

Jesús laughs and Tomás lights a cigarette.

'If you could put some money in the bucket over there, that'd be great. The astronomer in Vicuña says he'll soon find out exactly when the world will end so we need to keep raising funds.'

'Sure, of course,' Matilde says with a smile. 'Where's Lucas?'

Jesús laughs and turns to face the dance floor.

'Look at him, just look at him. It's like he's doing the robot or something. He hasn't stopped since he arrived.'

Matilde laughs because Lucas is dancing all stiff with an old goth who's a real good dancer, but he still swings his handkerchief and stomps and his shirt's half open and the sweat on his chest shines blue and red with the disco lights. Matilde and Tomás put some change in the bucket.

'Why organise a *fonda* so early?' Tomás asks Jesús as he makes himself another *piscola*.

'Well, we want it all done by Christmas, right? And we'll start selling shit,' he shows Tomás his rings, 'in October. The earlier you party the more money you make, and people give more when there's a reason to party,' he says between sighs, and then he goes to the dance floor and starts dancing in front of another dude with a tight necklace full of spikes. Matilde laughs too.

Tomás looks at Lucas doing the robot *cueca*. He will definitely get laid because if a girl stays with you while you look like that, then it's a done deal. The song ends and everyone claps and Lucas gets a kiss. Even without any music he just keeps on dancing.

'Oh – my – God,' Matilde says, laughing harder.

Tomás downs his drink and gets another. Then, as always, he has nothing to talk about so he downs four *piscolas* more and he leans on the drinks table and neither of them say a thing. But then the guitars start a sad slower tune and the guy sitting on the wooden box starts playing a pan flute and then they sing:

272

A country I'm leaving with lost,
A country I'm leaving with lost.
When I sleep it appears to me,
In my dreams like an enemy.
As if in my chest there struck
A sea that gives into silence,
And to my eyes there looms past,
The life I just lived.

. . .

IDEAS BOOK P. 81:

A sports game. ~~Isn't it odd that they're called sports games when really you're binging on Doritos and~~ What makes them so popular? What makes people buy pretty much the same game every year? *Fifa* 11, 12, 13, they will go on forever. But the box says it all. The last two years have featured Messi on the box art. They're popular because unlike platformers and adventure games, they're a constant reference to the real world. When you buy a *Fifa* game, you buy into ~~corruption and tax avoidance~~ becoming Messi, into his ability to make otherworldly plays and improbable pirouettes. You buy your way into becoming players that outperform you in every way.

And how will our version be any different? ~~How will it change the game?~~ Well, we'll take the realism one step further. We won't be able to afford official patents (it will be, after all, a 'free' mobile game) and so we'll simulate school sports instead. It will only feature one mode: Career Mode. You will be given a random character with a set of random attributes (it has to seem random but really you'll be a fat nerd with acne issues no matter what you do) and no one will like you. The taller, better-looking kids will never pick you for their teams. You will be everyone's last choice. They will roll their eyes at you when no one else remains by the schoolyard wall. Your jersey is too tight (they only had up to XL) and you look like a fucking burrito, a burrito limping this way and that until they put you as goalkeeper, but only because you take up so much fucking space... And still the other team scores a goal, one where the ball hits you on the shins before going in, and you can't hide it, because you got those red fat-people slap marks which take bloody ages to melt away back to skin colour. We could even use a remodelled version of Bimbo the elephant for the protagonist. It might save Jaime some time.

And then, just when you think things will never improve, a new kid arrives, a French kid, and SHIT THERE IS A GOD, this kid is twice your size, twice the Bimbo. He is so fat his steps leave a low hum echoing in the Andes, so fat your nerdy science classmates find him to be an interesting source of negative energy, a walking stellar devourer, a black hole with its own gravitational pull that is so strong the moon looks a little larger tonight, and shit you feel cool, shit you ARE cool. This is you:

You: THE SHIT   Him: dookie

And no one makes fun of you anymore. The controls that at first seemed so stiff are now smooth extensions of yourself. You score goals. Your friends, FRIENDS, tell you that they're going out for drinks after the game and they invite you, and fuck it, you go and you get hammered and all because of that fat fucking bastard that you now find yourself hating as much, no, MORE than your FRIENDS do, and you want him dead... And on the next game you shoot a real hard fireball shot to his face and *connard!* you burn him up, leaving behind only the puddle of goo that was his life.

And you turn around and everyone's cursing at you in French, laughing at your fat feet full of ash.

·   ·   ·

And then the guitars get loud and the pan flute blasts high notes and Tomás can't breathe, he can't drink, and all the people moving about shining in frozen poses with the strobes of light, all of it makes him want to cry. But he doesn't, because just at that moment, when the lyrics get repeated louder *As if in my chest there struck* and the dancers join in, *A sea that gives into silence* Matilde taps him on the shoulder and faces him with two paper napkins hanging from her hand. *The life I just lived.*

'Let's go,' she says, and she takes his hand and walks straight into the middle of the crowd. He's dizzy and she gives him a napkin and starts dancing in front of him so he starts swinging the napkin and stomping to what he believes is the rhythm, and he closes his eyes and hears the crowd shouting the lyrics and he feels light, so light he could disappear. And suddenly it makes sense to him that The End of the World is this, it is here starting already, a *cueca* always ending and everyone singing and dancing and then disappearing and then...

Matilde turns with her napkin behind her and then comes closer to him, smiling and looking at him. They switch places as soon as the singer shouts *Vuelta! Turn!* and everyone else does the same. Then, Lucas and Jesús come dancing next to them and Lucas hugs Matilde and Tomás is left dancing with Jesús, who also looks at him with a smile.

All four of them stomp their way through several songs, and then Tomás goes back to the drinks table to light another cigarette and have another *piscola*. He's sweating and he wishes he could be home, naked and inside the tent. He looks at Matilde dancing with Jesús and Lucas, still clapping and singing and Tomás thinks that she's beautiful, her black dress spreading out at the knees when she turns as if she had wings, and this is beautiful, this is what it's like to be young.

After another *cueca* ends and two *piscolas* later, Matilde appears next to him.

'Everything OK?' she asks.

'Yeah, I'm totally going to quit smoking after this.'

'He's wasted,' Jesús says behind Matilde, who is also finding it hard to stand without swaying backwards.

'I'll never smoke again!' Tomás shouts. 'I'll never be boring.'

Matilde and Jesús laugh.

'Thank you for the surprise. But I'm going to have to go home,' Tomás tells Matilde.

'No, no, your surprise comes now. Let's go. I just wanted to party one last time with them, to say goodbye, you know?'

'I know!' he says.

'Let's go,' she says waving at Jesús, and she takes Tomás by the arm and they walk out of the room. The stairs are hard and Matilde walks slow next to Tomás, still holding onto him.

'Thank you,' he says, and when they reach the bottom, he leans towards her and tries to kiss her but she moves him into a hug instead.

'Sorry,' he says, now feeling so sober he could... 'It's just, the dark stairs, drunk, you know?'

'It's OK, don't worry, I know.'

They come out of the house and the streets are empty and quiet and Tomás's ears are ringing and his mouth's real dry and he's cold and tries to walk straight along the lines in the pavement.

They get to the Vespa and Matilde takes his helmet out of the box at the back and he puts it on. When he breathes out, he can smell the booze and it makes him sick. He swallows hard.

'Don't worry, we'll get there quickly. It'll be worth it, I promise.'

'OK,' he says, concentrating on his swallowing.

He sits behind her and they tremble with the engine.

The darkened lights, the spots beaming past like shooting stars all silent and gold, the stone bridges arching over the Mapocho. He can hear it, he thinks, he can hear the river of shit, but it's really just the fact that he knows it all too well, but he's still surprised that at night it looks blue. At night it becomes a real river, that is, just like any other river.

They get to Plaza Italia and Matilde parks next to a lamppost facing the *Feria Artesanal*.

'Come,' she says, opening a thick padlock with a key.

They walk into the long outdoor corridors where all the shop counters are now covered by tin curtains that rattle in the wind. They get to Abdul's shop. Matilde lifts up the curtain and walks in. Inside and in the dark everything looks different. The shelves that in the day are so full it's impossible to find anything now look empty, invisible, and they're all alike, just stands holding shadows pushing against one another. And the hanging crucifixes and rosaries and the tiny wind-bells sway slowly but he can still hear them. They sound like wood creaking about to break.

'Here,' she says by the red door in the corner, the one Abdul keeps locked.

'I don't think we're meant to go in there.'

'It's fine,' she says, showing him a lock of Abdul's hair with the key attached to it.

She goes in and Tomás follows her.

'Close the door.'

'OK,' he says and closes it. In the dark and with the damp heat inside the room, Tomás thinks for a moment that he's home in his flat, and that the different door at the entrance, like the river, can change at night but inside everything's always the same.

.   .   .

What is it about the beach that makes it so inviting? Is it the waves? There are studies out there suggesting that the frequency of the crashing waves, their tonal evolution from the low fall of water to the high sizzle of the foam is not unlike the sonic transformations we undergo the moment we're born. And so the sea is as close as we'll ever get to birth again, the beginning of it all, the first connections of your inner wiring, the creation of your very own universe. But, again, what about the beach, the part that the water refuses to touch? Why build houses, no, whole towns, why watch the tides in and out, maybe even the sunset, if what we really want is to drown under the crushing immensity of our first memories?

Tomás is looking at the beach house with Eva's old telescope. It has a front porch with hanging flowerpots arranged under two neat windows. Daisies, there are a crap-ton of daisies in the pots and lining the walls of the house.

'We could stay there for a while,' he tells her.

'If that's where the sea is taking us, then sure, fine by me,' she says.

The ship keeps getting nearer, breaking ice as it does so. The noise is unbearable. It's the volume, the tension, it's what an amplified tooth-removal surgery would sound like, and so Tomás feels it at the ends of his mouth.

They are too close to the island for the ship to keep going. They will have to row their way there with one of the safety boats that Serge keeps on board. Tomás has never had to row before. 'It's simple,' Eva explains, straightening her back against the front of the little wooden boat. 'You pull back, use your legs, stretch your legs and then use that weight to move your arms. It's not really your arms doing it all, it's the things you do before the oar even touches the water that count.' Tomás does it, out of synch, and they start to turn instead of advancing. Eva just watches him. She believes in him, in his capacity to get them both wherever she wants to be, which is where he also...

He's getting the hang of it now. He stirs past dead ice, past the bulks of rock that stick out like black frozen tumours, like gathered piles of ash in a smoker's basement, secret and unnecessary, and he rows until his back aches, his arms ache, his butt and his legs ache, and what level of pain do you have to be in before you can say that you, the whole of you, your very soul or any of that shit that you believe is located at your very core, how much pain until you can announce to the world that you hurt, that your soul aches?

Tomás has only been rowing for twenty minutes or so and he's ready to give up. But Eva motivates him, 'Go,' she says, 'we're so close,' but Tomás has no way of knowing how close they really are. She told him to keep rowing and to keep facing the ship they left behind with Serge waving at them and making an O, a U, and an I with his arms. Then a C and… 'We're so close.'

Suddenly, they hit land. It's a surprise to Tomás that when he turns around, the once tiny island is now just part of a much larger world, where ancient civilisations have come and gone, where strange animals he's probably never seen before will have evolved according to their instinctive desire to make even the most secluded of places their homes. But even then he knows, just as much as she does, that right now they are completely alone.

'Look at that house,' she says. 'That's our house. We can get settled in and keep searching for the holes in the ice from here.'

'That's our house,' he repeats.

'It has daisies.'

'And a front porch.'

'You could write your stories here.'

'And you could live yours.'

'Right, but first I'll make us something to eat.'

Tomás takes a *Zelda* beach towel from a stack of *Zelda* beach towels in the corner of their bedroom. He lays it flat on the sand and takes his IDEAS book out. He'll write something about her, something better than *Zelda*, and as he begins to brainstorm ideas about saving people, saving Eva, he notices that the ice caps are breaking, splitting with a thick and dark crack that leads straight into the setting sun which this time, he just knows it, will set for good.

·   ·   ·

But then Matilde lights an old gas lamp. Surrounding the room is a shelf filled with cassette tapes, old cameras and reels of film. And in the centre, there's a red couch and a film projector on a coffee table. The projector is facing a white bed sheet spread out over a clothes hanger line attached to both ends of the room. On the floor there are old toys, a train set, farm animals and plastic soldiers, and old rubber truck wheels, like those in the shop, piled up in the corners.

'What is this?' he asks.

'My dad made this room when Mum died. He used to be a filmmaker. I mean, that's what he said when he was young and she was still around but he never finished a film. He's been trying to make one ever since. Pretty sad isn't it? The way old people never move on, and become so ashamed of it they lock it all up.'

'Yeah,' he says, stepping carefully past the toys on the floor to sit on the couch.

'Anyway, I found this for you,' she says, showing him an old reel of film.

'What is it?'

'I told you, it's a surprise.'

'OK.'

'But first,' she says, walking to a stack of shelved old records. 'Stravinsky or Max Richter?'

'What?' Tomás asks back, not knowing who the fuck Max Richter is.

'Just answer the question.'

He supposes that like any question between men and women who do not know each other well, it is a trick question. He also supposes that it has to be about a contrast, for the answer to mean completely opposite things, or she wouldn't ask it. In fact, he doesn't know much about Stravinsky either, but he thinks he was most active in the 20s or near the 20s, or was it maybe... Matilde is asking him how old he is, how old he feels, if he is also active and part of *his* 20s, or if he relates to the classics as if they were his contemporaries, but none of it matters. Listen to Stravinsky's Elegy on cello in Santiago and the streets will still cry out songs meant for Swiss Springs and somehow make sense and...

'Max Richter,' he says.

'I fucking knew it,' she says.

He will have to hear the city in another way now, in ways meant by Max, and whether the guy was barely a caveman hitting skins with bones or a trendy twenty-first century German electronica genius, it doesn't change the fact that the streets will still sing HERE – NOW – ALONE – OLD whenever you are here, now, alone and old.

And she knew it. She fucking knew it. And what does that even mean? Should he have surprised her? He remembers that Eva once said that you can only surprise someone once you really know them. She didn't say how long this took or how you decide you really know someone. He asked her. He said, 'Surely when you first meet someone everything's a surprise. Don't you think this is why they call it honeymoon phase? Surely you fall in love because you like the surprises. They like books? Wow, you do too. They like coffee black and out of an expensive capsule machine? Wow, so do you. You like fucking from behind because it's rough but do not mean any disrespect? Wow, you are soul mates!' He had said all of this during breakfast and Eva just watched him as she spread Bonne Maman apricot jam on her halved baguette. She paused for a few seconds, sat up straight, and then she said, 'You don't know the difference between discovery and surprise, Tomás.' She only ever used his name when he'd done something wrong, and it made him feel like a child. 'You might never understand it,' she continued, and he intervened. He said, 'But what about all those forty-year-olds, those tired, sad-looking sleepwalkers who can only ever talk about getting up, getting their children up, going to work, what they had for lunch – always the same – and how they sleep – always badly? What about them? How are they supposed to be surprised?' Eva looked at her halved toasted baguette and put it back on her small plate. That's right, he took her appetite away. Then she said, 'After all those years, what people miss are the surprises, not the discovery,' and she stood up and left him to pay for their uneaten breakfast.

Matilde fixes the needle on the record player and Max Richter comes on in a dark ambient hum. She puts the film reel in an opening on the side of the projector and turns it on, and then switches the lights off and sits by him on the sofa, covering him and herself with an alpaca blanket. It's a silent film, and it starts with writing:

> It is possible to only give a brief mention
> of the hardships of that perilous
> journey down the great ice-fall.

Onscreen: a black and white ship full of people and horses and dogs. The sailors are dancing while the ship remains stationed by the harbour and people outside are waving handkerchiefs like one massive *cueca* dance by the sea. Eva must have shown everyone her new ballet moves on her way there, she joined a ballet school and... Then there's a sailor getting a haircut and he laughs as the hairdresser passes him a mirror because he just lost all of his hair.

> Oh, I think he should stick to grooming the horses
> before trying his hand with the Captain.
> They were the happiest days for the company.
> And then they left New Zealand and there was
> silence and the loneliness of the vast ocean.

The image of the ship fades out and the title screen shows up: THE GREAT WHITE SILENCE. Tomás is worried. Not because of the silence or the vastness of the ocean. No, what he's worrying about is the fact that there are only men on the ship, and they're all good dancers and then there's the loneliness of the ocean which, like the loneliness of the city, would break anyone given enough time in those circumstances and then love and fucking would become a logical... Eva on a ship full of men and full of loneliness, like anyone else, would find it easier to forget about him and then she had stopped smoking, got herself new... Of course, he's worrying for nothing because he's pretty sure she left on a plane, or even better (because it's less crowded), a helicopter.

> During the next ten days, they had
> to fight for their lives. More than once they lost
> their way, and found themselves in ice that
> for miles was broken by pressure
> into the most appalling confusion.

'Imagine how scary it must have been to get completely lost out there on your own,' Matilde says.

'Yeah, but it's kind of their fault for leaving.' Max Richter is still looping the wave of piano notes. The melody never changes. Is there a melody? The volume, what they can and can't hear, the direction of the notes and the origin of arpeggios, that's always changing.

She laughs but he really means it. Why must people always try to prove how far they can go? Is it because they can then come back and tell you that you've always had everything and that you should appreciate even the things you hate because actually, they're not so bad, not as bad as the EXTREME things they've done. Must we really have a death wish so we can then say we, and everyone else, should love life? That's right, he'd been right all along. Eva left just so she could then come back and tell him, as she always did, that he complained for nothing, that gas bills don't matter. But then she'll say that she actually even missed them on her time away. And just like you can't argue with the dead, you can't argue with those who come back from nearly dying. All these sailors, all these male sailors, when they got home, they spent their time proving that everyone else's lives were small and petty and stupid and they can prove it by preaching the unarguable sadness of the sea.

'I bet they missed their homes so much. I'll miss Lucas and Jesús and my dad so much. It'll be hard,' she says. 'You know something, I'll even miss you.'

'So don't go,' he says, 'stay here.'

'There's nothing here for me to do though. I can't stay here my whole life.'

> At times it was almost impossible to find a way
> out of the awful turmoil in which they found
> themselves. Then, we saw one solitary penguin
> Roosting in the rays of the midnight sun.

'You can't possibly know that,' he says, 'that there's nothing here for you.'

'Don't judge me. You're leaving too. And at least I'm leaving because I worked my ass off to leave. I want stuff to write about. You're just going for a girl.'

'That's not entirely true,' he says, wondering what the hell he can say next but he doesn't have to say anything because it's dark and no one wants a long and full explanation in front of a movie screen. He looks at her with the lights of the film making shadows under her eyes and under her nose and mouth and she's looking straight at the screen, so beautiful and dark she could be anyone and Tomás could kiss her. But then, the loud noise of waves breaking against the ship fills the secret room.

> If the ship failed to break the ice,
> she was put in a stand some distance away.
> Then, with more way on her,
> she would ram again, and usually split it.

The ship breaks the ice and sails past the cracks leaving behind it nothing but floating ice cubes in what used to look like part of a whole continent. Tomás doesn't understand how such a miserable sight could make anyone happy.

Matilde's holding her knees up to her chest and she's so still.

'Sorry,' Tomás says. 'I think I'm just nervous about leaving. But it looks like an amazing place. Thanks for showing me this. It makes me want to go even more and you're right, there's nothing for us to do here in Santiago.'

She looks at him and smiles but Tomás knows that despite her meaning well, she's smiling because she made his life here seem pointless even before she's even left.

> We took risks, we knew we took them.
> Things have come out against us and
> therefore we have no cause for complaint
> but bow to the will of providence.
> We are weak, writing is difficult,
> But for my own sake I do not regret
> this journey...

And then the film cuts to a handwritten note left by some sailor who died trapped in a snowstorm saying the same thing: I DO NOT REGRET THIS JOURNEY...

'Tragic, huh? It kind of bummed me out,' Matilde says as the violins kick in mixed with Max Richter's piano. The film comes to an end without even a credits screen. Then, the projector comes to a stop too and the end of its hum leaves the dark room feeling empty.

'Thank you,' he says.

'I thought you'd appreciate it. How did it make you feel?' she asks, lifting the needle from the record player.

How did it make him feel? The ship leaving, the on-board dancing, the splitting ice and the lonely ocean, how did it all make him feel? He has no fucking clue but he...

'I feel like I'm there already,' he says.

She takes his hand again and they hold hands in silence for a few minutes.

'What are you going to do now?'

'What are you going to do?' she asks back, looking at him with the same shadows on her face as before.

'I'm going to go home.'

'Then I'll go home with you.'

19

The Blue Drum Kit

So you like thinking you're special, right? You like thinking that some-how your interpretation of the activities you share with others, the same daily routines, is different to everyone else's, yeah? You love that, admit it, no one here will listen, and you love it even more when there's music and the singer really gets you, you really get them, but no one else does. Now imagine you want to tell the girl or guy you're fucking exactly what you do and don't like. You love the weirdest things, you tell yourself. If you were honest you'd say you like blowjobs, handjobs, fucking from behind, slight pain, eating pussy, having them eat your pussy, choking, being choked, unprotected cocks, anal, and big firm tits, big firm cocks, and they ask you what you like again and you tell them it's just too weird to say, that they'd think you're a creep, a maniac, a sociopath, but this only makes it more interesting and they keep asking you and asking you and won't let go... So you tell them, you give them the whole list, and it turns out they like the same things as you do and tell you that every person they've been with before likes those same things too. And now you wish you hadn't said anything, and you realise you don't even remember the lyrics to the songs you call your own, only the choruses, and you let some random tune playing in the background dictate the movement of your hips, which are the same as every hip in the planet, so you stop altogether and they look puzzled. You keep still. A minute, two minutes pass by, but you don't move and they look even more puzzled. Then they laugh and tell you that no one in the world fucks like you now.

So Tomás doesn't wait to ask and Matilde doesn't stop to answer.

.   .   .

IDEAS BOOK P. 86:
Another game. Though this time it's a RHYTHM game. Like all of these types of games, it will have you quickly react to an animated screen, which varies according to a soundtrack or rhythmic setting, and you have to press a button or a sequence of buttons in perfect timing in order to win.

Guitar Hero is probably the most popular example, and it became the best-selling one for a reason. It completely took you off the controller and gave you a guitar-shaped input, a toy, so that you really fucking felt awesome clicking the colours of a fret board along with those on the screen. When you rocked out in *Guitar Hero*, when you were winning, the crowd would go mental, clapping and cheering as you shook your plastic fake guitar. When you were losing, the amp feedbacked and the crowd booed you and became restless. And so the design behind *Guitar Hero* isn't to simulate playing an actual guitar (unless you're a total retard you would never compare the two), but to simulate the high you get out of giving the masses exactly what they want, at the precise moment in which they want it. That's what true pop stars do.

So our version, which will be 'free' on mobile platforms (though every song will be halved and you'll have to pay to unlock them whole), will need you to touch the screen in time with the music. ~~We'll also sell you a plastic guitar to play it while you ride the bus~~ We won't be able to simulate rock and roll stardom or anything involving a stage. Jaime

288

just won't be able to do it. In fact, it will involve the opposite. You will listen to your protagonist's own music, and you will tap your finger to the rhythm of frustration, self-doubt, suicidal tendencies, alcohol abuse, drug addiction, dentist appointments, doctor's appointments, plastic surgery, photo shoots, dairy allergies, more photo shoots, memories of when you were NOBODY, photos, memories of when you decided NOBODY was just not good enough, pics, memories of your now dead parents, snap snap, then of the girl you fancied at school, and meeting said girl in the present and finding her the ugliest person alive, and shopping for guns, learning to shoot guns, playing Russian roulette on your own open mouth, and laughing at your luck, and then getting on cabs with nowhere to go, and going to expensive clubs and buying others drinks because they recognised you, and then getting another cab and the crowd cheers when you come out of it, and you're unsure of just how much money you left the driver, and then entering the concert hall, and more cheering, more photo shoots, and the game ends with one last tap of the screen, just as you enter the stage, which if Jaime could program it, would have beams of green light across clouds of smoke which fade to black as the song also ends.

But that only happens if you get a Perfect Score, if you have a perfect sense of rhythm, and you're playing on Hard Mode (Hard Mode will be sold separately as Downloadable Content: DLC).

·　　·　　·

He receives a text message on his phone and his head still aches. To his side, Matilde is still asleep and he sighs. They're inside the tent inside his flat on the sleeping bag and she has her head on his chest. She's not naked at least and they were very drunk. Isn't that why people get drunk anyway, to do things that they can count or discard when needed? Yes, oh my God, he doesn't remember a thing… Jesus, man. And she'll probably say that too and it will be as if they had disappeared from any moment they shared, leaving them still alone and silent and wishing to leave this fucking city.

He looks at his phone trying not to move too much and Matilde turns to sleep facing the other way and starts snoring, so he sits up to read the text. It's from Yiyo and it says:

Hey, I need to talk to you. It's important, so important.

Come to the guitar shop as soon as possible.

Love you dude. X!

What could this be about? Even stranger, what could it be if Yiyo, the coolest and most apathetic human being he's ever met, thinks it's 'so' important?

His band Fármacos were on the radio so maybe they finally did it, they got signed without him and he will never be able to play with them again because anything he does in comparison will be just another amateur attempt, another hobby that cannot be taken seriously. He should have never left. But what really bothers him is the fact that anything he's not a part of, any story he leaves behind, suddenly becomes successful. Shit, that's the thing that gets to him. Things end well without him. But Eva is different. After all, he never chose to leave her and he's always been present despite what she may have once thought... And the trip will only prove that and then she'll know that everything can end well with him because...

'Hey,' Matilde says, turning to him yawning.

'Hey,' he says, sliding away from her. 'Hey, we didn't...'

'Yeah, it was awesome, I needed that.'

'What?' he says, unzipping the tent flap.

'Only messing with you, man. You just fell asleep when we were just... I don't remember much either.'

'Yeah. I don't remember anything at all.'

He gets out of the tent and changes his T-shirt. He hates sleeping with his clothes on because no matter how much he sleeps in the next morning, it always feels like he hasn't slept at all. He puts some water in the kettle but then remembers he has no electricity so he just stares at it instead.

'What's wrong?' Matilde asks, appearing behind him and touching the edges of the broken piece of his ceiling on the living room desk.

'The kettle doesn't work,' he says, hoping she doesn't try to turn on anything else.

'Don't you have a pot or something? Put it on the hob.'

'Oh,' he says, taking out his one pan and pouring the water from the kettle in it. Then, he places the pan on one of the two electric hobs and, well, just stares at it.

They wait by the hobs and she looks around his kitchen. She moves the stack of pizza boxes by the bin with her foot and lets out a quiet laugh.

'So, is it ready?' she asks. 'I could really do with a cup of coffee right now. Let me get the mugs.'

'It's not working for some reason. Damn electric hobs, you know?'

'That's OK, I'll wait.'

And just as she starts to check the pan and the hobs, his computer under his desk starts to ring and his mum's picture, the one with all the beige furniture, appears on the screen.

'I really need to take this,' he says.

'Sure.'

'Would you mind staying here and not coming out?'

'Um, OK?'

'Thanks.' He goes under his desk and answers.

'Hello,' his mum says. 'How're you?'

'I'm busy Mum, as always. How's India?'

'I won't bother you for too long.'

'Thanks.'

'Just called to see how you were. You never call me, you never e-mail.'

291

'Sorry, I'm just very busy.'

'After your dad died, I don't have anyone to talk to.'

'Sorry Mum. But how's Angela and Alejandro?'

'They're fine. Though I think they're insane. They gave their shoes away to the poor. I bought them new pairs. And they did it again! Can you imagine? Where are you? You look like shit. Have you been eating well?'

'Yes, everything's fine.'

'Are you under a table?'

'No.'

'Ah… How's Eva? Is she back from her trip yet? Is she feeding you well?'

'Mum, I don't need feeding and—'

'Well, that's not what I see.'

'I'm fine. Eva's fine. We went to the San Cristóbal Hill on the weekend and now she's cooking.'

'Something French? Always so sophisticated…'

'Yeah, something called a *cassoulet* or something.'

'Like *casuela*? I can make you *casuela* when I get back.'

'No Mum, it's French.'

'Well, can't she come and say hello? It'd be so nice to see her.'

'Mum, she wouldn't go to India. And hey, you know how she gets with the whole cooking thing. I'm not even allowed to go into the kitchen.'

And then Matilde comes out holding the frozen chicken and laughing.

'What the fuck is this?' she asks.

Tomás waves her off but she just stands there.

'Is that Eva?' his mum starts. 'Hi Eva!'

Matilde looks at him with a frown.

'Hello, how are you?' she says at the computer.

'Your voice has changed so much! You should stop smoking!' his mum shouts and then Tomás closes the laptop and looks at Matilde from under the desk.

'She still thinks you live with your ex... That's healthy...' Matilde says, rolling her eyes.

'Hey, my dad died very recently. She couldn't take any more bad news.'

'Oh, I'm sorry,' she says. 'The coffee's ready,' she adds, pointing at the kitchen table with the frozen chicken on it by the microwave.

'How did you make it work?' he asks.

'I don't know. It just did.'

Even hobs work better when he isn't around. He sighs and they go back into the kitchen and he gets two straws and then...

'Should we wait for the coffee to brew?'

'It all tastes the same to me,' she says, putting the frozen chicken back in the freezer, which is the only part of the kitchen that somehow still works.

'Alright,' he says, and presses the coffee down before fitting in the straws.

They walk to his room and they sit leaning on the windowsill and he lights a cigarette. They take turns on the coffee.

'How come you don't have a bed?'

'I haven't had time to build it. I only just moved here.'

'Oh, well, I can help you build it if you want.'

'It's OK, I'm fine with the tent. I figured if I'm going to the Antarctic, I—'

'You do know they probably have housing over there with full heating and all.'

'I'm preparing for the worst.'

They look outside and it's raining hard.

'Do you think spring will ever come?' she asks.

'I don't know. But you're leaving soon so what does it matter if it doesn't?'

'I guess you're right, nothing really matters until I'm gone,' she says, passing him the cafetière.

'Yeah, exactly,' he says. But can that be true? Can she expect nothing here (can't she?) just because she chose to leave? And could anyone just stop living in the present in one place because they have the promise of a life somewhere else? And if that were true, then when do people really start leaving, and when do they arrive? Maybe, like him, she's already on her way.

They face each other in silence until they finish the coffee.

'What are you doing today?'

'I have to go empty my office.'

'Rough.'

'And then I'm going to go see Yiyo.'

'The Fármacos guitarist, right?'

'Yeah, him,' he says, getting up.

'Can I come? I can help you carry your stuff back.'

'I guess that would be fine. It's near Plaza Italia anyway.'

'We'll go on my bike.'

'Alright, let's go.'

They get on the bike together and Tomás notices that the other mirror's now gone too.

'Should you be driving at all? What happened to the other mirror?' he asks, putting on his pink helmet.

'Fucking cars, you know?' she says, starting the engine.

They drive up the Kennedy Avenue again. Santiago is a different place in the daytime. But it's not just the lights or the amount of people or cars. No, it's something else, like the difference between having a shower in the day or at night, or how cold pizza is better in the morning. It's the pace, it's what it makes you be to keep up with it, it's what it makes you think and feel. In that sense, Santiago is you and right now it is him too.

'Where do I turn?' she shouts.

'It's near Blue Peace.'

'And where's that?'

'Over there! By the protesters.'

She turns into the smaller street and gets on the pavement and avoids people with signs still showing floods with photographs of children in their school uniforms with water up to their bellies.

'It's here,' he says.

She stops and they take their helmets off. She locks her bike by a lamppost and shakes it to see if it holds.

'Will my stuff get stolen here?' she asks.

'They're hippies. They don't ride motorcycles,' he says.

A woman with a military jacket (even though she must be in her mid-fifties) is shouting about the rain through a megaphone in front of them, and a guy who looks just like John Lennon gives them banners. Matilde shakes her head while Tomás takes one.

'Just take one. They won't leave you alone if you don't,' he tells her.

She sighs and takes a banner. John Lennon gives them a fist salute and moves on and they walk past the crowd and into the office building. The elevator's finally working but Tomás doesn't notice it. He takes the stairs and Matilde follows him until they reach the door that leads to the university lobby.

'When we get in, run to the corridor to the left. Don't stop running,' he tells her with one hand on the doorknob.

'Why? I'm pretty sure they'll understand that you're coming to pick your stuff up.'

'No… Listen to me. I know these people. Just run.'

He opens the door and he starts running but Anna isn't at the front desk anymore. He stops and walks up to the new receptionist. Matilde turns back and leans on the reception counter.

'Where's Anna?' he asks the much younger and thinner receptionist.

'Who's asking?'

'An old friend.'

'Oh, well, she had her baby, she's on maternity leave.'

'Oh.' He taps the counter twice and then turns to his old corridor. 'Thank you anyway,' he says and starts walking.

'Shouldn't we run?' Matilde asks laughing.

'No, not anymore,' he answers with a sigh. But as soon as they cross the door that leads into the corridor he hears steps behind them.

'Hey, you can't just come in here.'

'Run!' Matilde says, and they both start running down the corridor.

'You don't have an appointment!' the receptionist shouts, trying to walk quickly on her heels.

'Which one, which one?!' Matilde asks.

'Four hundred and five.'

'Here,' she says. 'What's the code?'

'Four zeroes. Quick!' he says, looking at the receptionist waving her arms at them.

'Done.'

They stumble in and Tomás locks the door from inside.

'I'm calling the cops if you don't come out!' the receptionist shouts from outside.

Tomás thinks of an answ... But Matilde covers his mouth with her hand, her whole hand, and they stay like that, quiet and catching their breaths as they hear the footsteps outside moving away.

'Right then,' she says, laughing and rubbing her now wet palm on her coat. 'We better hurry.'

'They won't call the cops.'

'How do you know that?'

They leave the banners by the door. He opens the window and the noise of all the people outside protesting fills the room.

'The cops never come here when the hippies are out,' he says, looking down at them all.

He checks around the office for things he may have left, and is too embarrassed to admit that apart from a pencil Eva had given him (that's right, not even a pen) with a metallic figurine of the Eiffel tower at one end, and a plastic Space Invaders folder (as empty as Eva had bought it), he had forgotten that there is nothing else here that is his.

Instead of picking up his stuff, he crouches down and lies under the desk. He waits for Matilde to ask, to tell him he's completely lost the plot now, but she doesn't say a thing. She kneels down and lies besides him and they both look up at the bottom of the table. But there are no constellations, no chewing gum, nothing.

'You OK?' she asks.

'There used to be chewing gum here.'

'What?'

'There was a lot of chewing gum under the desk.'

'So?'

'So nothing... There just was, and now there isn't any. I used to spend hours looking at it.'

She laughs.

'Don't laugh, it's true,' he says, noticing that the troll doll's back on the shelf facing the desk. This time it has clothes on.

'Fine, fine.' Then she breathes out and a few minutes pass and she reaches down to her pocket. 'Gum?' she asks holding out a wrapped piece of gum towards him. They smile at each other and they both have one.

'Hey, I never asked you. What's your writing about? What's your story about?'

'To be honest, really honest, I have no fucking clue,' she says.

'So how did you get accepted into NYU?'

'I wrote a story about Pinochet and magical children. *Gringos* go crazy for shit like that.'

'Oh, fair enough.'

'Yeah, but I have no clue what to write about now. I hate most of what I write.'

'Me too,' he says with a sigh. 'You'll be fine.'

'Doesn't it scare you to leave?'

'No, not really... Actually, I don't know. How about you?'

'Yeah. It's not so much the leaving as it is the coming back. I'm afraid everyone will be different, that everyone just move on without me and that my friends won't need me.'

'I think Lucas and Jesús will manage to end the world just fine by themselves.'

'No, I mean it,' she says, sitting up and leaning on her elbows.

'Look, since you don't really know me that well I'll promise you one thing... When you come back, if you come back, I promise I'll be the same, just because, I guess, because you don't know me.'

She smiles at him and takes her chewing gum out of her mouth and stretches it between both her hands.

'Look,' she says, as she cuts a gumball off and sticks it above them. Then, she does it again and again and he joins in too and in just a moment they fill the desk with chewing gum constellations in no particular order. No squares, no circles, just shapeless stars and Tomás looks across at the troll doll and he swears its smile just grew a little.

'They look like stars,' she says.

'They do.'

But then they hear steps outside and someone trying to get in.

'Hey, it's me, Jaime. Let me in!' he says, knocking.

Tomás comes out from under the desk and stretches his hand to help Matilde up but she gets up without looking at him.

'We better go,' he says.

Tomás unlocks and opens the door. Jaime's wearing a suit.

'Did you bring back my umbrella?' he asks, but then looks past Tomás and to Matilde and frowns. 'What are you doing here?'

'What are you doing here?' she asks him.

'I work here...'

'Oh,' she says, taking Tomás's hand. 'Let's go.'

'I'm here with my new girlfriend too, in case you're wondering,' Jaime tells her, adjusting his tie.

'I wasn't, but good for you,' Matilde says. But as she pulls Tomás towards the door, Fran appears playing with a pair of scissors.

'Oh, you so fast a one,' she says to Tomás. 'How count many that is already? Two, three girl? Who know, yes? It not like is you are keeping no count,' she says to Tomás, snapping the scissors close.

'By the way,' Matilde tells Fran, 'if he tells you that he writes stories, that's all a lie. He's only in charge of the gameplay mechanics.'

'Let's get out of here,' Tomás says, and Matilde nods and they start running down the corridor and they hear Jaime shouting 'Text me!' and then arguing with Fran but Tomás keeps running: past reception, down the stairs, through the hippies and their banners and then finally they get to Matilde's motorbike.

'Sorry you didn't get your stuff,' she says.

'I can't believe you went out with Jaime.'

'Let's go,' she says, unlocking the bike chain.

'I mean, he could be your dad.'

'He's as old as you, Tomás, and you went out with…'

'Hey, he's at least two years older.'

'Fuck,' she says, looking at her bike.

'What happened?'

'Look on the other side, the hippies sprayed it.'

Tomás looks at the other side of the motorcycle and sees a large neon pink 'CO2' painted at the back.

'Crap.'

'Yeah.'

'At least it goes with my helmet now,' he says, putting his pink helmet on.

'You're an idiot,' she laughs.

'Yes, but you went out with Jaime.'

'And you went… Alright, alright… Where to?'

'Just round the corner. Yiyo works at AudioPop.'

'The glass building with the strip club in the basement?'

'I think they call it pole fitness.'

'Sure they do. Let's go.'

She starts the motorbike but this time she drives straight on and all the hippies standing against rainfall have to move to the sides. Matilde almost runs over John Lennon and they all wave their arms and call her a bitch and a *huevona* but she doesn't care. She doesn't give a shit. She just drives on, and he holds on to her.

She turns at the avenue and for the first time in his life, Tomás sees it empty and large and open and he wonders, how could anyone ever want to leave this? But, as always, the ride doesn't last and they get to AudioPop and Matilde chains up the bike again and they head into the shop.

Yiyo's inside playing guitar for a group of schoolgirls in their uniforms gathered in a semi-circle around him. He's using a delay effects pedal that makes any note he plays fill the shop. Tomás can hear the rattling of loose snare drums until it all ends in feedback and the crackling noise of a loud amp that sounds like a car radio under a tunnel.

It can't be too urgent if Yiyo hadn't come to find him himself. Matilde walks over to the harps section and fingers random strings. Tomás waits for the girls to leave once Yiyo starts packing up the guitar gear.

'Hey man,' Tomás says.

'Oh, hey,' Yiyo says, dropping a wire as he turns to Tomás.

'What happened?'

'I don't know how to tell you, dude… I don't want you to be all upset about it. I just thought… Well, maybe, I don't know if…'

'Wait, I know… You got signed. Is that it? You finally got the band signed. Don't worry, man, I'm happy for you, really.'

'Um, yeah. Thanks. We did get signed. We start touring in a month actually. You should come with us. You could always play the keyboard or something. Textures, you know, dude? It's all about textures.' Tomás imagines himself playing keyboard arpeggios no one will hear whilst wearing a black turtleneck that no one will see.

'Textures? But you don't have keyboards,' Tomás says.

'But we should. And—'

'I'm fine man, really. I won't be here anyway. I'm going through with my trip to see Eva.'

Yiyo hangs the guitar up between other guitars and just stands there facing the shelves and touching single strings. Behind them: the perfect scales of a harp and the laughter of schoolgirls who are looking at each other's phones.

'You know, man, I sold the drum kit. That fucking blue piece of shit drum kit,' Yiyo says, looking sad. 'Dude, you have no idea how much I wanted to sell that piece of shit.'

'I know man, I know.'

'And for such a long time.'

'I know.'

'Like, I don't think you do. It's just now, like the band and everything, like I don't really care much about it. I don't even enjoy the songs that much. And it started when I sold the fucking kit. We got signed and all, but we're not coming up with new material. It's like, harder for some reason. I even fucking called the new owner you know? To get it back, I mean. I know it sounds mad, but if I could have it back, then maybe, I don't know, maybe it would change stuff back to—'

'Man, don't worry, you'll be fine, you always are.'

'I don't know man. Anyway, that wasn't why I called you here. I wanted to talk to you about Eva,' Yiyo says, without turning back to face Tomás.

'What about her?'

'Well, dude, she's like—'

'Hey, would it be OK if I got your autograph?' Matilde asks Yiyo. She's over in the corner of the shop, playing with a small harp.

'Um, sure, do you have a paper or something?'

'No.'

'Get some from the printer at the counter.'

'Hey, what's going on?' Tomás asks; he watches as Matilde steps away, looking for paper.

'Oh, yeah, sorry...' Yiyo says, turning back to the guitars. 'She, like, came back.'

'What?'

'Eva, she's back in Santiago. She told me not to tell you, but I thought you should know in case you ever run into her or something.'

'She's back. Eva's back. Like, right now she's here...'

'Yeah.'

'Where is her flat?'

'You know where.'

Matilde comes back with an A4 sheet of paper and as Yiyo grabs it to sign his name on it Tomás starts running. He runs out of the shop, he runs past the motorbike, past the crowds of schoolchildren gathering for another protest, past the kiosks and the hippies with their anti-rain banners and the traffic jams and the puddles full of rain and the sky-scrapers all in gold and he keeps running because tonight everything will change, and he needs to make sure that he's ready for it. And by change he means that he will get back a life that for a moment he thought he had lost, which then isn't change at all but WHO THE FUCK CARES, she had crossed an ocean, an OCEAN, just as he would have done for her, and they will show each other that nothing, no matter how frozen and cold, not continents and not even time, can stand between them. He just runs and runs and hopes that she's still wearing the same yellow dress that she was wearing back when...

He stops by another music shop and the blue drum kit is on sale.

20

The River of Shit

But nothing happened. They ate *canard à l'orange* and fucked just liked they've always fucked, Eva on top first until she comes, and Tomás on top after that until he comes. And they fell asleep so tired from the whole trip, the ocean and the fucking, that they didn't wake up for another two days.

By the time Tomás got out of bed, Eva had already left the house. He now walks out onto the front porch and finds her gearing up (a helmet, a camping bag with hooks and rope and boots with spikes on the soles) at the beach, sitting on a *Zelda* towel. He waves at her and she waves back.

'Are you ready?' she asks him.

'I've just woken up,' he says, combing his hair back.

'Then you're ready,' she says, tying a final knot on her bootlaces. 'I found the ice hole, Tomás, I found the entrance and who knows what the hell we'll find down there.'

He nods because he wants her to find it too, but not because he believes they'll find anything even remotely interesting, but because he wants her to stop, to stop looking at the ground for answers, as if the whole fucking universe was a question mark, a puzzle that needed solving. He wants her to look at him with the same sense of wonder, though he knows that once this is over, there might not be any wonder left in the…

But he nods anyway, and he follows her down the beach, up a hill, down a hill, and then, in the midst of a clutter of bushes on top of the dunes, a frozen cave, a hole, like an abandoned well. Tomás picks up a handful of sand and drops it inside. No sound whatsoever.

'You first,' she says with a big smile.

'I don't think so,' he answers.

'I'll meet you down there. I always will.'

Would you go down first? Would you jump? And if so, would you do it under any circumstance, without any gear or plan as to how you'll get back up afterwards? Or a better question would be, what if you don't want to get back up afterwards, what then? Can anything prepare you for the stupid, the silly, the uncomfortable, the downright self-destructive leaps that people take for love?

Tomás isn't thinking about any of these questions. His only worry is finding Eva once he's down there, but she hugs him and kisses him, '*Je t'aime*,' she says, '*je t'aime vraiment*,' and he jumps and slides through the icy tunnel which, to his surprise, isn't dark at all even though it looked it from the outside. He can even see his own reflection opposite him and he's no longer afraid. He doesn't even feel like he's falling, but flying, flying down, down and turning and down some more and he's gaining speed, going so fast that every time he tries to think about Eva he gets forced into a new turn, a new fall, a new direction which needs all of his attention because he could get stuck in mid-flight, he could crash and crack the walls he needs to keep intact for her to fly down too, and then, suddenly, he drops to a room, the frozen belly of the Earth, and there's a frozen table in the centre with service for two. Tomás sits and waits for Eva and then he…

But she doesn't arrive. He can't even hear her. He starts to eat the bread left on the table, drink a glass of white wine as slowly as possible:

the things people do to pretend they haven't been stood up. He notices that Serge is down here with him and he pours Tomás some more wine. 'Oui, ça,' Tomás tells him, 'she will arrive any minute now,' he adds, 'you'll see,' and Serge just smiles back in silence.

And what comes down the tunnel, after five mini baguettes and a full bottle of wine isn't Eva, but a rope ladder. Tomás is tired, so tired, but Serge points at it and then takes away his plate so Tomás knows he has to climb it. What had felt like ages falling now only takes a few seconds in reverse. It was so shallow, he thinks, so shallow, and he's out in only seven steps.

'You didn't jump,' Tomás tells Eva, now sitting in front of her.

'No, I couldn't.'

'Why not? I was waiting for ages.'

'You're always waiting for me.'

'I meant down there.'

'I know. But I couldn't. What would be left of us if I had followed you? What would we do then?'

'But it's what you wanted.'

'Yeah, and I always will.'

And then they walk back to the house by the beach.

'I'll make us something to eat,' she says.

'I already ate.'

'Alright then, I'll fix myself something.'

'I'll stay here and work,' he says, spreading out a *Zelda* towel on the sand.

'So how was it? I don't want to know the details, just your opinion. Was it wonderful?' she asks him, with such a big smile, with such large eyes that it is impossible for him to betray her expectations, despite him feeling that she just betrayed his.

'It was wonderful,' he says.

'Thank you,' she says, and then walks off to water the daisies in their flowerpots before going inside.

Tomás sighs and watches the setting sun. '*Je t'aime*,' she said, 'I couldn't do it,' she said, and the sun blackens out into a sphere of ash that falls apart at the very last waves of the ocean. He gets up. He sits back down. The daisies she just watered are the first to die. Would she save him?

·   ·   ·

He's sitting down in front of his desk with his head on his crossed arms, and the back of his neck is wet from the dripping ceiling above him. His phone is lit up and he sees Matilde's name on it, which no longer matters.

Instead, he opens his laptop and goes on Facebook and lights a cigarette. He looks for Eva's profile but it isn't there. He clicks on Yiyo's and checks the Common Friends list and scrolls down to find it but nothing. He looks through his contacts list on his phone and presses on *Eva del mundo* and he's surprised he had forgotten he used to call her that. He presses on her number and waits for it to start ringing. He holds his breath and his face feels hot and he readies his voice and then…

'Please leave your message—'

'Eva,' he says, as soon as the answer machine lady speaks for her. He hangs up and throws his phone at the wall and it makes a dent and a paint crack, but it doesn't break like they do in movies. Of course, he should have predicted that this would happen, that she'd make sure to show him how much she's changed, how much she's learnt about herself, how much better than him she now knows she can be. Yes, because like most people who suddenly claim to have found themselves, she has erased her Facebook profile.

He gets up and leaves the flat. It's only just past eleven at night and she never goes to bed before midnight. He can get there quickly if he runs. He must see her, he needs to know that she's really back, that she remembers him and that she still…

·   ·   ·

So games nowadays cost more money to make than ever. Most triple-A titles, the big corporate hitters, cost more money than Hollywood movies. But if they do well, they make much more than movies do. In the race to maximise profits and add value to a game with very little effort, studios introduced a new type of media content: Downloadable Content (DLC). With DLC, studios can sell you an unfinished, unpolished turd of a game and then make you pay for additional packages of information so that you can then finally play the game you think you bought. ~~If you don't have internet shoot yourself, you're fucked, though if you don't have internet DLC is the least of your worries.~~

This is how it works. Your avatar is wearing brown and grey rags while he destroys dragons or some other dragonny shit like that. But there's a DLC out there, an ad popping up each time you pause to save your game. It offers you a new costume, a ninja costume, a zombie costume, a golden fire sword and a shield with cool mirror lighting effects. Now you feel shit about wearing dirty rags so you buy it all and now you're happy, only you just saw another guy riding a fucking unicorn across the sky when all you have is a pet worm. DLC: Unicorn. Buy. Check. And so on.

~~And so Jaime wants to do a game with DLC and unicorns~~ How about making a game about DLC? The game starts you off with nothing but a naked avatar and 500 coins. To get more coins you need a job. The DLC to get a job is 250 coins. And that's just for an interview. You'll need clothes: 50 coins, and you'll need to go to university, another 199 coins. Now a month passes and you have one coin to do everything from exploring to hanging out with your friends, to dating (all of them separate DLC: Friends packs) and what do you do? We sell you 500 coins more for the price of the full game, though now you've spent so much time and money on it that you might as well, and you even think it's an investment.

And then our servers break and all you paid for gets taken away and Jaime will be laughing his ass off with his pockets filled with your tears, because the funny thing about DLC, of being able to add and subtract content from a game, is that deep down you know you never owned it in the first place.

.　　.　　.

He puts his headphones on and tunes to Sonar Radio and it's playing Javiera Mena's 'Como Siempre Soñé'. He runs to the beat trying to not step on the lines in the pavement. It amazes him how different songs make a different city, *I get near to you, without being able avoid it,* how unrecognisable something that's been there forever can become, *You don't know that I looked for you throughout the city,* and then in a matter of minutes, then, just like that, *your eyes before you sleep,* all come to an end.

He gets to the bridge in Baquedano and ignores the river and the plastic windmill salesman offering him another windmill, *I looked for you without knowing where to go,* and he crosses over towards Bellavista. He can hear himself breathe over the music so he turns it up, *The streets I walked randomly, the places I have been to,* and keeps running towards the San Cristóbal Hill, and he crashes against a crowd of ceviche eaters out in a bar terrace, *Let me come home with you so that I,* and they shout things he can't hear but none of it matters because the music makes anything that happens part of the same scene, the same story, and *I'm going to take one step that takes me…*

He gets to Neruda's house and the graffitied wall is filled with 'Fármacos' posters. Yiyo's face is on some of them, but that's fine, it was all meant to happen and he whispers Javiera Mena's lyrics, *going to take one step* and crosses an empty stone fountain and gets to Eva's violet house.

He rings the bell. There's a light on in one of the flats and he tries to look for moving silhouettes inside but he can only see a chair next to a lamp. He rings again, twice, three and four times but nothing, and then the radio dies out and the song ends and the world without music is so disappointing and quiet and he's just another person in Bellavista, another dude looking for...

He sits on the pavement opposite to wait and lights a cigarette, and just as he manages to turn the radio back on, a black SUV pulls over in front of him. A woman comes out to open the gates. She's getting drenched and it takes Tomás a few seconds to understand that it's Eva who's smiling whilst she opens a door to somewhere he's not yet been to, it's her he's not kissing, and that it's him who she did not see.

He can't stand at first. He can't call her. She's changed so much, he thinks, without being able to point out any specific changes. Maybe it's the hair, much shorter than it used to be. Or maybe it's how much thinner she looks. Or it might just be the makeup. But it could just be the rain. Whatever it is, he can't get up and he notices he dropped his cigarette into a puddle and he doesn't have any more left and...

Shit, he can get up! He gets closer to her but he still can't... Is it even possible? Is it even her? He can't yet see because the sky is fucking falling, the rain is heavy in the puddles, rivers forming at the edge of the pavement, and to see her, to really see her he has to hear her too, and ask her, is it really you? Is it... And only when she says yes and holds him and invites him into the house, and into the non-cream-coloured flat, and asks him if he'd please just stir those damn vegetables for the *canard à l'orange* and then asks him about his latest games, his latest stories, and she tells him about the holes of the Earth, the icy caves that reminded her of him all this time because they lead, well, they lead...

And she steps besides her car after the lock-button makes him appear in its orange flash. The rain makes them both look like standing shadows, no, not shadows, because shadows live, and neither of them moves at all, not an inch.

Tomás takes a deep breath and a step towards her. Even her shadow form is the best shadow form. His feet are soaking wet. His hair won't stop dripping. He feels the weight of his jacket, getting heavier, heavier, heavier and what does his shadow even look like? He walks right up to her and he can finally see her eyes, the green eyes which remain calm despite everything. And so he remains calm too, but not for long, because he takes another few step towards her and now they are face to face and he can finally hear her breathing... Does she remember his breathing too? And it's right now where Tomás wants to tell her about so many things and all at once: the dead bird at the office, the dead leaves of dead Serge stuck on repeat, the Satanists and The End of The World, his meaning to meet her all the way down in Antarctica, on a ship with as much hope as crew members, and his dad's funeral, and then the second plane crash, the coffin crash, and his new friends, his new friend, his new... So much he finds it impossible to tell her about any of them.

'Hi,' he says instead.

'What are you doing here?' she asks, dropping her handbag on the tiny rivers on the pavement. 'I can't believe it. I honestly can't believe you sometimes.'

'I never thought I'd...'

'You shouldn't have come. What are we meant to...'

'Do you know, do you...'

'You need an umbrella. This is ridiculous.'

'But, wait, I mean, sorry, do...'

'Tomás, how is this good for either of us?'

'Well, it, you know, I still...'

'No. Don't say it. You can't just turn up. What did you think would happen?'

'I don't know. Maybe, something, I don't know.'

'I... I'm speechless. You need to leave.'

'But I think we should...'

'Please, Tomás, please leave.'

'But it's been too long.'

'Not long enough.'

'When is that? How does that make sense?'

She looks up at her window. He wonders if she ever looked up at his window. Did she ever see the HI – I HOPE YOU'RE WELL ☺ sign? He knows it's stupid as hell, but he wishes he had it with him to show it to her.

'Has it always rained this hard?' she asks instead.

'Sometimes harder. But, I wanted to…'

'I need to go and get ready. It's late. Tomorrow I'm…'

'Why are you…'

'Um… It was really not good seeing you. I don't think you should come here again. Take care. Keep well.'

Tomás can't move again. He wants to move but he just can't. What is it with the rain that once it has you, you almost forget that it's falling? Is it perhaps that it is then you finally realise that it is water, only water, and that it falls just as violently on any floor, roof, person and animal? Does it take a storm for you to finally realise that none of it was really meant for you? But Tomás isn't thinking about any of these questions. In fact, he isn't thinking much at all. He can only repeat the final words. Keep well, keep well, keep… And then he turns round and heads towards the river of shit.

Tomás is trembling and his hair drips. If this moment were a videogame it would be a bug, a game-breaking bug, in C++ it would be a dash, GAME OVER, Insert Coin… And no story would be able to save it.

He picks up a cigarette from a puddle and tries to light it knowing that it won't work. He takes his headphones off and sighs. He's surprised by how life without a backing track has no drama, no opening tune to new situations and no tragic climaxes for an ending. It's just small sounds: the birds and the wind through the tree leaves, the traffic always humming, and the banal percussion of breaking branches, steps on the pavement and the creaking wooden tiles of the old Bellavista bars. But that's fine. Tonight, Tomás has no choice but to be a part of that city, the lifeless city, the real Santiago.

He walks away from Bellavista and gets to the bridge in Baquedano again. He goes to the kiosk at the end of the bridge to buy some cigarettes.

'Hey Tomás, how are we doing tonight, *po' huevon*?'

'Hey Matías, not good, not good at all.'

'Oh, shame, shame. You know what my mother always said? When things turn to shit, buy expensive alcohol.'

'She said that?'

'Yes, always. Lucky for you I have very expensive alcohol.'

'Can I just get some cigarettes?'

'Of course. You know I have boxes of ten again if you'd like… Although, if I may say so myself, I recommend not getting those. I mean, imagine running out and not being able to give one to a lady at the disco. I wouldn't want to be you, that's for sure.'

'Twenty will be fine, man. And no one says "disco" anymore.'

'Thank you, thank you. And what do they say then? Here,' he says, handing Tomás the packet.

'I'm actually not sure.'

'Disco it is then.'

'Bye man.' Tomás waves and walks to the centre of the bridge.

He looks down and he remembers that he's done this before, but he isn't sure which part, because he should have predicted this would all happen and maybe new things from now on will seem like memories. Is this what happens when you turn old? Life should be counted in hours, in seconds, just so everyone could know how old he feels right now. The water under him swallows all the noises of the city and he's glad he doesn't have to hear any of it for as long as he stays there. Everything disappears at the bridge and even though he knows rivers erode the edges of their flow, he is sure that this one has stayed the same and will carry on changing nothing long after he's gone.

He starts his walk home and it feels like the longest walk he's ever had to do. Then, when he gets to his corridor he can hear Jesús's heavy metal playing through the door. He notices that his own door is open.

'Fuck my life,' he says, banging his head against it. The piece of cracked ceiling isn't on his desk, the rug's dry, and there's no trash on the kitchen floor. And on his desk there's a full French press with two coffee cups beside it. One of the cups is the naked woman cup he got at Abdul's. The tent is still there and he tries to see if anyone's inside. Nothing.

'Hello?' he says, lighting his way in with his phone.

He hears someone walking in his room at the end of the corridor, so he gets the axe by the fridge and tiptoes his way to the noise.

'Hey!' he shouts.

A girl screams in his room and then laughs.

'What are you doing?! It's me.'

'Oh,' Tomás says, putting the axe down by the door. 'What are you doing here?'

Matilde walks up to him.

'I was with Lucas and Jesús. You weren't answering my texts. So I knocked and noticed the door was open so I thought I'd fix your flat a little. Look, you have a bed now. Well, it's still just half a bed. These manuals do not make it easy, huh? Want to give me a hand?'

'Look, I've had the worst fucking... I need to be alone.'

'Come on, give me a hand,' she says with a smile, showing him her hammer.

'I just want to sleep.'

'That's fine, but at least sleep on a bed tonight. Come—'

'Please, leave. Leave. I didn't ask you to do anything. Nothing fucking works. Nothing gets fixed. Get out. Have fun in New York. Just know that no one will give a shit about stories over there either. No one gives a shit about anything.'

She lets the hammer fall and puts on her coat. She makes her way past the corridor and she doesn't say a thing. At his door, Lucas and Jesús are waiting for her without coming in.

Lucas gives him a long stare before they all disappear and he can lock the door, which he bangs his head against several times.

He goes inside the tent and puts on his ski goggles and he's glad he's wearing them, because with them on he won't have to know if he's crying or not if he passes by his own reflection on the windows. He stays on the sleeping bag straight and starts his radio again but it's playing Fármacos and for once he prefers to cope with the silence. The world has no echoes, no delay, no distortion and no release. It's just streets in Santiago, and most nights they're empty. His life is this, he thinks as he lies down on his side, it is this and nothing else.

21

One Day The Sun Sets

It's almost 5am and Tomás is sitting by his window smoking and drinking coffee. And even though he now has two coffee cups, he still drinks straight from the French press because washing the cups is too much of a hassle now that he's so used to not having them around.

Through the night, Tomás marked all the student papers he hadn't even looked at and gave everyone higher marks than they deserved. He's decided that he will go to the university to try and get his job back. He doesn't have a plan as to what he'll say or do when he gets there, but he's hoping the high marks will prove that he was a good teacher and that they do not want to lose him. He needs it or he'll have to live with his mum and see more of his sister and her fucking friends when they come back this week, and he can't stand proving any of them right about the mess he… On his way out he'll have to go through the bank and check what he needs to do to get that inheritance money, which should last him at least three months if the job falls through.

Always so much to plan, so much to do, even during times that should be epilogues, the echoes of an ending, a few lines leading to absolutely nothing. But in real life this just doesn't happen. And so he has a shower and shaves for himself and then waits by the window for the city to light up in sunrise. It doesn't though, because it starts to rain AGAIN instead, and he can't even see the mountains or the hills and it's all blinking lights on rooftops and aeroplanes AGAIN appearing and disappearing through the clouds.

He leaves his flat at 7am without his coat and when he's locking his door he hears Lucas and Jesús opening theirs.

'Hi,' Tomás says.

'Hey,' they both say, frowning at him.

'Off to the shop?' Tomás asks, just to say something.

'No,' Lucas says, 'we're going to meet Matilde to say goodbye for the last time.'

Jesús nods.

'Oh.'

'Yeah.'

'Well, tell her to—'

'We have to get going.'

Tomás nods with a sigh. Lucas and Jesús leave and Tomás waits by his door so as to not have to see them again downstairs.

He then walks down and starts making his way to the metro. He looks around him in the street, watching out for black SUVs in the roads, and then checking people's faces when he gets to the station. How is it that a single person could turn into the backdrop of a whole city? She could be anywhere, and he could miss her even if they were on the same wagon in the metro and he'd never know... And wherever he turns he has the sensation of having just missed her, as if it were his own lack of attention that's keeping her hidden in the crowds.

He looks up at the metro station names instead, even though he always takes the same line. This time, however, something bothers him. Jaime is in one of the metro ads lit up orange and green. People start getting off at Baquedano and he tries to look over the crowd at the ad and he forgets that he should also be leaving. The doors close and he reads it over and over on his way to the wrong station...

On the poster, there's an 8-bit rendition of Fran holding a pair of scissors in a dim-lit bedroom. Under that, Jaime's signature appears by the App Store logo. How clever of him, Tomás thinks, for Jaime to finally come to terms with how bad a programmer he is. And Tomás isn't referring to Jaime's use of 8-bit graphics (which is just an attempt to grapple with the retro-loving douche mainstream going on right now). No, no, it's the fact that he made a game about people so unfixable, a game about two bugs of humanity, so that any mistake in the coding would end up being poetic. The protagonist jumps and defies all laws of gravity? It must be how he feels. She won't let go of the scissors? Of course she won't, because that's how she feels... Still, who knows, it might be a good game and he's glad he didn't have to come up with its story.

He comes out of the metro one station later and decides to walk instead of taking another metro back. That way, he can also pass by the bank and see what's up with his inheritance cash.

As soon as he's out of the station he can hear student protesters chanting on the streets and he starts to push through them and then starts running towards the bank. They jump and laugh and shout as if it weren't raining at all, and most of them aren't wearing coats either. One guy dressed in a penguin costume gives him a banner that says PENGUIN REVOLUTION – PRESENT, and Tomás takes it and keeps running.

He goes inside the bank and shakes off the rain, but before he can reach the lobby, a guard stops him.

'No protesters in here, *huevón*. Get out.'

'I'm not protesting.'

'Go play Che Guevara somewhere else.'

'This isn't mine,' Tomás says, looking at the penguin with a Che Guevara T-shirt on his sign.

'It is yours because you're holding it. Hi ma'am,' he says to a woman coming in.

Tomás sighs and goes back out into the street but he can't find anyone who doesn't already have a banner, so he just throws it onto the pavement and a group of protesters start taking pictures of him and shouting.

'Capitalist pigs in the bank, just like always!'

'Terrorist!'

'Banks always polluting everything!'

'Don't you have a mother?!'

And Tomás sees the mob coming towards him so he goes back into the bank, which, like sunlight to vampires, instantly makes the hippies turn away at the door.

'Welcome, sir,' the guard starts again.

'But you saw me a second ago.'

'No, I saw a protester.'

'I'm not—'

'The lobby is that way,' the guard says, pointing inside. Tomás sighs and pulls out a ticket.

When his number comes up on a screen on the wall, he walks up to one of the office counters with a young clerk dude with a yellow smiley badge pinned to his chest, just to the side of a skinny tie.

'Um… Do you have some ID, please?'

'Yes, here.'

Tomás gives him his ID card.

'Um… Thanks… So what can I do for you?'

'I just wanted to ask if there's been some attempt to deposit on my account recently. I'm expecting inheritance money from a cheque or something,' Tomás answers, and the clerk keeps typing.

'Um… OK.'

Tomás wishes he could smoke here.

'So?' Tomás asks.

'Um… Yeah… Nothing. It says it attempted deposit. But something failed somewhere. It's procedures. The system. Computers. Something.'

'Oh… But aren't you managing the computer?'

'Have you got it with you? The cheque?' he asks.

'No, sorry.'

'Well, then I can't help you then, can I?'

'The cheque should be on your system somewhere. Check again.' He just doesn't want to have to come here again. He has so much to do, so much to think about – though he could be back tomorrow (or the day after), but he had set tomorrow aside, the whole week aside, to write a whole story based on all his notes.

The clerk slides the papers back to Tomás and the guard comes to take him outside by the arm. Tomás and the guard look at each other in silence.

'It's procedures, my friend. Why can't some people just understand?' the guard says, shaking his head.

When the guard deposits him outside, a protester comes and takes a picture of him.

'Banker assholes! Treating our people always like shit! Enjoy it while it lasts. This will end, you will end!'

Tomás sighs. He's back with the revolutionary penguins. He has his last cigarette on his way to the university offices.

When he gets there he sees a blue Vespa attached to a lamppost amidst all the Blue Peace hippies. But when he walks closer to it to check if it's Matilde, one of the hippies hops on it and leaves.

He makes his way up to the office and the new secretary frowns at him and stands from her seat.

'You again,' she says.

'I need to talk to the Head of School. Or Jaime. Is Jaime around?'

'He's teaching.'

'And Pedro?'

She sighs and picks up the phone.

'Someone's here to see you... Sure? OK.' She looks at Tomás and sits back down. 'What are you waiting for? He's in there waiting for you.'

'Thanks.'

Tomás walks his old corridor and readies the old student papers out of his bag. He knocks but no one answers, so he just goes in. Inside, Pedro is holding a skull and facing the row of embalmed birds in bell jars on his bookshelf.

'Come here Tomás, come here.'

Tomás walks over by the window and he can see all the hippies shouting downstairs.

'Do you know why I keep these?' Pedro asks pointing at the birds.

'Nope.'

'They remind me, every time I come into work, that one day I will die too and all that will be remembered of me will be short moments frozen in time and all out of context.'

'Alright... Well, I brought you the marked papers.'

Tomás puts them on Pedro's desk. 'I was hoping we could talk about—'

'No, no talk. Look at them outside.' Tomás look at the hippies and he spots John Lennon shouting into a megaphone on a stage.

'What about them?' Tomás asks.

'They want to be remembered too.'

'So?'

'So you never had your great idea. Jaime told me you never came up with the story. You don't get a place in my office Tomás, because you leave and then you're forgotten.'

'So I can't have my job back?'

• • •

CHAOS CREW: Urban Revenge. LIGHTNING SQUAD: Arma-fucking-geddon. NUCLEAR WINTER: Hot Shots. DOOM. QUAKE 3: Arena. CALL OF DUTY 4: Modern Warfare. WOLFENSTEIN 3D.

What do these all have in common (apart from their generic titles)? Well, they're all big hits and they're all First Person Shooters (FPS), in which you run around killing people or aliens (or both) in first person, that is, never seeing your avatar's reaction to all the killing you make him or her do (in some old ones you do get a tiny face at the edge of the screen, but the only expressions available are rage and fear). In fact, they often create *ludonarrative dissonance,* a conflict between gameplay mechanics and story elements, because sometimes you can even kill your digital partner or innocent civilians and just go on with the story as if nothing had happened. *Bioshock* is one of the few that do it on purpose, since the game world is a bonkers under-water capitalistic utopia gone wrong, and yet you, as the player, are locked into a gameplay format which lends itself to self-interest, and can only really focus on one point of view (a capitalistic utopia).

But what could we do differently? We could change the setting and take the format away from wars and conflict zones. There was once an unofficial *Wolfenstein 3D* clone (*Wolfenstein* is about escaping a Nazi castle ran by mecha-Hitler, part machine, part Hitler) called *Noah's Ark 3D*, in which you are Noah and instead of a gun you use a slingshot to shoot at sheep trying to attack you. It was a piece of shit, but at least it tried to take the violence out to appeal to a younger, and crazy evangelical audience. Now the question is, can we make a non-violent (and non-evangelical) FPS?

First, we'd have to disarm you. You no longer have a Glock, or a P7 or a Desert Eagle. No M16s or AK-47s and definitely no grenade launchers or anything that could blow up an opponent.

And there'd have to be no opponents because you won't have guns and… No, you will have to run away. You will be a digital Ghandi and just take a few bullets until the baddies run out of ammo and start chasing you to punch you in the gut and... Now there's violence again so no... In this game you understand, you UNDERSTAND that the baddies are not baddies but just regular people who expect a regular wage to live their regular lives and that it's nothing personal, there are no hard feelings, in the fact that they would like you dead... And again... More violence... Now they don't want you dead. They just want to talk to you, you know? But you don't want to talk. You have no guns and the thought of having a long chat with a computer character is so embarrassing that you keep running away... But they still want you to chat with them. They even send you an invitation: CHAT WITH US. You ignore it in your inventory: *Ludonarrative dissonance.* But then you wonder what is there to do in the game. If you can't shoot, if you can't kill or hurt anyone, why would the game do it to you?

And then you die.

·   ·   ·

Tomás leaves and he makes his way to the bridge in Baquedano to buy more cigarettes. But when he gets to the middle of it, he decides to just stand there and look at the water. No job, no girlfriend, and likely to move back with his mum. What a fucking cliché. He should be in the Antarctic, on some boat breaking sheets of ice like in that movie Matilde showed him. But no, Eva came back and she brought him nothing. They probably didn't even discover what was at the bottom of those underwater ice caves that she always mentioned. It wasn't about the results, they'll say, it was about being able to come up with more questions, with a way to ensure that no one could ever again be certain of anything that goes so deep into the ocean. Instead, he's here in Santiago, and despite the fact that he might never leave, he finds himself missing it. And it's not about the distance, not about how far he is from all the skyscrapers around him, or how the river at night can only be beautiful from the bridge, or even how rain sounds better from the inside of a bedroom. It's about time, so much time, because even from the top of the San Cristóbal Hill, even when the whole world's under him and he can see it all, it is made up of so little. It's the things he remembers. The walks in the park. The benches they sat on. The plans they were making. It's about Paris! And the silence of a look before a kiss and the way she always broke them off when she heard someone else near. But he can't put the images into order, and the more time that passes the more Santiago will be filled with the things he's forgotten. Such a waste of time. And isn't that what moving on means, to agree to waste time, to declare yourself absent from this fucking city?

He walks to the kiosk to buy cigarettes but it's another salesman who greets him.

'Hi,' Tomás says, 'where's Matías?'

'Who?'

'I'll just have a twenty pack of Camels please.'

'Here you go.'

'Thanks.'

'You should probably try to give up, my friend. These things will kill you.'

'You're right, I should,' Tomás says, thinking that he needs to start buying his cigarettes somewhere else.

He takes the bus home to avoid the crowds of protesters. They never go on buses and he doesn't know why, but it might be that no one can look threatening waiting for a bus driver to open doors only wide enough for one person.

On the bus, he looks for his phone in his pockets but can't find it. He had been an asshole to Matilde again, and although he's sure she'll understand (Jesus, man), she must still be waiting for him to answer her texts. He presses the button for the bus to stop but it doesn't work. An old lady with a trolley sighs and looks at him and presses it again and it makes a loud TING.

'Thanks,' he says, standing up.

'Men today,' she says with a sigh, 'so utterly useless.'

When he gets home he takes his phone from under the table and lights a cigarette. The last text from Matilde says, 'I guess we did what I wanted. I will go and I will forget the week ever happened. I should thank you but I won't. x.' Then he reads a text from Yiyo, 'LP launch party tonight in Bellavista. We're going touring after that. Come say goodbye!' Below that, it says his phone's memory is empty and two other texts come up with Matilde's name but they're blank. He goes over the photographs on his phone to make space and most of them are about Eva: her showing their apartment keys in front of her parents' fig tree, DELETE, her posing with a new summer dress she bought herself for a New Year's Eve, DELETE, her showing him the miniature Eiffel Tower statue, DELETE, her pretending to be testing something out of a pan with her finger, DELETE, her with her back to the camera looking down at the city from the hill, DELETE! He doesn't see the rest and just deletes them until the phone says that he has no more photos to look at, and that he should try using the new filters to make everything better and worth keeping.

Matilde's texts don't appear and Tomás readies himself to go see Yiyo (which is to say he puts his shoes back on). But at the door he turns and opens the freezer and takes the frozen chicken out. He looks at it all contorted and sighs.

'Fuck you, you fucking douchebag fucking chicken,' he tells it and bins it and it falls like a brick and just as it hits the end of the bin, his phone rings with Matilde's name bright blue on the screen and a bird commits suicide by banging its head on his smoking window.

·   ·   ·

And Eva has stopped breathing but he hasn't. In fact, as the tidal wave takes over the world, he finds he's able to breathe even better under water. It's pitch black now, there is no up or down or anywhere to go. He doesn't know where Eva is. He doesn't know where he is. He can't light a new cigarette to pass the time, or write a new game idea, which may or may not make him a millionaire, because the waves take, and they take and take and spoil and spoil everything with their unexpected sways. There is sometimes a flicker of pink and green, but it's far, so far into the deepest places of the ocean or the sky, and he knows then and there, that the dying fireworks of the world are dying forever. So he waits for the last explosion of colour, the last time he'll see the remainder of the world he used to know and… BANG! He can only breathe, breathe deep into the lack of air and let the currents take over while thinking shit man, one day the sun sets and on the next you have nothing.

.   .   .

In Santiago every shadow is triangular, edging past pavement cracks and bending over walls to end on sharp peaks that stick out like knives. When he stands still, he looks like a triangle too, and he cuts the peach-lit walls into darker parts and then he knows, and she knows, she knew, that even shadows leave permanent marks that divide the world into little intangible bits of information like the stillness of a misremembered anecdote, or the sound of his own breath before voicing her name.

Outside the Bar Loreto, there's yet another queue of goths. Some of them must be in their forties because they have velvet capes and top hats and they're smiling instead of being ashamed of dressing up like children playing wizards.

He queues behind them and sees Jesús at the door, stamping hands. Beside him, a faded red and pink poster that says 'Fármacos: TO THE END' and behind the band name there are rows and rows and rows of… Tomás can't stop looking at them.

FARMACOS: TO THE END

$5000

'Hey, it's you,' Jesús tells him, adjusting his top hat.

'Hi,' Tomás says. 'How much is it to get in?'

'For you, ten thousand.'

'Oh, but it says five,' Tomás says, looking at the sign by the door.

'First off, why do you ask then? Second of all, it's five for the general public, free for my friends... And you're neither, man. You're more like Lilith, fucks with my friends and then leaves them alone.'

'Who the fuck's Lilith?'

'It's ten thousand pesos.'

Tomás looks inside his wallet and he has nothing.

'Hey, look dude, my friend Yiyo's playing inside. He expects me to be there.'

'Yeah, well, a lot of people expect you to be there.'

But then Tomás sees Yiyo pass by the entrance.

'Hey!' Tomás shouts and Yiyo comes out to hug him.

'Dude, come in, we're about to play.'

Jesús lets him through with a frown. Inside, it's the familiar thumping of the bass and the strobes of green and red through clouds of smoke, and groups of people dancing and drinking and keeping their distance with other groups doing the same. Yiyo leaves him in the middle of the dance floor and Tomás looks at his phone. He should answer Matilde's text message. Particularly that last text message. He wants to tell her that it's fine, that even though most people will tell you that any second, any random moment could change your life forever, most outcomes are predictable and have been programmed full of bugs and mistakes, and it isn't even destiny or some bullshit belief in the afterlife. No, all it takes is the knowledge that the spark of the moment does not light anything you didn't know was already there, and that stars and all their constellations have never spoken to you, even though you speak for them every night. But he doesn't write anything and looks up at the empty stage. He notices that everyone around him is wearing a black T-shirt with a white print of troll dolls that says 'Fármacos' under it, and Tomás laughs and wishes he were under his desk at work again.

He looks for Jesús to ask him about Matilde, as if by apologising to someone who knows them both he'd be easier to forgive. And lighting a cigarette in the middle of the crowd gathering at the dance floor, he suddenly has an idea. Fármacos come on the stage and all the people in troll doll shirts start screaming and whistling and Tomás makes his way out against the pushing crowd.

Outside, he finds Jesús alone.

'I'm sorry,' he says, but Jesús just looks at him. 'I wanted to ask you... Has she left? Has Matilde left already?'

'Why would I tell you?'

'So she's still in Santiago?'

'I don't know.'

Tomás sighs and drops his lit cigarette inside his satchel. Jesús laughs as Tomás tries to find it. And it's there that he takes out the folder with the inheritance cash information and blows the cigarette ash out of it.

'Wait, how much do you still need?' he asks Jesús.

'From you? Ten thousand.'

'No, no, in total… For the End Of The World, I mean.'

'Well, the guy in Vicuña is charging just under a million. Last I heard, he found out that there might even be a 2% chance that the comet could end it all in 2018. Why?'

Tomás smiles. 'Here,' he says, showing him the folder. 'Here's the money you'll need. Read it, and call me later.'

Jesús opens the folder and reads the number on the first page.

'So you are actually mental.'

'No, seriously, just take it and call me. We'll sort it out. Where's Matilde?'

'Oh, she's in a hotel called Valle Bonito,' Jesús says, putting the folder in a backpack behind him. 'Are you serious about this?'

'Yes, I'm serious. Where's the hotel?'

'Right, it's just past Plaza Italia, in front of the park by the river. You'll find it if you just follow the road. Dude, thanks so much for this. I'll make sure to tell you how everything ends.'

Tomás nods and looks around for a way to get to Plaza Italia quickly.

'Hey,' Jesús says, 'she left me her motorcycle to take care of it while she's gone. It's over there by the bins. Here are the keys. Bring it back safe.'

'I don't have a license.'

'But can you drive one?'

'I don't know.'

'It's like a bike. Don't be such a pussy,' Jesús says, handing him the keys.

'Thanks.'

'Oh, wait,' Jesús says, reaching down to a cardboard box behind him, 'here, take a shirt for you and Matilde.'

Tomás puts on the troll doll shirt on top of his other shirt and runs to the bins to get the motorcycle. He turns the engine on and runs it against a lamppost and breaks the front light but it doesn't matter. He pulls it out and to the side, gets on and accelerates and there are no mirrors, and so he just has to imagine what's behind him or forget about it and just ignore it. Not being able to look back and guiding himself by the lights around him, he thinks that this is what it must be like to learn to fly and his dad would...

The streets are all moving silhouettes and the sound of wheels sliding on rain. Drops keep bouncing at his face as if it were raining backwards and he uses his shoulder to wipe himself. When he's past the ceviche assholes of Bellavista, the avenue opens wide and he turns to follow the river, with only the light of the buildings and the silver shine on the pavement allowing him to see into the road.

He sees the hotel but he drives past it. Trying to brake into the side of the road he ends up crashing against a parked car and its alarm goes off. He stays there staring at it for a few seconds. People look at him, at the car, and he turns around and starts running to the hotel.

When he gets there the lobby is empty. He rings the reception bell, waits a few minutes, rings again. Nothing. Tomás sighs and he turns to leave but before he crosses the glass doors out...

'Hey.'

He turns around and it's Matilde and Abdul.

'Hey, I need to talk to you,' he says.

'What about?'

'Your message. About how to end your story, about the characters on the San Cristóbal Hill.'

Matilde sighs and looks at her dad.

'I'm not leaving. I have to wear a baseball cap now, after you cut my hair and stole my keys because of him. And just look at him, dressed like a gay,' Abdul says, pointing at the troll doll on his T-shirt.

'Dad,' Matilde says with a sigh.

'Alright, alright, I'm just fucking with you. I'll be at the bar.'

Abdul leaves and it's just Tomás and Matilde in the lobby.

'Should we go to your room? Or somewhere private?'

She lets out a quiet laugh. 'I'm fine here.'

'OK.'

'You were such a douche to me.'

'I know, I'm sorry.'

'Do you know though?'

'I think so, yes—'

'You think,' she says, turning away from him.

'Wait,' he says. 'About your message, I agree, you shouldn't change it.'

'Why?'

'Because if they don't stay on top of the hill your story wouldn't make sense. They need to feel small and the city's the largest place they know.'

'And you came here to tell me that? To talk about plot points?'

They walk out of the hotel and cross over to the park to look at the river.

'When are you leaving?' he asks.

'Tomorrow morning,' she says.

Tomás looks down and it's so dark the river appears still, frozen, and nothing in the world would be able to break it.

'Why are you wearing such a stupid T-shirt?' she asks, not looking at him.

'You know, I have one for you as well. Tonight, I found out when the world will end. It's in 2018,' he says, giving her a shirt.

'What?'

'It will end in three years.'

'But how? How can you know something like that?'

'I just do, OK? And it ends just like this, at night under the rain, the river standing still and everyone saying goodbye.'

She smiles at him and holds his hand.

'I might never see you again.'

'I know.'

'It's starting to snow.'

'I think it's just rain.'

They stay looking down at the frozen river and the plastic windmill salesman walks by pulling the old trolley. They see him sit down and write graffiti on the nearest bench. When he notices them watching him, he offers them a windmill by blowing on it but they both apologise, they say they're sorry for not wanting anything, nothing at all, and they try to spot the stars but it's all fog and even the largest cities can disappear behind passing clouds but that's fine, that doesn't matter. They look up to Santiago, to its blurred streets, to the invisible corners they know will reappear tomorrow all changed and new, and they wish the river would for once just stop.

GALLEY BEGGAR PRESS

We hope that you've enjoyed *We Are The End*. If you'd like to find out more about Gonzalo, along with some of his fellow authors, head to www.galleybeggar.co.uk.

There, you will also find information about our subscription scheme, 'Galley Buddies', which is there to ensure we can continue to put out ambitious and unusual books like *We Are The End*.

Subscribers to Galley Beggar Press:

- Receive limited black-cover editions (printed in a run of 500) of each of our four next titles.
- Have their names included in a special acknowledgments section at the back of our books.
- Are sent regular invitations to our launches, talks, and annual summer and GBP Short Story Prize parties.
- Enjoy a 20% discount code for the purchase of any of our backlist.

WHY BE A GALLEY BUDDY?

At Galley Beggar Press we don't want to compromise on the excellence of the writing we put out, or the physical quality of our books. We've been lucky enough to have had quite a few successes and prize nominations since we set up, in 2012. Over three-quarters of our authors have gone on to be longlisted, shortlisted, or the winners of over 20 of the world's most prestigious awards.

But publishing for the sake of art and for love is a risky commercial strategy. In order to keep putting out the very best books that we can, and to continue to support new and talented writers, we ourselves need some help. The money we receive from our Galley Buddy subscription scheme is an essential part of keeping us going.

By becoming a Galley Buddy, you help us to launch and foster a new generation of writers.

To join today, head to:
https://www.galleybeggar.co.uk/subscribe

FRIENDS OF GALLEY BEGGAR PRESS

Galley Beggar Press would like to thank the following individuals, without the generous support of whom our books would not be possible:

Stuart Armstrong · Martin Bainbridge · Edward Baines · Jaimie Batchan · Rachel Barnes · Alison Bianchi · Mark Blackburn · Edwina Bowen · John Brooke · Max Cairnduff · Stuart Carter · Leigh Chambers · Paul Crick · Alan Crilly · Jonathan Dawid · Paul Dettman · Janet Dowling · Gerry Feehily · Lydia Fellgett · Robert Foord · Simon Fraser · Paul Fulcher · Elaine Glaser · Neil Griffiths · Robbie Guillory · George Hawthorne · David Hebblethwaite · Penelope Hewett Brown · Ann Hirst · Sandra Horn · Sylvia Horner · Bex Hughes · Ruth Hunt · Heidi James · Alice Jolly · Diana Jordison · Riona Judge McCormack · Lesley Kissin · Wendy Laister · Sue and Tony Leifer · Philip Lane · Jackie Law · Philip Makatrewicz · Anil Malhotra · Tom Mandall · Cerith Mathias · Adrian Masters · Jon McGregor · Malachi McIntosh · Leona Medlin · Marilyn Messenger · Tina Meyer · James Miller · Linda Nathan · Dean Nicholls · Catherine Nicholson · Seb Ohsan-Berthelsen · Liz O'Sullivan · Eliza O'Toole · Victoria Parsons · Radhika Pandit · Roland Pascoe · Alex Preston · Richard Price · Polly Randall · Bronwen Rashad · Barbara Renel · Pete Renton · Ian Rimell · Jack Roberts · David Rose · Libby Ruffle · Ellie Rycroft · Richard Sheehan · Matthew Shenton · Chris Smith · Michael Spoor · Nicholas Stone · Ashley Tame · Preti Taneja · Ewan Tant · Justine Taylor · Sam Thorp · James Torrance · Eloise Touni · Anthony Trevelyan · Kate Triggs · Anna Vaught · Stephen Walker · Steve Walsh · Rosita Wilkins · Eley Williams · Bianca Winter · Emma Woolerton · Ben Yarde-Buller · Ian Young · Sara Zo · Rupert Ziziros · Carsten Zwaaneveld